THE NEXT NEW WORLD

ALSO BY BOB SHACOCHIS
Easy in the Islands

THE
NEXT
NEW
WORLD

**STORIES BY THE WINNER OF THE
AMERICAN BOOK AWARD**

BOB SHACOCHIS

CROWN PUBLISHERS, INC., NEW YORK

Grateful acknowledgment is given to the following magazines where stories in this edition originally appeared:
"Stolen Kiss," copyright © 1982 by Bob Shacochis, originally appeared in *Paris Review*. "Where Pelham Fell," copyright © 1985 by Bob Shacochis, originally appeared in *Esquire*. "I Ate Her Heart," copyright © 1986 by Bob Shacochis, originally appeared in *The New Virginia Review*. "Celebrations of the New World," copyright © 1985 by Bob Shacochis, originally appeared in *Chicago Magazine*. "The Trapdoor," copyright © 1984 by Bob Shacochis, originally appeared in *Telescope*. "Hidalgos," copyright © 1988 by Bob Shacochis, originally appeared in *Harper's*.
Author's Note: The first line of "Les Femmes Creoles" has been lovingly pinched from the novelist Richard Hughes's 1928 classic, *A High Wind in Jamaica, or The Innocent Voyage*.

Published by Crown Publishers, Inc., 225 Park Avenue South, New York, New York 10003 and represented in Canada by the Canadian MANDA Group.

CROWN is a trademark of Crown Publishers, Inc.

Manufactured in the United States of America

Library of Congress Cataloging-in-Publication Data
Shacochis, Bob.
    The Next New World: stories by the winner of the American Book Award / by Bob Shacochis.
        p. cm.
    I. Title.
PS3569.H284C4   1989   88-14113
813' .54—dc19

ISBN 0-517-57067-x

Design by Lauren Dong
Cover art by Connie Nelson

10 9 8 7 6 5 4 3 2 1

First Edition

*In memory of Bob Thompson and
Linda Maltsberger; writer, wanderer; wonders.*

CONTENTS

THE
NEXT
NEW
WORLD

LES FEMMES CREOLES: A FAIRY TALE

The two old Miss Parkers lived in bed, for the Negroes had taken away all their clothes: they were nearly starved. This happened in 1923, a year before the occupation, which was meant to set everything right, ended. They lay together in an upper-story room at Derby Hill, in the ornate mahogany bed of their parents, its headboard decorated with ormolu. On the same prickly feather mattress too where they had been born, six years apart, in the estate house built by their father in another century, those days when musicians came from New Orleans to play in the ballroom on Boxing Day, the servants were rewarded with hams, and their mother wore dresses that were heavy to carry, absurdly unsuitable to the climate, and took a year or more to arrive from seamstresses in London.

Out any of the three banks of windows in the room where the sisters now reigned, the unpeaceful contours and eruptions of land daily grew more wild across the once-industrious plantation. They spent hours in a state of

1

enraptured emptiness, watching shadows parade off the hills and stall in the destitute fields of guinea grass, muster along the horizon of mangrove to drown in the sea once filled with ships waiting to load coffee, syrup, and cotton.

Outside the south row of windows grew an immense gnip tree, laden with fruit. Birds would flock in it, overcrowding the branches, and make quite a disharmonious racket at the crack of dawn, and Mary Elizabeth—M.E., or Emmy since birth—who was afraid of birds, would throw the last of her costume jewelry to chase off grackles that landed on the sill. Margaret Gloriana prayed for the birds to cock their iridescent heads at her sister, to have the pleasure of seeing the hoard of cheap necklaces and embarrassing rings pitched out the window. Fare-thee-well to that whore's brooch, she would cheer—to herself, of course, since she didn't want to hurt Emmy's feelings. So much wretched tin and sixpenny glass. There went that awful tiara, the tarnished pendants, the gilt-painted earrings—how they made Margaret Gloriana's hands tremble for the few real objects they had replaced, the treasures they had been forced to sell one by one to the Syrian in his vile shop, inhaling his turpentine odor.

Yesterday, or perhaps the day before—the sisters were not at all interested in counting—Mary Elizabeth had stood in one of the south windows, her wizened body visible like a stick drawing underneath her muslin nightgown, and leaned out to pick a cluster of gnips for breakfast.

"Sir, sir," Margaret Gloriana had heard her sister calling matter-of-factly to someone below. Emmy had seen a barefoot old black man dodging behind the base of the tree. He was wearing dress pants, a white shirt that was too big, a black necktie that was too short, and a bowler hat with crescents cut through the dusty dome to keep his head from heating up. What's more, he had been sketching a *vévé* in the dirt with his walking stick.

"Sir," Emmy said, waving. "Behind the tree. I saw you." She implored him to gather her bird ammunition and toss it back into the room.

Margaret Gloriana sprang out of bed, forgetting both her age and her nakedness. Throughout her life she had preferred to sleep with nothing on against the cool linens, and so when all was lost she was left without even a nightshirt to cover herself. "Who could you be talking to?" she wondered out loud, wrapping herself in the single sheet they shared. Everyone they knew was dead or gone away. Everyone they didn't know was unkind. She came up behind her sister, who was flapping like a scarecrow, went to the next window over, and squinted her sharp blue eyes at the figure below, who had stepped halfway out from behind the gnip tree to marvel at them.

"Who are you?" she demanded to be told, and then decided since she was speaking to a man out in the yard, it was more practical to use outside language. "What you want, jack-o, snoopin' about? Who give you permission to draw *vévé* in we dirt?"

With a jolted expression, the man below looked at the two crones, from the ethereal Mary Elizabeth to the shroud-bound Margaret Gloriana, the long white braid of her hair dangling over the sill like a hangman's rope. One spirit beckoned him forward, one scolded him like a fierce archangel—the windows of temptation and retribution. In the excitement, Margaret Gloriana forgot that she wore no clothes; she opened her hands to brace herself and the sheet slipped to the floor. The old man's eyes enlarged even with the brim of his hat, his knees had dog-shake, he took a nervous step backward to learn if this was what they were waiting for to kill him, and then he scuttered off into

3

the bush, convinced he had seen twin harpies, a very ungodly apparition.

"White people ain' need no wanga magic," Margaret Gloriana shouted as he fled. "No carabee spells." He was the first soul to come poke around since the last family of servants had disappeared one rainy midnight, hauling what remained in the house, and the first man to have a good square wake-up-Maggie-it's-Christmas-morning look at her body, such as it was, since her days of childhood. Well, she felt giddily unashamed about it, and now that she was shouting, she had the impulse to shout more, to shout something scandalously satisfying.

"Backra bubbies on sale today!"

She felt the blood rising in her mossy cheeks, fermentation in her delicate stomach. She tried again, exhilarated by the advance she had willingly made toward shandyism and disgrace. She craned out the window, her emaciated backside thrust toward Emmy, her breasts like a mauga dog's swinging in the air.

"A fart fill your sail, you Guinee rouge!" she cried out, making a bony fist, and collapsed back into the room, alarmed at how extraordinarily good it felt to raise her voice, to say something nasty and speak in the rough island dialect she had heard all her life.

"*Margaret Gloriana!*" Emmy, blushing and tittering, had stooped for the sheet. She spread her arms, opened like linen wings to receive her sister. They promenaded side by side back to the bed. "Where are your principles! You sound like a *filibustier!*"

"Oh, get on," Margaret said, unconcerned. She propped herself with their one pillow, pulled out her braid, set it on her chest, and began to unwind it. It was her favorite, most gratifying act, brushing the length of her pale brittle hair, blowing the broken strands off her fingertips to the floor.

LES FEMMES CREOLES

She had a desire for a glass of ginger wine, or sherry, which she had never tasted.

"I sound just like Father, that's who."

"Thank you, I don't need to be reminded," Emmy sniffed. "Still, it's very shocking to hear it from you."

"You will live your life," Margaret Gloriana sermonized, "and I will live mine."

Emmy slid down flat and wiggled her stiff toes, imagining she was a fish at the bottom of a mustard yellow lake, which was the color left in plaster patches on the walls of the room. She tried to remember her father ever saying anything nice or gallant or uplifting to anybody. He had once traded a young female servant for a sow, the price determined by matching the girl's weight against that of the pig's. Of course, the pig was worth more. She went through the ordeal of sitting back upright, weary from being at the bottom, the austere and lonely bottom, of a yellow lake.

"Do me now, Maggie dear," she said, touching the hawksbill shell of the brush which, with their enamel chamber pot and two cracked Worcester cups, was the extent of their common wealth.

"You have such pretty hair," Margaret Gloriana said, stroking her sister's silvery, ever-slackening curls.

"Oh, but it's not as pretty as yours." The two old Miss Parkers had been saying so to each other since the beginning of time.

<hr>

After several hours of tying and untying two threads she had unraveled from the hem of the sheet, the younger sister, Mary Elizabeth, announced her momentous news.

"Don't be upset," she forewarned. "I have a lover."

"You do?" Margaret Gloriana, who had been staring at a blue beetle on the ceiling, sat straight up. "How can you?" Out of respect for her sister's sensitive circumstance, she looked merely doubtful, although her reaction could have been far more dramatic.

"Why, yes, I do," said Emmy, intransigent, feeling revitalized with confidence now that her secret was out in the open. "He has a gold tooth."

The present vacancy of life expanded out of focus. Margaret Gloriana folded her weightless hands and thought for a minute before she spoke again. "You have given yourself back to Christ Our Lord," she concluded, famous at Derby Hill for her uninspired good sense. "I thought you'd gotten over that ages ago. When they burned the church."

"I did," Emmy agreed. "What good is it to love someone if you can't even go to his house and have lovely conversations with his guests? I don't see the point."

Margaret Gloriana shifted restlessly, her shoulder blades scraping against the headboard, and made a second guess. "Is it Papa? Didn't he have a gold tooth?"

"He had eight or nine, I think." Emmy shrugged with her awkward matchstick arms. "No, it isn't him. How could it be? I always, always hated Papa. Why should I love him now that he's dead? What is there to love about the dead, except that they're not in your way? What strange ideas you have."

"Well then," Margaret Gloriana snapped. "Who is it, who can it be? There's nobody."

"He's coming." Emmy's eyes had an unsettling starry luster to them, entirely inappropriate for a woman her age. "You'll see."

Margaret Gloriana looked incredulous, wheezed—she couldn't help it. The sound created a brassy vibration in the hollow expanse of the room. Her sister was a ninny, always had been, anyone could see, disrupting their fragile serenity, threatening their sistership with youthful fantasies.

"And when he comes, what will you do with him, you old moth?"

As much as they had seen of life, they had not seen much of men. They were not beauties, but they were not without their feminine merits either. Even so, year after year, they were condemned never to be more to any man's life than their father's maiden daughters, and the island itself conspired with this destiny. Once, on the Queen's birthday, they had both danced the quadrille with a Captain Selcroft, ashore off one of the trading ships, but their father spoiled it by belligerently insisting he be told which one Selcroft intended to marry; and when the Captain balked, challenged him to an affair of honor; and when the Captain refused to raise a pistol on the grounds that the daughters, as fair as they may be, weren't ladies enough to die for—an opinion to which *pere* Parker brutally conceded—challenged him to a horserace, which Selcroft accepted, but finished the loser with a broken neck. Only a Napoleon was foolish enough to fetch away an island girl.

"When he comes, then I shall die . . . and happily," Emmy confessed. She crossed her forearms over the washboard of her ribs as though she were practicing to be stuffed in a hole. "Not a day sooner."

But how unfair, thought Margaret Gloriana, who by virtue of being the elder felt she had every right to die first. Besides, Mary Elizabeth would appreciate the upper hand, late as it was to come to her, and who in the world would tend to her corpse and save her spirit from wandering about if not Emmy.

"What shall you die of, then?"

"Is it at all true what they say, that you can die of love?" Emmy whispered in ghostly repose, her hands clasped over her flaccid bosom. "That would be the least I could do for love, after all this time. Wouldn't you think?"

Margaret Gloriana groused for a bit, unimpressed. "You always want everything perfect," she said.

They were without oil lamps or candles but it didn't matter. When the sun, only minutes from setting, dropped into the western windows in the late afternoon, the glare was a powerful soporific; it absorbed their reservoir of strength, disordered their thoughts, and put them almost instantly to sleep: the deepest, most forlorn, most uninhabited sleep they had ever experienced. They were also in the habit of waking hours later, simultaneously, like a pair of zombies, in the middle of the night. Then they would use the chamber pot and patter back to bed, nestled together but trying not to move, listening to the gunfire in the mountains while they waited for their wistfulness to turn to a second, more benevolent sleep. For years (they didn't know how many exactly) the island had been occupied by foreign troops (they didn't know whose, really) and a resistance movement had organized against the outsiders (they weren't actually sure why) but they did know that the men only fought after dark, which the sisters thought cowardly and of a fiendish design. Eventually they would close their eyes again, the translucent lids lowering shut, and enjoy separate but identical dreams: the *vévé* the old black man had scratched in the dirt under the gnip tree, a cross-hatched heart pierced by two swords. Now it was being inscribed by Captain Selcroft.

Not the following day but not long after, perhaps a day or perhaps two, Mary Elizabeth was kneeling on the sill of a south window, her insubstantial waist encircled by Margaret Gloriana while she stretched as far as she could—not very far because she was characteristically timid and her sister was making her do it anyway, so her heart wasn't in it—stretching to reach a second group of ripe gnips, the first and closest already eaten in weeks past. Birds dashed from branch to branch with dizzying speed, mocking her. She leaned a few more inches, then for no apparent reason and without warning, Emmy blasted the fresh morning air with one of her girlish screams. Margaret Gloriana hugged tighter—all their lives they had been lean healthy women, not weak (though Maggie was tall), and now they each weighed no more than a basket of sorrel blossoms. She tried to pull Emmy back in but couldn't; her sister spread herself out like a cobweb in the window, opening her knees and grabbing hold of the shutters and vines. "Are you falling?" Margaret Gloriana asked. "You don't seem to be."

Emmy quit resisting and floated in her sister's arms. Margaret Gloriana helped her down quickly from the sill, afraid she was being stung to death by jack spaniars or assaulted by the birds. Once she was on her feet again, Emmy, her face feverish, her jaw quivering, took one guilty glancing look at Margaret Gloriana and burst into tears. She gestured toward the south as if she were shooing mosquitoes.

"There's a man on horseback coming," she wailed miserably.

The older sister rushed to the window. "Where?" There was nothing much wrong with her sight, but she could see no man on horseback near or far.

"He's a white man," blubbered Emmy.

9

"Impossible," Margaret Gloriana clucked. "Inconceivable. You're making-believe again." She peered into the green-tangled distance where disciplined groves had once stood, as sweet to the eye as rose gardens. Nothing was out there anymore but a spiteful jungle re-creating itself. Not a chicken or peacock or guinea fowl, not a goat or black-bellied sheep, not an ox or cow, a donkey or a horse, and certainly not a backra man, which would be terribly disconcerting, for neither of them had seen or spoken to a white man in years, and they would sooner transform themselves into *crapauds* than prepare for a civilized visit. It was an indecent idea.

"Stop bawling," Margaret Gloriana said, leading her sister back to bed. "It's very tiresome to hear you go on like this. No one's coming." She cuddled her sister to her breast and rocked gently, as she had so many times in the past. Who would come this far into the abandoned countryside to gape at two old women with flesh like salt cod and not a stitch to wear? Who even knew they were alive, and why should anyone care, and if they cared, what business was it of theirs, she'd like to know.

"My lover," lamented Emmy, reading her sister's mind, a skill she had been explicitly forbidden to use long ago. "If only I had some violet water."

"Oh dear, let's not start up with that." Were they even alive? Maybe someone would come and tell them if they were one way or another.

"Or a gown. Or just a ribbon for my hair."

Not much was wrong with the old sisters' hearing either, and they were both startled by the muffled impish laugh of a whinny, still miles away on the serpentine path that traversed down palisades, dipped into ravines, wove through vaulted tunnels of ceiba trees, vanished across irrigation canals grown solid with lily pads—yet close

LES FEMMES CREOLES

enough to make their hearts flutter. Emmy felt her sister's long nails dig into her shoulders and she squirmed to the other side of the bed.

"I told you," Emmy despaired. "Dear God Almighty Jesus, what shall I wear?" She begged her sister to go back to the window to see how near the rider had come.

"No, I can't bear it." Margaret Gloriana rasped her disavowal of whatever might happen next. She began to shudder and pulled the sheet up to her chin. "I don't want to see a white man. You go."

But Emmy herself was too distraught to move except to yank her own side of the sheet up to her face, so they lay there quaking, their dehydrated skin turned clammy. The horse whinnied again, much nearer, then after a while snorted, nearer still, and not a minute later the day—which had been like so many others and not worth complaining about, because what had been done was irreparable—was being praised in a booming voice that seemed to cause a rumble in the stone foundation of the house.

"Good day, good day, good day!"

"I'm fainting," said Emmy in a barely audible sigh.

"So am I," answered Margaret Gloriana. "He's your lover. Tell him to go away."

There was a knocking—though not at the door, for the servants had sprung its hinges and taken it too.

"Hello, halloo, *bonjour*, anybody home?"

"He has a powerful voice," noted Emmy.

"He sounds to me like a *cinquantaine*," Margaret Gloriana replied, hissing. She had no precise idea of what a *cinquantaine* actually was, only that it was her father's most relished label for whomever he didn't like. He had been a man delighted with the abundance of his enemies—Irish rebels, Gallic Protestants and Papists, Scottish Covenanters, Quakers, Puritans, and all manner of psychotics, convicts, and deportees, not to mention the Dutch, the Portagee, Jacobin French, and barbarous Spaniards. The intruder down below would likely be representing one or more of these diabolic traditions.

"A hairpin," murmured Emmy, "a teaspoon of scented powder."

"If he comes in the house he'll murder us," said Margaret Gloriana. "That's what kind of white men show their face these days."

He came in the house, stamping his boots on the fractured terrazzo, crunching a path through broken table legs and chicken bones and the busted machinery of clocks. They listened to him playing football with coconut husks, they heard the tintinnabulation of porcelain and pottery, shattered on a night of inscrutable liberation. What made them all the more apprehensive was his dreadful whistling, a low-pitched melody like none they had ever imagined, a sinister bold and bumpy rhythm. When he reached the wooden floorboards of the dining hall he became an earthquake, and when a foot thundered down on the first step of the main staircase, and then the second thundered down on the next step, and so on to the top of the landing, the two Miss Parkers whipped the sheet over their heads and lay petrified, immobile as plaster saints. Throughout the halls and passages the repercussing amplified to apocalyptic proportion; he clomped from room to room like a nosy Goliath until at last he clomped into theirs and halted at the foot of the bed. The whistling ceased, but the atmosphere still rang with his noise.

"Are you alive?" he inquired politely.

He repeated the question in Spanish, which confirmed Margaret Gloriana's cutthroat fears, and then in French, which made Emmy shiver imperceptibly in anticipation, because she had always known the French to wear such provocative hats. Receiving no response, the man began to pull ever so cautiously at the sheet, inching it down farther and farther until he saw one grizzled and one flossy mop of hair, pinkish scalps, and the glossy crowns of two foreheads, liver-spotted and additionally marred by the scarlet dappling of sun-made cancers. He took a steadying breath and continued: a double set of eyebrows astonishing for their coal-black thickness, and then, regrettably, the pure but lifeless eyes, wonder-stricken by the beyond. His face saddened, he drew his hand back from the sheet and crossed himself, muttering in a language neither sister could understand but which sounded like groans and smacks. He went to a window and sagged against its peeling frame, staring out at the vast and savage terrain.

Contained within the slightest exhalation of breath, a sound not different from the natural silence of the house, Mary Elizabeth spoke to her sister.

"He's wonderful."

Margaret Gloriana puffed back, an insufflation as soft as blowing into a baby's ear. "He's much too young—and thin."

"He's very handsome."

"He has a nose like a Jew."

They did not think it odd or offensive that the young man had a carbine strapped across his back, for on the island men had always carried guns, even to the dinner table, and they did not perceive that his soiled gray blouse and stained flannel pants were in fact a uniform. But through the weave of the sheet, Margaret Gloriana, at least, could taste the bitterness of cordite that enveloped him, and smell the familiar sorrow of blood, and knew without having to ask that he had come fresh from battle.

13

Emmy would have registered this evidence too, for her senses were equally refined by solitude as her sister's, but she was drifting, overwhelmed, pursuing vague memories of passion through the museum of her heart.

The young deserter went from window to window, surveying the dense panorama, and assured himself he had not been followed. He wished he had discovered the two old women alive and prosperous, quick to offer him a plate of lamb and pudding, and he would sit, assuming they owned a chair, and confess the peculiar fate that had befallen him and they, poor withered figs, saturated with long experience distilled to wisdom of the world, would advise him what to do. They would tell him how to undo what history had done to him: how he, a Flemish village boy who aspired to play in the most renowned beer gardens and cabarets of Europe, lubricating the dreams of the masses with new and dangerous music, how he, who until yesterday had masqueraded as the heroic Charlie Andrews, might recross the ocean and repatriate himself to the ravaged continent as his civilian self, the Liege *savant* by the name of Josef Krunder, who since the age of three could play the *Marseillaise* or any of a dozen anthems on whatever instrument he was handed. He, Josef Krunder, who was Charlie Andrews risen to First Lieutenant's rank, a member of a great army that had been victorious in a great war, now doomed by an invisible momentum to tidy up jungles and deserts, islands with names no one ever heard.

On the other hand, he had participated in splendid adventures, and increased his repertoire of popular songs tenfold—but enough was enough.

Throughout the exotic diaspora of sinners where he had campaigned, he had viewed uncountable dead, the majority of them flayed and mutilated, and he had stumbled upon more than a few old women like these in the bed, but none so intimately. They were like forsaken goddesses who had outlasted their value, dispossessed by their celebrants and allowed to spoil, unworshipped, suspended in purgatory between a fallen world and one as yet unborn. He returned across the room to replace the sheet as he had found it, taking a last gaze into the soul of their eyes, inanimate as miniature pale-blue doll parasols. Swept by profound homesickness—what, after all, had become of his own mother?—he marched out of the bedroom, downstairs, and then outside into the heat, from a cistern splashed water on his face and neck and began to police the grounds in search of a shovel, obligated by a Christian upbringing to bury the hags before he rode on to the sea.

After a time he gave up the hunt, having discovered nothing in the dilapidated outbuildings of any use save a hoe blade with its shaft broken and a cutlass filed as sleek as a rapier. Back to the house he went, through a rear entrance that passed him into a library strewn with excreta and goose feathers, its remaining volumes flowering a slick vivid mold, and he thought to himself that he would say a prayer over the stiffs and leave it at that. Belated last rites. But the day had progressed too far for traveling hostile territory, and he reasoned he should stop the night until the moon rose, and then go on. His village superstitions, however, argued against such a plan: pass the evening with two dead women and get attached to whatever curse lingered over the violated estate. Yet to think of the world this way, so vulnerable to mystery, was no longer possible for Josef Krunder Charlie Andrews. His conscience chided him, he was taunted by the imperatives of manhood, and so he resolved to stay—and to quicken the time he would offer a requiem, so that the dead might look down from heaven and know they had not been, for once, forgotten.

In the final hour of daylight, the sisters as unconscious as logs, he ascended to the sun-swept upstairs room outfitted like a junk dealer. From the ubiquitous trash of devastation, he had combed three galvanized pails with their bottoms partially rusted out, a length of cedar planking hanging by its last nail from one of the sheds, a half-burnt spindle from a ladder-back chair, and from his saddle an army-issued wool blanket and a paraffin plug of candle. Near the foot of the bed he went to work, set the cedar plank spanning two of the pails, upturned the third as a stool cushioned by folding his blanket into a pad. Out the windows, the evening's stridulation of crickets and frogs began to saw at the tranquility of twilight. He lit the candle and took his seat, gripped the charred point of the spindle, and with it reproduced a crude outline of a keyboard upon the surface of the cedar plank, minus the highest and lowest scales for want of space. He flexed his hands, practiced several finger exercises, limbering the knuckles, and called the notes in his head but to his surprise they came as sterile letters, not tones, until he pictured the clefs like a charge of helmeted troops, advancing through the scales from bass to treble.

His countercharge, the requiem. He was ready to perform.

"Eternal rest grant upon them, O Lord," he sang in a tenor's voice. His spidery hands crept along the board in a solemn cadence, the calluses tweaked by splinters, fingertips blackened by char. His amateurish preoccupation with striking the correct keys; a panic as the formal sequence of the mass temporarily faded from memory—these shortcomings slowly dissolved and he was transported by the

literal resurrection, impoverished as it was, of music. As his instincts revived and intensified, he concentrated less on the act itself and more on abstract appreciation, oneness, union. He smiled mournfully upon his subjects, aware that they and they alone could hear the divine orchestration that resonated with such compassion within the chamber of his mind, but as he approached the *Dies Irae,* he was spontaneously delivered back to his youth into the slicing scrubbed hands of his choirmaster father, a bloody bastard he was, and he inhaled again the frankincense of suffocation of the church, and felt its smothering robes on his shoulders. His hands slammed clumsily on the plank, he glowered at the two desiccated crones and their whiffy mattress, his eyes raked their loathsome morbid shapes. And as he played on, his nails indenting the wood, he realized something was different—wrong—about the arrangement of the corpses. He squinted through the dim and shifting illumination, his voice rose until he was bellowing in Latin. The noise outside the windows churned like the engines of a mighty factory. Was he mad, or had the geometry of their bones been reformulated? Then he had it: When he had first looked down upon them earlier in the day, they were aligned in bed like two fallen fence posts in a snowy field. Now they had thaumaturgically branched. Now their parallel arms formed a chevron. They were holding hands.

"The hell with this, ladies," Charlie Josef sang, and with a flourish of vaudevillian chords, bridged over to a ragtime dirge, putting himself in a sweat. Then he gave the two possums love songs, folk songs, drinking songs, ballads from operettas, every music-hall ditty that came to mind, songs in Flemish and Celtic, Finnish and German, torch songs, war songs, minstrel songs and shanties, verse upon verse, chorus and refrain, one after another on into the night until his mouth was paste and his throat nostalgically raw, the candle extinguished to a frozen puddle and the room flooded with satin mists of moonlight.

With throbbing fingers and stiffness in his knees, his thighs cramped from riding all last night, down from the mountains, he got to his feet, refastened his rifle over his shoulder, and approached the head of thc bed. Tenderly, he turned back the corner of the sheet, exposing Mary Elizabeth's smitten expression, and bent over.

"How far is the coast, madame?"

"Two leagues southwest," peeped Emmy to the relief of Margaret Gloriana, who was sure her sister had fulfilled her own premonition by dying hours ago when she had released her water into the mattress, and her hand had gone limp and cool. Still, she didn't think it necessary to converse with the man in French, like a soubrette. He leaned over and turned the opposite corner of the sheet, but Margaret Gloriana clung to inexpression, refuting any notion of her continued existence.

"Can I do something for you, *Gran-mere?*"

Emmy asked that he send her a pair of black crepe drawers, if he'd be so kind.

She remained in an ecstatic trance for days, effervescing upon occasion, uttering endearments at the birds, fragmented lyrics, frivolities about gold teeth (which she hadn't verified) and artistic temperament, until Margaret Gloriana was disgusted with her pretense, the latest of many perpetrated by her younger sister since they were children. She contrived a list of mortal sins the singer had most likely committed in his young life, but Emmy wouldn't listen, and so in frustration over losing her company, she fought fire with fire and declared that she too had a lover.

In Emmy's eyes, the cloudy bliss instantly clarified, her nostrils dilated with the restorative vapors of rivalry. "Why, I don't believe it," she protested. "I would be so happy for you, but I don't believe it at all."

"Yes," Margaret Gloriana held firm, although she herself didn't believe a word that rolled from her mouth, "and he will come very very soon."

"How do you know? Can't you tell him there's no hurry?"

Emmy felt her sister meant to punish her for luring the singer to Derby Hill with her yearning. Ever since his nocturnal concert, all Margaret could do was malign his innocent talents, point to the smudged board across the pails (which she dare not touch) as if it were a pagan altar, diminish the gift he had endowed to her memory. He sang such devilish things, Margaret Gloriana accused daily. Oh, they were so much fun, Emmy would defend. His intention was to rob all that was left in the house, and that could only be their eternal spirits, her older sister retorted. But that was fine with Emmy; she said he was welcome to hers.

"I know because the shooting has stopped at night." The end of the conflict seemed to have occurred the evening before the white man appeared to beguile them with evil crooning. "The war is over," Margaret Gloriana improvised. "He has done his duty valiantly. He is free. I won't say another word about it."

They lay together at a standstill for several more days, fatigued by the smallest exchange of civilities encouraged by this new tension. They sucked on the creamy orange pulp of gnips, sipped cistern water from cracked cups, and tried to speak of other less selfish things. Of their mother, for instance, who became ill when they were twelve and six and returned to her homeland for treatment. They could not remember the illness she suffered, but the treatment administered apparently had great healing power, for it cured her of being a colonist's wife.

"She sent for us and sent for us," recalled Emmy.

"But she died."

"Father wouldn't agree."

"But he did. We couldn't leave, though, unless she came to claim us."

"She never came."

"She couldn't. He would have hacked her to pieces."

"Would you have gone?"

Their remembrance of their mother consistently ended with this uncomfortable question, each of them shy to answer for fear of distressing the other, and they would move on to other events.

"The November hurricane was the worst day of my life."

"It killed Alexander Brumfield." Emmy threw a gnip seed at a trio of grackles on the sill.

"You were too young to remember."

"I remember. The servants picked cuttlefish out of the trees."

"Alexander was cut right in half. Something flew in the air and hit him, but it went so fast no one saw what it was."

"Alexander was going to marry you."

"You can't remember, you were only three."

"I was four. The fishermen never came home, but their boats did. I remember we made coffins from them."

The sisters conjured up the scouring stones along the river bank, the eddies of moss-green water. The stones were flipped like pancakes during an earthquake and ruined for laundering for at least another century, their smooth lye-bleached surfaces, burnished by so much cotton, replaced by slime-coated coarse undersides. The same catastrophe had rocked the Virgin Mary from her chapel pedestal, breaking the statue into three pieces and releasing an egg snake that had lived in the hollow of the casting. Their father had it caught, and kept in a grass basket on a table in the parlor, and only white men were permitted to look at it. The sisters saw the workers in the fields fanned out like a line of ragged infantry, bent to the ground in a torturous advance, as if searching all day for a dropped coin. And the painter from Italy who resembled, in their opinion, a Biblical shepherd. The servant women were rendered too merry and independent by his brush, with faces like voluptuous moons, and no one purchased the canvases. They reminisced about the itinerant professor, his smokehouse pungency; his thin frock coat, his mustard shirt with too few buttons, the gray trousers with a black stripe down the outer seams; his green flat-sided carpenter's pencil; his purse a soda-cracker tin with a rope strap, stuffed with papers. He left them untutored except through mimicry, scattered lines from *Othello* and *The Tempest*— "Hell is empty, and all the devils are here" and "Do that good mischief which may make this island thine own forever"—and schooled them in the details and habits of foreigners, a class that excluded no one. They remembered the dentist in the capital who repaired their teeth with caulking compound; the charcoal-makers who cooked entire trees like pigs in the soil; the vomit smell of grinding houses and the caramel smell of boiling houses; the taste of the baked spheres of cheeses, stuffed with prawns, sweetbreads, and pigeons; tamarind butter, sunbonnets, and whale oil lamps; the vulgar little monkeys that would shit on the veranda; the parrots, now extinct, and the carnival flamboyance of their plumage.

The campfires of the laborers, the ululation of their legends. How many empty columns of time had passed since they had admired the handsomeness of their father's *paso finos*, the best of them raced in Jamaica? And before the instrument was outlawed by the last governor, the frantic seductive sound of the *tambu,* drumming from inside the mountains? Neither of them could say how many years it had been since the week-long poisoning epidemic, which first took their father's bulls, then his mastives, then the man himself; they could remember the last drought because of the pink-and-black-petaled strawflowers that bloomed only during periods of exceptional dryness. And they could hear their mother teaching them the alphabet as if they had savored the queer vinegary edge of her breath—she drank red wine—only yesterday:

A is for Albion; B is for Berkshire and Buckingham; C is for the Crown and Cruelty; D is for Devonshire, Drake, Decadence, and the Damned; and E is for Eternity, which is the length of any day under this roof.

But the alphabet failed to subvert the sisters. Their mother could not persuade her daughters that they were prisoners in a world confounded by an inexhaustible capacity for sin; she could not teach them not to call it home.

———

And so he came, as he must given the unwitting prescience of the sisters, the thinning of the veil stretched across the future. He was one of the freedom fighters, a black man come out of the mountains after untold years of struggle. He hung with filthy rags; one leg bled from an undressed wound, and the flesh around his left eye was slack from an invisible injury. There were no more bullets for the rifle he carried, but he didn't need them anyway for he had triumphed over his enemies, over all adversity, and was now untouchable. He limped through the broad shadows of waning moonlight. With eyes most keen after sundown, he inspected the *vévé* at the base of the gnip tree; other signs throughout the yard—the skeleton of a land turtle, an erebus moth that flew against his cheek—warned him that Derby Hill was haunted. But he knew as well already, it was why he had come, and he praised the gods for this opportunity, this further evidence that he had been chosen, that his trials were divine, that now he must wage peace on the dead as successfully as he had waged war on the living. He had returned to his place of birth.

The two old sisters, in between their first and second sleep, heard the sawboning of the jungle cease and knew he had arrived, passing over the grounds and into the house with no more disturbance than a stray breeze rising off the sea. They listened carefully and for some time heard nothing, nothing distinct other than the tremulous presence of his breathing in the kitchen, until finally there was an anguished cry, and the house echoed with his grieving.

"Why does he weep?" Mary Elizabeth asked in a whisper.

"Oh, how should I know?" Margaret Gloriana said, acutely agitated. She wanted this fellow to come up, present himself with expedience, then go about his business elsewhere. She was feeling especially old and frail tonight, weary of this recent plague of males, tipping the sublime calibration of the scales of sisterhood. Nevertheless, she felt compelled to defend him. "And why shouldn't he weep?" she said. "It's no worse than the other one's singing."

Yet it was worse, much worse, this tragic outpour, and it resounded through the ruin of the house and into the surrounding countryside like the mourning of a nation. "I wouldn't say he's terribly pleased to be here," Emmy observed.

"Quick to judge, quick to apologize." Her sister lowered herself off her elbows.

There was a natural rhythm to his baritone keening; before long the sisters had accustomed themselves to its aqueous surges, its failing ebbs, and were lulled back into their twin dreams of Captain Selcroft. They woke at dawn to the same sobs, which had lost none of their vigor. All through the day the man's marathon sorrow continued unabated, afflicting the two old Miss Parkers with its depth of wretchedness and preempting their sisterly discussions, but as the sun balled its light and simmered down toward the western windows, the crying stopped and Emmy, who was first to see him enter the bedroom, made a ravenous gasp for air as if she had been submerged underwater and had almost drowned. Thus alerted, Margaret Gloriana sat up in bed and, mortified by what she saw, just as quickly slumped back down.

"That's not who you think it is!" she blurted out.

"Mother of God," said Emmy, "you're in love with a darkie." So much of the time through the years there had been scant else to do but look in the opposite direction, not merely away from the tribulations of the blacks, but from the extravagances of the whites as well, and half the world was too full of wonder, the other half constricted by manners and taboos, to have extra room for temptation. And so Mary Elizabeth marveled at how impetuous her sister had become at the end of her life.

Margaret Gloriana, however, was hardly capable of speaking. "Absolutely not," she croaked without her customary authority. "That's his servant." But she knew this was no more true than her original announcement, that

this feral being poised inside the door was no more another man's servant than he was or could be her swain,
real or imagined, if at all a man himself, and yet despite
his lycanthropic eyes and beard, and the mien of a beast
who feasted on human virtues, from the sound of it he
had wept as other men do, with a crushed heart, a
long-suffering spirit, and a lust for the infancy of pain.
In this regard his humanity was more outspokenly noble
than their father's ever had been, their father who had
lived in a closet of avarice and moral certainty and had
died roaring hatred for all peoples, including his own
kind. Still, Margaret Gloriana surmised, she had stupidly, childishly, summoned a nemesis, the only lover
that would ever come for either sister—the brilliant sol-
itaire, their death.

As for the black maroon, whose name was Alvaro Toussaint Parker—no blood relation but the surname of a slave
brand inherited from his ancestors—he took one freezing
look at the sisters, the prominence of their yellowing teeth,
the transparent skin varnished around their skulls, the
witch's locks, the purpled eyepits, the beaks of nose, and
addressed them as if they were indeed already dead, though
of a more privileged caste of duppy than the other ghosts
he had sought to communicate with during his time in the
house. Falling to his knees at their bedside, he spoke to the
spirits as a supplicant.

"I might ask you to ask my mother to forgive me," he
said.

Straight off, the sisters were too amazed by the formality
and dignified tone of his speech to reply. He had mastered
their own language, the house language and empire's language, but emitted from so swollen a mouth it struck their
ears as a masquerade, a subterfuge. It so spun around
Emmy's thoughts that she changed roles and responded in

the patois that was or should have been his own, maintaining a most irregular social symmetry.

"I hear now, Moses, who you muddah?" she squeaked and, aghast, clapped her hand over her mouth.

Margaret Gloriana yawned, willing herself to remain composed, yet she began to feel drowsy. "Why don't you go on your way and ask her yourself?" she suggested. She blinked uncontrollably and yawned a second time.

"My mother was Lydalia Parker, laundress," Alvaro Toussaint Parker answered the first sister. Throughout the past infelicitous hours he had spent in the house, that's all he had done: asked his mother directly for forgiveness for betraying his eight brothers and four cousins by conspiring with the occupation troops, because you can persuade yourself of many crimes when you know you cannot win, nor your cause prevail, and so he had led his comrades into ambush. All night and all day he had offered contrition, beseeched his mother for absolution. Instead of acknowledging him, she would not come away from her scouring stones at the river, where she slapped massa's wet linens against the whitened boulders, kneading them like dough with her muscular arms, singing hymns of resurrection. He felt he would go mad begging her to come to her feet and comfort him, her youngest son, in his grim passage of leadership.

"Lydalia Parker, laundress," he droned balefully, "Lydalia Parker, mother of her country."

Lydalia's family *was* big, I recall, thought Emmy as she sank into unconsciousness. He bowed his leaf-flecked head to wait for the dead to deliver his penance, craving pardon so that he might resume his self-appointed mission without malediction. He remained kneeling, full of remorse; the sisters fondly remembered the laundress Lydalia Parker but had ceded the power to speak; the western windows blazed like doors thrown open to a hellish furnace. Blood-red glorioles irradiated the phantoms in the bed; Alvaro raised his eyes and saw the spirits reduce glimmer by shrinking glimmer back into nothingness of inert flesh. In the deluded mind of Alvaro Toussaint Parker, their departure was a merciless disconnection. The *loas* had rejected his plea, they would not enter as his advocate into the netherworld and intervene on his behalf. He bounded to his feet, vowing this was the first and last time he would petition backra spirits for their charity. He noticed the cedar plank on its pails, deciphered its smudges, and Alvaro Toussaint Parker condemned himself for not foreseeing the full and malicious range of plots he was up against. He crawled from the house, on hands and knees, sideways at times like a crab, to search for his mother's grave.

⁓

They awakened at their habitual hour, in the middle of the night, not to the distant pops of gunfire, or the chirring of the insects, but this time to the labor of muffled chopping, and they rose together, Ladies Lazarus, and went to stand in the northern windows. There was another, more fluid sound reaching them, like blankets being shaken out, and now they located its source, the high fire on the nearby hillside within the low stone walls of Derby Hill's cemetery. The shape of a man jerked between flame and shadow, lifting an arm, a skull balanced in its hand.

"It's the professor," Emmy said. He had been given to campfire reenactments of *Hamlet,* staged on the dirt between the cluster of servants' huts.

"What's he doing back, do you think?" Margaret Gloriana wondered—out loud or to herself, it no longer mattered.

"I suppose no one told him that everything's different now."

Hand in hand the sisters wobbled back to bed a last time.

Alvaro Toussaint Parker dropped the skull of his laundress mother into the conflagration, gathered the leathery scales of her skin, the kindling of her bones, and threw them in as well. He withdrew from the plot of his ancestors and slunk farther up the hill to its crest and renewed his digging, sinking the hoe blade with the broken shaft at a furious pace, as far into the rich ground as he could drive it. *Go on,* he heard the sisters urge in their transcended voices, and he struck open the old patriarch's coffin and cast his poison-twisted bones into the flames. *Go on,* the sisters urged through the night, *Go on,* as he persevered, emptying grave after grave, until by dawn he had spent his obsession, tarred by mud and ash and crumbs of dead peoples' clothes, and there was but one grave undisturbed in the cemetery, its marker carved with a sailing ship.

"Go on," exhorted Margaret Gloriana in the black man's ear. "That one too."

"Him especially," said Mary Elizabeth.

With all the strength of those before him who had been bonded to the land, Alvaro Toussaint Parker obeyed this ultimate command and hoed as long as it took to finish the job of enthrallment forever. Then, exhausted, he stumbled to the river, past the scouring stones with their dark sides turned up, stripped the abomination of rags from his body, and washed himself. Energy crackled back into his flesh and he returned to the grounds of the manor house and stood below the gnip tree, adorning himself with peddler's jewels. Naked but for these cast-off ornaments of his destiny, he reentered the shambles of the house and mounted the stairs, wrapped his waist with the threadbare sheet, tore the sleeves from the muslin nightgown and dropped it over his head like a vestment, and descended once more to the outside world to begin his long arduous pilgrimage across the island, to the capital where he would rule his people in the lunatic passions popular to this day, leaving the two old Miss Parkers curled on the mahogany bed of their parents, the windows filled with curious grackles, the *vévé* cleaned away by the advent of the rains, a graveyard readied for the future, the sisters hand in hand with expressions isolated from possibility but as if poised to fall faithfully under the influence of an irresistible attraction.

STOLEN KISS

On an inside day in November, a smoke and cider day, Burton Glass found a white greasy kiss stamped against the black post of the sun porch he was painting at the shore, off-season in Rehobeth.

It pleased him. Look at that, he said.

He worked facing the sea, which today was friendless, dulled by empty grandeur and an early winter. He saw only where his brush pointed, where the textures changed. In the cold his hands were dumb animals, struggling and stupid, pushing against their task. He wanted them to be stronger, to remember a better day, remember a woman or a fire. His leather gloves made him feel clumsy, so he took them off after the first few strokes.

Behind the DuPont place up the beach the geese on Silver Lake cried: the unmusical chorus, the tock of migrating wings, the splash of the spinning gadwalls and pintails on the restful water. The noise came across the dunes to Burton as if there were no distance between the lake and the porch, and it comforted in a powerful way and kept him company.

Burton finished the south post and moved over to the middle one, starting at the base. The darkly stained wood was dry, saturated with salt, rough but not splintering. He pecked at it with his brush, stooping to also take his pipe from where he'd set it on the deck. Too much of the season came through into his lungs as he sucked the cold stem. The ash was dead and bitter. He paused to relight it, gazing out along the strand. The sea was pocked, coarse like steel wool, full of dimension. As he concentrated on the match, a wave rose above the tidal slope, held up by the wind and feathered backward, splitting to the sand. He turned back to the post. Half the way up there was the kiss, circled by a glossy halo of oil that seeped out from the image.

Burton examined the mark. He had not expected such a thing. Tamping the lid back on the bucket of paint, he squatted down on it to meditate, to smoke his rum-flavored blend. He could not readily come up with anything to think about, then recalling it was the kiss that stopped him, Burton dreamed a little about the private act of a woman, into August and blood-hot air, skin blistered beyond appeasement but finally soothed by cream and lotion, smeared onto the face, over red cheeks and burnt lips. Little wordless dreams saying nothing, just feelings and fragrances that pushed their blessed way through into the day.

This was not his house. He rarely had talked with the women—mother and daughter—who weekended here, both dark haired, distant bodies he had stared at on the beach, admiring how much they might have given or how much more they could. The husband was a lawyer from

New York. As caretaker, Burton received his check, carelessly inscribed, and the checks of many others—lawyers,
bankers, businessmen—on the first of each month. The mail
had no immediacy for Burton anymore. For the past year he
only made bi-weekly visits to the post office—once for the
money, and once to collect the letter from his own wife, who
still lived in the Washington suburbs. She was faithful in her
writing. Her letters usually arrived the second week of each
month. They were chatty and honest and full of little news.
Burton enjoyed reading them as a diversion.

Maybe it was the fellow's wife, Burton thought, looking
again at the kiss. She seemed happier when her husband
didn't come down with her and the girl. There was never
that forced gaiety about her, never the staged manners;
even the clothes she wore were more casual and free when
the man wasn't there. But Burton could not discount the
daughter. The source of the kiss might have indeed been
her. He had seen how her breasts and hips had grown in
the past two or three years, how the boys had found her
out there on the sand, sometimes had heard the faint,
wonderful language she used, at night in the dunes, as she
marked her discoveries. She shrieked once when his dog
surprised them back there; Burton heard a young man's
voice bringing the girl back into his arms. It was easy to
love these things about people he did not know, but he
couldn't look at his own life like that. After thirty-two
years in Washington, it was hard to see what was genuine
and what was not. You had to decompress after being
down into it for so long, the *it* a state of affairs not unlike
the cold mud shore around the lake, gray and smelling of
decay, an airless trap. He had sat behind his desk all those
years knowing he was in the wrong place. The beach
became his tonic. To now work with one's hands, to scrape
and callus them, to be next to the sea when everyone else

had abandoned it, to preside over quiet cottages full of the lives of others—this was good, this made sense, to see and feel what you do.

Burton arose from the bucket, a familiar pain soaking his legs, to stand before the kiss. The lips of the woman or girl had set a perfect print. He touched the surface. It did not smear; the wood had taken it in, would hold the kiss forever in sterile ownership. He leaned out over the rail of the porch to knock the crumbs and dust from his pipe.

This was enough for now. Burton wanted something in his belly, a nugget or flame that would warm his blood. He cleaned out the brush so it would be ready for his return, passed through the French doors directly into the master bedroom—her bedroom. Usually he would keep going, but he stopped this time to turn up the thermostat. When he finished the porch he must work in here, replace a closet door. The bed was quilted, the pillows uncased. He saw small things he'd never bothered to notice before: a clean ashtray made from a cockle shell, a blue fountain pen and bottle of pills on the night table, a metallic tube of lipstick on the dresser next to a hand mirror. Why, he did not know, he could not tell himself, he had never done a thing like this, but he slid open the top drawer of the dresser— nothing. He opened another—bobby pins and ribbons, a tortoise-shell clasp. In the next one down were sheets, linen pillow cases, army blankets. The bottom drawer— two sweaters, lemon and pink, a folded nightgown, and a bra, the elastic in its straps warped from many washings, so many doings and undoings. Burton picked it up, held it, brought it to his nose to smell—ah, so clean. There was a slow, nervous thrill that came from the silken touch. Before replacing it next to the gown, he held each cup in his palms and imagined the breasts that once filled those crumpled, unshaped spaces.

STOLEN KISS

Taking the stairs down to the first level, he left the house, walking up the beach toward town. The lake was visible between the dunes, the noisy congregations of waterfowl, squadrons circling above, constant arrivals and departures. Not long ago he'd had a good dog, an Irish setter, and the dog died there in the lake. He didn't want to think about it.

The boardwalk began just past the DuPont place. Burton stepped up on it, into more wind, his high-laced boots booming down on the wood, the wind harmless against his stiff white hair trained since boyhood into three patrician waves that rolled straight back from his crown. His wife once said—it was soon after the war— she said, Burton, when you take off your clothes and stand the way you are now, turned just a bit around from the way you're going, you look so handsome and hard. It's your hair, I think, you have the best head of hair, and your nose and the color of your body. How did you get so tan all over? What did you do there in Italy? What was it like? You don't know how much I missed you.

I can imagine, he had answered, but in fact he rarely thought about her when he was over there.

The love between them lasted a long time, longer than he thought it would. It was still there, although they couldn't live together anymore. At least they hadn't used each other up to the point where they wanted nothing, where any desire wasn't worth the effort. It seemed to get that way at times—those middle years when they managed their love as if it were an anemic bank account. Now those days were over. Thank God for letting us be apart and at peace with the loneliness.

His eyes watered in the wind, his chest tightened under the woolen Pendleton. Onto Atlantic Avenue, he passed the shuttered guest houses, the pew-like rows of benches that faced back toward the ocean, the statue of angry Neptune, a lone bicycler in scarf and stocking cap. Inside the Sportsmen's Tavern, his eyeglasses fogged as he moved instinctively toward the first empty stool at the bar. He took a paper napkin to wipe his glasses clean, saw the blurred shape of Carl approaching.

"Burton."

"What?"

The proprietor ambled the length of the counter, stopped to remove a bottle of whiskey from the shelf, and then stood opposite Burton, pouring both of them a shot.

"Your wife called looking for you."

"She leave a message?" The whiskey brought back everything the wind had taken from him.

"She said to tell you that John Warner's left Liz for her. They're running off together."

"What, again?"

"Hah!"

"What did Carole want?"

"She says she can't make it this weekend and she hopes you won't mind. Somebody gave her a ticket to an opening at the Kennedy Center. She said call her back if there's a problem. You want something to eat?"

"If there's chowder, I'll have that."

After he returned from the kitchen and set the steaming bowl in front of Glass, Carl came out from behind the bar to sit. The two men had known each other for many years. Burton sipped the liquid delicately from his spoon.

"Get a new pup yet?" Carl asked.

"No."

"A fellow up in Henlopen has a setter bitch that just had pups. You should have a look."

"All right. Maybe this weekend."

"Rachel was a fine dog. Going to be hard to replace her, Burton."

"Good dog, sure. Dumb though. Rather not have a dog it if can't stand up to a goose."

They had debated the point several times since it happened. Burton said the dog got into the lake, chasing the fowl back and forth, finally swam into an army of Canadians that converged on her. Carl insisted the dog was just old, too old to swim that much, and a goose would be shy of a dog anyway. Red-haired Rachel must have drunk salt water and drowned, in Carl's opinion. Burton no longer cared how it happened, he wouldn't have another dog. Next time it would be the dog that was left behind, can't leave a stupid dog behind.

He stared into his bowl. The milky chowder was the same color as the kiss he had discovered on the porch post. "Carl," he began but stopped himself. He was going to tell about the kiss but thought better of it because when the words started to form they felt like a betrayal, like blabbing about the most intimate moments shared with somebody.

"What?" asked Carl.

"The chowder's good. It's what I needed."

He thought about Rachel. Can't have another dog, but maybe I should. Maybe that's the way my wife is feeling. She didn't put up any fuss. She said, Burton, I've known for a long time that's what you wanted, but I can't spend the rest of my life up there. It's too quiet for me. I can't fit into a place like that after living in a city that has everything. That's too much to ask, but you go on. I'll spend the summers there with you. The summers are good. And we'll visit each other, like lovers. That's the only way I can do it.

"You all right?" Carl asked. "You're not getting a cold, are you?"

"No."

"Another whiskey?"

"No, I'll be getting back now."

~~~~~

He stretched out on her bed and watched it happen, let the breeze turn warm again, the heat invade the day. He had a vision of her out there on the sand. She has tried to read her book but cannot focus; the words rise and recede on the page, throb behind her eyes, enter into her as some unintelligible force. She falls asleep on her towel and is unbothered. When she wakes she feels as if she has lost all privacy, that she has been possessed too much, too long, too hard, and every movement now brings pain.

The house is quiet, empty. Her husband never comes with her anymore. The girl is somewhere else, in town parading the boardwalk maybe. The woman enters the room. Although she is still beautiful, still unaged, her face looks battered and blank, untouchable. She carefully removes her top and Burton is startled by her white breasts, so white they no longer seem to belong to the rest of her body. An elegant, enameled fingertip tests the sore red line that vees to the middle of her chest. Her nipples exaggerate the touch. The tight pressure of her skin makes the woman grimace.

Burton thought that now her husband might come and provide a motive for the kiss. He kept still and watched.

But she remains alone despite the expectation that Burton felt in the room. Her hair is swollen and scattered, lightened softly in places where the sun held, where it slowly branded her. Her abdomen is stretched taut, a small, dimpled drum, smoldering underneath the surface. Legs, arms, and cheeks flame brilliantly, her lips pouted and raw as if they have been roughly, persistently, kissed. She twists the lid from a blue jar. Feverish and dizzy, she sinks her fingers into the cream, digging round and round. There is a burning that feels as if it drains her. She stands before the French doors looking out upon the water. Burton saw the strap lines on her back like perfect cuts where her torso had been separated by the sun. Below the horizon, the moon begins paddling the ocean, stroke by stroke across the shadowed water. The woman steps from bedroom to porch, bending down to draw down the bottom of her suit, the clear unsunned flesh unnaturally luminescent, almost transparent, in the dying light. She rubs the cream onto her scorched body, where it melts and sucks the coolness from the rising moon. Standing before the sea, she opens herself to this redemption and sways gratefully, one hand clutching the middle post, pressing her creamed lips against the wood.

~

Burton paused to study the lines, the ridges and cracks, the thin black space between full halves, this language of the past season, another life. He had loved his wife, Carole, through thirty-nine years, four children and as many homes, a career that seemed more vague with each new day away from it, and now this, their negotiated freedom.

He dipped his brush into the fresh black paint and looked again at the white kiss in the middle of the post. It spoke so much for love when all else tried to ignore it. He traced a finger along the outline, withdrawing his hand finally with irritation. He thought he heard a phone ring somewhere and stopped to listen. It was only the tide coming in, rattling shells together in the trough at land's end. Burton stepped forward and kissed the kiss, glancing to see how closely his lips matched those on the wood. Then he painted over it.

WHERE
PELHAM
FELL

Less than a year after Colonel Taylor Coates had been
told not to drive, he was behind the wheel again, smok-
ing Chesterfields, another habit he had been warned not to
pursue, clear-headed and precise in his own opinion, holding to the patriotic speed limit north on Route 29 away
from Culpeper in a flow of armies and horses and artillery
across the battlefields of Virginia. On one flank the landscape pitched toward a fence of blue mountains, on the
other it receded through the bogs and level fields of Tide-
water, and as far as Colonel Coates was concerned, there
was no better frame for a gentleman's life. There never had
been, there never would be, which wasn't just a guess,
because the Corps of Engineers had made him world-sore,
a forty-year migrant before they discharged him in the
direction of the Piedmont.

The confederate John Mosby came onto the road at the
Remington turnoff and galloped alongside the car for a
mile or two, spurring his Appaloosa stallion. The Colonel

decelerated to keep in pace. Mosby pointed to a field map clutched in the same hand that held the reins. His boots were smeared with red clay, the tails of his longcoat flapped, and he held his head erect, his beard divided by the wind. Colonel Coates rolled down the car window and shouted over into the passing lane. *You!* Mosby arched an eyebrow and tapped an ear with his map, leaning to hear the Colonel's voice in the thunder of a diesel truck poised to overtake them. The breeze flipped the Colonel's walking hat into the passenger seat, exposing the white brambles of his hair, blew cigarette ash into his eyes. *That coat you're wearing,* he said, pointing. *Your grandson honored me with a button from the cuff.* The Gray Ghost, as Mosby was known to those who loved or feared him, saluted and rode off onto the shoulder of the pike. The truck rumbled past between them, followed by a long stream of gun caissons pulled by teams of quarter horses showering froth into the air.

Well now, in the presence of consecrated ground even the imaginations of simple men are stirred to hazy visions, and Colonel Coates wasn't simple, only old, recuperating from the shingles and a number of years of puzzling spiritual fatigue, having been given too many years on earth. Brandy Station, two miles south of Elkwood, was where Colonel Coates really headed when he deserted his slumbering wife to replenish the supply of dog food at home, a legitimate errand that he automatically forgot in favor of cruising Fleetwood Hill. The hill was the field of war that engaged him most thoroughly, for there was fought the greatest cavalry battle ever on American soil. The site, virtually unchanged since the mayhem of 1863, had the smell of clover and apple blossoms at this time of year, a nostalgic blend that floated a man's thoughts through the decades of Aprils he'd survived. The Colonel studied accounts of the conflict, knew its opposing strategies, its advances and countercharges, flankings and retreats. He preferred to sit atop a granite outcropping on the knob of the rise and, with an exhilarating rush of details, play out the twelve-hour struggle for himself, the harsh sputtering rake of the enfilades, the agonizing percussion of hooves, swords, musketry. Here the sons of America had devoured one another as if they were Moors and Christians. Here slaughter within the family was an exquisite legend. History could be scratched by the imagination and made to bleed on a few hundred acres of greensward and farmland fouled magnificently by violence.

Almost a year without independence had made Colonel Coates lust for a prowl at Brandy Station. After the war between North and South, that was all the aristocracy had left, the right to remembrance. Taylor had claimed this right and felt obliged to it; his vigil registered in the bloody heart of the land as if he himself—his existence—were the true outcome of the fray: a florid, half-bald man alone in a rolling pasture, hitching his loose pants up repeatedly to keep them above the horns of his failing hips, stricken by the deep blue plunge of loss for those things he wanted but now knew he would not have; for those things he possessed and loved but whose time was past; for myth and time itself, for what was, for the impossibility of ever being there.

And yet he would return from the battlefield uplifted.

Out on the road, however, the Colonel was distracted by the withdrawal of federal troops back across the Rappahannock, and he bypassed Brandy Station, not realizing his mistake until he spotted the marker post commemorating Pelham on the east side of the highway. Major John Pelham commanded Stuart's Horse Artillery until he fell at the battle of Kelly's Ford, mortally wounded by shrapnel that ribboned his flesh and broke the forelegs of his sorrel mount. The skirmish was between cavalry charging blindly through a terrain of deep woods and dense scrub along the banks of the river, the riders cantering through trackless forest, squads of men blundering into tangled thickets, the legs of their coarse pants cut by lead and briar thorns. Down went Pelham as he inspired his men forward, and the event was memorialized many years later by a roadside marker at a junction on Route 29, erected near Elkwood by the United Daughters of the Confederacy, informing the curious that four miles to the southeast the young major had been martyred to the rebel cause.

Abruptly and without signaling, the Colonel veered to the shoulder and turned onto the country road, grim but unrepentant of the nuisance he made for the traffic behind him. Before the privilege of mobility had been taken from him, he had spent one afternoon in aggravated search for the location of Pelham's slaying. The direction of the marker was vague—four miles to the southeast—and the road that supposedly went there split, forked, crossed, and looped through pine and hayfields without bringing Taylor to the ford of the river. Sixteen miles later he threw up his hands and jogged west, eventually arriving at a surfaced pike that returned him to Route 29.

It was now or never again, the Colonel rationalized. From the diaries of the generals he had learned that an opportunity renewed by destiny could not be prevented. The soldiers themselves often hastened forth under the influence of such patterns through the same geography, wandering here and there until suddenly foes met and clashed. The paths they followed were subject to mortifying change. What was right yesterday might be wrong today. But that was the nature of rebel territory—a free-for-all. The Colonel, in slow reconnaissance, took the road to a T intersection, craning to see the houses at the end of their lanes, under a guard of oaks, evergreens, railfences. Virginia, he thought, was the abattoir of the South, mother of the destruction. These were the estates that sent their young men to war, the houses where the lucky wounded returned to expire, where the enemy plundered, where the secessionist ladies wept through the night as the armies marched by. What did people in the North know of the residue of terror that had settled in the stones and beams of these estates? Where in America were there such noble structures, one after another after another, league after league, each a silent record of strife and defeat? It was not an exaggeration to say that the Colonel adored these houses.

At the intersection the pavement ended and an orangeish gravel lane ran left and right. Taylor calculated a southeast direction by examining the sun. The odometer had advanced three miles. He swung left, pleased that the road soon curved, auspiciously by his reckoning, to the south, over swampy ground created, he was sure, by its proximity to the river. For four miles more the road wormed through this low, wet countryside reeking of bog rot, switched its designation twice, and then ascended to higher land, no river in sight, no water crossing, no defunct millhouse, no aura of hostility, nothing but the warm hum of springtime.

By God, I'm missing in action, the Colonel thought, confused as to his whereabouts. And that was how he met President Trass and ended up in possession of the bones.

Cresting a ridge, he sighted the glint of running water a half mile in the distance. The road he was on went off away from it, but there was a narrower track burrowing through a strand of hardwood that appeared as though it might drop in the right direction. On the opposite fringe of the grove, the Colonel saw he had blundered onto private property—and a trash haven at that. The track wasn't a road at all but a drive dead-ending in ruts around an unpainted frame house, the center of a cluster of shanty-like outbuildings and rusted junk. An ancient pink refrigerator stood sentry on a swayback porch, the only color in the monotony of gray and weather-hammered boards. A hound scrambled from under the foundation and barked an alarm. Colonel Coates tried to reverse back through the woods, but he wasn't up to such a maneuver. The rear wheels went off the packed dirt into a spongy muck at the same time the front fender debarked the trunk of a hickory tree. The station wagon lodged across the track, the Colonel demoralized and flustered.

It must be understood that the Colonel was not a man who was unaware, who had no insight into his behavior. He knew full well that he was becoming more spellbound by both the sacred and profane than ever before. Contact with the world at hand was lost or revived on an inscrutable schedule. So distressed was he by this condition, he had devised a plan for its rougher moments: If you get confused, sit down. If you sit down, stay put until the mind brightens.

He remained where he was, smoking Chesterfields with pointless determination, the ashes collecting in his lap. Picket lines formed in the underbrush beneath the skirt of trees. Then the guns played on him, and an ineffective hail of grapeshot bounced across the hood of the wagon. The Colonel withstood the onslaught, battling against the failure of the vision. Then came his capture and subsequent imprisonment at Fort Delaware, the parole, and at last the shameful journey home.

President Trass was a tolerant man, but eventually he became annoyed that his bird dog was baying itself hoarse.

WHERE PELHAM FELL

When Trass came out on the porch of the house he was born into, the Colonel noticed his advance and ducked down onto the car seat, felt immediately foolish in doing so, and rose back into view. He cranked open the window, shouting out with as much vigor as was left in his voice.

"I'm unarmed."

President Trass halted in front of the station wagon, wary of tricks. No telling what was up when a white man blockaded your drive. "Yeah?" he said suspiciously. "That's good news. What y'all want 'round here?"

The Colonel admitted his mission. "I'm looking for Kelly's Ford, where Pelham fell."

"That a fact," President Trass said. He slowly pointed in the direction the Colonel had come from. "You way off. You about two miles east of the crossing."

"Is that so," said the Colonel. "Much obliged." He stepped on the gas. A volley of mud kicked into the air over President Trass's head. The rear wheels spun in place.

Colonel Coates was invited into the house to wait for President Trass's neighbor to bring a tractor over for the car. They sat in the parlor, the Colonel on a threadbare sofa, President Trass in an overstuffed wingback chair. Neatly framed pictures were tacked in a well-sighted line across one wall: four tintypes of nineteenth-century Negroes; a sepia-toned group portrait with a Twenties look; an array of black-and-white snapshots, some of the subjects in the caps and gowns of graduation—presumably President Trass's ancestors and offspring.

To Colonel Coates's eye, President Trass looked like an old salamander in bib overalls, a slick, lymphatic edgelessness to the black man's features. President Trass thought that the Colonel, removed of the hat squashed onto his skull like a bottle cap, resembled a newly hatched chicken hawk, hot-skinned, old-ugly, and fierce at birth. They faced each other without exchanging a word. The longer President Trass considered the Colonel's *there*ness in the room, the more he began to believe that it was no coincidence, that something providential had happened, that Jesus had sent him a chicken hawk to relieve the Trass clan of the macabre burden they had accepted as their own for more than a hundred years, the remains of the soldiers President's granddaddy had plowed up on the first piece of land he cleared as a free man, a sharecropper in the year 1867. President Trass licked the dry swell of his lips, looked down at his own cracked hands as if they were a miracle he was beginning to understand.

"What you 'spect to see at ol' Kelly's Ford anyway? Ain't nuthin' there worth even a quick look."

"Eh?" said the Colonel.

"Say there ain't much there."

"That so."

President Trass kept his head bowed and prayed himself clean: Shared a lot of jokes, Jesus, me and You. First white man I ever *invite* through the door and You lettin' me think he some kinda damn cracker angel. Why's that, Lord? Well, I ain't afraid no more somebody goin' take this all wrong, leastwise this ol' chicken hawk.

"What's worth seein', I got," said President Trass.

The Colonel coughed abruptly and squinted. "I'm not the man who would know," he said.

"You come lookin' for soldiers, you must be the man. They's yo' boys, ain't they?" said President, and he led the Colonel out back to one of the cold sheds and gave him the bones that four generations of Trass family couldn't quite decide what to do with.

So the Colonel had defied Dippy, his wife, sneaked out onto the road ostensibly to buy dog food, and was returning home with two dirty burlap sacks full of what President Trass had described to him as noisy bones. Bones they were, laced with rotted scraps of wool and leather, too sacred for canine bellies, and tasteless anyway. But no noise to them the Colonel could detect, other than the dull rattle and chalky shift they made when he and the old black fellow carried them out of the shed and hoisted them into the rear of the station wagon. President Trass had what he and the Colonel agreed was accurately called a nigger notion: The bones talked too much, jabbered like drunk men in an overcrowded rowboat; the men whose flesh had once hung on these disjointed skeletons were still in them, like tone in a tuning fork, refusing the peace of afterlife in favor of their military quarrels. "That's a voodoo I never had use for," the Colonel grumbled. "Men our age always finding queer ways to pass the time." "I ain't yo' age as yet," President answered back, "and I never said I had trouble fillin' a day like some folks I know."

Colonel Coates wasn't a man to heed mere telling, nor to concede to age what age had not yet earned or taken. "All right," he said to the black man. "With all respect for your habits, I am duty bound to recover the remains of these brave boys."

"That's right. Take 'em," President said. "You might just be gettin' some nigger notions yo'self. Prob'ly do you some good."

"I've been waiting half my life for a younger fellow to set me straight," the Colonel said, "and I don't reckon you're him."

"Well, Colonel," President Trass said with a tight smile, winking at the sacks of bones in the car. "You finally get in with the right crowd to tell you a thing or two."

49

Since turning eighty, Dippy Barrington Coates slept more during the day, catnaps on the sofa in the den, a quilt pulled over her legs, not because she was tired but because her dreams were more vivid and interesting than they had ever been before, and nothing she witnessed in them frightened her. She hadn't slept so much in daylight since 1942, when she was always tired. Awaking from those naps back then she had been miserable. The extreme loneliness of the dead seemed in her, as if she had been spinning in solitude through the blackness beyond the planets. That ended, though, when she left the house to become a nurse. After the war Taylor came home from Europe. It took some time for him to become her friend again, to settle in his own mind that he wasn't going anywhere without her the rest of his life. The migrations began again, so many places, so many homes she created only to dismantle them a year or two later.

But none of the early years were as hard to endure as the three before the last. Taylor, infirm but alert, first his prostate and then the shingles, which left extensive scars across his shoulders and chest, issuing orders from bed: I want this. I want that. Goddamn the pain, let it off for sixty blasted seconds. You're a nurse, do something. Dippy, have you fed the dogs? Has the *Post* been delivered yet? Did you hire a boy to pick the apples? Dippy, come up here and tell me what's happened to your ability to fix simple egg and toast.

The house and lands were too much for her to manage alone. She had secretly put herself and the Colonel on the waiting list at Vincent Hall up in Fairfax. There were days when she wished to God that He would make Taylor vanish into history, which was what the man had always wanted anyway. Just as she became acclimated to the regimen of his illness and moods, he popped out of bed one day fifteen months ago, announcing he would occupy his last days touring the fields of battle in the area. He recharged the battery in the Ford pickup and motored down the cedar-lined drive on his excursions, to be grounded semi-voluntarily three months later after what seemed like, but wasn't, a premeditated string of collisions, mad acts against authority. He plowed into a Prince George County sheriff's patrol car, a state-park maintenance vehicle, a welded pyramid of cannonballs at New Market. None of these accidents injured more than vanity and metal. Each occurred during a low-speed drift, the Colonel mesmerized by the oblique and mystical harmonies played for him by Fredericksburg, by Manassas, by New Market, where the cadets had fought.

She had made him sell the truck rather than repair it. Taylor sulked and groused for several weeks, the pace of his recuperation slackening to a plateau. He entered a year of book reading, map gazing, talking back to the anchormen on the television news, typing letters to the editors of papers in Washington, Richmond, and Charlottesville, disavowing the new conservatism because its steam was religious jumpabout, lacking in dignity and too hot-blooded for an Episcopalian whose virtue had never faltered to begin with. *Are we cowards?* one letter inquired about a terrorist attack on an embassy. *Many Americans today seem to think so. We are afraid we are, but I tell you we are not. What the true citizens and families of this nation have learned is not to abide by courage wasted.*

Writing in his study on the second story of the antebellum brick farmhouse, Taylor could look out across hayfields and orchards to the Blue Ridge. He found the gentility of the view profoundly satisfying. On stormy days the mountains were purple. Dramatic shafts of light would pierce the clouds, and the Colonel was reminded of the colors of the Passion and Golgotha. For his grandchildren he penned accounts of the clan, the Coateses and the Barringtons and Tylers and Holts and Hucksteps, hoping to seduce them into a fascination with their heritage, the precious ancestral silt deposited throughout the land. *My grandpa*, he wrote, *was Major Theodore Coates of the Army of Northern Virginia. He was assigned to General Early's staff and fought valiantly for the Confederate cause until the Battle of Antietam, where within an hour's carnage he was struck directly in the ear by a cleaner bullet. The wound itself was not fatal, but it destroyed the Major's inner ear, denying him his equilibrium and orientation and causing him to ride in front of his own artillery as they discharged a salvo over the lines. The charge lifted horse and rider far into the air, so witnesses said.*

When one of the grandchildren, a boy at college in New England, wrote back that the rebellion, not to mention the family's participation in it, was too disgraceful and produced in him a guilt by association, Taylor responded, *You might reasonably suppose that your forefathers were on the wrong side in this conflict, but I assure you they were not wrong-minded, no more so than the nation itself was. White men weren't slaughtering each other because of black men, that was clear from the start. Read about the City of New York during those years. When you go into Boston on your weekends, what is it that you see? Do you really mean to tell me that Northerners died to save the Negro from us?*

What do you think of communism? he had asked a married granddaughter last Christmas. It's foo-foo, she answered, and afterward the Colonel decided he had communicated enough with the newest generation. Altogether it was a serene year Dippy and Taylor had passed in each other's company, and neither of them had much desire to go beyond their own land. When once a week she took the station wagon into Culpeper to shop, Taylor would occasionally come along, and he did not protest being demoted to the status of a passenger.

She knew last night had been a restless one for him, though. Troubled by a vague insomnia, the Colonel had slipped out of bed three or four times to listen to the radio, stare out the window at the silhouettes of the outbuildings in the Appalachian moonshine. When he urinated he said he felt as though the wrong stuff was streaming out, not liquid waste but vital fluid. Nights such as this he felt were nothing more than waiting to kick off into eternity, to blink and gasp and be a corpse. At breakfast his shingles burned again and his breathing was more constricted. He had difficulty concentrating on the morning paper. He complained that his tongue seemed coated with an aftertaste of medicine that even her coffee couldn't penetrate.

After lunch Dippy snoozed on the couch, the afghan she was knitting bunched on her chest. When she awoke she went right to the kitchen door, knowing he was gone. It was wrong of Taylor to do this to her. Trusting him had never been much of an issue in the course of their marriage except when the children were growing up, and only then because he played too rough with them, wanted them to learn reckless skills, and showed no patience for the slow art of child rearing. He had once knocked out Grover when the boy was twelve years old, demonstrating how to defend yourself. Throughout his life the Colonel had been a good enough man to admit his shortcomings, by and by, but now he had survived even his ability to do that.

She walked nervously around the house, emptying the smelly nubs of tobacco he had crammed into ashtrays, thinking about what she might do. Nothing. Phone the sheriff and have the old mule arrested before he banged into someone and hurt them. That would serve him right and placate the annoyance she felt at Taylor's dwindling competence, three-quarters self-indulgence and willful whimsy anyway, she thought, the man trespassing everywhere, scattering his mind over too much ground. It was as though the Colonel had decided to refuse to pay attention. If he hadn't returned within the hour, she would call Taylor's nephew in Warrenton for advice. In the meantime she couldn't stay in the house alone, marking his absence.

She put on her black rubber boots, cotton work gloves from out of a kitchen drawer, a blue serge coat over her housedress, wrapped a red chiffon scarf around her tidy hair and knotted it under her chin. On her way out she turned the heat to low beneath the tea kettle. In the yard the dogs ran up to her and she shooed them away, afraid their clumsy affection would knock her down.

Behind the house the pasture was sprayed with wildflowers for the first time she could remember, the result of a Christmas gift called Meadow in a Can from one of the grandchildren. She walked out into it and the air smelled like sun-hot fresh linen. She went as far as the swale, sniffed at its cool stone dampness, and headed back, the dogs leaping in front of her, whirlybirds for tails. She went to the tool shed and found the rake and garden scissors, thinking she'd pull what remained of last autumn's leaves out of the ivy beds, and cut jonquils to take inside. Below the front veranda, where the boxwoods swelled with an aroma that Dippy associated with what was colonial and Southern, she tugged at the ivy with the tines of her rake, accomplishing little. Then the Colonel came home.

The station wagon bounced over the cattle bars sunk into the entrance of the drive and lurched ahead, slicing gravel. She looked back toward the road, wondering if Taylor was being chased, but certainly he wasn't. Dippy reached the turnaround as he pulled in, swerving and skidding, making white dust. One of the front fenders was puckered from the headlight to the wheel well. She stamped over and rapped with the handle of the rake on this new damage Taylor dared to bring home.

He remained in the car, veiled behind the glare on the windshield, his hands clawed to the steering wheel, reluctant to drop them shaking onto his lap while he suffered his pride. The dogs barked and hopped into the air outside his door as if they sprang off trampolines. Dippy kept rapping on the fender with the rake, harder and harder, drumming shame. His jaw slackened and his shoulders seemed no longer able to sustain the gravity of the world in its orbit. He prayed for composure, for the muscle of his feckless heart to beat furiously against their damn devilish luck, the fate that had made them two living fossils, clinging to the earth with no more strength than moths in a rising breeze.

The Colonel rolled down his window. "Stop that," he ordered.

"You are a hazard, old man."

"Stop that. I won't stand for this Baptist behavior."

"Come out of there."

"Here now, stop that and I will."

Well, Dippy did cease her banging on the fender, but she didn't know what to do next to emancipate the sickness that came when she realized Taylor had launched himself back onto the highways where he was likely to murder himself. She jabbed at the fender with the rake once more.

"What was so important you had to sneak off like a hoodlum?"

"Bones," he said too loudly, "bones," followed by a sigh. He had jumped ahead and had to backtrack his explanation.

"Dog food," he corrected himself. She knew better and he had to tell the truth. "I wanted to see where Major Pelham fell, that's all."

She wanted to cry at this irony—an old man's irrepressible desire to see where a young man had died—but she could only shake her head. Taylor coaxed his limbs out of the car and she listened skeptically to him tell the story of what he had been up to. "Noisy bones?" she repeated after him, becoming alarmed. This was not the sort of information she took lightly. He brushed past her to open the tailgate on the wagon. She frowned because inside she felt herself straining to hear the muddled end of an echo ringing across the boundlessness. Was a message being delivered here or not? Her longevity had made her comfortable with the patterns of coincidence and happenstance that life enjoyed stitching, cosmic embroidery on the simple cloth of flesh. She tried to make herself extrareceptive to this peculiar sensation of contrivance, but nothing came through.

"I think you've finally gone cuckoo, Taylor Coates," she said.

"None of that. These are heroes." He patted the sacks. "Gallant boys."

Dippy was bewildered. Goodness, she thought, what sort of intrusion is this? Who's to say how she knew, or what sense was to be made out of it? A bridge formed between somewhere and somewhere else, and Dippy understood that the man who had given the Colonel the bones was absolutely right—they were *noisy* bones, not the first she had met either. Oh, you could call those invisible designs by so many names: intuition, spirit, and ether, witchery and limbo. Don't think she didn't reflect endlessly about the meaning of each word that could be attached to the force of the unknown. Even as a child her life had been visited by startling moments of clairvoyance and fusion. Each instance felt as if she had just awakened at night to someone calling through a door.

"Look," the Colonel invited, and peeled back the lip of burlap to reveal the clean dome of a skull.

She had dreamed and redreamed such a thing. There were occasions in Dippy's life, each with its own pitch and resonance, chilling seconds when she attracted information from the atmosphere that translated into impulsive behavior: refusing to allow children out of the house, once persuading Taylor not to buy a horse because she sensed evil in the presence of the animal, sending money to a Buddhist temple she had entered briefly when they lived in Indonesia. She avoided riding in cars with Connecticut license plates if she could. As a nurse at Bethesda Naval Hospital during the war, she watched a sailor die on the operating table after hearing her son's voice say, *He's a goner, Ma.* What about you? she thought. You're dead too now, aren't you? And then she held her tears while still another dying patient was wheeled in.

There are a few things you don't know about me, she had said to the Colonel in February when he saw her mailing a letter to a scientist she had read about in the paper, a man at Duke University who researched these phenomena.

That's not right, he answered. After all this time.

Yes it is, she said. Secrets are what crones and children thrive on.

The Colonel pawed through the bones, exhibiting a look of sanctified pleasure. Warriors in a sack, seasoned messengers of glory. Conscripts from the republic of death. Dippy cursed them like any mother or wife. Dog food indeed. Why else were the bones here but to tantalize the Colonel with their chatter?

"I suppose we better call the police."

"The police!" the Colonel said. "Never. I'm going to find out where these poor boys belong."

"There's only one place bones belong," she said.

"They'll take their seat in history first," Taylor insisted, shuffling the bones he had pulled out back into their sacks. He straightened up, frail and indignant.

"God wants those souls placed to rest."

"No. He don't, Dippy. Not yet He don't. Not till I find out who they were."

Rally them, Colonel, rally the boys.

As Dippy expected he would, given his interests, the Colonel became obsessed with the bones, the necroscopic opportunities they presented, and she readjusted her daily life to accept the company of both the living and the dead. Because she had forbidden Taylor to bring the two burlap sacks inside the house, he spent his time in the workshop that adjoined the garage, paying little attention to much else than his mounds of dusty relics. Every two hours she brought the Colonel his medication. At noon she brought him lunch and tea, and at four o'clock each afternoon, for the full five days he spent in the workshop, she took him a shot of brandy to tire him out so he'd come willingly back to the house, complaining of the heaviness in his arms. Between trips to the workshop she'd fuss with needless cleaning, cook, or nap, instantly dreaming. She dreamed of her first daughter's elopement in 1939 with a German immigrant who later abandoned her. Once she dreamed of the good-looking doctor who plunged his hand into her drawers when she worked at Bethesda—she woke up smoothing her skirt, saying,

Whooh, that's enough of that. And she dreamed of the two of her children in their graves, a little girl from influenza, the boy who died during the liberation of France. They would stay in her mind all day after she dreamed them. Not so great a distance seemed to separate them now, and she took comfort in the sensation of a togetherness restored. Even a long life was daunted by its feeling of brevity and compression.

And Taylor out there in the garage, history's vulture, pecking through the artifacts. She dreamed him, too, atop a horse, leading his skeletons toward the fray into which they cheered. They cheered, and the extent of her sadness awakened her.

"How do we teach our souls to love death?" he asked her in bed the evening of the second day, the fumes of wintergreen ointment rising off his skin.

"Who says you have to bother," she said. "Leave those bones alone."

"They'll be placed with their own," he answered. "I'm working on it."

What do you remember of your life? the Colonel had asked President Trass in the shed. It ain't over yet, President said. But I remember everything—the gals, the dances, the weather. What about white men? the Colonel was eager to know. President answered, They was around. Then he told the Colonel about his nigger notion and said take the bones because there wasn't a Trass alive or dead who was willing to put them to rest. Not on Trass property anyway.

The Colonel cleared his worktable of underused tools and spread the contents of the sacks across the length of its gummy surface. He turned on the radio, lit a Chesterfield, and surveyed what he had. He counted twelve pelvic cradles but only ten skulls and nine jawbones. One of the jaws had gold fillings in several of the bare teeth, evidence attesting to the integrity of hate passing through generations of Trass caretakers.

Well, twelve men then, a squad, a lost patrol, eighteen complete though fractured legs between them sharing twenty feet, one still in its boot. The first and second day the Colonel reconstructed what he could of twenty-three hands from two hundred and sixteen finger joints. He divided the ribs up, thirteen to a soldier.

Something curious happened, but he didn't speak of it to Dippy. Metal objects in the workshop began to spark him, fluttering his heart when he touched them, so he put on sheepskin gloves and wore them whenever he was out there. His hands became inept and the pace of his work slowed. He started the third day aligning vertebrae into spines but gave it up by lunch. His interest transferred to those material objects that fell from the sacks: the boot with its rattle of tiny bones, a cartridge box with miniballs intact, a flattened canteen, six belt buckles (five stamped CSA), a coffee can he filled the first day with copper and fragile tin buttons, indeterminate fragments of leather, and scraps of delicate gray wool.

On the fourth day he brought to the workshop a wheelbarrow-load of books and reprinted documents from his study in the house, prepared to concentrate on the forensic clues that would send the boys home. The weather changed, bringing a frost, and his legs cramped violently. Dippy helped him carry a space heater up from the cellar to supplement the one already glowing in the shop. When she delivered his lunch on the fifth day, she found him on a stool bent over the table, his reading glasses off-balance on his nose, a book opened across his thighs, lost in abstraction as he regarded the buttons arranged in groups of threes. He appeared not to notice when she set down the tray. The radio was louder than usual. Easter was a week away and the announcer preached irritatingly about the sacrifices Christ had made. Dippy turned the sound off. Taylor looked up at her as if she had somehow thwarted his right to sovereignty.

"I'm close, damn it all," he said, scowling, and yet with a fatigued look, the remoteness quickly returning. "These are General Extra Billy Smith's Boys." His voice became unsure. "The Warren Blues, maybe."

"You don't have to tell me how close you are," she said. "I can hear the racket they're making."

The Colonel waved her away and she left. Dippy did not think his devotion to the bones morbid or absurd, only unnecessary, wasted time for a man with nothing more to spend. She could have told Taylor, if he believed in what could not be properly understood, the nature of the noise the bones were making. The bones were preparing to march. She loathed the clamor they made, a frightening, crazed exuberance. She returned to the house and suffered the grief of its emptiness.

That night a thunderstorm moved in from the west, blowing down the eastern slope of the mountains. The Colonel couldn't sleep. He stood at the bedroom window and peered out, seeing atomic sabers strike the land. He slid back under the covers with his wife and felt himself growing backward. His muscles surged, youth and confidence trembling once again in the tissue. Here too was Dippy, ripe in motherhood, squirting milk at his touch. And here were his school chums, the roster of names so familiar, Extra Billy's Boys one and all. *Company D. Company K.* Fellows he grew up with. Well I'll be, he said to himself in wonder. I went to school with them damn bones.

On the sixth day Dippy went to the workshop shortly after Taylor, disturbed by the extreme volume of the radio music coming across the drive. Pushing open the door she was assaulted by a duet from Handel's *Messiah,* the words and music distorted by loudness. The Colonel was on his feet, at attention, singing with abandon although his lyrics were out of sequence with the broadcast of the performance for Holy Week:

O death, where is thy sting? O grave, where is thy victory?

His face turned red and waxy as she watched in anguish. His shirttails flagged out between his sweater and belt, the laces of one shoe were untied. The Colonel seemed trapped between euphoria and turmoil, singing to his audience of skulls propped along the table. His voice became cracked and tormented as he repeated the lines, faster each time and with increasing passion. Dippy, thinking the Colonel had gone insane, was scared to death. She hurried to the radio and pulled its plug from the wall. Taylor gradually became aware that his wife had joined him. He felt a funny pressure throughout his body, funny because its effect was a joyous feeling of weightlessness—he could levitate if he chose to. He tried to smile lovingly but knew he failed in his expression. Dippy stared back at him, mournful, one hand to her mouth, as if he were a creature unfamiliar to her. Then a calmness came to him.

"Dippy," he bargained feebly. "I don't wish to be buried in my blue suit."

She helped him back into the house, insisted he take a sleeping pill, undressed his dissipating body, and put him to bed. She couldn't raise him for supper, nor did he stir when she herself retired later in the evening. She woke the following morning startled by the sound of the station wagon leaving the garage. By the time she reached the window, there was nothing to see. She telephoned the police to bring him back, covered herself with a house robe, and went to the kitchen to wait.

Two hours later the curator at the Warren Rifles Confederate Museum in Front Royal observed an old man enter the building and perform a stiff-legged inspection of the display cases. Afterward, the same old man approached the curator with a request to view the muster rolls of the 49th Regiment. There was nothing unusual about the old man's desire, and the curator agreed. He offered the gentleman a seat while he excused himself and went into the archives, but when he returned to the public area with the lists, the old man had left.

As he waited for the curator, the Colonel was overwhelmed by a sense of severe desolation. The room seemed all at once to be crowded beyond capacity. He felt claustrophobic and began to choke. The noise was deafening, unintelligible, and he was stunned to think how Dippy and President Trass could tolerate it.

In the car again he felt better, yet when the road ascended out of the valley to crest the Blue Ridge, suddenly the Colonel couldn't breathe the air for all the souls that thickened it. He died at the wheel, his hands grasping toward his heart, the station wagon sailing off the road into a meadow bright with black-eyed Susans, crashing just enough for Dippy to justify a closed coffin. The undertaker was a childhood friend of Taylor's, loyal to the military caste and the dignity of Southern families, understanding the privacy they required when burying their own. With discretion he gave her the large coffin she asked for, assisted her in carrying the two heavy satchels into the mourning parlor, and then left, closing the doors behind him without so much as a glance over his shoulder to witness her final act as a wife, the act of sealing the Colonel's coffin after she had heaped the bones in there with him.

She was dry-eyed and efficient throughout the service and burial in the Coates's family plot outside Warrenton. Children and grandchildren worried that she was holding up too well, that she had separated from the reality of the event, that when the impact arrived she would die too. She could have told them not to concern themselves. She could have told them how relieved she was to be the last Southern woman, the last of the last to lower the men who had broken from the Union into their graves, how relieved she was to hear the Colonel exhorting the bones, *Keep in ranks, boys, be brave,* until the terrible cheering grew more and more distant and their voices diminished and she was finally alone, free of glory.

I ATE HER HEART

It was a wretched act of love and greed. I was in Galveston, playing the mouth harp with the Stank Brothers Band and crewing on the shrimp boats when they wanted me. She was another woman from Dallas who figured she'd look hurtfully sweet and sexy with the Gulf of Mexico as a backdrop. My Starlene, she was right. I fell for her hard. There was a miserable turn of circumstances. I made an irresponsible decision and took a bite from her heart. It was a sour thing.

Lord, how I suffer the loss of her. My Starlene was an inspiration to me. She smelled like a lime tree and had legs like a movie star. I never had it so good.

We met at the Wildcatters Picnic, where the Stank Brothers were providing the noise. Me and the brothers noticed her right off down in front of the stage. It looked like she was reading our message loud and clear. Playing in a band you get used to a lot of girls being friendly. When the music picks up speed, they start behaving like they got lightning in their pants. She was parading herself in green terrycloth short-shorts tugged right up into her Alabama, and a tube top of similar color wrapped tight around her bosom. Her legs were so long it looked like it would take all day to run your tongue down them from hipbone to heel. After a few songs this old boy came up to dance with Starlene. He was swinging and dipping her. They were moving fast to the rag. I thought, My God, those boobs are going to pop and sure enough one did. Without breaking step she tucked it back in like I might do my shirttail. I remember nodding to Roy Stank and saying, That's a fine woman there. I remember him nodding back and smiling like a weasel.

She settled in my mind right then. I thought of her as I played. My music started coming through in a purer form than it ever had before. I blew the Texas dust through those reeds. I sucked in the frontier and the longhorn steers and the Alamo. I spoke a version of Spanish and Apache and rattlesnake. I courted my mother's mother, charmed from her her toughness and suspicion. I took all the bums of the range up the tracks to Kansas City and back. My lips were burnt and bleeding by the time I finished.

She found me over by the van liquoring up between sets. I like my liquor, God knows I do, and that's a part of this story. I've always handled it well, but when you start chasing grief with booze you're in for a second world of trouble all your own.

Well, she comes up to me. The Brothers were inside the van, and they began to caw and squeal when they saw her. The Stanks knew no restraint. They're in the back of the van hitting up methiolade and sniffing canisters of Freon they tore off old refrigerators. I saw in her eyes that this woman had some tenderness to her, so I said, Let's you and me take a walk, thinking I'd never have a chance with her if she got in the van. She did poke her head through the door and say, Boys, you make it all worthwhile. They grabbed for her but she declined their invitation with a wise little laugh. I put my bottle-free arm around her high waist and we promenaded through the parking lot.

She said, "Mouth man, you've got a talent that makes me wonder what you're truly like. You've got a style."

I appreciate words like that, and I told her so.

"You're a good-looking man too, a good-looking ugly man."

"I know how you mean," I said. It took a long time for my ugliness to smooth out into something beneficial.

"They're the best," she said. "They don't suffer without good cause."

I knew what she meant. She was talking to the history of my heart.

She stopped by a willow tree, told her name, and pressed against me. I put my face into the curve of her neck. Her skin smelled like lime, a sweet, fresh, citrus sting. My nose is a weak part of me. More than once it has led me into love. I could feel it happening again.

"Mouth man," she whispered in my ear, "I'll bet you know how to treat a woman fine."

I let my hand crawl up her back and explore her curly hair. She lifted one of her long legs and hooked it behind me. We kissed and rubbed together. "I do," I said. "I do."

Starlene expected a lot out of those words, and I'll be damned if I didn't give it. Knowing what fame was for, I took her home with me that night and bedded her. In the morning fame went right out the window, and love swept in like new air filling a dead space. We spent the day licking on each other. By the time the sun went down, and I fixed her coffee, I wasn't the Mouth Man anymore, I was just me, Parris Deaks.

67

You know the course of such passion. She moved into my place, came with a suitcase full of pretty clothes, a big box of shoes, a transistor radio, and a bag full of stuff that filled every spare inch in the bathroom. She cleaned things up, though in a disregardful way, and put a picture of her daddy on the shelf next to the bed. None of that bothered me. My life had taken a step up. I was grandly in love. I had been in love with women before, but I couldn't recall when or where or who or how. Starlene seemed like the one and only. Women have always been important to me. I need to treat them like queens, but I never had one before who knew what she needed from me. Starlene needed the queen treatment, and I gave it to her.

At dinner I'd cut her steak up into little pieces to save her the trouble. When she took a bath, I'd scrape her skin soft and pink with one of those Japanese sponges. She'd get her monthlies, and I'd go into labor pains out of sympathy. She'd sneeze like a little kitten, and I'd get on the phone to the doctor.

The way I felt, I couldn't do enough for Starlene. I'd smell her smell, or ponder those legs, and get in a helpless state of giving. Her fondness for cocaine, I'll say, was not to be denied, and I did my best to accommodate her with what little money I had. She'd dope up a lot, but I never said anything. It seemed to bring her so much pleasure. She didn't usually get far off like some dopers do. As I said, I go for the booze, so I'd just sit beside her and drink until she fell into my arms. We'd drag into bed, undressing as we went. She'd turn on my unit and stick in a tape, always the Bonecrushers or Nellie Slit. She'd take the headphones and put them on. I'd nuzzle down between her thighs and have my ears clamped by her burning flesh. Locked in like that, I'd play her night lips in a harmonic fashion. She'd shove into me as if she wanted to be swallowed up. Occasionally I'd look and see the ecstasy of her face on the horizon.

Do you get what I'm saying here? I was in love. I was way down in love and never wanted to come out. It was the best thing that ever happened to me, and the worst.

After a couple of months she said to me, "Trailers ain't a decent place for life to advance."

I hadn't thought about it before. "Right," I said. "What did you have in mind, honey? One of those condo things? A cabin in the woods?"

"I like the water," she says. "I like the smell of it and the way the sun moves around like mercury on the surface."

I searched about and found an old houseboat docked at a marina in Trinity Bay. The guy wouldn't rent it but said he'd sell cheap. I was cash poor, so I called up my shrimper friends Jim and Joe (not their real names). They were organizing a run to Mexico and took me along as a favor. Everything but shrimp ended up on that trawler. My cut was large enough to buy the houseboat and something special for Starlene.

When I came back eight days later, she wouldn't go with me to the band jobs anymore. "Why'd you have to be away so long?" she said. "The Brothers sound like birdshit without you, Parris."

I held her in my arms and told her how much I missed her.

"I hate being alone," she said, looking at me straight. "You were always in my heart, Parris." She let go of me and placed my hand over her left breast. "Right in here, kicking like a baby. I never forgot about you for a second."

I said I wouldn't leave her again. I gave her the ghetto blaster I had bought her for a thousand bucks—a high-technology unit that sent out enough sound to kill everything in a forest or sustain life in the barrios. My hands trembled when I gave it to her. She said, Oh my, oh my, and cried.

"No one, Parris," she said, "not ever, has been this nice to me. I've always felt like property in a war zone, seized and abandoned, over and over."

"Aw hell, Starlene," I said, petting her hair.

"I suppose it's my fault. I need a lot of love and attention. Love me, Parris. Pack my heart full."

I told her I would.

"Forgive me my sins," she added.

I told her she was without sin in my eyes, that the devil wouldn't dare come near a soul like hers.

I leased this rundown dock in a secluded part of the bay for our houseboat. We seemed alone together in the world. I could piss off the side in the daylight if I wanted. She could sunbathe bare-assed, expose her real estate to the wild blue yonder. With a fishing pole or crab net, she'd snare creatures from the deep and transform them into spicy gumbo. The best thing for Starlene was when our house rocked cradle-like in the wake of a passing motorboat. It got to the point where she craved that rocking more than anything.

One night she said to me desperately, "Oh dammit, Parris. I don't think I can sleep with everything so still. Even these quaaludes won't take me out."

We made love, but still she kept her edge.

"Maybe it's the coke making me so restless," she moaned.

I'll see what I can do, I told her. There wasn't much I could do. I tried holding on to the dock and jumping up and down, but the hull had too much concrete in it to move that easily. The next day I drove over to the wharves, where an old buddy of mine worked on the supply end of a drilling team. He sold me a crate of dynamite at a pirate's

I ATE HER HEART

price. After that I'd blow a stick in the water whenever Starlene had trouble sleeping. We'd get about a fifteen-minute roll out of it, and if she wasn't out by then, I'd blow another. I never heard a complaint from anybody on the bay except once from a rich lady about the dead fish in the water. I said it was my intention to eat those fish, and it was no business of hers.

Sometimes we'd sit out on the deck at night slapping mosquitoes and stargazing. We'd count UFOs. The sky always seemed full of them. If the mood was right, I'd spit some blues through my harmonica. She'd hum a lazy counterpoint that would amuse me. I forget how long we had been on the boat by then, but it was during a peaceful night like this that I asked her a question that she'd been avoiding.

"Starlene," I said. "Nobody has a thirst for music more than you. When you going to come with me to another job? We're booked at Gilmore's Friday night."

The way she said *Never* made we wonder what was on her mind. Then she recovered. Her face came out of a shadow into the light of a candle that burned between us. I could tell by the set of her eyebrows that she was ready for finding fault in the world. "You ask that awful Roy Stank for a raise. Do that, Parris," she said.

I was low on cash again, had been thinking out loud that very day on what chance I had to get on a shrimper. I knew Starlene had a good point. But I wasn't deaf to the basic revelation of her words. "What's wrong with Roy?" I asked. "You've not said bad about him before."

"Never you mind."

"What in the dickens does that mean?" I said. It was the only time I raised my voice to the woman. "Roy do something to you while I was away? He make a move?"

"No such thing," she insisted, clipping her voice. "It's

71

you he's doing something to, Parris. Roy ain't giving you what's due."

I said, "Now honey, that's Roy's band. I don't play on every song. I don't have loans out on fancy equipment. I may be the best harp man in the South, but what's fair is fair."

"We need more money," she tells me.

"Cocaine ain't salt," I said. "You have to slow down."

She changed tack on me. "Parris," she said tenderly, "I can't have you going off on those boats. I was never meant to be alone."

"Neither was I."

"Then stay," she said, moving toward me for an embrace. "Roy will give you more money. That band pulls in a lot. Where would they be without the weight you add to their sound?"

"The question is, where would I be?" I told her. We didn't talk about it again that night.

About a week later, when we drove home from dinner at the Evil Enchilada, I noticed that the old boat had suffered damage—she was down a foot in the water. I got a bilge pump going, but the best I could do was stabilize the situation. Starlene was crying, and I hated to see that. Whenever she slipped into tears it made me feel like a dog.

"Must've been the dynamite," I said sadly. "The shock waves must've cracked the cement of the hull."

"Aw Parris," she bawled. "I loved our home. I love the creak and the sway."

"Don't you worry, baby," I said. "We'll have her hauled out and patched. You'll see."

"Homeless again," she sighed.

"Now don't worry," I told her. "We'll stay in the van until the work's done."

We rolled up our pants to keep dry and went below to

I ATE HER HEART

collect our clothes. She spent some time in the bathroom doing something to improve her mood. When she came out she was smiling what I'd call indiscreetly. Thinking back, I'd say she was calculating how to survive the narcotic hunger she lived with.

"We can stay with Roy," she said. "He'll put us up."

I didn't think that was a good idea. Roy wasn't much of a man without a guitar in front of him, and Starlene herself had applied the word *awful* to the fellow. The van would have been fine with me, but I went along with the scheme because I wanted her to have what she wanted, no questions asked.

We got over to Roy's place around midnight. The Brothers were just waking up. The house, a stuccoed old-style thing with red tiles on the roof, stubby palm trees and motorcycles in the yard, used to be nice but the boys had turned it into a pigpen. Between the needles and the dogs, the wall-to-wall shag was unkind to bare feet. One of the band's fans had taken a blow torch and written FUCK YOU and ROCK OFF in fire all over the walls. Two stereos were going at the same time, playing different numbers at top volume. Living with Starlene, I had become accustomed to a certain level of cleanliness. The Stank place was reprehensible. I thought maybe I could take it for a day or two. I suppose you have to live hard to sing right.

The Brothers were gathered in the kitchen for what they called their breakfast. There was no table, but they stood around eating vitamin pills. They had no other form of nourishment that I ever saw besides Buckhorn beer and orders of ribs from Smiling Goofus McTeez, that barbecue place run by some old black guy gone crazy on his Scottish ancestry.

Anyway, Roy was combing the knots out of his hair

with his fingers. He looked unrested for just getting out of bed.

"Roy," I said. "Bad luck's come upon Starlene and me."

He became very concerned. He wanted to help us, he said, in any way he could. I was a brother, he said. Starlene asked for a vitamin. Donnie threw some capsules in her mouth. I took a beer from the fridge but had to wipe brown sludge from the top of the can before I could drink it. One of Roy's hounds ran through the room so fast he skittered all over the linoleum, then crashed out a small hole in the back screen door. We made powerful music together, but I sure didn't like socializing with the Stanks. Their habits were lethal. They had minds like a trash dump on fire.

I opened a second beer. There was some disjointed small talk that came right from outer space. Everybody's eyes seemed connected to a rheostat—they just kept getting brighter and brighter. Starlene's too. She said, Oh dear, this is *good,* and giggled. The Brothers grinned like jackasses. Buzz found a ukulele in one of the cupboards and started strumming out this calypso shit. I was bored, tired, and uncomfortable.

I said, "Starlene, let's go lie down and nap."

She looked at me like I was spoiling her party. Her pupils had dilated fully, her flashing green eyes eclipsed by dark moons. Her face explored a series of expressions until it found something right, something serious and deliberate.

"Ask Roy now," she said.

"Ask him what?"

"Ask me what?" Roy joined in.

"You know," she said to me. She was by my side now, holding my arm with both hands. "Ask him."

"Ask me what?"

I ATE HER HEART

"Starlene," I said gently. "This isn't the right time. We're here enjoying this man's hospitality." What the hell was she doing? Maybe she wanted to be sure I wouldn't leave her alone again, but the way she kept going, I had to think it was deeper than that.

"Ask me what?" Roy persisted.

"A matter of business, Roy. Nothing much at all. We'll talk about it another time."

"Go ahead. Ask me."

"Naw, Roy. Some other time."

"Go ahead, brother."

Starlene took over, or we might have gone on like that all night. Her voice was squeaky and vicious. "Roy," she said. "You're going to have to pay Parris more money, or he'll have to leave the band."

"Well, honey, come on now," I said, like it was a joke. "That's not true."

Roy was rather delighted by Starlene's proclamation. "Is that right?" he said, looking at her, not me.

I tried to intervene. The two were making a kind of connection I couldn't break. "Roy, forget what she said. Donnie, what'd you give her?"

"Is that right?" Roy repeated.

"Yeah," she said. "You know it."

Roy howled and clapped his hands, a gesture that made me think he was a maniac. "Well, how 'bout that," he said. He was just tickled pink. "Donnie!" he yelled without ever turning away from Starlene, "how 'bout that?"

"Shame on you, Mister Deaks," Donnie said.

"Buzz, how 'bout that? What do you think?"

Buzz pouted his lips. "This ole boy is pussywhipped."

"How 'bout that? Lester, you have some thoughts on this?" Lester didn't. He had laid down on the floor with his eyes closed. He was in poor condition for talking.

75

Starlene was smoldering, and she broke out in flame. "Roy Stank, you are a worm," she hissed.

"But you like that, don't you, gal?" he said. He smiled wickedly and finally dropped his stare. He turned to me instead. "This little bitch has got you fooled, Deaks."

"Roy, don't say such a thing," I told him.

"This girl likes to gallop up the side of heaven and shout at the angels. Starlene's in love with the snowman, Parris. Ask her what she was up to when you was out on the Gulf."

I don't like fighting, but I was ready to strike the man. Starlene commenced to tug me out of the room. "We can't stay here," she said. She said it over and over again until we were at the door. I heard the Stanks back in the kitchen laughing ungallantly. "My honorary Brother," I heard Roy shout after me. "Just say the word and I'll take her off your hands."

"Come back anytime, Star Queen," one of the other Stanks called out. "You know how generous the Brothers can be."

Starlene ran across the driveway ahead of me, shaking her head and screaming, *Damn, damn, damn.* When I caught up with her, she spun around. "Hit me, Parris," she said. "Go ahead."

I'd never do that.

"I fucked up," she said. "I did you harm. You must hate me."

I held her, cuddled her head to my chest, smelling that scent of fresh lime behind her ears and along the tense curve of her neck. "You did no harm," I told her. "You own my heart. That devil tried to twist his way in, but it didn't work."

"Jesus God, don't ever leave me, Parris."

"I'd never do that," I said.

We had the houseboat hauled out of the bay and put in

dry dock. I parked the van next to it, and we quartered there. I said no more to Starlene about what happened because I knew no good would come from talking of it. For me the glory of the Stank Brothers Band was no more—I had to seek other employment. I went to see Ed Chiles of the Kamikaze Kowboys. He said the Kowboys were going into the studio in another month or two to cut their next album, and they could use me then. I did some roustabout work in the oil fields for about a week. The boatyard finished repairing the houseboat and handed me a hell of a bill. The yard wouldn't release the boat, though, until I paid in full. Starlene had no patience for anything. One day she took a job as a waitress at a nice seafood restaurant nearby but quit before her shift was over. She stayed in the van more and more, nodding to the tape deck, then at night when I was there she'd whine and complain. The tan on her legs began to pale. It didn't prejudice my love for her. I only became more determined to set our world back in balance.

To be precise, it wasn't more than eight or nine days like that until Jim and Joe (not their real names) showed up in the yard the same time I was arriving from work. They talked a lot of vagueness and indirection, as all of these fellows do, but from what I gathered they were doing something big and needed me along to replace a member of the crew who had misbehaved publicly and gotten thrown in jail. On an operation like this sums of money are not clearly discussed beforehand, but I was made to know that I would earn enough money to buy a new dick if I wanted one after the run was over. I discussed it with Starlene. She said no, she wouldn't be alone again. I said to her, Honey, this is the windfall we need to live a life free and unmolested. She sulked all night but finally gave in. I left before noon that next day.

Being with Jim and Joe can get dangerous because they don't give a shit what they do. Smuggling wetbacks, guns, heroin, pot—it's all the same to them.

This particular run was a junket for six Mexican thugs who couldn't afford the formality of airports and borders. We picked them up in Cancún, off the Yucatán. They gave Jim a garbage bag full of money for their passage.

I watched them come aboard at night. I know a little Spanish, so I asked them who they were.

"Nosotros somos Los Huevos Grandes," they said audaciously, as if I was breathing air only because they allowed it.

I thought that *huevo* meant egg, but I didn't laugh. People from other countries just don't think the way we Americans do.

These greaseballs were well-heeled. They all wore silk shirts of the most terrible colors. Their underarms smelled like overcooked chili. Two of them had briefcases handcuffed to their hairy wrists, and each of them wore more jewelry than I've ever seen on any woman except a back-alley whore. They were going to Galveston to deposit money in special bank accounts, get checked out at the gringo VD clinics, visit the cathouses they owned in the barrios, break the arms of the upstarts that were trying to move in on their action.

These Huevos liked to touch their knives and shout at each other. I tried to keep away from them as much as I could, but they were bad headlines from the word go.

Halfway through our cruise the passengers were having trouble relating to each other. A boat's not a place for people with no tolerance. Toward the end of the voyage I was fool enough to try to break up a fight

between two assholes in the galley. The one they called
Aguila took more than his share of rice and beans at
lunchtime. One of his buddies stabbed him in the hand.
I stepped in, and immediately there was a switchblade
pressed across my throat. Another guy came up and
wanted to slice off one of my ears to teach me the big
lesson—don't interfere in the business of Los Huevos
Grandes. He was laughing and thought it would be a
great prank. Jim walked on the scene just in time. He
told the Huevos that if any of them fucked with the
crew, they could tear up their round-trip tickets. That
message twice saved my life.

Bad weather drove us in near Port Lavaca, which is by
car not more than three hours south of Galveston. The
Gulf is big, the Coast Guard small—you're always bank-
ing on luck in a deal like this. We snuck into the inter-
coastal waters and anchored in a tiny hideaway cove in
Tres Palacios. On shore you could see the sandy tracks of
a fisherman's road winding through the dunes down to the
water.

After we set anchor, Joe tuned in the short wave and
contacted one of his local men for some transportation.
The plan was for me to escort the passengers to a roadside
motel, check them in, and pay for the rooms. Then they
were on their own to get to Galveston any way they could
to rendezvous with the ship in about ten days. I could do
whatever I wanted until it was time to head south again. In
the meantime, Jim and Joe would enter the harbor to wait
for better weather and then move the shrimper up to home
port.

Joe gave me fifteen one-hundred-dollar bills. I was to
pass a thousand of that to the wheels man, pay for the
motel, and keep the rest for pocket money. I ferried the
Mexicans ashore and told them to lay low in the dunes

until the transportation arrived. Rain kept falling the whole time. I longed for Starlene. I wanted that lime smell to open my nostrils. I wanted those sleek legs wrapped somewhere around me.

Jim came along the last trip and returned the Zodiac to the boat. From shore I watched the props churn up mud as they reversed out of the cove. I was alone with the six goons and didn't much care for it. I was also dying for a drink, a little taste to relax with. Nobody had much to say to me. I tried to be as polite as I could because I knew damn well there wasn't five seconds worth of trust among us. Paranoia isn't something that bothers me much, but this group wasn't exactly the Jaycees. I knew I had to be careful.

Los Huevos passed reefer back and forth and talked in shrill, bitch-like voices. Then one of them, Aguila again, the fellow with the appetite, found a sea turtle. It was a female. She had recently crawled up on the beach, probably thinking it was a quiet enough spot to scoop a hole for her young. They chopped her open and ate the eggs. When they were through, they stood around telling one another how virile they would all now be. I thought to myself, These savages make the Stank Brothers look like young Republicans.

What there was of the sun was fading into general bleakness by the time the transportation arrived. A big International Harvester all-purpose vehicle, its side and back windows blacked out, came roaring across the sand flats to where we were in the dunes. We packed in and got the hell out of there.

"Jim says there's a motel you know of that guarantees privacy," I said to the driver. He nodded once, kept his eyes straight ahead. We bumped and banged our way out to a surfaced road that led to Point Comfort.

"When you see a liquor store, stop," I said. "I got to buy a bottle or I'll go crazy. These egg fellows are bad on my nerves." He offered me some reefer but I passed it up. That stuff makes me sleepy and loosens my overall confidence. I had a night ahead of me and needed to be in control.

We stopped at a small bait and lure shop with a package store attached. I bought a fifth of whiskey. The Mexicans bought a couple cases of good Scotch, a case of Winstons, and a box of beef jerky. I was impressed by the quality and quantity of their thirst.

At the motel we came to everybody waited in the vehicle while the driver went inside. I considered going with him but then thought better of it. I looked like a tramp, un-shaven, clothes dirty and wet, smelling like diesel fuel. I cracked my bottle and drank from it like it only held water.

The driver reappeared. "Gimme four hundred bucks," he said. I did. He left and came back within a minute, handing me a single room key.

"What's this?" I asked.

"Waz thees?" one the Huevos echoed, his voice full of hostility. I had the sense this guy wanted to start a war.

"That's all the man had. Be thankful for it, buddy."

"This is bad," I said. "These boys are already claustro-phobic from the boat."

"Keep a low profile now," the wheels man said as he returned to his seat. "Don't bother other guests. Every-body's got to be out of there in three days."

I paid him off and escorted the passengers across a dark patio to the room. They griped a lot among themselves about being forced into one room, but they didn't pester me with it. As soon as we got in there they began to fight over who was going to use the bathroom first, who was first on the phone, who would get to sleep on the twin beds. I told them not to be so loud. They told me something that I believe meant fuck off and die. I began to worry that being with them was becoming bad for my health.

Bring us food, one of them told me.

"All right," I said. "What do you want?"

They wanted Kentucky Fried Chicken. A lot of it.

"Right. Try to hold it down while I'm gone," I warned them quietly. Like I said, I was just trying to be a nice guy, do my job, and get back to Starlene, as quick as I could and in one piece.

The motel was on the edge of a commercial strip. Once I was outside, I placed a long-distance call to Starlene from a booth across the street. I phoned the boatyard and had somebody go get her on the line. Her voice sounded very weary when she asked me where I was.

"Starlene," I said. "I'm with a bunch of people I don't like. Come rescue me."

I gave her directions and hung up. It was about eight o'clock. I walked down the road a ways and bought three buckets of chicken and a tub of coleslaw. By the time I got back to the room, the Mexicans had dug into the booze and were celebrating their safe arrival in Los Estados Unidos. They wolfed down the chicken and slaw and were soon noisy again. I tried my best to pacify them, but it was useless. Each of them had his own bottle of Scotch. A few of the guys were tying off their veins and shooting up. Somebody came toward me with a hypo, but I waved him away. He threw the thing at me as if it were a dart. I dodged, and the needle stuck in the lampshade behind me. He laughed, and I joined in nervously to let him know I could take a joke. If I had any sense I would have gotten out of there, but I figured I was safe, that business is business, and Jim had warned them not to harm me.

I lay on one of the beds drinking heavily from my bottle,

I ATE HER HEART

my nerves all jangled, wondering if I should stay in the room until Starlene showed. By ten o'clock I had finished my fifth but didn't feel the way I wanted. I started in on some of the Mexs' Scotch. The head honcho, who still had a briefcase locked to his wrist, kept dialing the phone, making contact with his people in Galveston.

This gang liked a fast track. They didn't impress me as being a tightly run organization, though. You can never trust low-life to stick together, even if they are goddamned eggs, or Big Balls, or whatever the hell Huevos Grandes is supposed to mean. I had not before been with men of such petty and brutal character. One of the junked-out boys accidentally burned Aguila with his cigarette. A knife was drawn and brandished. He was talked out of using it, but everybody wanted to yell about the incident. From what I could tell, they were trying to convince each other they were the nastiest lot of people on the planet. Aguila was an exceptionally swarthy man, a guy with droopy ears and nose and a mustache that looked as if it were coated with shoe polish, who usually hung back from everything. But whenever he joined the action, it was like throwing nitrate into a toilet bowl.

I didn't want a part of what was going on, but I didn't know what else I could do. I was drinking away my discomfort, pining for Starlene.

Eleven-thirty.

Twelve o'clock. She loomed in my mind like a big wave about to crash down. She wasn't there yet. I stared at the door as if it were my future, trying to understand what went wrong. Whenever I looked around at Los Huevos, all my eyes could see was blood lust.

By one o'clock I was itching I needed her so bad. Then I heard the knock that would provide my salvation. The fiesta shut down in an instant. The Huevos hopped up, dug out their guns and knives. The atmosphere was suddenly pure poison.

"It's all right," I said with confidence. "That's a friend of mine."

She came through the door. Roy was with her. They were both going a thousand miles an hour.

"Roy, you skunk," I recall saying. "What the hell you doing with Starlene?" I looked at Starlene for an answer, but there wasn't much to see on her face. She was on the moon.

"She wanted company, man," Roy said. He was dirtier than me and without good reason. He had an outlaw face, stained mustache, bad teeth, patched blue jeans, odoriferous T-shirt. I hated everything about him now, even his long beautiful fingers that could play a guitar so fine.

"Don't say another word, Roy," I said. "I'm in a dark mood." I gave him a hundred-dollar bill for fare back to Galveston and started to throw him out the door. He didn't resist. Roy had a big build and a lot of meanness deep in him, but I wasn't afraid. One of the Huevos moved up behind me. I looked at him and realized he was going to jump on Roy if Roy remained in the room another second.

"It's all right, it's all right," I said. "No problem. Just a friend who's leaving." I guess the Mexican considered Roy's presence a threat to their operation, especially after they saw how I behaved toward him.

Just as I had Roy outside, he squealed, "Starlene's gonna sing with the Brothers. Fuck you, Deaks." I knocked him in the side of the head with my fist and slammed the door on him. Starlene had been absorbed into the midst of the Mexicans. I forgot about Roy and went after her, grabbed her cold hand roughly.

"Is that true, honey?" I asked, tears forming in my eyes. The booze had gotten me into a terrible state of release.

I ATE HER HEART

"What?" she said thickly. "Oh."

"You singing with the band now?"

"I am?" she asked. She was all confused. No telling what Roy had gotten into her.

My heart was pumping strong for her. She was dressed in a dainty peach-colored sundress. Her curly hair frizzed out from under a sharp-looking straw Panama. I wanted to be alone with her and cuddle, drop Roy from my mind. One of the Huevos grabbed her ass. I pushed him gently away. My adrenaline couldn't find its way through all the alcohol in my blood.

"None of that," I said. "Time to go. I'll see you boys in Galveston."

We reached the door right as Roy was coming back through it, talking a supersonic line of apology and regret. If he had had the time, I think his intent was to beg a ride with us back to Galveston, seeing as how Point Comfort is at the back edge of nowhere, but the world jerked ahead to his speed before he had the chance to make amends. Los Huevos came in on us before I knew what was happening. Roy fell dead or dying into the room, his neck opened by Mexican steel. A grinning Huevo swung his knife at me but then restrained himself, allowing the blade to penetrate my chest only superficially right above my heart.

He immediately threw his hands up in innocence. "Meestake, beeg meestake," he said, still grinning like he had only stepped on my toe. He pointed at the door and said, "Gal-vees-ton."

I looked at the Huevos standing over Roy. Strange, but only Aguila hadn't been in on it. I stood up straight, feeling no pain, and went for the phone. Somebody put his hand on my shoulder, and Starlene began to scream.

"No policia," the Huevo with his hand on me said. It was the same guy who had just cut me.

"Right," I answered him. "No policia. Just an ambulance, that's all." I dialed the operator.

The Mexican took the receiver away from me, yanking the cord from the wall outlet. Starlene was still screaming. I turned in time to see Aguila lurch out of his corner. He was smiling wickedly. He wrapped a fat hand around Starlene's pretty lips, and they commenced to wrestle. I was a step apart from them but never made the distance. I felt no pain, only the blow from behind and my nose squashing as I hit the carpet.

This is the trouble that can visit a peaceful man sometimes.

The place was silent when I came to. The Huevos had cleared out of there. It seemed like I should have been dead, but I wasn't. Starlene was stretched out on the bed like a forsaken angel, her peach dress ragged up and blood-soaked, a tired smile locked on her bruised mouth. I bolted the door and went to her.

"Don't look at me so cold, Starlene," I said. "You know how sensitive a man I am."

I lay down next to her on the bed. I kissed her, squeezed her. There was no smell of sweet lime on her like there always was before. It wasn't good, she wasn't for it anymore. She was gone.

That fact grieved me deeply. I let her rise up to heaven on my grief. As I pressed her against me, my left hand caught in a hole just below her armpit. I pulled my fingers out of the chilly flesh and looked at them, then at her. She was slashed everywhere, as if the Huevos all needed to get inside her at the same time. Knife language—this was the only tongue the Huevos spoke fluently.

I reeled up from the bed and started drinking the liquor left in the room until I was as crazed as a man could get. Then I lay back down next to my love. I wept without

I ATE HER HEART

shame. I cried, Don't leave me, baby. I lost consciousness. When I woke up, it must have been hours later. The room was shadowy and smelled foul. I wept again. I cried, If you go, Starlene, you take too much of me with you. I gave you more than I knew I had.

The drunkenness had left me, but I had fallen into a delirious condition. There was a large pain in my chest, and I imagined it was the loss of Starlene's love. This was how it felt when two hearts were separated forever. I knew that if there was any love left, it would have to be located in her. That's where I would find it and restore myself.

I settled down and considered these thoughts. She had a long cut right below her breastbone. I stuck my hand in there and wiggled it up under the ribcage until I gripped her heart muscle. I just held it, waiting for something to run back into my veins. I fell asleep that way. The rest might be a dream for all I knew. When I withdrew my hand, I thought I had found what I was hoping for. In my palm was a hard little pearl. I studied it and thought, This is me, this is my part, what I gave her, the seed that got inside like a grain of sand in an oyster and grew to be love. I bit into it, believing that I had to get it back circulating in my own flesh. I spit it out, it was such a sour thing. The agony in my chest remained unsoothed.

This is all I'm going to say about it. It's been bad enough already. I spent three days alone with her and my wretchedness until they busted the door down and dragged me out.

They tagged me for conspiracy to aid and abet the illegal entry of aliens. The cannibalism charge that was finally dropped got a lot of attention from the press. I had to take the heat for Jim and Joe, although Los Huevos now conduct their business from behind bars.

My lawyer was expensive and encouraged the judge to

show compassion in the end. I'm not in prison or the nuthouse but spending six months on a model farm with a high reform rate.

Oh Starlene, I miss you sorrowfully.

Not too long ago this tweedy fellow drops by asking me if I've changed. Yes sir, I have, I answered him. I'll never do a foolish thing like that again, I swear. Do you regret your deeds? he asked. Mister, I don't, I said. Except in a legal way. He left and I went back to watching the soaps on TV.

I stay up all night thinking things over. I'm not a bad man. I didn't hurt anybody, no one died by my hand. I guess I've been around the wrong sort of people too long. Somebody's been a poor influence on me. Maybe it was just her, the way she made you believe you were giving so much, and it was paying off, like you were making smart investment uptown. Isn't there a Mexican saying that goes something like, You eat the heart, or the heart eats you? Maybe I was thinking of that when I ate the damn thing.

I think somewhere there's a woman who'll understand what I did, the right and the wrong of it, and come to comfort me.

Honey, get in touch. I'm ready for love again.

CELEBRATIONS OF THE NEW WORLD

It is July Fourth and my mother-in-law has decided that since Lorraine and I were married in a courthouse without family present, now is the time for the two households that are joined in us to come together. I am not happy with the idea, especially since my own mother has turned that basic, intimate idea into an extravaganza.

We will meet at my wife's parents' house in the Chestnut Hill district of Philadelphia. My side comes east a week early to sightsee in Washington. They drive in for the occasion from Moberly, Missouri, and thereabouts in two station wagons, a Monte Carlo, my father's kelly-green Cadillac, and rented Winnebago—except for Uncle Alabard, who flies into Dulles Airport from the West Coast the day before the reunion.

My parents stay with me and Lorraine and the baby in our town house near the Torpedo Factory in old Alexandria. The rest of the folks, the aunts and uncles and cousins, the nieces and nephews and grandchildren, stay at the

Marriott Inn in Rosslyn. They linger at breakfast each morning, enchanted with the view of the city from the rooftop restaurant. I am there also, their tour guide, waiting to herd them across the river and march them along the streets of the capital.

Together my relatives represent a substantially homogenized group. They are clean and slow, responsible and readily impressed. My father became rich during World War II mining fire-brick clay from the rolling, unimaginative landscape of central Missouri. Only when he first started the business did he really have to labor at it. Afterward he took life easy, fishing and hunting, raising bird dogs, and watching my mother, the perfect small-town matron, organize charity fund-raisers at the Moberly fire station. He would send her off on days-long shopping sprees in St. Louis, Kansas City, or Chicago, and he took these opportunities to drive down the road to Columbia to attend the basketball games and to flirt harmlessly with the girls at the university.

As for the rest of them, I can't remember exactly who does what. My uncles (except for Alabard) and cousins are, I believe, farmers, and I suspect my father has bankrolled each and every one of them as restitution for not allowing my mother's side of the family into his business. I am grateful to my father for having had the imagination not to farm. It's no secret that I have never appreciated my Midwestern heritage. As I grew older, the dusty streets of Moberly seemed like bars across my life. I felt like an eagle stuffed into a shoe box, a symphony played on a Jew's harp. I am still sensitive about it, but that seems to be gradually passing now that I am relocated and independent, have a family of my own, and look forward to making a name for myself in the maze of corridors on Capitol Hill.

The kids all want to stay in town for the Fourth to pack in one more visit to the new Air and Space Museum and to hang around until dark when the fireworks go off at the Washington Monument. I align myself with the kids, but it's the matriarchs who have the final say, as they always seem to do when family business is at stake. My mother thinks it's a grand idea, an *inspiration,* to wrap up their trip with a dinner and celebration in the City of Brotherly Love—the sponsor of the Constitutional Conventions and home of her favorite forefather (you know who, and she never misses an opportunity to quote him saving pennies). Although Lorraine's mother, Rose, has organized this, and although she really had something smaller in mind when she talked to Gloria, my mother, on the phone in December, she has accepted Gloria's single-minded vision and even joined in the spirit by inviting her husband Bernie's cousins from New York City and sending Uncle Joachim Elrojo (Bernie's last living brother) a round-trip ticket to fly up from Mexico City. Rose herself is an only child—her parents died in a car accident in the Fifties—so she stands alone against the onslaught, especially since Bernie has started to slip away from her.

Lorraine and I make it a point to be the first to arrive in Philadelphia to help Rose with the preparations. Uncle Alabard, my father's only brother, wants to ride up with us. I haven't seen him since I was a boy, but I know that he usually lives in Las Vegas, taking his chances with the money he earned originally by investing in Dad's mines thirty-five years ago. In the car, Albie (he asks us to call him that) amuses the baby with coin tricks and celebrity imitations. His Peter Lorre is pretty good; his Jerry Lewis, appropriately clumsy. Lorraine and I both fall in love with the guy. At the tollbooths on the turnpike, Albie rolls down his backseat window and tries to talk the attendants into flipping a silver dollar for double or nothing.

"Where I come from, see," he says in the voice of Jimmy Cagney, "anything goes."

We reach the Schuykill Expressway by noon. A yellowish dome of humidity and pollution presses down into the city. Albie talks about staying an extra day, renting a car, and driving over to Atlantic City to see some fellows he knows who have maneuvered casino gambling onto the ballot in November. What a dream, to get in on the ground floor of that one, Albie tells us. I turn away from the downtown area and count the stoplights to Jefferson Boulevard.

I pull into the Alazars' long driveway. We are relieved by the coolness of the shady oaks and maples and ever-greens. The smell of boxwoods is colonial and delicious. The flagstone house stands up out of a girdle of ancient azaleas and rhododendron. Double chimneys rise above the steep black-slate roof at both ends of the house. It was built in 1821 by Rose's great-great-grandfather, who fled his native Cork County in Ireland, accused of the murder of a queen's magistrate. Rose insists that the man was guilty only of patriotism.

I park and walk around the car, and Lorraine hands the baby out to me so she can get out. Lorraine is her usual bright, dynamic self. She gets frantic, and she gets meekly depressed, but I have never seen her sour. Since she cut her black hair boyishly short at the beginning of the summer, her dark, moist eyes (like her father's) dominate her face, foreign and penetratingly mystic.

Rose's two poodles are out on the lawn. They run up yapping and sprinkle my sandaled feet with excited drops of pee. Albie mistakes them for ankle biters and is reluctant to leave the car. Curiously, it is Bernie, not Rose, who answers the doorbell. Lorraine and I are fully aware of

Bernie's condition; for the past year now, Rose has found something to occupy him when she expects visitors. Bernie's face is set, as if he's waiting for us to come to the point. A white frost has settled deeper into his hair since we saw him several months ago.

"Rose," he calls back into the house, "the pizzas are here. How much is it?" he says, fishing into the pockets of his baggy trousers.

"Hello, Daddy," says Lorraine, stepping forward to hug him. "How are you feeling?"

Bernie looks quite fresh, quite alive, deceivingly healthy. "Hello," he answers, looking at us closely, polite and then puzzled. I realize that he still doesn't recognize us, that he is foraging in the expanding wilderness of his brain, cast out from those friendly habitual places that made the world fit tightly together, and there is no spark of cognizance, no electricity flushing across the terrible dark gaps. When his expression turns to desperation, I imagine that while his heart pushes toward us he is furiously searching the margins of his mind for a note of information, an imperishable root, to verify his weak sense of knowing us. Rose's voice calls to us from somewhere in the house.

"Is that you, kids? You're early. Come back to the kitchen. If Bernie's there, bring him with you."

I throw my free arm around Bernie's shoulder and pat his back, guiding him along. We no longer seem a mystery to him. He bends toward the baby in my other arm, inspecting her, his face awkward. He pats her silky head softly, lovingly.

"Do you know who I am?" Bernie asks the baby. "I'm your grandfather."

Behind us Lorraine sighs with relief. She teasingly says, "Don't forget your daughter, Bernie. It takes one of those to make grandchildren, you know."

"Oh, yes," says Bernie without looking around.

We find Rose busy at the stove. All of the gas burners blaze with blue flames; a light on the microwave oven blinks on and off like a warning signal on a rough high-way. Lids clatter against pots overboiling with steam and the rich, exotic aromas of cumin and garlic, olive oil and lemon. Rose wears an ironed flower-print apron over her brown cotton slacks and white sleeveless blouse. She looks harried but beautiful. Besides her daughter, she is the most energetic, capable woman I know. Because she chose to have a small family, she was able to have a career of her own, away from the house, away from Bernie. Now she's a special assistant to the president of Temple University, a job she loves. I can see her at the conference table, her elegant hands folded atop a black binder of statistics, her reddish hair igniting the hearts of her male colleagues.

Unlike Lorraine, however, Rose often gets carried away with her sense of duty. Lorraine has told me stories of Rose beating her on the head with an espadrille for the usual childhood offenses. I suppose that was the hot blood of her ancestors pulsing to the surface. I like Rose, though; she has always treated me like one of her own, but she has a way of assuming you agree with her, and forcing it when you don't. She is generous enough to ask my opinion (Gloria won't ask), but like my own mother's, her mind is always predisposed toward the rigid or the unpredictable.

Rose sets down her big wooden spoon to kiss us and hold the baby while I introduce her to my uncle. She is eagerly affectionate toward Lorraine, taking her daughter's hand in hers and not letting go, interested in how things have been for us. Bernie and Albie are looking at each other as if they don't know what to do.

"Bernie, this is Albie," I say. "Albie, Bernie."

"Alazar," says Bernie.

"Yeah?" says Albie. "I met this guy once at the Stardust who called himself Sheik Alacazar. Money was like sand in the desert to him. Couldn't play cards, though."

"Bernie's Lebanese. His father was ambassador to Washington after World War One," I tell him. "Bernie used to teach foreign affairs at Columbia."

"No kidding?" says Albie. "Say, you like to play cards?" he asks, pulling a fresh deck from the inside pocket of his pastel sports jacket.

"Sure," says Bernie.

The two of them sit down across from each other at the kitchen table. Bernie appreciates my uncle's card-shuffling ability. His eyes become the eyes of a priest fingering through a racy magazine, trying to concentrate and be casual and indifferent simultaneously. Albie smacks and pops the cards and they dive together like trained fish. Rose puts the baby into our portable crib and takes Lorraine by the arm. The two of them disappear into the expanse of the house.

"What'll it be, Bern?" asks Albie.

"Blackjack?"

The cards fly forward and I am at the liquor cabinet fixing myself a rum and tonic when the baby starts to cry. "She's hungry," Lorraine yells from the back of the house. "Her formula is in the blue bag."

I liberate a burner on the stove to warm the bottle. While I am waiting, I inspect the food that Rose is preparing. She fancies herself a superior cook of Middle Eastern cuisine (Bernie's magnanimity has encouraged this). She has created her specialties for our get-together. I wonder about this choice since the members of my family are corn-fed people and not generally adventurous or curious about what they put in their mouths. I sample the kibbeh and pine nuts—overspiced and mediocre. The grape leaves are pasty inside.

Bernie ignores his cards momentarily to pick up the baby. She stops crying. He sits back down with her in his lap, propped up straight against his chest.

"Hit us," he tells Albie. Albie lays a nine on Bernie's king.

"Bust," says Albie.

Bernie slowly draws his down card toward him and shows it to the baby. The kid instinctively grabs it. Bernie carefully unwraps her fingers and tosses the card face up on the table. It is a two of diamonds.

"Twenty-twenty-twenty-one," says Bernie. He smiles bashfully.

The bottle is ready and Bernie insists on feeding the baby while she sits with him. I watch for any signs of trouble, but he remains attentive to both her and the cards. His dusky, Eastern eyes are serene. His freshly shaven jaw relaxes. I open cold bottles of White Horse ale for the two men and fix myself another drink. As a team, Bernie and the baby play against Uncle Albie. It is a rare, beautiful picture, something to hold on to, to preserve against the days ahead. I decide to go to the car for my camera and photograph the three of them together.

On the way back to the kitchen, I look through the bay window at the rear of the long living room and see the screened shadows of my wife and mother-in-law sitting in deck chairs on the porch. Beyond the house, the grounds are lush and thickly green, overcome with trees and filled with flower gardens. The strong, natural peace of what I see disturbs me in a way I do not fully understand. Perhaps it's only knowing that on the far side of the barrier of woods, less than a mile away, an urban nightmare, a monster of trash and neon and stone, is winding up for a holiday spree, and all leaves of absence on the Philly P.D. and Fire Department have been canceled. I return to the kitchen wondering what the two women are talking about.

"Your father-in-law is beating the pants off me," Albie says.

"Thatta boy, Bernie," I say. The baby has fallen asleep on his lap and he has set her bottle next to his own on the table. I take a light reading and snap away. Bernie starts talking in what sounds like German.

"*Der spichken vonbringst mein stubberflappen,*" he says. "*Lipshitz.*" He goes on and on.

"You go to school in Germany or something?" Albie asks him.

Bernie does not stop to answer. His magnetic eyes jump from Albie to the cards to me, confident that we understand what he says.

"*Ott blashauden meister,*" Bernie says. Suddenly he is quiet, his teeth clenched, the lines on his forehead pinched in confusion. "I don't know what that means," he says. But then he smiles cheerily.

Albie looks at me to confirm his guess that Bernie is playing a joke. I am laughing, and now Bernie is laughing with me, and I can only shrug my shoulders.

"He's getting old," I say.

"Geez, he don't look any older than me," says Albie.

"I have a disease," Bernie says indifferently. "Alzheimer's disease."

"No kidding." Albie doesn't know what else to say.

"Bernie's all right," I tell him. "In fact, he's in good shape. They fear this man out on the golf course."

"That's right," says Bernie.

"Sometimes he just forgets things," I say.

97

"You want to deal?" Albie asks, his one sure gesture of compassion.

Bernie deals. Rose bursts into the kitchen, with Lorraine several steps behind her. Their presence creates an ambiguous tension. I try to look at Lorraine, but she seems to be staring into space.

"Oh my God, look at the time!" Rose shrieks. It is one P.M. "Uncle Joachim's flight arrives in twenty minutes. You'll have to pick him up for me, Jack."

"That's no problem."

Lorraine says she will stay behind to help with the cooking and to greet the relatives when they arrive. She looks as if she needs to get out of the house, but there's no sense asking her to come along. Because Rose has never met Joachim, I ask Bernie what he looks like.

"He's red," says Bernie. He will say no more on the subject; his meaning is indecipherable. Rose adds what little she can.

"He's four years older than Bernie. In the Thirties he left Paris, where he was studying something peculiar—maybe it was linguistics—and followed Trotsky to Mexico. He even changed his name from Alazar to Elrojo. From the letters that he writes Bernie, he seems to be a very dedicated man. Nobody in the family has seen him since 1938, when he spent a year in Pittsburgh organizing the steelworkers. Just keep an eye out for a little old Lebanese-Mexican man with more nose than a face deserves."

Under a daisy pushpin, she finds the flight number on her bulletin board and gives it to me. Lorraine follows me out to the car. Her skin glows in the dappled watery light soaking through the trees. Her eyes are red. I can see she's been crying.

"Rose says Daddy's much worse," Lorraine tells me.

"You could see it when he answered the door. He didn't even know us."

"In the kitchen he was talking like a German, making the words up. Uncle Albie finally began to answer him. You would have thought they were at a beer hall in Dusseldorf playing pinochle."

Lorraine laughs and tries to hold on to her lightheartedness. She usually can and she does again. Her long fingers pick at the buttons on her blouse.

"Oh brother, Jack, what am I supposed to do? He's loony. My distinguished poppa's becoming a loony bird. Rose says that she always has to keep an eye on him now. Last week he was supposed to play in a tournament at the club and he put his golf bag in the car and drove around and around while his partners waited all morning for him to show. The first thing he asked Rose when he got home that night was, what were his golf clubs doing in the backseat?"

She pauses to emphasize what she is going to say. "A *policeman* had to bring him home. He couldn't find the street by himself. This from a man who has influenced American foreign policy. He'll put on his coat and start out the door without any idea where he's going. Rose had a special lock installed on the front door to keep him in. She lets him out in the back and he digs around all day like a mole and cuts flowers to bring to her."

"I should leave now or I'm not going to make it," I say.

"You've got to talk to Rose when you come back," Lorraine says. "Mom says that as long as he knows her she won't let him down, but I think she can't take it anymore and that means she'll commit him. She's searching for an answer, Jack. She feels so guilty."

I reassure Lorraine that I will talk with Rose, although if there is any decision to be made, I'm sure she has already

99

beaten us to it. As I pull out, a black Continental with New York license plates squeals into the driveway. Its radio blasts out the Yankees game. Bernie's cousins from Queens, undoubtedly. They are very, very swarthy-looking, dangerous in my suburban imagination.

The holiday traffic around the city is heavy. I arrive at the airport late, my shirt drenched in sweat, but the flight is delayed. I wait in the bar, distracted, my thoughts occupied with those portions of Bernie's cerebrum shrinking like old grapefruit. I made a pilgrimage to the hospital on a Sunday afternoon in November with Rose and Lorraine and Bernie, an unpleasant family outing that ended in passing around a sequence of Bernie's CAT scans as if they were album snapshots. His brain appeared in the negatives as large cross sections of cumulus cloud rising out of celluloid, each of us marveling not at the growth of, say, a niece or nephew, but at the implosion and irreversible retreat of Bernie's moribund gray matter, crumbs of it plaqued and fallen in like sinkholes in a Missouri pasture.

About a month ago Rose wrote us that the doctors believed Bernie was approaching a crisis stage, a fork in the road where he would either become docile ("exquisitely passive" were the doctors' words—"Sure, as exquisite as a goddamn turnip!" Lorraine snapped when she read that) or quickly degenerate into unmanageable paranoia.

Now that we have seen Bernie, I know what direction his chemistry has taken (for how long, nobody dares to say), and that the country of his soul remains green and unviolated. There is still room for a man to live there.

I make my own sense out of Rose's determination to unveil Bernie, bring him out of the closet to parade clownlike before my embarrassed kin. In the past, she has outmaneuvered plans to bring us together as we are today.

CELEBRATIONS OF THE NEW WORLD

Bernie was always out on the golf course with some statesman from Washington, or recovering in bed from the flu (she even made a point of saying *Russian* flu, hinting at some greater intrigue), or deer hunting in the Poconos. Rose now must have encountered her own Rubicon. Bernie's growing need for attention surpasses what she can give, threatening her job, which I know excites and fulfills her in a way that being a mother again does not. The dinner is a scheme to establish her pride and save her own life as her husband drifts away from his. Perhaps it is admirable and brave and honest. I think she wants to impress upon everyone what a banana Bernie has become. I think she wants to win our sympathy and then give him up as I suppose she must. And she wants Lorraine and me to say, Yes, Rose, you're doing the right thing.

Uncle Joachim's plane arrives. It is painted a tropical, ridiculous yellow. Through the waiting-room window I watch the passengers disembark. I am unable to spot any likely candidates to be Uncle Joachim Elrojo. Then, after the plane seems emptied, two stewardesses appear at the top of the mobile stairs. Between them the women are holding a very thin, very happy Kriss Kringle outfitted in a perfectly tailored white linen suit, a black string tie flopping below his neckline. Even from a distance I see that the man looks much like Bernie, and as the trio comes closer I can see the wrinkles on Uncle Joachim's face spread out from his eyes like feathers in a wing.

The stewardesses seem distraught and anxious, and seek relief from their charge. Uncle Joachim leans forward in their arms at a precarious angle as they descend the steps off the ramp. As they come through the gate, the flight attendants carry Joachim along with them; he's lifted right off the ground, still at an angle, and his feet seem to float up behind him. I am the only one left waiting there, and the stews bring him right to me.

"Hello," I say. "Was it a good trip?"

"If he's yours, sir," one of them says, "please, please take him. This old man has a nasty mouth."

"Not only that," says the other. "He thinks he's here for a revolution."

I marvel at Uncle Joachim's hair. It's as though someone has glued white fluffy goose down around his ears, under his nose, along his cheeks and chin. The aquiline nose on such a face cuts the air aggressively, and he stretches forward in the women's arms like a rooster ready to strike.

"Uncle Joachim?" I ask.

"Joachim Elrojo ha llegado," he says. *"No tenga cuidado."*

"Quite the contrary," the stewardess on his left tells me. "You've got a lot to worry about."

I don't understand Spanish, so I don't know what she is referring to. Joachim's voice is gentle, the tone as soothing as a hymn. The stewardesses release their hold on my uncle-in-law and he glides into my arms. We hug one another: I have embraced a soft plant, a fern, but his cheek is like the floor of the desert sanding my face. I look into his strong eyes as we pull away from each other and they sparkle with tears.

"Don't let him fool you," the stewardess says. I am beginning to dislike her unforgiving attitude. "He speaks English as well as you or me, and he's bilingually abusive."

"Trilingually," says the other. "You forgot what he said in Italian."

Looking at Joachim's unculpable, if not sleepy, smile, I cannot believe their accusations. He hooks his weightless arm around mine and we take slow, short steps toward the baggage area. He does not respond when I ask for a description of his luggage, so we wait silently among the animated crowd until there are no more people, and no more bags riding the circular conveyor belt. Uncle Joachim is untroubled by this mystery. I escort him to the claims office, where the old Trotskyite still refuses to speak, but the agent checks his manifest and announces that Mr. Elrojo had no luggage on the flight. Christ, I think, Uncle Joachim is quite a prankster.

Walking out through the main terminal, Joachim stops in front of the dark entrance to the cocktail lounge. He backsteps around until he has changed our direction and we are both facing it. The name FLYING HIGH pokes out of the painted clouds above the glass door.

"Let me buy you a cool one," he whispers.

I am delighted that Uncle Joachim has decided to speak to me, and in English, but I tell him we are running late, that traffic is bad, and the collective family awaits our arrival. Still, we drift into the lounge. Uncle Joachim is, I feel, and has been, in perfect inscrutable control of the situation. We advance to the bar and he asks for two ice cubes placed in two paper cups. He must repeat the request several times before the bartender can hear his light, accented voice. Joachim keeps one of the cups, gives me the other, and we leave.

In the car, Joachim digs behind him and pulls a silver flask from his hip pocket. I can see engraved on its front a falcon gripping a hammer and sickle in its talons, a serpent squirming in its beak. He tells me the flask was a gift from Trotsky.

"We were brothers," Joachim says. "I was speaking at a *campesinos'* meeting in Merida the day Stalin's dog tore him apart with an ice ax." He unscrews the cap and pours a clear liquid into my cup. It melts the remainder of my ice cube.

"Here," he says. "Just a taste for the road. Leon loved his vodka. Cheers. *Salud. Skoal. Prosit. Aloha. Pax vobiscum.* Here's to absent friends."

He downs his; I test mine, resting the cup between my legs. I pay the lot attendant and pull out into the fast lane. While we stood at the baggage area, I had explained to Uncle Joachim who I was, but he had not been interested. He did not know me, nor did he care. It was enough for him that I was there, that we had found each other, and that whatever it was we were doing was going smoothly. He had, I guess, long ago accustomed himself to nameless contacts, and esoteric arrangements that need not be mentioned twice.

Now he gazes straight ahead through the windshield at the cityscape smoldering in front of us. "Do you know," he says. "Do you know?" But I don't know if I do or not because he forgets me. I don't understand why the stewardesses were so critical of him. To me he is an old, leathery seraph, a veteran of tireless campaigns whose vision has trimmed all superfluous fat from body and mind.

I turn on the car radio, but Uncle Joachim immediately flicks it off and startles me by breaking into song:

> "*King Borria Bungalee Boo*
> *Was a man-eating African swell . . .*"

He switches to verses from *The Mikado* and I realize he is singing Gilbert and Sullivan songs I have not heard since I was in grade school. His voice is clear and firm, though a bit off pitch. He swings his arms up on each chorus and looks over at me as if he expects me to join in. After ten minutes, his enthusiasm falters.

"Those fellows," he says. "Bourgeois as hell, but they made people happy." He spends the remainder of the trip with his hands close to his eyes, inspecting the fingernails.

CELEBRATIONS OF THE NEW WORLD

Despite all the distance between them, I begin to see that Joachim Elrojo is truly Bernie's brother. He is another jewel in the family *fleur de lis,* a prophet called away from the bedside of Utopia. And, like Bernie, he seems to be a step or two beyond the rest of us.

The roads are jammed and by the time we turn into the Alazars' driveway it is late afternoon. Two entire teams of uncles and cousins and nephews play whiffle ball on the shadowy front lawn. They are all dressed in Bermuda shorts and madras seersucker short-sleeved shirts. White gym socks and black oxfords protect their feet from the zoysia. The women sit on lawn chairs in a sunny spot, gossiping or thumbing through sections of the *Inquirer.* My little nieces torture the poodles with affection, tying red, white, and blue ribbons to the dogs' collars.

Bernie's New York Lebanese cousins are nearby, spread out on military blankets, looking very much like gangsters and opium smugglers. As we come to a stop, they line up in a stiff row in front of us, heavyset and wordless, their wraparound sunglasses very threatening. My father has his movie camera whirring in his hand and films us getting out of the car. I keep a nervous eye on the Lebanese.

"Comrades," Joachim proclaims. He strides forward, a *comandante,* and gives each of his silent recruits a pat on the shoulder, a kiss on each cheek. They seem satisfied with this and march back to their blankets. I wonder what's going on; they are Joachim's cousins too, but I doubt if he's ever met them before. Joachim waves my father away.

"*Por favor,* no cameras," he says.

"You don't understand—" my father begins, but Joachim turns his back, beckons to me, and jerks his thumb at my dad. I guess Joachim wants me to throw him out.

"He's official," I explain. "He's one of ours."

"Okay," says Joachim. "But tell him to film from behind. Only from behind."

Rose steps out the huge front door of the house with a tray of bottled beer in her hands; Bernie is right behind her, and Gloria follows them both with a pitcher of iced tea and a pack of star-spangled Dixie cups. Bernie has not noticed our arrival. He remains in Rose's shadow while she delivers the beer to the ballplayers. When she finishes, she sets down the tray, takes Bernie by the hand, and leads him to us. She stops him in front of his brother, and the three of us—Rose, my father, and I—wait with anticipation. Joachim looks him over.

"He'll do," says *el comandante*.

Bernie's attention ascends through the trees, over the gardens, across our smiling faces, and alights on the Winnebago in the driveway.

"Say, whose is that?" he asks, taking a step toward it. "What do you call that thing?" Rose pulls him back.

"Bernie, look at this man. He's come a long way to see you."

Bernie looks right at Joachim without seeing. Then, degree by degree, Bernie falls into himself.

"It's Yusef, my brother Yusef!"

Uncle Joachim, too, finally comprehends the exact nature of this, his latest, expedition. Emotion bruises his eyes and spreads tears across his face in the many channels of his creased brown skin. The moment has such impact that my father lowers his camera in respect. The two brothers embrace and kiss each other again and again. Bernie is so much larger than Joachim and he holds his elder brother's delicate head to his shoulder. Sobs squeeze up out of Joachim's withered throat, an anthem to Alazar history.

"It's okay," Bernie tells him. "It's okay. It's okay."

Forgetting our presence, they release each other but

continue holding hands like two schoolboys. Joachim keeps his free hand over his eyes, and I wonder if behind the callused palm he sees the years that were never theirs together, and the early years long ago that were. They walk across the side lawn toward a bed of flowering peonies. Bernie sits on the grass and pulls Joachim down next to him like a lover. We can still hear him consoling Joachim. Rose observes them for several minutes and then turns to me. Her eyelids flutter spasmodically over her green eyes, little electrical twitches.

"Jack," she says. "I've got to talk to you." There is anguish in her face, or rather her mouth, which is pale and tight.

"I think I'll go see what Albie's up to," my father says.

"No, please stay," Rose tells him. "I need you to hear me too."

My father acquiesces; he chooses to bow his head so that his presence is minimal. I already know what Rose will say, and because she is going to say it, I feel genuine— what?—not love, but genuine *something* for her. Perhaps it is love, and I worry that I will become emotional.

"Jack," she says to me, "what should I do?"

Of course, I tell her that she must think for and of herself. But I doubt the credibility of my own advice. I try to read my own heart—I don't know what I feel. Or what I should say, how I should act. Maybe I'm afraid, but then what's to be afraid of?

"Yes," she says. "You're right. But it's so hard to do that after thinking of everybody else all this time. At least I hope I was thinking of them and not just myself."

I nod my head to comfort her.

"And I have to tell you," she says, "if you don't know already—it may be hereditary. From what I've seen of Joachim, I'd say it was."

107

"I know," I say. "And Lorraine knows too. We've seen the statistics."

Rose looks at my father to check his reaction to the news, for this thing in the Alazar blood has swum generations to find his grandchild. My father raises his head to meet her troubled eyes. Never have I seen his face so benign and glistening, so overtaken by the anima. This is a part of my father that has been denied me.

"I reckon they're like two kids," my father says, "dressed up like old men." He reflects on this in his slow, Midwestern way, which so many of his business competitors have misjudged in the past. Averting his eyes, he says, "This is a nice way for a man to close up shop. There are not many fine endings left. Who dies happy these days?"

Without knowing the full story, my father seems a little envious of Bernie and Joachim. I see no sense in outlining for him the terminal features of this dry-brain disease. They are no blessing. I suppose he imagines they will be spared the sharp peak of lucidity that perhaps washes through the soul before the knock and entrance of death. My father will not. He has survived one heart attack and lives in fear of the second.

"But it's wearing me down," says Rose. "I'm getting tired."

"I understand," my father says: the voice of a minister about to fly up to heaven.

"I know when I'm unhappy," she says. "Some people don't. They just let themselves be mean."

"Hire a nurse," I say. My innocuous suggestion pierces the air around us and there is a moment of brittle, conspiratorial silence. I realize suddenly that through Rose I am rehearsing my own future with Lorraine.

"Believe me," she says slowly. "I've thought and thought about that. I just can't keep watching him."

"The nurse will watch him."

"No," she says. "I mean before my eyes. I can't take Bernie losing his mind right before my eyes. I can't watch *it*."

"I understand," my father says.

"I better see how Lorraine is doing in the kitchen," she sniffs. In a minute she calls from the doorstep that dinner is ready.

My father rounds up the sweaty ballplayers, the gabby aunts, the chubby nieces. He understands, and I suppose I do, and Lorraine does, but my mother, I know, will not. She will pounce on Bernie's illness like a small girl rescuing a bird with a broken wing. She believes that people are unloaded into rest homes the minute their hearing goes bad or are hidden in institutions the second time they misplace their car keys. This represents a great un-American crime to her. No family, I have heard her insist, can ever divide itself if its members truly love one another, which they should if they're related. Common blood is like Super Glue to Gloria. I have also heard her say she doesn't worry about old age because she knows her children will take care of her as she once did them. She's wrong.

I collect Bernie and Joachim from the peony garden. Bernie's eyes are bulging forward into the diminishing sunlight like ripe olives, and phlegm speckles his bright lips. Apparently a word has stuck at the back of his mouth. His effort to overcome the dysnomia sends only preverbal vowel sounds sliding carelessly off his uncooperative tongue. He has never appeared more witless to me. Joachim reminisces about their boyhood together in the District of Columbia, frequently interchanging Bernie's name with Leon's. His use of the present tense makes me instinctively look ahead of him into the clouds of flowers to see what he sees there.

"We take the streetcar out to Hains Point," Joachim

says, "to line fish for bass and scoop out the herring with our nets when they're running. You are afraid of the water and afraid of the colored people. When we get home Poppa says to you, 'What did you catch, Leon? What fish is that I smell?' "

"It's okay," Bernie finally says. He can say whatever he wants as long as it isn't *Help*.

"Time to eat," I tell them.

I stand them up and brush the pink petals off their pants from the blooms they have unconsciously picked apart while talking. We are the last ones into the house. The downstairs bathroom has been invaded by relatives crowding the marble-topped sink. The upstairs bath presents too much of a challenge for my slow-moving companions. I take them to the kitchen sink and turn the water on for them to clean up. Lorraine is there, spooning food into silver chafing dishes raised above disks of transparent flame. The bowls look sacrificial, antediluvian; they glimmer with ceremonial potency.

Uncle Albie is uncorking brown bottles of wine. Rose removes a large crock of chilled cucumber soup from the refrigerator. Joachim cups his hands under the faucet and splashes the cool water onto his face. Bernie thinks this is a good idea and does the same. Lorraine stands by, shyly waiting to meet her uncle, but the two brothers are still throwing water around.

"*Ver gut*," says Bernie.

"*Que bueno! Que delicioso!*" Joachim declares. By the time he turns around, the shoulders of his suit are soaked gray and his hair has turned to paste.

"Uncle Joachim," Lorraine says, taking off her apron, drying his face and then Bernie's. "I'm Bernie's daughter Lorraine. Ever since I was a little girl I've been romanticizing about you."

Out from under the apron, Joachim's head looks wrapped in cirrus, his fine, tousled hair wisping over the topography of his features. He takes her hands and brushes his lips against them in a gesture of Old World graciousness.

"Bernie," he says. "Bernie, you never told me you had a daughter. She looks just like Teresa." (None of us know who Teresa is. And Joachim has been told of Lorraine through the mail.)

"I have two daughters," Bernie says, and he looks around the room for the other one. Almost three years ago, the other one, Sherry, dropped out of graduate school and joined a group of Gurdjieff cultists in Oregon. Nobody in the family hears from her anymore.

We all move out of the kitchen toward the dining room. Lorraine and I take baby steps to accommodate Bernie and Joachim. The doctors refer to this in their more affected moments as *marche à petit pas*. The maple table has been pulled apart and four leaves added to its middle. It now extends from the rock fireplace at one end of the room to the French doors that frame the sunset at the other. The golden rays flash off the silver and china and crystal arranged on the table. Everything looks very proper, very special. The fragrant steam rising from the food smells like incense and spice in an Arabian marketplace. I begin to worry.

From her purse Gloria has taken a plastic bag of miniature American flags, and she runs from place setting to setting sticking the toothpick poles into marshmallows also dug from her purse. These novelties are placed in the center of each dish. She charges when she sees us come into the room.

"You must be Bernard's brother Hokum," she says, prying loose Joachim's hand from Lorraine's to pump it. "Isn't this just marvelous, all of us together on this great day. Just imagine, our forefathers sat down to a dinner like this, right here in this very city, two hundred years ago. It makes me feel like I'm part of history."

Joachim's expression is blank but his voice is full of gallantry when he replies to her in Spanish. I don't know the true extent of what he says; I catch only one word—*capitalista*. Of course, my mother doesn't understand him either. She doesn't understand people from New York or Atlanta, for that matter.

"Oh dear," she whispers to Lorraine. "Do you think he wants a Stars and Stripes at his setting? He really wouldn't appreciate it, would he, being a foreigner?"

"Everybody please sit down. The food's getting cold," says Rose.

"Maybe we should leave a copy of the Declaration of Independence on his plate," Lorraine tells Gloria, smiling. It has taken Lorraine a long time to feel comfortable around my mother, to realize she can insult her and get away with it and feel better because of it.

"No, no time for that," Gloria says. She forgets about Joachim. "Oh dear, everyone doesn't have a flag yet."

We take our seats, my father shouting at Gloria to sit down and stop bothering people. By my count there are twenty-nine of us, not including the baby, who is asleep upstairs. Bernie sits between Gloria and Uncle Albie at the middle of the table. Across from them, my father is flanked by Rose on his left, me to the right. At the far end of the table by the fireplace, Joachim and Lorraine are seated among the teenagers and children. The New York Lebanese cousins occupy the opposite pole, silhouettes against the sunset. The rest of the folks fill in the gaps. One of the uncles on my mother's side of the family, Uncle Vince, picks up his wineglass and proposes a toast to the Alazars, and then continues on into grace.

"Dear Lord, our Savior, we thank Thee for our bounty, and we ask Thee to bless this generous home, and to let Your love shine upon it and fill it with happiness and wealth." (My mother barks "Amen" to this.) "And we thank Thee for our good health and for bringing us safely together to rejoice in Your glory and to sing the praise of this great nation. Let us now drink a toast to our forebears; let us salute their forbearance, and never let us forget or cease to honor the courage and the dream of men like George Washington—"

Joachim interrupts him. We get a demonstration of the fireball the stewardesses had warned me about. He picks up a celery stick and points it like a shiv at my surprised uncle.

"Washington could never unbutton his pants by himself," Joachim announces. "Do you know what that means?"

No one dares to answer, although I think I hear the New Yorkers grunt. After a moment, Joachim goes on.

"Hamilton's fingers always stank from playing with his own ass. His father was a Portuguese pimp who washed ashore in the West Indies. I say God bless Tomás Jefferson. He was confused, okay, but he was honest and he knew what men needed. To hell with Lenin and Ike. None of the bastards, not a one, understood Lorenzo of *The Plumed Serpent*. So what did you expect? Eh? *Viva la revolución de los corazones!*"

"Oh my God," says Rose.

"It's okay," Bernie shouts down to Joachim.

"Amen," says Lorraine and starts the soup around a silent, mortified table. Everybody tries to concentrate on the food, to be polite, to forget what they have heard, but I can see that Uncle Vince's fuse is lit and an outburst is imminent. He holds off until everybody has his soup, and then explodes.

"Look here you—" he says, rising up out of his chair to yell at Uncle Joachim. There are tears in the old Trotskyite's eyes; Joachim wipes at them with the cuff of his jacket.

"Why don't you just keep quiet, Vince," my father calmly tells his brother-in-law.

"Hell no, I'm not gonna keep quiet," Vince says. "No tamale-eating scoundrel can come up here to the U.S.A. and blacken the name of the men that made the best country in the world."

"Why don't you just settle down, Vince," my father says. "The old fellow was making a joke, that's all."

Vince looks at his sister Gloria for support, but she is staring at her cucumber soup, probing it with her spoon. Vince slumps back into his chair. I think he owes Dad too much to resist him. He will go only so far for his country; likewise my mother for her family. As far as Gloria is concerned, the interchange never took place. This is her special gift: to blind herself to dissension, diffuse the obvious.

Joachim is stirred by Vince's challenge. He snatches up a butter knife and brandishes it.

"Hey, *gringo,* let me tell you something," he says. "The only thing Columbus ever discovered was the clap."

Vince turns a rather brutal shade of purple, but before he can do anything, Lorraine breaks up with laughter, deep and heartfelt with no edge to it. She tries to take the knife away from Uncle Joachim; he won't give it up. Instead he stretches forward to dip it into hommos, which he spreads on a piece of pita bread. Lorraine laughs louder. Her eyes are closed and I can see she's releasing all the tension that's been building. Bernie joins her, his short, coughing laughs an exclamation to Lorraine's flowing melodies, and I finally wise up myself. Soon we are all laughing and everybody seems to relax a little. Lorraine teases both Vince and Joachim about their hot blood. Gloria finishes exploring her soup.

"This looks marvelous, Rose," she says.

Gloria lifts a spoonful to her shiny lips, blowing to cool it off. She says nothing after she swallows it, but from the expression on her face she might have put a dead fish in her mouth.

"Oh goodness," she says. "How wonderfully different. But everybody's been talking so much it's cooled off."

"It's okay," says Bernie. "Rose makes it for . . ." But the words swim away from him. He works the muscles in his cheeks and jaw in frustration, waiting for the sensation of loss to pass, for redemption, for the tide of his thoughts to return the words. I can see that it is killing him. Gloria has turned expectantly, grateful that Rose's husband is finally speaking to her. Because they do not know better, because in their innocent eyes Bernie is still the head of the household, the Missouri relatives also offer him their formal attention. Lorraine, my father, Uncle Albie, and the cousins from Queens keep right on eating. Something washes up on the shore of Bernie's brain. He is clinging to a lectern, authoritative in his prime, Rose's sweet "professor-type" once again.

"If we are to believe Mr. Dulles," he says, "the Cold War was not the result of imaginary fears or the eagerness of the intelligence community, but of a direct and genuine threat to the security of Europe, and consequently, the United States."

Joachim looks up from his plate. *"Mierda,"* he says. "Forget that crap, Bernie."

Rose comes to Bernie's rescue this time. "I make it especially for hot summer days," she says. Bernie unbends like a man being pulled from a small hole.

115

"It's so refreshing," my mother lies. "I never would have thought of such a thing myself."

"I think it's great, Rose," says Albie. He shows us an appetite that made him my grandmother's favorite son. Even my father is enthusiastic as he inspects the bowls of tabouleh and couscous, the platters of hot pita and feta cheese, the yogurt, skewers of shish kebab that Rose had Albie grill outside on the patio. My other relatives look on in self-pity. There is nostalgia in their expressions for corn on the cob and country ham. They take complimentary portions of each dish and poke the spoonfuls like children ordered to eat liver and lima beans.

"Where's my hot dog?" one of the kids whines. His mother shushes him.

"Lookit that guy," says another kid, pointing at Uncle Joachim. His head is down over his plate and he stuffs kibbeh into his mouth with all ten fingers. Everybody turns to watch.

"Was your brother born Mexican originally?" Gloria asks Bernie.

"*Landstadt en gimmler pooksny,*" Bernie replies. He has abandoned the English language, or it has forsaken him as if it too can judge when a man no longer needs something. My mother's eyes narrow. She slices at her mouth with a napkin.

"Are you mocking me, Mr. Alazar?" she says icily. "Because if you are, I want you to know that I've just about had enough of these people out here in the East."

"He's sick, you goddamn bitch; you're so blind!" Lorraine screams. She pushes away from the table, looking at me defiantly, but I would applaud her if I could. When she is Rose's daughter, when her Irish blood rises and shows itself, she is stronger than me and I need her to teach me the secret of that power. My father gets up, glares at his wife, and goes to soothe his daughter-in-law. Lorraine excuses herself before he reaches her; the baby probably needs changing, she says, and hurries out of the room. Gloria winces but I know she feels triumphant. She has discovered the leverage that will restore her sense of well-being and confidence.

"I'm so sorry, Rose," she says. "Can you ever forgive me?" Her sympathy is phosphorescent, like certain worms, giving only a dull light and no warmth. I see she plans to say more, but Uncle Albie stops eating, reaches across in front of Bernie, who seems to be meditating, and knocks a glass of red wine off the table into Gloria's lap.

"You wicked pool-hall tramp!" Gloria shrieks. "You did that on purpose!" She looks toward my father for support, but he won't even acknowledge her complaint. The Missouri relatives are frozen, fearful of being attacked if they make the slightest move. The New York Lebanese terrorists are devouring great heaps of food.

"Oh!" Gloria is crying. "Oh, Lord!" An obscene magenta stain expands below the waist of her sky-blue summer dress. She jumps up from her seat and runs out of the room. Uncle Albie excuses himself to make a phone call. Rose seems impassive, under a spell; the kids squirm where they sit. Outside there is a muffled, distant explosion. It is followed by a whistle and then another boom.

"Fireworks!" the kids yell to one another. "Let's go!" They race for the front door and out into the darkness. The aunts and uncles each take a last token nibble of Rose's cooking, congratulate her on its excellence, and apologize for their concern over the children's safety. They, too, then leave the dining room, their chairs scraping guiltily across the hardwood floor. Bernie's cousins remain to finish off the meal.

"Stay calm, *amigos*," advises Joachim. "The day has come. We've nothing to worry about. And tomorrow, tomorrow . . ." His voice fades.

Rose looks at him as if she'd like to yank his tongue out. Joachim wipes his hands delicately with his napkin and then proceeds to buff down his fingernails on the stone surface of the hearth, stopping occasionally to check his progress. My father leaves to search out my mother. I suspect he'll have an apology ready by the time he finds her—maybe she deserves one. Rose is not aware that Bernie has also exited. She puts her elbows on the table and her head in her hands, fingers raking the limp hair as if this were a way to exorcise her fears.

"I don't have room for this in my mind," she says, but not to anyone in particular. She looks up in time to see Bernie with his winter coat on, headed for the door.

"Jack," she says. "Don't let him go. Stop him."

I reach the door when he does and have to pry his hand from the knob. His flesh loosens in my grip like a ripe peach. "Where are you going, Bernie?" I ask. He doesn't know. "Why don't you stay here, then, with Joachim?"

"Okay. Sure."

Albie is standing quietly there when we turn around. He is studying Bernie; I feel he wants to say something, but it takes a moment and first he must clear his throat.

"Unless they be like little children," he says, "they shall not find heaven, or something like that. Shit, imagine me trying to quote the Bible."

"My heart is losing gravity," Bernie says. "I can feel it lifting right up."

Albie smiles and nods at him, shakes his head sadly. He says to me, "Look, Jack, explain things to your folks and Rose and Lorraine. I've called a cab to take me out to the Coast. You know how it is."

"Yeah," I agree. "Good seeing you, Uncle Alabard."

"Bernie," he says, taking three cigars from his coat pocket, "here. I want you to have these." Albie turns to me and confides, "I gave him one in the kitchen and he loved it."

I say good-bye and he leaves. The front yard reverberates with the sharp clacks of firecrackers and bottle rockets that my relatives have imported with them from the untamed Midwest. The celebrations shift into high gear.

Someone outside is screaming wildly—whether from pain or great joy, I do not know. Cherry bombs blast from one end of the property to the other and Rose's poodles yelp hysterically. Perhaps big skyrockets are being tied to their collars now for an airborne pooch finale. A barrage of Roman candles sends an aura of multicolored light through the window of the door; it fades across our faces.

I tell Bernie to hang his coat back in the hall closet, but he wants to talk to Joachim first. We shuffle back to the dining room. Bernie's cousins still scrape the serving bowls, but Rose has disappeared. Joachim's fingers are raw and bloodied from rubbing them against the stone.

"And Poppa says, 'What did you catch, Bernie, stink-fish?' And he makes the maid scrub you with lanolin and throw out your clothes to save you from Momma's sensitive nose. You were a great fisherman, Leon."

"It's okay," Bernie says tenderly. He puts his arm around his brother and sits down beside him. I leave the two of them together and hunt for Lorraine. I find her in the upstairs bath. The water is running in the sink, but she won't let me in. She tells me she'll be downstairs in a minute. I wander back toward the dining room, but on the way I hear voices coming from inside the hall closet. I pull back the door and clouds of pungent smoke press into my face. Bernie and Joachim squat on the floor of the big walk-in closet, quietly puffing on the cigars that Albie bequeathed them.

"We're celebrating our reunion," Joachim tells me.

I squeeze in with them. Bernie hands me the last cigar and I light up. Lorraine finds us a few minutes later.

"Jesus Christ, you're going to suffocate in there." She reaches in and flicks on the ventilation fan. In a moment the smoke has cleared. "You want to come out and sit somewhere comfortable?" she asks.

"No," I say. "Come in and close the door behind you."

She slides in with us. Her shirt is lifted and she is nursing the baby. She hands me the kid and puts her arms around her father's neck.

"It's okay," says Bernie.

The only sounds coming from the darkness are the heavy breaths of Joachim, a sigh from Lorraine, the round, milky bird noise of the baby, like a morning song. Outside, the rockets are bursting in air.

for Barbara Azar Davis

THE TRAPDOOR

ONE

Like the unambitious towers of the New World, the play-houses rose before the passengers to a modest height and then stopped unconvincingly. The pilot tied off the skiff to the landing and waited to be paid. The first gentleman out turned back to offer a hand to the lady, lifting her up by the elbow onto the boardwalk stuck into the muddy bankside. Resisting the urge to return with the ferryman to London, Sir Philip's guest, the privateer Captain Relsworth, stood up in the bow of the unstable boat and gracefully leapt ashore, a hand on his rapier to keep it from banging between his legs.

There, like the towers of Santa Marta, of Maracaibo, of Havana, the Captain said to himself, looking up the bank: squat white hives close to the earth, afraid of heaven but brilliant in the afternoon sun, somehow begging faith in their solidness and invulnerability. The Spanish had no time to build proper defenses, no apparent need to build them high. The golden tropic sun ruined one's sense of

121

proportion: Men were not men in the Indies but gods and animals. Drake's culverins had been able to lob nine-pound shot into the towers like a child dropping raisins into a fish basket.

"You see, Captain," Sir Philip said, his palm held out in front of him, "there to the left is the *Globe*, bearing the sign of Atlas, and there the *Rose* in the middle, and there is the bear-baiting ring in the trees, you see?"

The woman had turned, with a coy expression, to witness that the Captain did in fact see, so that she did not know they had come to the end of the boards, where there was a drop to the grass. She missed her step and tripped. The high heel of her shoe snapped off and she would have fallen had she not caught her escort's arm. The Captain frowned. He did not like the ostentatious woman with her affectations, her lemon velvet, her hair dyed pale orange and crisped so that it erupted from her temples, her jewels of colored glass. She was a trull as far as the Captain was concerned. Whether or not the court was willing to acknowledge its demimondaines now that Elizabeth was dead, Sir Philip was still a fool to have such a woman on his arm.

"Oh, la," she was crying. "Wait. I've broken it. We must go back. The louts shall have a laugh at my uneven step."

Sir Philip sought to calm her with sugary words. She stood pouting, raised on her left toes to compensate the loss of her heel. A few forced tears loosened the paint in the corners of her eyes, leaving black-rimmed trails along the sides of her nose. The Captain thought the woman looked and acted absurdly, but he wanted to agree with her, he wanted to return to his office in London and finish the business that had brought him to the city. Sir Philip took her hand and stroked it in a fatherly fashion.

"Surely, my lady, this is a small misfortune. The Captain rarely comes to see us. You haven't been to Bankside since before we built the *Fortune,* have you, sir? Ah, surely not. Shall you deny him his pleasure for a heel, my lady?"

"Sir Philip," the Captain began, "my satisfaction would be as great—"

"Tush, sir. Tush! Thou dost not stop a carriage because the horse has muddied itself."

He continued to hold her wrist as if she might run away.

"The groundlings'll whistle at me," she said miserably. "I shall bobble like an old goose."

A flush of choler tightened the features of Sir Philip's face. He lost his patience and demanded her other shoe. The woman stubbornly obeyed, leaning over to pluck it off. The heel and toes of her stocking were mildly soiled. The Captain watched indifferently as Sir Philip took the good shoe and broke the long square wooden heel from it. It cracked like a chicken bone in his hands. The woman made a sound as if she had been pinched. Sir Philip bowed graciously and returned the shoe to its owner.

"There," he said victoriously. "They are equal. I will buy you new ones."

To hide his weak smile, the Captain petted his shiny black mustaches. He wished the woman had had her way. If he must come to Bankside, he would rather attend a bearbaiting. As they walked up the grassy slope, he could smell the beasts' bitter, exciting stench coming from the ring. A gutty snarl crescendoed to a roar, children screamed, and the mastiffs whined and bayed in their blood lust. Was that a lion? he wondered. Didn't they sometimes have lions on Sundays? He would like to see *that,* by God. That would be a story to tell his men.

They were coming up to the horses. The white pins of jugglers spun in the sky beyond where the animals grazed.

Somewhere someone was strumming a lute or cittern, he couldn't decide which. If there were music, the Captain thought, he could endure the afternoon. Music or beasts, but not, for God's sake, speeches. The woman, much smaller now without her heels, ordered one of the horse-boys to remove his charge away from the footpath. He made an ugly face at her but complied, tugging the massive, liver-colored stallion farther down the lawn. The Captain thought, I should spring up on its back without a word to Sir Philip and gallop down the lonely green roads to Plymouth, back to the sea. He would rather be in Plymouth, where his ship was being careened and its hull tallowed for speed than waste an afternoon watching players beat the air for a horde of twitching landsmen. He belonged back there, overhauling the gear and refitting the rigging with his crew. Or sitting in the *Salt and Sugar* on the sea-slapped quay, the seagulls rioting over scraps on the cobbles while he drank the rum he himself had pirated from the Spanish.

He would most like to be back on the sea, where he had spent his life, where the wind did not smell like the gutters of London or a gallant's perfume, where he was not servant but a master in the most masterful fleet on the globe. Better there than here in London, where the fashions changed in a fortnight and a soberly dressed gentleman was treated as a foreigner. He was weary of the clucking of Sir Philip and his Providence Company and their misinformed rush to colonize, to follow Spain's lead. Years ago Raleigh had proven the madness of that course. Like the clergyman's *Gloria Patri,* the word *gold* shaped the lips of every agent on Fleet Street into a round prayer. There was no more gold, save where the Spanish were. The crown's treasury had been fattened through piracy and slaving and trade. Now oily-haired men who had never set a finger on a nautical chart talked as if the New World were paradise. If it was, it wasn't a place for an Englishman to live unless he was raised naked and senseless. God knew Ireland was full of savages; let them populate the hellish jungles, the frozen marshes. No, the Captain decided, the merchants would never lure *gentlemen* there. As for himself, he would always return upon the mercy of the Lord to the roses of England, the exquisite white puffs and red daubs, delicate as the heart of a virgin.

Aye, he told himself, either the British coast or the heaving of the sea—but here, they were entering the tower. Sir Philip was passing a shilling for a gentlemen's box. The Captain resigned himself to Sir Philip's love of the players.

TWO

It was a large cage for birds too occupied with each other or impressed by their own finery to fly out the unbarred top. Perched in two tiers around and above him, coxcombs and courtiers and Fleet Street moneymen pushed toward their seats, creating a reeling spectrum of queer colors—cornflower blue and magenta like a spray of fuchsia, a lusty, improper yellow, pease-porridge tawny, green and silver stripes, popish reds. Here and there in the flock ostrich-like ladies twisted and bounced, the gray and scarlet plumes of their headdresses swaying above them, their hips made mighty with wire hoops. The yard to his side, for Sir Philip had led them to a box at stage right on the ground level, was like a marketplace spinning with East End cockneys and drunkards, weaselish fops in the most eccentric styles, beggars, bullies, and hucksters peddling apples, hard pears, rock sugar, chestnuts, and beer, or advertising less honorable entertainments that would commence at dusk in Soho.

Sir Philip hailed a fat, unhappy man who sold them wine of questionable quality. Still people squeezed into the pit. The Captain surveyed the thousands of playgoers with disgust. The masses carried the plague on their tongues and spit it into the stale air. He did not particularly enjoy crowds unless he had license to beat at them with a stick or cutlass. He was hot and uncomfortable and drank his wine quickly to relieve his spleen. Their party had not arrived early enough and they were forced to share the box with two men who played monte bank on square boards set across their knees. Sir Philip, who had sat down next to them, greeted them coolly, suspicious of their common blouses. The Captain felt trapped between the woman and Sir Philip, who sat rigid and focused, as though someone were painting his portrait. Long metallic curls of hair spread like coils of ash on the starched surface of his ruff, and his beard lay out on it like a sleeping dog. The Captain did not share this urbane fondness for shackling one's neck in the stiff, hideous things, propping up the layers with forks and wires—a clean linen collar or a simple mantle were genteel enough. The single indulgence the Captain permitted himself was a gold cross earring he had torn from the lobe of a *hidalgo*, a *son of something*, on a pinnace they had captured off the shores of Tortuga.

The woman was restless. With every breath she took she shuffled or wriggled, straightened her neck in its high collar or jerked her hips to find the position they wanted, and every movement she made caused the gold and white tissue of her skirt to crackle. The closeness of the woman nauseated the Captain. She had doused her breast and shoulders generously with lilac perfume, a scent he abhorred for its sweetness, but through the disguise of lanolin her fingers smelled of fish when earlier he had kissed her hand. The Captain took a slender white clay pipe from a pocket in his cape, tamped it with tobacco he carried in a leather pouch, and struck a flame to the bowl. His head swelled. The blend he smoked was a gift from a Carib chieftain. The Captain let the heavy smoke curl from his mouth, filling his mustaches and nose with its penetrating aroma. He felt better, his melancholy rounding off to a narcotic glow, mild and pleasant.

Sir Philip suddenly abandoned his pose and placed a hand on the Captain's broad back, tilting over to speak in his ear. A trumpet sounded before the words were out and he pulled away.

"Mark that," he said with good humor. "The first toot! The players are ready, God bless them."

The Captain looked up to the hut on top the tall, narrow house that closed the stage from behind. The call had come from above. The stage resembled a portico; two painted columns rose from the outer corners and supported a high canopy that partially obstructed his view, but he had seen the silver flash of a trumpet up there against the circle of blue sky held by the roof's thatching. Some of the crowd had begun to cheer.

Sir Philip continued with what he had wanted to say. It was a matter of business, as the Captain suspected, a clucking reprimand in praise of thrift: Provision the ship with beer in place of wine, less fresh fruit, less beef, less dried mutton, and more grains. Without expression, the Captain replied he was tight enough. Frugality was an absolute on the uncertain world of the water, but he would not cause his men to increase their natural sufferance. A request for higher crew wages abruptly stalemated the discussion.

The woman decided she had eaten enough of an apple and pitched the core into the yard, hitting, intentionally it seemed, a man who wore a short green jerkin with multi-colored ribbons sewn across the chest. He slowly turned and acknowledged the woman with a wicked smile, showing teeth blackened by a taste for molasses.

"'Tis Richard Kinch," she said. "I shall never forgive his manners. Oh, stay! He's coming over. He is a fop, a stroller, a wag, a roistering vagabond. Go away, you."

She leaned over the rail of the box to scold him in a voice full of invitation. Sir Philip did not tolerate this for long. He hauled her back beside him, perhaps too firmly, for she protested and he was compelled to kiss her cheek. The Captain marveled at the brashness of so public a kiss. The second trumpet sounded. The two strangers in the box put away their deck of cards and untied leather cases shoved beneath the bench, taking out leaves of paper, a bundle of quills, and two flat bottles of ink stopped with corks.

The Captain had emptied his flagon of wine and called for another, carefully counting out the copper pennies. The vanity that fluttered about, the Spanish lace, the French embroidery and pendants, the pompous German cuts, the Morisco gowns and loose Barbary sleeves adapted from the Turks—this misadventure in taste, this bastard sartorial rainbow had begun to amuse him. To the Captain, the crowd was all parrots and peacocks, gallant, plumed, primped, and feathered creatures that must even wing and pinion the shoulders of doublets and hop about like birds that had never flown. The Italians understood dignity in dress. There was enough color and perfect design in the world without mocking God's creation—*there was the third blast*—and thank heaven that between reason and passion there was only one London.

The clear trumpet note died away to shouting and full applause. At each end of a black arras stretched across the back of the stage, doors opened and a player advanced. The two men met in the middle of the stage and bowed. A boy followed behind them, turning out along the balustrade at the perimeter. He stood to the audience across the way from Sir Philip's party, holding up a painted board.

"Elsinore!" shouted that part of the crowd. The word echoed out over the Bankside. The Captain waited until the boy had circled the stage and faced their box. "Elsinore," the Captain read aloud, satisfied. He liked the Danes. They were a sensible, clear-headed people. He could trust them at sea.

THREE

"My father's ghost will not speak, nor wave his arm like this one," the Captain whispered. He had gripped the oak railing of the box and sat forward until his ruddy face and knuckles were in the plane of the retiring sunlight.

"What dost thou say?" asked Sir Philip politely.

" 'Tis nothing, sir. The play has found me."

"Ah! Though art entwined in the illusion," Sir Philip said proudly, as though he were responsible for the Captain's earnest attention.

The ghost rising from the center of the stage had chilled the mariner's heart. It wore rusty armor wrapped in a loose gauze of black muslin, a mist of the underworld. Its face was a terrible white in which the eyes were desperate islands, and a snowy beard splashed down the front of its corselet like a waterfall. Up from hell the phantom rose, a menace to the living, and then vanished behind the arras, reappearing when the third man joined the soldiers of the Danish King. Against the Captain's will, the apparition lifted up from deep within him, carrying with it the ghost of his own father. Just as the groundlings strained forward or shoved back from the stage in morbid attraction or dread, his mind worked against itself to foil the vision as it leached through the void. But then cannon firing from above in the tower house had sent it back to its hole.

Now once more the thing drifted out from the black curtain, reaching into his past, his blood bolting through him like a school of frightened mullet—*into every brain that looks so many fathoms to the sea and hears it roar beneath*—and he watched transfixed as the ghost and Hamlet (whose first entrance had caused the woman to swoon with the name *Burbage* on her lips) confronted one another at the edge of their gallery—*if thou dids ever thy dear father love*—where the Prince looked to throw his arms around the unnatural form of the dead King, his father—*Revenge his foul and most unnatural murder*—but embraced only the night air of the battlement.

Oh, horrible! O, horrible! most horrible!

Adieu, adieu, adieu! remember me.

He had forgotten. How many years now had it been? Fourteen? Fifteen? Fifteen this month, was it? He had been holding his breath through the scene, it seemed, and exhaled wearily, returning from the rail to sit upright on the bench, the sea foaming beneath him. My father's ghost never spoke to me, the Captain repeated to himself, and no one else would swear to seeing it.

It had followed him over the oceans to the West Indies and to Panama, to Cathay and Tartary and the Northern Territories, through the Straits of Magellan, pulling it together out of the moist night, knitting the wind and fog into a familiar shape, bent as it once was with dysentery, long cheekbones drawing the face into sadness, a luminescent grief.

The Captain had been a young cannoneer on Frobisher's flagship when the Armada was first sighted off Plymouth in 1588. His father had been a Lieutenant Commander with Drake on the *Revenge*. For years, the Queen had managed her navy scandalously. She had failed to provide her sailors with ammunition and denied their wages with the shake of a jeweled glove. Meat and wine were replaced with a pauper's fare of peas and saltfish, rancid oil and old beer. Men were rotting as they fought, his father among them, thinned and pale beyond the son's recognition.

The first day there was a westerly wind, the seas pushing higher and higher as night fell. The Armada lined the horizon like an eagle with outstretched wings, bloody in the sunset. In the morning Frobisher, the Welch mystic, set upon them with his necromancy, dipping like a sparrow, there and gone before the Spanish could come about, stinging the slow galleons with well-aimed broadsides. At dusk in heavy seas that scattered them, the Spanish fleet ran up-channel for Calais, the Queen's ships in pursuit. Drake was in the lead, bearing the lantern. But without signaling, he had broken off with the *Bear* and *Mary Rose* to prey upon stragglers. At sunrise Sunday, the unsuspecting English saw that the light off their bows was not the *Revenge* but a galleon. They were in the center of the Spaniards but quickly jibed. Frobisher and the other admirals reconnoitered at a safe distance, returning to pluck one by one—like feathers from a bird, Sir Hawkins had said—the ships of the Armada. They did not see the *Revenge* that day; by nightfall the boy had learned that Drake had captured the disabled *Catalina*, her four hundred men and fifty-five thousand ducats. The boy's father was among the boarding party.

On Tuesday, with a change of wind to the south-southwest, Drake rejoined them and they fought the Spanish together throughout the unending week. For the young cannoneer, the world around him was broken and reduced

131

to salt and blood and flame in the wooden vault of his post. He felt he must die than fight another day; his hands, chest, and face were covered with black blisters from the heat of the gun. But by the week's end the Armada was decimated and the Lord Admiral knighted Frobisher. In port the boy borrowed a skiff and rowed over to the *Revenge*. His father was not aboard. None of the crew had seen him since the capture of the *Catalina*. He assumed his father was lost in action. No, he was told, the galleon had surrendered without resistance. That night Frobisher accused Drake of treason for refusing to divide the *Catalina's* gold among the fleet. The boy lay awake in his hammock wondering if his father were in heaven or hell.

The Captain had forgotten the love he still held for his father until this moment, unexpectedly pushed forward through a passage that had closed in his memory, into a revelation of the fleshless remains of his father and his own torn being where the true life of a man was a stage amusement for which you paid a shilling. The Captain's emotion seemed to squirt out onto his tongue.

"Aye, revenge!" he shouted to the actors. It was a burst of tropical suddenness that soon evaporated. He quickly sat back, silent and remote, surprised by himself.

Sir Philip was stirred by the Captain's show of enthusiasm. The play was a revival; he had attended an earlier performance at Oxford when the children took over Blackfriars Inn. Sir Philip felt the need to point out the *significance,* the hidden meaning, of the production to the Captain.

"They say," he said with authority, "that our own headless Essex and Southhampton formed the mold of this Hamlet and Horatio, and Leicester's the treacherous pretender."

The Captain nodded his head blankly, uninterested,

struggling to concentrate on the players through the gaps in his consciousness where the seas rushed madly over the image of his father. Sir Philip had noticed the blood come into his guest's sunburnt face, staining it dangerously bright. He hailed a wine vendor, fearing an attack of apoplexy in the Captain.

The woman's attention was circling the play; she was intrigued for the moment by the noblemen in the surrounding galleries. Her focus, however, would always return to Hamlet. She wondered how she might persuade Sir Philip to introduce her to Burbage, whom he often drank with. The two peculiar men at the end of their box annoyed the financier, yet he could not help but notice them. Each man was mouthing the words a second after the actors, scribbling intrepidly in what appeared to Philip to be a code of some sort on sheet after sheet of paper which mounted on the floor. The Captain too had glanced over earlier and seen them bent across their boards, lips moving in silent recitation, the quill pens skipping and gliding like flying fish. They had drawn a circle with a dot in its center when the word *gold* was spoken by a player. Sir Philip stared in vexation at the pages filled with broken symbols, a milieu of frozen insects with legs sticking every which way. What language is that? he asked them. But they didn't look up from their work.

The Captain was studying the ghost. It was leaving, dropping from sight in the middle of the stage. The Captain felt shame. It was true; until this moment his father wasn't even a memory, only a shadow he would turn from at sea many years ago.

FOUR

He gave the third *adieu—remember me*—and ducked his head under the stage too quickly, bumping the crown of his helmet.

He hurried, but it was difficult to move with sureness or grace in the heavy armor. Crouching halfway down the ladder, he pulled at the trapdoor to set it back in place, closing himself in darkness. He called softly for the stage boys, but no one answered so he continued backing down the steps unassisted. His foot missed the last rung: a wrench of the ankle in its soft inner boot, and pain as he crashed down onto the dirt. A groan followed, venomous cursing under his breath. Where were the boys? He wished them boils on their arse, snakes in their bed, chancres on their lips. He even swore at his foot as if he could insult away the injury. Ghosts should not have to crawl back to the tiring-house.

"My lord?" It was a pretty voice.

"My lord, indeed, my lord! Thy lord and master. Where are thou, boy? Must thou hide to play dice?"

The ghost's eyes adjusted to the weak light filtering through the black curtains that enclosed the base of the stage. In the outermost corner he could see a silhouette rise and move hesitantly toward him through the forest of oaken supports.

"My lord, art thou hurt?"

"Come up, boy. Thou art sluggish enough." The weight of his voice drew the figure onward. The ghost lifted off his helmet. It scraped his ears.

"God-a-mercy! Who is this in a maiden's costume?"

"A maiden, sir."

"Marry, a maiden! A rare thing in London since our Queen has left the world to wed our Lord, if He suits her."

THE TRAPDOOR

"A woman then, and not so rare."

"Ah, a woman, God's grace to you. Art thou named, woman, or dost a man call only 'woman' to call thee?"

"Virginia Fields, my lord."

"And why dost thou crouch down here with the devil?"

" 'Tis a fitting place as any, sir, for a woman—to be underneath and the world above."

"Why, well said! You are not so simple," he said, in praise of her defiant words. "Mark! The cue. I have forgotten the actors." He pulled himself off his elbows to a sitting position and bellowed, *Swear,* startling the girl. His round, bald forehead shimmered like a moon in the gloom around them. *Swear!* he yelled again in a mock deep voice that made the girl snort with suppressed laughter.

"Nay, be quiet. Take this headpiece and thump it thrice on the bottom of the front stage so that it rings. Wait till I speak."

She moved off into the shadows while he carefully listened to the faint words above. She had to stoop to keep from bumping her head on the trusses. There was the cue again. He hissed at the girl to warn her.

Swear by his sword.

She banged against the floorboards.

"Psst. Holla, lady. Enough!" She groped her way back to him.

"I pray you, dear Lady Fields, sweet angel of this cave, the unlighted belly of the world, pull this iron from my chest. The buckles line the side."

She was charmed by his flattery but still timid, afraid to come too close. He seemed like a gentleman, but she knew how sudden the mood of a man could change. Even in the poor light she could sense an ambiguity in his hard eyes that the sun would not affect. He peeled off his beard. Underneath were clean cheeks and a perfect chin. Then he put his head back as though he were trying to swallow the muffled noises that sank down to him from the stage.

"Once again," he whispered hoarsely. And then, *Swear!*

"More!" she cried. "My lord, the stage master has punished thee."

"How so?"

"He must loathe thy face and company to cast thee in a role so lonely and distant from the surface. Thou art on the wrong side for men to appreciate thy talent."

"Aye, I must speak to him about my position, and tell the gatekeeper to hold a better seat for thee tomorrow."

"Thanks, my lord," she said, despondent. "Shall you swear again?"

"No more."

He lifted his arms and she knelt by him and pried the breastplate from his chest, forcing it open like a clamshell. Off came the girdle of mail, the brassards, the thigh guards, and finally from his shins the steel jambs, tossed aside in the dirt. Underneath it all he was dressed in galligaskins and garter stockings and a cambric blouse. He stretched forward to rub his ankle. Now that she had finished, she turned away, forgetting him for a more portentous matter. Unexpectedly he was stern and she cringed as he assumed a manner of formality.

"Hast thou seen my boys?"

"Too much."

"A short and bitter fact you make it. Where did they wander?"

"I know not, my lord."

"Prithee, go and call them."

"No, my lord."

"What's this! You'd make a beggar of me?"

"No, my lord. I cannot go. I am banished like thee to hell."

THE TRAPDOOR

There was a flourish of trumpets from above them. The girl jumped up and cocked her head to listen. She began to rapidly suck in air until she could contain no more and exhaled weeping.

"There he is! Oh, I cannot bear it."

"Shhh. Who?"

"My heart."

"Where?"

"Atop us. Mark that voice. Thy Queen!"

"My Queen? Surely not."

"Aye, thy Queen. Hamlet's mother, Gilly Nashe—the King's boy. Your duckling about to break his egg. Mark that voice with the sap rising to it. His hour upon the stage shall soon end. He has outgrown his skirts and grown a beard, and I have gained his loss."

"Thy wit is pregnant, lady. You give me pause."

"My wit? Nay, sir. My belly."

Out of despair, she fell down beside him, the tears running again, her forehead braced against his shoulder. He tried to comfort the wretched child, patting her back as he would his own daughter, embarrassed. Though language was the water he most liked to swim in, he could think of nothing to say to her. Then her spirit seemed to shift; she was herself again, and angry.

"And thy same Gilly's—my Gilly's—soft words have caused it."

"Words! I think not, lady. They lack the proper essence."

"Nay, my lord, words were enough. For two years he has courted me, and swore he would marry at the season's close. 'Ginny, my flower, my rose, let me taste once from this table,' says he, pulling my buttons, 'or I shall surely starve.' He took his fill, my lord, but now he's abused my trust and innocence. I came at midday to greet him and

137

threw my arms around his neck to kiss the untimely news into his ear. He broke away from me as if I had bit him and forbid my presence at the playhouse. I ran to hide my grief and found shelter in the dimness here, and had fixed my mind to kill myself when I heard a coarse oath about snakes and such and found thee in the dirt growling."

"Go to—kill thyself!"

"Aye. Nay, I shall kill him instead."

"A husband would be more fitting than an angel, child. Seek to impress him with his obligation and, one hopes, love, rather than lift him beyond it."

"He's thick-hearted, my lord."

A door creaked and footsteps cluttered down the stairs from the tiring-house. Two indistinct figures stumbled about the murky chamber, calling his name. It was Nozzle and Harry come to find him. Their boyish faces loomed out of the shadows.

"Ho, stop there or you'll walk on us."

"Master? Ah, hallo. Henslowe said to discover what became of thee. Oh, in faith, sir. We did not know you were so engaged, now did we, Nozzle? Your pardon, sir, we pray you."

They started to fade back into darkness.

"Stay, Harry. Give me your hand. I've bruised my foot and can't step on it. The lady's acquainted with our boy-Queen Gilly."

The stage boys looked closer, recognizing the girl. They had often seen her hanging on Gilly Nashe, and Gilly on her. They straddled the ghost and raised him, his arms wrapped over their shoulders, the rest of his weight shifted to his left foot.

"Farewell, my lord. Thanks for your charitable ear."

"Nay, come with us, Virginia. Hurry, while your boy-man's still on stage. We'll fashion a plot to set a vision of conscience into Gilly. Pray, follow. He cannot stay Queen forever."

"He has proved that."

Their entrance backstage in the tiring-house was little noticed through the urgent confusion that is natural to such a place. The narrow room smelled of grease and sweaty wool and talc. Players hurried to change costumes wherever they could find space in makeshift stalls between props and racks of clothes. For the girl, coming here was like entering an alchemist's workshop, where simple specimens of humanity like herself could be refashioned into a king, a queen, a Moor, a great lover, or a witch. Only she was a woman, something less than these simple men, and the magic of acting was taboo to her sex. Her bleak fate weakened her and she wanted to stop, but the wounded ghost, in a kind and tender manner, urged her forward past the thrones and chairs and stools, sets of armor like the one he himself had left underneath the stage, into a thicket of halberds and lances ornamented with streamers and out again into a passage hung with caps and bonnets and headdresses on which feathers waved and bristled from a breeze that gusted through an open window. Then a row of coat stands hanging with robes, silk and velvet and fur-trimmed, purchased from the servants of dead nobility. Despite the visual busyness, every human motion was dreamlike, folded up and hidden in silence; the unseen presence of something greater seemed to press upon it all and soften the texture without diminishing it.

He was all right, he insisted, and dismissed the boys back to their duties after Harry had brought him a crutch. The girl waited for him while he hopped one-legged to speak with a man who sat on a stool by the stage-right entrance, shuffling through a mound of papers in his lap. The man listened with a puzzled expression on his face to her benefactor's instructions, trying to understand what it was his ghost wanted. He leaned over and pulled down the actor's stocking to inspect the puffy ankle. Then, with soundless, shaking laughter, the man seemed to consent, and the ghost hobbled back to her with a luster in his eyes.

She followed him to a small anteroom behind a vertical stack of lumber. He quickly urged her forward and shut the door behind them. Moments later someone was tentatively knocking at it. She gasped when she heard the voice and put her hands over her mouth.

"Master, are you fit? Henslowe says you have lamed your foot."

"Go away, Gilly, while I pray for quick healing. You'll see me in the closet scene."

The ghost did not know who was right, or how the matter finally should be settled. Perhaps the girl was a strumpet, but he didn't think so. Gilly must confront the issue nevertheless. And here was a fine test for Burbage's courage and greatness, a diversion to complement their ale afterward at the Boar's Head. He called the girl over to a chair behind his writing table. In the light she was not pretty, nor unpleasing. Her dark appearance, her man's nose, her fat cheeks and small bosom, but ah, he noticed, those lively eyes would not lack suitors in hungry London, and her wit was not easily matched. She was of the type that, dressed in the right clothes, would attract wealth and station.

"Remove thy slippers and put these heeled boots on to raise thee. Do they fit?"

"Nay."

"No matter. You shall not walk far with them."

"My lord?"

"Aye?"

"The stage-master will not allow your game."

"I think not, Virginia. 'Tis my play, and mine to play with."

Her dress was straight and plain, without the layers of petticoats or architecture of a farthingale to swell it out like a pumpkin. She would not have to remove it.

"Now, my lady," he said, catching up her long auburn hair, "let me tie this back with a ribbon. None shall know thee save those that know thee closely."

FIVE

The music startled him back into the play. The stretching moan of the sackbuts was like a fat finger pressing in to his emotions. The plaintive bass viol deepened the sense of loss that had been hounding him since he had seen the ghost. He would rock on the sea for months with never the desire to stand and check himself in front of a looking glass, but here he must sit idly by and watch men full of airy gestures and long speeches open him up and unsettle his peace. He had never been a man of words, of lady-pleasing or beguiling phrases. His course was sudden and deliberate action, as was England's. Hamlet's indecisiveness challenged him; the man's defective will burned against the Captain's instinct. The Dane was casting his father deeper into diabolic misery. And Sir Philip obviously approved.

"Hamlet's a fool." The Captain sneered. "He's content to tease the villain with a troop of loobies. Now the tragedy will double."

"Don't believe so hastily," said Sir Philip. "Hamlet is a man of cunning humor. He'll trip the King with cords of distraction."

"Hamlet finds no difference between the nut and the shell. The part he pretends is real; thus there is no pretending, but a wind that blows from all directions."

Sir Philip paused to think about this. The Captain jumped up before he could reply.

"Mark that! The visiting players have set a fire under the King—he flees and all doubt follows. Mark that, I say. If Hamlet is a fox, let him bite. After him, man. What, he stays. God save thee, he only wants to hear his words match each other."

The Captain swung one leg over the railing of the box. This effort mortified Sir Philip and he grabbed the hem of the Captain's tabard.

"Here, where are you going?"

The Captain was not sure.

"I beseech you, sit back, sir. Let the amusement run its course."

There was a growing noise in the pit. Several groundlings clambered up the balustrade of the stage as the King exited. Burbage still strutted about behind the milieu, taking pleasure in responding to catcalls. Rosencrantz and Guildenstern marshaled the intruders from the stage. The Captain sat down with a sigh. After a moment there was music again, bird sounds puffed out of recorders. The sun now divided the stage in half. The Captain blew his swollen nose vigorously into a silk handkerchief and bought more wine, regretting that this was not his fight, more eager than ever to get back to sea. Sir Philip remained fascinated by the men in the corner of their box, still hoping to decipher their code. He imagined they were spies, Knights of Malta, collecting information on the Providence Company. Perhaps later he would have them arrested. The woman had been teary ever since Hamlet first spoke to Ophelia. She dabbed at her eyes with a scarf tied to her wrist. "How brutal," she said under her breath, "his love is."

SIX

The Captain's second sense had alerted him. He felt the tension of blood ready to be released. There was a strike, and the old milkweed Polonius fell from behind the arras dead. There's the first. There was no stopping it now. The Captain was satisfied. He was accustomed to and strengthened by danger, sensitive to plans gone astray; his life depended on intuition. The ghost had reappeared and something felt wrong, off balance. The Queen was behaving oddly. The person subdued within the actor seemed to show himself, to jut out for a moment like a white knee through the folds of a robe.

SEVEN

The beard itched and the paint felt like mud on her face. The boots he had made her wear were like pails strapped around her feet. She crossed the stage, clumping each foot down, thinking she must throw her arms around Gilly, but he was backstroking away from her, and Burbage had slid between them. She froze from the clarity of the actor's eyes, the impatience of his mouth. She thought she must run offstage, but then he smiled and seemed to bow slightly in acknowledgment:

A king of shreds and patches—Burbage stopped, licked his lips and howled,

"Risen in a most unnatural form," he added with a wink;

Save me, and hover o'er me with your wings,

You heavenly guards! What would your gracious figure!

Alas, he's mad, said the Queen, but her voice broke in a mulish tone like a viola da gamba stroked with an unresined bow. She grabbed at her throat, stunned, and sat back unladylike on her bed.

Hamlet spoke to the ghost of his father:
Do you come your tardy son to chide,
That, lapsed in time and passion lets go by
Th' important acting of your dread command?
O, say!
Her beard bobbed up and down, but her lips were speechless. The words roared out in a familiar voice from behind the curtain:
Do not forget this visitation
Is but to whet thy almost blunted purpose.
But, look, amazement on thy mother sits:
Speak to her, Hamlet.
How is it with you, lady?
The Queen did not stir. She had pitched back on the bed and was staring wall-eyed at the signs of the Zodiac that whirled about the stage's canopy.

EIGHT

He beckoned the girl offstage. The crutch pinched his underarms, but the sensation vanished as he listened to his Hamlet. Burbage could not be bully-goated, he could not stumble. Given the opportunity he would wag his tongue at anything, and each spontaneous phrase was a miracle of rhythm and concise beauty. Since the Queen would not finish her lines, Burbage was full of wordplay, floating the plot on a tide of wit. The world stopped to hear his fluency. Behind the curtain, the ghost listened quietly to the flowering of the language, musical and complete, as though it had always existed, and would forever.

SQUIRRELLY'S GROUPER

A fish story is like any other, never about a fish but always about a man and a place. I wouldn't even mention it if I thought everybody knew. When you cut down to the bone of the matter, a fish is just Pleasure with a capital P. Rule of thumb—the bigger the fish, the bigger the pleasure. That's one side of the coin of fishing, the personal best and finest, but this is Hatteras, and there's that other side. On the Outer Banks of North Carolina, you can't pitch a rock in the air in the morning without rock-throwing becoming widespread ruthless competition by the time the sun goes down over Pamlico Sound, and that is because we go to sea for our living, and because commercial fishermen think they are God's own image of male perfection. I've seen it go on all my life here on the coast, each generation afflicted with the same desire to lord, bully, and triumph; doesn't even matter where they come from once they're here, north or south or bumbled in from Ohio and beyond like Willie Striker. So that's the other side, where size counts, wakes the sleepyheads right up, subdues the swollen-head gang, and becomes everybody's business.

~~~~

We saw the boats off that morning like we always do, and near an hour later Mrs. Mitty Terbill came in the marina store to post a sign she had made, a little gray cardboard square she had scissored from the back of a cereal box. It said: LOST DOG. YORKSHIRE TERRIER. NAME—PRINCE ED, MY SOLE COMPANION. REWARD, and then a number to reach her at.

"What's the reward, Mitty?" I asked. It was five dollars, which is about right for a Yorkie, measured by appeal per pound. Mitty Terbill is not an upright-standing woman, but then considerable woe has befallen her and keeps her squashed into her pumpkin self, allowing for only brief religious ascension. She spent that much plus tax on a twelve-pack and trudged back out the door, foot-heavy in her fishwife's boots, going back to her empty house on the beach to sit by the phone. Well, this story's not about the widow Terbill, though plenty of stories are since she lost her old man and her dope-pirate offspring two Januarys ago when they ran into weather off Cape May, up there flounder fishing I believe it was. That's just how I remember the day settling down after the dawn rush, with Mitty coming in, some of the fellows cracking jokes about how one of the boys must have mistook Prince Ed for bait and gone out for shark, and although Mitty likes her opinions to be known and gets the last word in on most events, let me please go on.

Life is slack at a marina between the time the boats go out early and vacationers get burnt off the beach about noon and come round to browse; then in the afternoons all hell breaks when the boats return. Anyway, after Mitty stopped in, Junior left to pull crab pots; Buddy said he's driving out to Cape Point to see if the red drum are in on the shoals with the tide change; Vickilee took a biscuit breakfast over to her cousins at the firehouse; Albert went down to the Coast Guard station to ingratiate himself to uniformed men; Brainless was out at the pumps refueling his uncle's trawler so he could get back to the shrimp wars, which left just me, my manager Emory Plum, and my two sacked-out Bay Retrievers in the place when I hear what might be an emergency broadcast on the citizen's band, because it's old grouch Striker calling J.B. on channel seventeen. Willie Striker has been one to spurn the advancement of radio and the charity of fellow captains, not like the other jackers out there bounced wave to wave on the ocean. They yammer the livelong day, going on like a team of evangelical auctioneers about where the fish aren't to be found, lying about how they barely filled a hundred-pound box, complaining how there's too many boats these days on the Banks and too many Yankees on land, in a rage because the boys up in Manteo are fetching a nickel more for yellowfin, and who messed with who, and who's been reborn in Christ, and who knows that college girl's name from Rodanthe, and who's going to get theirs if they don't watch it. Willie Striker has something to say himself, but you wouldn't find him reaching out. He kept to himself and preferred to talk that way, to himself, unless he had a word for his wife, Issabell. Keeping to himself was no accident, and I'll tell you why if you just hold on.

J.B. J.B. . . . come in, Tarbaby, I hear, and even though an individual's voice coming through the squawk box fizzes like buggy tires on a flooded road, you know it's Willie Striker transmitting because his words had the added weight of an accent, nothing much, just a low spin or bite on some words. Like mullet, Willie Striker would say, *maul*-it.

Tarbaby Tarbaby . . . come in. That was the name of J.B.'s workboat.

I was restocking baits, ballyhoo and chum, my head bent into the freezer locker, and Emory, he was back behind the counter studying delinquent accounts. "Turn her up a bit there, Emory," I told him, "if you please."

He didn't need to look to do it, he's done it so many times. He just reached behind and spun the dial to volume nine, put a hailstorm and a fifty-knot blow between us and the boats. "Well, who's that we're listening to?" Emory yelled out. "That's not our Mr. Squirrel, is it?"

Some twenty-five years it'd been I guess that Willie Striker had lived among us, married Issabell Preddy, one of our own, came south it was said sick and tired of Dayton and a factory job, and from the day he showed his jumpy self at Old Christmas in Salvo, folks called Striker Squirrelly. If you've seen his picture in the paper, you might think you know why. Squirrelly's got a small shrewd but skittish face with darting, then locking, eyes, a chin that never grew, some skinny teeth right out in the front of his mouth, and his upper lip was short, tight, some called it a sneer. The top of his head was ball-round and bald up to the crown, then silver hair spread smooth like fur. But like any good made-up name that fits and stays, there was more to it than manner of appearance.

Way-of-life on Hatteras Island has long been settled, that's just the way it is. A couple dozen families like mine, we lived together close back to Indian times, wreckers and victims of wrecks, freebooters and lifesavers, outcasts and hermits, beachcombers and pound netters and cargo ferrymen, scoundrels and tired saintly women, until they put the bridge across Oregon Inlet not long after Willie moved

SQUIRRELLY'S GROUPER

down. Outsiders meant complications to us one way or another; the truth is we don't take to them very well—which used to have significance but doesn't anymore, not since the herd stampeded in the last ten years to buy up the dunes and then bulldoze the aquifer. That's the island mascot these days, the yellow bulldozer, and the Park Service rules the beach like communists. That's one thing, but the fact is Willie Striker wouldn't care and never did if a Midgett or a Burrus or a Foster ever said, "Fine day, iddn't Skipper" to him or not. He wasn't that type of man, and we weren't that type of community to look twice at anything unless it had our blood and our history, but Issabell Preddy was the type of woman inwardly endeared to signs of acceptance, which you could say was the result of having a drunkard father and a drunkard mother. Issabell and her brothers went to live with their Aunt Betty in Salvo until they finished school, but Betty had seven children of her own, a husband who wouldn't get off the water, and no time to love them all. I went to school with Issabell and have always known her to be sweet in a motionless way, and not the first on anybody's list. She had one eye floating and purblind from when her daddy socked her when she was small, wore hand-down boys' clothes or sack dresses on Sundays, her fuzzy red hair always had a chewed-on aspect about it, and her skin was such thin milk you never saw her outside all summer unless she was swaddled like an Arab. Back then something inside Issabell made her afraid of a good time, which made her the only Preddy in existence with a docile nature, and the truth is a quiet girl who is no beauty is like a ghost ship or a desert isle to the eyes of young and active men: No matter how curious you are you don't want to be stuck on it.

One by one Issabell's brothers quit school and took off,

joined the Navy and the Merchant Marines, and Issabell herself moved back down the road to Hatteras, rented the apartment above the fishhouse and got employed packing trout, prospered modestly on the modest fringe, didn't hide herself exactly but wouldn't so much as sneeze in company without written invitation. The charter fleet was something new back then; there were not-unfriendly rumors that Issabell upon occasion would entertain a first mate or two during the season. These rumors were not so bad for her reputation as you might expect in a Christian village except none of us really believed them, and it would have come as no surprise if sooner or later one of our crowd got around to marrying Issabell Preddy, but the island had temporarily run out of eligible men by the time Terry Newman met Willie Striker in a Norfolk juke joint and brought him back with him for Old Christmas in Salvo. Old Christmas all the long-time families come together to feast by day, to game and make music and catch up with the facts of the year; by night we loudly take issue with one another and drink like only folks in a dry county can, and of course we fistfight—brother and cousin and father and godfather and grandfather and in-law; the whole bunch—and kid about it for three hundred sixty-five days until we can do it again. A few years back a lady from a city magazine came to write about our Old Christmas, called it culture, and I told her call it what the hell you want but it's still just a bust-loose party, gal, and when the night fell and the fur started to fly she jumped up on a table above the ruckus, took flashbulb pictures, and asked me afterward why Hatterasmen liked to brawl. I told her there's nothing to explain, we all think we're twelve years old, and if it was real fighting somebody'd be dead. Anyway, Terry Newman showed up that January with his twenty-four-hour buddy, Willie Striker, and it was the year that Terry's brother Bull Newman decided Terry was good-for-nothing and needed to be taught a lesson. One minute Bull had his arm across Terry's shoulder laughing, and the next he had knocked him down and out cold, continued through the room rapping heads of all he perceived to have exercised bad influence on his younger brother, including the skull of his own daddy, until he arrived at Willie, nursing a bottle of beer off by himself at a table in the corner. Bull was a huge man but dim; Willie Striker was no young buck but was given to juvenile movements the eye couldn't properly follow— twitches and shoulder jerks and sudden frightening turns—so even as he sat there holding his beer he seemed capable of attack. Bull towered over him with an unsure expression, a dog-like concern, trying to determine who this person was and if he was someone he held an identifiable grudge against or someone he was going to hit on principle alone, and when he swung Willie dodged and lunged, laid Bull's nose flat with his beer bottle without breaking the glass, threw open the window at his back, and scrambled out.

"That'll teach you to go messin' with squirrels," someone said to Bull.

No one saw Willie Striker again until a week later, raking scallops in the Sound with Issabell Preddy. The way I heard it was, Willie got to the road that night about the same time Issabell was headed back to Hatteras from her visit with her Aunt Betty, driving a fifty-dollar Ford truck she had bought off Albert James, her Christmas present to herself, and even though Willie was hitching back north, she stopped and he got in anyway and went with her south, neither of them, the story goes, exchanging a word until they passed the lighthouse and got to the village, everything shut down dark and locked up, not a soul in sight of course, and Issabell said to him, so the story goes,

151

that he could sleep in the truck if he wanted, or if he was going to be around for the week he could come upstairs and have the couch for thirty cents a night, or if he had plans to stay longer he could give her bed a try. Willie went the whole route: truck, couch, Issabell Preddy's lonely single bed.

In those days scalloping was women's work, so it was hard to raise any sort of positive opinion about Willie. He was a mainlander, and worse, some brand of foreigner; out there wading in the Sound it appeared he had come to work, but not work seriously, not do man's work; he had moved into Issabell's apartment above the firehouse and burdened her social load with scandal; and he had clobbered Bull Newman, which was all right by itself, but he hadn't held his ground to take licks in kind. He had run away.

The following Old Christmas Willie wedded Issabell Preddy in her Aunt Betty's kitchen, though for her sake I'm ashamed to say the ceremony was not well-attended. She wanted kids, I heard, but there was talk among the wives that Willie Striker had been made unfit for planting seed due to unspecified wounds. For a few years there he went from one boat to another, close-mouthed and sore-fingered, every captain and crew's back-up boy, and Issabell scalloped and packed fish and picked crabs until they together had saved enough for a down payment on the *Sea Eagle*. Since that day he had bottom-fished by himself, on the reefs and sunken wrecks, at the edge of the Stream or off the shoals, got himself electric reels a couple of years ago, wouldn't drop a line until the fleet was out of sight, wouldn't share Loran numbers, hoarded whatever fell into his hands so he wouldn't have to borrow when the fish weren't there, growled to himself and was all-around gumptious, a squirrel-hearted stand-alone, forever on guard against invasion of self, and in that sense he ended up where he belonged, maybe, because nobody interfered with Willie Striker, we let him be, and as far as I know no one had the gall to look him straight in his jumpy eyes and call him Squirrelly, though he knew that's what he was called behind his back. Whatever world Willie had fallen from at mid-life, he wound up in the right place with the right woman to bury it. Maybe he had fallen from a great height, and if the plunge made him a loon, it also made him a man of uncommon independence, and so in our minds he was not fully without virtue.

Squirrelly finally connected with J.B., who bottom-fished as well, not possessing the craft or the personal etiquette— that is to say, willingness to baby the drunken or fish-crazed rich—to charter out for sport. Likewise, he was a mainlander, a West Virginian with a fancy for the rough peace of the sea, and for these reasons Willie, I suspect, was not loathe to chance his debt. They switched radio channels to twenty-two in order to gain privacy and I asked Emory to follow them over. Up at their trailer in Trent, Issabell had been listening in too; hers was the first voice we found when we transferred. She questioned Willie about what was wrong; he asked her to pipe down.

"What you need there, *Sea Eagle?*" J.B. squawked. After a moment Willie came back on; hard to tell through the greasy sizzle, but he sounded apologetic.

"*Tarbaby,*" he said, "(something ... something) ... require assistance. Can you ... ?"

"What's he say was the trouble?" Emory bellowed. "I couldn't tell, could you?"

153

"Roger, *Sea Eagle*," J.B. answered. "Broke down, are you, Captain?" Willie failed to respond, though J.B. assumed he did. "I didn't get that, Willie," he said. "Where the hell are you? Gimme your numbers and I'll come rescue your sorry ass."

"Negative," we heard Willie say. "Report your numbers and I come to you."

So that's how it went, Striker ignoring his Issabell's pleas to divulge the nature of his trouble, J.B. staying at location while the *Sea Eagle* slowly motored through three-foot seas to find him while we sat around the marina, trying to figure out what it meant. Squirrelly had a problem, but it didn't seem to be with his boat; he needed help, but he would come to it rather than have it go to him. J.B. was about twenty miles out southeast of the shoals, tile fishing; likely Willie was farther east, sitting over one of his secret spots, a hundred fathoms at the brink of the continental shelf. We heard no further radio contact except once, more than an hour later, when Striker advised J.B. he had the *Tarbaby* in sight and would come up on his starboard side. Back at the marina the Parcel Service man lugged in eighteen cartons of merchandise and we were fairly occupied. Then past twelve J.B. called into us, jigging the news.

"Diamond Shoals Marina," J.B. crowed, "y'all come in. Dillon," he said to me, "better clean up things around there and get ready for a fuss. Squirrelly caught himself a fat bejesus."

I picked up the transmitter and asked for more information but J.B. declined, claiming he would not be responsible for spoiling the suspense. I slid over to channel twenty-two, waited for Issabell to stop badgering Willie, and asked him what was up.

"*Up?*" he spit into the microphone. "I tell you *up!* Up

come victory, by God. Up come justice . . . Going to seventeen," he muttered, and I flipped channels to hear him advertise his fortune to a wider audience. "Ya-ha-ha," we all heard him cackle. "Cover your goddamn eyes, sons of bitches. Hang your heads. Age of Squirrelly has come . . ."

We had never heard him express himself at such provocative length.

⁓

The island's like one small room of gossip-starved biddys when something like this happens. People commenced telephoning the marina, took no more than five minutes for the noise to travel sixty miles, south to north to Nags Head, then jump Albemarle Sound to Manteo and the mainland. "Don't know a thing more than you," Emory told each and every caller. "Best get down here to see for yourself when he comes in around three." I took a handcart to the stockroom and loaded the coolers with Coca-Cola and beer.

Now, there are three types of beast brought in to the dock. First kind are useless except as a sight to see, tourists gather round and take snapshots, Miss Luelle brings her day-care kids down to pee their pants, old stories of similar beasts caught or seen are told once more, then when the beast gets rank somebody kicks it back into the water and that's that. I'm talking sharks or anything big, boney, red-meated, and weird. Second style of beast is your sport beast: marlins, tuna, wahoo, barracuda, etcetera, but primarily billfish, the stallions of wide-open blue water. This class of beast prompts tourists to sign up for the Stream, but Miss Luelle and her children stay home, as do the rest of the locals unless a record's shattered, because these are regular beasts on the Outer Banks, at least for a few more

155

years until they are gone forever, and after the captain and the angler quit swaggering around thinking they're movie stars, I send Brainless out to cut down that poor dead and stinking hero-fish and tow it into the Sound for the crabs and eels, and that's that too. The third style of beast is kidnapped from the bottom of the world and is worth a ransom, and that's what Striker would have. He wouldn't bring anything in for its freak value, he was the last man on earth to recognize sport—all he did day in day out was labor for a living, like most but not all of us out here—so I figured he hooked himself a windfall beast destined for finer restaurants, he'd weigh it and set it on ice for brief display, then haul it to the fishhouse, exchange beast for cash and steer home to Issabell for supper and his bottle of beer, go to bed and rise before dawn and be down here at his slip getting rigged, then on the water before the sun was up.

First in was J.B. on the *Tarbaby,* which is a Wanchese boat and faster than most; J.B. likes to steam up a wake anyway, put spray in the air. Already the multitudes converged in the parking lot and out on the porch, elbowing in to the store. Vickilee came back across the street with her cousins from the fishhouse to start her second shift; Buddy led a caravan of four-wheelers down the beach from Cape Point. Packers and pickers and shuckers shuffled drag-ass from inside the fishhouse, gas station geniuses sauntered over from the garage. Coast Guard swabs drove up in a van, the girls from Bubba's Barbecue, Barris from Scales and Tales, Geegee from the video rental, Cornbread from the surf shop, Sheriff Spine, Sam and Maggie from over at the deli, the tellers from the bank, Daddy Wiss leading a pack of skeptical elders, and tourists galore drawn by the scent of photo opportunity and fish history. Before three all Hatteras had closed and come down, appetites inflamed, wondering what the devil Willie Striker was bringing in from the ocean floor that was so humongous he had to defy his own personal code and ask for help.

J.B.'s mate tossed a bowline to Brainless; took him in the face as usual because the poor boy can't catch. J.B. stepped ashore in his yellow oilskins and scale-smeared boots, saying, "I can't take credit for anything, but damn if I can't tell my grandkids I was there to lend a hand." Without further elaboration he walked directly up the steps to the store, went to the glass cooler, and purchased one of the bottles of French champagne we stock for high-rollers and unequaled luck. Paid twenty-eight dollars, and he bought a case of ice-colds too for his crew, went back out to the *Tarbaby* with it under his arm, going to clean tile fish.

"Well, come on, J.B.," the crowd begged, making way for him, "tell us what old Squirrelly yanked from the deep." But J.B. knew the game, he knew fishing by now and what it was about when it wasn't about paying rent, and kept his mouth glued shut, grinning up at the throng from the deck, all hillbilly charm, as he flung guts to the pelicans.

Someone shouted, *He just come through the inlet!* The crowd buzzed. Someone else said, *I heard tell it's only a mako shark.* Another shouted, *I heard it was a tiger!* Then, *No sir, a great white's what I hear. Hell it is,* said another boy, *it's a dang big tuttie. Them's illegal,* says his friend, *take your butt right to jail.* One of our more God-fearing citizens maneuvered to take advantage of the gathering. I wasn't going to have that. I stepped back off the porch and switched on the public address system. *Jerry Stubbs,* I announced in the lot, *this ain't Sunday and this property you're on ain't church. I don't want to see nobody speak-*

ing in tongues and rolling on the asphalt out there, I said. *This is a nonreligious, nondenominational event.* You have to take things in hand before they twist out of control, and I run the business on a family standard.

Here he comes now, someone hollered. We all craned our necks to look as the *Sea Eagle* rounded the buoy into harbor waters and a rebel cheer was given. Cars parked in the street, fouling traffic. The rescue squad came with lights flashing for a fainted woman. I went and got my binoculars from under the counter and muscled back out among the porch rats to the rail, focused in as Willie throttled down at the bend in the cut. I could see through the glasses that this old man without kindness or neighborly acts, who neither gave nor received, had the look of newfound leverage to the set of his jaw. You just can't tell what a prize fish is going to do to the insides of a man, the way it will turn on the bulb over his head and shape how he wants himself seen.

I went back inside to help Emory at the register. Issabell Striker was in there, arguing politely with Vickilee, who threw up her hands. Emory shot me a dirty look. Issabell was being very serious—not upset, exactly, just serious. "Mister Aldie," she declared, "you must make everyone go away."

"No problem, Mizz Striker," I said, and grabbed the microphone to the P.A. *Y'all go home now, get,* I said. I shrugged my shoulders and looked at this awkward lonesome woman, her floppy straw hat wrapped with a lime-green scarf to shade her delicate face, swoops of frosty strawberry hair poking out, her skin unpainted and pinkish, that loose eye drifting, and Issabell just not familiar enough with people to be used to making sense. "Didn't work."

Her expression was firm in innocence; she had her mind

set on results but little idea how to influence an outcome. "Issabell," I said to her, "what's wrong, hon?" The thought that she might have to assert herself against the many made her weak, but finally it came out. She had spent the last hours calling television stations. When she came down to the water and saw the traffic tie-up and gobs of people, her worry was that the reporter men and cameramen wouldn't get through, and she wanted them to get through with all her sheltered heart, for Willie's sake, so he could get the recognition he deserved, which he couldn't get any other way on earth, given the nature of Hatteras and the nature of her husband.

Issabell had changed some but not much in all the years she had been paired with Squirrelly in a plain but honest life. She still held herself apart, but not as far. Not because she believed herself better; it never crossed our minds to think so. Her brothers had all turned out bad, and I believe she felt the pull of a family deficiency that would sweep her away were she not on guard.

Her hands had curled up from working at the fishhouse. Striker brought her a set of Jack Russell terriers and she began to breed them for sale, and on weekends during the season she'd have a little roadside flea market out in front of their place, and then of course there was being wife to a waterman, but what I'm saying is she had spare time and she used it for the quiet good of others, baking for the church, attending environmental meetings even though she sat in the back of the school auditorium and never spoke a word, babysitting for kids when someone died. Once I even saw her dance when Buddy's daughter got married, but it wasn't with Willie she danced because Willie went to sea or Willie stayed home, and that was that. I don't think she ever pushed him; she knew how things were. The only difference between the two of them was that she had an ever-strengthening ray of faith that convinced her that someday life would change and she'd fit in right; Willie had faith that the life he'd found in Hatteras was set in concrete. The man was providing, you know, just providing, bending his spine and risking his neck to pay bills the way he knew how, and all he asked in return was for folks to let him be. All right, I say, but if he didn't want excitement he should've reconsidered before he chose the life of a waterman and flirted with the beauty of the unknown, as we have it here.

"Mizz Striker, don't worry," I comforted the woman. Besides, a big fish is about the best advertisement a marina can have. "Any TV people come round here, I'll make it my business they get what they want."

"Every man needs a little attention now and then," she said, but her own opinion made her shy. She lowered her eyes and blushed, tender soul. "Is that not right, Dillon?" she questioned. "If he's done something to make us all proud?"

Out on the bayside window we could watch the *Sea Eagle* angling to dock, come alongside the block and tackle hoist, the mob pressing forward to gape in the stern, children riding high on their daddies' shoulders. Willie stood in the wheelhouse easing her in, his face enclosed by the bill of his cap and sunglasses, and when he shut down the engines I saw his head jerk around, a smile of satisfaction form and vanish. He pinched his nose with his left hand and batted the air with the other, surveying the army of folks, then he looked up toward me and his wife. You could read his lips saying *Phooey*.

"What in tarnation did he catch anyway?" I said, nudging Issabell.

"All he told me was 'a big one,' " she admitted.

One of the porch layabouts had clambered down dockside and back, bursting through the screen door with a report. "I only got close enough to see its tail," he hooted.

"*What in the devil is it?*" Emory said. "I'm tired of waitin' to find out."

"Warsaw grouper," said the porch rat. "Size of an Oldsmobile, I'm told."

"Record buster, is she?"

"Does a whale have tits?" said the rat. " 'Scuse me, Mizz Striker."

You can't buy publicity like that for an outfit or even an entire state, and taking the record on a grouper is enough to make the angler a famous and well-thought-of man. I looked back out the bayside window. Squirrelly was above the congregation on the lid of his fishbox, J.B. next to him. Squirrelly had his arms outstretched like Preacher exhorting his flock. J.B. had whisked off the old man's cap. Willie's tongue was hanging out, lapping at a baptism of foamy champagne.

"Old Squirrel come out of his nest," Emory remarked. I fixed him with a sour look for speaking that way in front of Issabell. "Old Squirrelly's on top of the world."

Issabell's pale eyes glistened. "Squirrelly," she repeated, strangely pleased. "That's what y'all call Willie, isn't it." She took for herself a deep and surprising breath of gratitude. "I just think it's so nice of y'all to give him a pet name like that."

The crowd multiplied; a state trooper came to try to clear a lane on Highway Twelve. At intervals boats from the charter fleet arrived back from the Gulf Stream, captains and crew saluting Squirrelly from the bridge. Issabell went down to be with her champion. Emory and I and Vickilee had all we could do to handle customers, sold out of camera film in nothing flat, moved thirty-eight cases of beer mostly by the can. I figured it was time I went down and congratulated Willie, verify if he had made himself newsworthy or was just being a stinker. First thing though, I placed a call to Fort Lauderdale and got educated on the state, national, and world records for said variety of beast so at least there'd be one of us on the dock knew what he was talking about.

To avoid the crowd I untied my outboard runabout over at the top of the slips and puttered down the harbor, tied up on the stern of the *Sea Eagle*, and J.B. gave me a hand aboard. For the first time I saw that awesome fish, had to hike over it in fact. Let me just say this: you live on the Outer Banks all your life and you're destined to have your run-ins with leviathans, you're bound to see things and be called on to believe things that others elsewhere wouldn't, wonders that are in a class by themselves, gruesome creatures, underwater shocks and marvels, fearsome life forms, finned shapes vicious as jaguars, quick and pretty as racehorses, sleek as guided missiles and exploding with power, and the more damn sights you see the more you never know what to expect next. Only a dead man would take what's below the surface for granted, and so when I looked upon Squirrelly's grouper I confess my legs lost strength and my eyes bugged, it was as though Preacher had taken grip on my thoughts, and I said to myself, *Monster and miracle greater than me, darkness which may be felt.*

J.B. revered the beast. "Fattest damn unprecedented jumbo specimen of Mongolian sea pig known to man," he said (he could be an eloquent fool). "St. Gompus, king of terrors, immortal till this day." He leaned into me, whispering, fairly snockered by now, which was proper for the

occasion. "Dillon," he confided, "don't think I'm queer."
He wanted to crawl down the beast's throat and see what
it felt like inside, have his picture taken with his tootsies
sticking out the maw.

"Stay out of the fish," I warned J.B. "I don't have in-
surance for that sort of stunt."

A big fish is naturally a source of crude and pagan
inspirations. I knew what J.B. had in mind: get my marina
photographer to snap his picture being swallowed and
make a bundle selling copies, print the image on T-shirts
and posters too. He could snuggle in there, no doubt, take
his wife and three kids with him, there was room. The fish
had a mouth wide as a bicycle tire, with lips as black and
hard, and you could look past the rigid shovel of tongue in
as far as the puckered folds of the gullet, the red spikey
scythes of gills, and shudder at the notion of being suck-
ered through that portal, wolfed down in one screaming
piece into the dungeon of its gut. Don't for a minute think
it hasn't happened before.

Willie wasn't in sight, I noticed. I asked J.B. where the
old man had put himself, it being high time to hang the
beast and weigh it, see where we stood on the record, have
the photographer take pictures, let tourists view the creature so we could move traffic and give the other fishermen
space to go about their daily business, lay the beast on ice
while Willie planned what he wanted to do.

"He's up there in the cuddy cabin with Issabell," J.B.
said, nodding sideways. "Something's gotten into him,
don't ask me what." Vacationers shouted inquiries our
way; J.B. squared his shoulders to respond to an impru-
dent gal in a string bikini. "Well ma'am," he bragged,
"this kind of fish is a hippocampus grumpus. People round
here call 'em *wads*. This one's a damn big wad, iddn't it."
As I walked forward I heard her ask if she could step

aboard and touch it, and there was beast worship in her voice.

I opened the door to the wheelhouse; ahead past the step-down there was Willie Striker, his scrawny behind on a five-gallon bucket, the salty bill of his cap tugged down to the radish of his pug nose, hunched elbows on threadbare knees, with a pint of mint schnapps clutched in his hands. If you've seen a man who's been skunked seven days running and towed back to port by his worst enemy, you know how Willie looked when I found him in there. Issabell was scooched on the gallery bench, her hands in front of her on the chart. She was baffled and cheerless, casting glances at Willie but maybe afraid to confront him, at least in front of me, and she played nervously with her hair where it stuck out under her hat, twisting it back and forth with her crooked fingers.

I tried to lighten the atmosphere of domestic strife. "You Strikers're going to have to hold down the celebration," I teased. "People been calling up about you two disturbing the peace."

"He don't want credit, Dillon," Issabell said in guilty exasperation. "A cloud's passed over the man's golden moment in the sun."

Here was a change of heart for which I was not prepared. "Willie," I began, but stopped. You have to allow a man's differences and I was about to tell him he was acting backwards. He cocked his chin to look up at me from under his cap, had his sunglasses off and the skin around his eyes was branded with a raccoon's mask of whiteness, and I'm telling you there was such a blast of ardent if not furious pride in his expression right then, and the chill of so much bitterness trapped in his mouth, it was something new and profound for me, to be in the presence of a fellow so deeply filled with hate for his life, and I saw

SQUIRRELLY'S GROUPER

there was no truth guiding his nature, I saw there was only will.

His face contorted and hardened with pitiless humor; he understood my revelation and mocked my concern, made an ogreish laugh in his throat and nodded like, *All right, my friend, so now you are in the presence of my secret, but since you're dumb as a jar of dirt, what does it matter,* and he passed his bottle of bohunk lightning to me. Say I was confused. Then he mooned over at Issabell and eased off, he took back the pint, rinsed the taste of undeserved years of hardship from his mouth with peppermint, and jerked his thumb aft.

"Where I come from," Willie said, rubbing the silvery stubble on his cheek, "we let them go when they are like that one." His face cracked into a net of shallow lines; he let a smile rise just so far and then refused it. "Too small." (*Smull* is how he said it.) "Not worth so much troubles."

I thought what the hell, let him be what he is, reached over and clapped him on the back, feeling the spareness of his frame underneath my palm. "Step on out of here now, Captain," I said. "Time for that beast to be strung up and made official."

"Willie," coaxed Issabell with a surge of hope, "folks want to shake your hand." He was unmoved by this thought. "It might mean nothing to you," she said, "but it makes a difference to me."

Striker didn't budge except to relight his meerschaum pipe and bite down stubbornly on its stem between packed front teeth. On the insides of his hands were welts and fresh slices where nylon line had cut, scars and streaks of old burns, calluses like globs of old varnish, boil-like infections from slime poison.

"What's the matter, honey?" Issabell persisted. "Tell me, Willie, because it hurts to know you can't look your own happiness in the face. We've both been like that far too long." She tried to smile but only made herself look desperate. "I wish," she said, "I wish . . ." Issabell faltered but then went on. "You know what I wish, Willie, I wish I knew you when you were young."

Issabell jumped up, brushed by me, and out back into the sunshine and the crowd. Willie just said he was staying put for a while, that he had a cramp in his leg and an old man's backache. He had let the fish exhilarate and transform him out alone on the water, and for that one brief moment when J.B. poured the victor's juice on his head, but the pleasure was gone, killed, in my opinion, by distaste for society, such as we were.

"Now she will despise me," Willie said suddenly, and I turned to leave.

<hr />

J.B., me, and Brainless rigged the block and tackle and hoisted the beast to the scales. The crowd saw first the mouth rising over the gunnel like upturned jaws on a steam shovel, fixed to sink into sky. People roared when they saw the grisly, bulging eyeball, dead as glass but still gleaming with black wild mysteries. Its gill plates, the size of trash-can lids, were gashed with white scars, its pectoral fins like elephant ears, its back protected by a hedge of wicked spikes, and it smelled to me in my imagination like the inside of a castle in a cold and rainy land. You could hear all the camera shutters clicking, like a bushel of live crabs. When I started fidgeting with the counterweights, the whole place hushed, and out of the corner of my eye I could see Striker come to stand in his wheelhouse window looking on, the lines in his face all turned to the clenched pipe. He was in there percolating with vinegar and stubbornness and desire, you know, and I thought, What is it, you old bastard, is it the fish, or have you decided Issabell is worth the gamble? The grouper balanced. I wiped sweat from my brow and double-checked the numbers. Squirrelly had it all right, broke the state mark by more than two hundred pounds, the world by twenty-six pounds seven ounces. I looked over at him there in the wheelhouse, and brother he knew.

I made the announcement, people covered their ears while the fleet blasted air horns. A group of college boys mistook J.B. for the angler and attempted to raise him to their shoulders. A tape recorder was poked in his face; I saw Issabell push it away. Willie stepped out of the wheelhouse then and came ashore to assume command.

You might reasonably suspect that it was a matter of honor, that Willie was obliged to make us acknowledge that after twenty-five years on the Outer Banks his dues were paid, and furthermore obliged to let his wife, Issabell, share the blessing of public affections so the poor woman might for once experience the joy of popularity, just as she was quick to jump at the misery of leading a hidden life, so ready to identify with the isolation of the unwanted that night of Old Christmas all those years ago. Willie knew who he was but maybe he didn't know Issabell so well after all, didn't see she was still not at home in her life the way he was, and now she was asking him to take a step forward into the light, then one step over so she could squeeze next to him. You just can't figure bottom dwellers.

Anyway, I swear no man I am familiar with has ever been more vain about achievement, or mishandled the trickier rewards of success, than Willie after he climbed off the *Sea Eagle*. The crowd and the sun and the glamor went straight to his head and resulted in a boom of self-importance until we were all fed up with him. He came without a word to stand beside the fish as if it were a private place. At first he was wary and grave, then annoyingly humble as more and more glory fell his way, then a bit coy I'd say, and then Bull Newman plowed through the crowd, stooped down as if to tackle Willie but instead wrapped his arms around Willie's knees and lifted him up above our heads so that together like that they matched the length of the fish. The applause rallied from dockside to highway.

"I make all you no-goodniks famous today," Willie proclaimed, crooking his wiry arms like a body builder, showing off. Bull lowered him back down.

"Looks like you ran into some luck there, Squirrelly," Bull conceded.

"You will call me Mister Squirrel."

"Purty fish, Mister Squirrel."

"You are jealous."

"Naw," Bull drawled, "I've had my share of the big ones."

"So tell me, how many world records you have."

Bull's nostrils flared. "Records are made to be broken, *Mister* Squirrel," he said, grinding molars.

"Yah, yah." Willie's accent became heavier and clipped as he spoke. "Und so is noses."

Bull's wife pulled him out of there by the back of his pants. Willie strutted on bow legs and posed for picture takers. His old adversaries came forward to offer praise— Ootsie Pickering, Dave Johnson, Milford Lee, all the old alcoholic captains who in years gone by had worked Willie like a slave. They proposed to buy him a beer, come aboard their vessels for a toast of whiskey, come round the house for a game of cards, and Willie had his most fun yet acting like he couldn't quite recall their names, asking if they were from around here or Johnny-come-latelys, and I changed my mind about Willie hating himself so much since it was clear it was us he hated more. Leonard Purse, the owner of the fishhouse, was unable to approach closer than three-deep to Willie; he waved and yessirred until he caught Squirrelly's eye and an impossible negotiation ensued. Both spoke merrily enough but with an icy twinkle in their eyes.

"Purty fish, Willie. How much that monster weigh?"

"Eight dollars," Willie said, a forthright suggestion of an outrageous price per pound.

"Money like that would ruin your white-trash life. Give you a dollar ten as she hangs."

"Nine dollars," Willie said, crazy, elated.

"Dollar fifteen."

"You are a schwine."

"Meat's likely to be veined with gristle on a beast that size."

"I will kill you in your schleep."

"Heh-heh-heh. Must have made you sick to ask J.B. for help."

"Ha-ha! Too bad you are chicken of der wadder, or maybe I could ask you."

Vickilee fought her way out of the store to inform me that the phone had been ringing off the hook. TV people from New Bern and Raleigh, Greenville and Norfolk were scheduled by her one after the other for the morning. Newspaper people had already arrived from up the coast; she and Emory had talked to them and they were waiting for the crowd to loosen up before they tried to push through to us, and one of then had phoned a syndicate, so the news had gone out on the wire, which meant big-city coverage from up north, and of course all the sport magazines said they'd try to send somebody down, and make sure the fish stayed intact. Also, scientists were coming from the marine research center in Wilmington, and professors from Duke hoped they could drive out tomorrow if we would promise to keep the fish in one piece until they got here. The beer trucks were going to make special deliveries in the morning, the snack man too. Charters were filling up for weeks in advance.

So you see Squirrelly and his grouper were instant industry. The event took on a dimension of its own and Willie embraced his role, knew he was at last scot-free to say what he pleased without limit and play the admiral without making us complain. He sponged up energy off the crowd and let it make him boastful and abrupt, a real nautical character, and the folks not from around here loved his arrogance and thought we were all little squirrelly devils. Issabell seemed anxious too, this was not quite how she had envisioned Willie behaving, him telling reporters he was the only man on Hatteras who knew where the big fish were, but she beamed naively and chattered with the other wives and seemed to enjoy herself, even her goofed eye shined with excitement. It was a thrill, maybe her first one of magnitude, and she wasn't going to darken it for herself by being embarrassed.

Willie left the fish suspended until after the sun went down, when I finally got him to agree to put it back on the boat and layer it with ice. Its scales had stiffened and dried, its brown- and brownish-green-marbled colors turned flat and chalky. Both he and Issabell remained on the boat that night, receiving a stream of visitors until well past midnight, whooping it up and having a grand time, playing country music on the radio so loud I could hear it word for word in my apartment above the store. I looked out the window once and saw Willie waltzing his wife under one of the security lightpoles, a dog and some kids standing there watching as they carefully spun in circles. I said to myself, That's the ticket, old Squirrel.

Life in Hatteras is generally calm, but Tuesday was carnival day from start to finish. Willie was up at his customary time before dawn, fiddling around the *Sea Eagle* as if it were his intention to go to work. When the fleet started out the harbor though, he and Issabell promenaded across the road for breakfast at the café, and when he got back I helped him winch the fish into the air and like magic we had ourselves a crowd again, families driving down from Nags Head, families who took the ferry from Ocracoke, Willie signing autographs for children, full of coastal authority and lore for the adults, cocky as hell to any fisherman who wandered over. A camera crew pulled up in a van around ten, the rest arrived soon after. What's it feel like to catch a fish so big? they asked. For a second he was hostile, glaring at the microphone, the camera lens, the interviewer with his necktie loosened in the heat. Then he grinned impishly and said, I won't tell you. You broke the world's record, is that right? Maybe, he allowed indifferently and winked over the TV person's shoulder at me and Issabell. When the next crew set up, he more or less hinted he was God Almighty and predicted his record would never be broken. After two more crews finished with him the sun was high; I made him take the fish down, throw a blanket of ice on it. Every few minutes Emory was on the P.A., informing Squirrelly he had a phone call. Vickilee came out and handed Willie a telegram from the governor, commending him for the "catch of the century." I guess the biggest treat for most of us was when the seaplane landed outside the cut, though nobody around here particularly cared for the fellows crammed in there, Fish and

Game boys over to authenticate the grouper, so we pulled the fish back out of the boat and secured it to the scales. Hour later Willie took it down again to stick in ice, but not ten minutes after that a truck came by with a load of National Park Rangers wanting to have individual pictures taken with Squirrelly and the grouper, so he hung it back up, then a new wave of sightseers came by at midafternoon, another wave when the fleet came in at five, so he just let it dangle there on the arm of the hoist, beginning to sag from the amount of euphoric handling and heat, until it was too dark for cameras and that's when he relented to lower it down and we muscled it back to the boat, he took her down past the slips to the fishhouse, to finally sell the beast to Leonard I thought, but no, he collected a fresh half ton of ice. Willie wanted to play with the grouper for still another day.

That's almost all there is to tell if it wasn't for Squirrelly's unsolved past, the youth that Issabell regretted she had missed. On Wednesday he strung the fish up and dropped it down I'd say about a dozen times, the flow of onlookers and congratulators and hangarounds had decreased, Issabell was as animated as a real-estate agent and as girlish as we'd ever seen, but by midday the glow was off. She had been accidentally bumped into the harbor by a fan, was pulled out muddy and slicked with diesel oil, yet still she had discovered the uninhibiting powers of fame and swore that she had been endowed by the presence of the fish with clearer social vision.

By the time Squirrelly did get his grouper over to the fishhouse and they knifed it open, it was all mush inside, not worth a penny. He shipped the skin, the head, and the fins away to a taxidermist in Florida, and I suppose the pieces are all still there, sitting in a box like junk.

Now if you didn't already know, this story winds up

with a punch from so far out in left field there's just no way you could see it coming, but I can't apologize for that, no more than I could take responsibility for a hurricane. About a week after everything got back to normal down here, and Squirrelly seemed content with memories and retreated back to his habits of seclusion, Brainless came crashing through the screen door, arms and legs flapping, his tongue too twisted with what he was dying to say for us to make any sense of his message.

Emory looked up from his books. I was on the phone to a man wanting a half-day charter to the Stream, arguing with him that there was no such thing as a half-day charter that went out that far. "When's that boy gonna grow up," Emory clucked. He told Brainless to slow down and concentrate on speaking right.

"They'se takin' Squirrelly away," Brainless said. He pointed back out the door.

I told the fellow on the line I might call him back if I had something and hung up, went around the counter and outside on the porch, Emory too, everybody came in fact, Vickilee and Buddy and Junior and Albert and two customers in the store. It was a foggy, drizzly morning, the security lamps casting soupy yellow columns of light down to the dock; most of the boats hadn't left yet but their engines were warming up. I don't think the sun had come up yet but you couldn't be sure. The boy was right, a group of men in mackintoshes were putting handcuffs on Squirrelly and taking him off the *Sea Eagle*. The other captains and crews stood around in the mist, watching it happen. The men had on street shoes and looked official, you know, as you'd expect, and they led Willie to a dark sedan with government license plates. One of them opened the rear door for Willie, who kept his head bowed, and sort of helped him, pushed him, into the car. None of us tried to stop it, not one of us spoke up and said, Hey, what's going on? He was still an outsider to us and his life was none of our business. None of us said or even thought of saying, Willie, good-bye. We all just thought: There goes Willie, not in high style. The sedan pulled out of the lot and turned north.

"He's a goddamn natsy!" squealed Brainless, shaking us out of our spell.

"I told you not to cuss around here," Emory said. That was all anybody said.

Squirrelly's true name, the papers told us, was Wilhelm Strechenberger, and they took him back somewhere to Europe or Russia, I believe it was, to stand trial for things he supposedly did during the war. The TV said Squirrelly had been a young guard for the Germans in one of their camps. He had been "long sought" by "authorities," who thought he was living in Ohio. One of his victims who survived said something like Squirrelly was the cruelest individual he had ever met in his entire life.

Boy, oh boy—that's all we could say. Did we believe it? Hell no. Then, little by little, yes, though it seemed far beyond our abilities to know and to understand.

Issabell says it's a case of mistaken identity, although she won't mention Willie when she comes out in public, and if you ask me I'd say she blames us for her loss of him, as if what he had been all those years ago as well as what he became when he caught the fish—as if that behavior were somehow our fault.

Mitty Terbill was convinced it was Willie who grabbed her Prince Ed for some unspeakable purpose. She's entitled to her opinion, of course, but she shouldn't have expressed it in front of Issabell, who forfeited her reputation as the last and only docile Preddy by stamping the widow Terbill on her foot and breaking one of the old lady's toes. She filed assault charges against Issabell, saying Issabell and Willie were two of a kind. Like Mitty, you might think that Willie Striker being a war criminal explains a lot, you might even think it explains everything, but I have to tell you I don't.

Now that we know the story, or at least think we do, of Willie's past, we still differ about why Willie came off the boat that day to expose himself, to be electronically reproduced all over the land—was it for Issabell or the fish?—and I say I don't know if Willie actually liked fishing, I expect he didn't unless he craved punishing work, and I don't know what he felt about Issabell besides safe, but I do know this: Like many people around here, Willie liked being envied. The Willie we knew was a lot like us, that's why he lasted here when others from the outside didn't, and that's what we saw for ourselves from the time he conked Bull Newman on the nose to the way he abused what he gained when he brought in that beast from the deep and hung it up for all to admire. He was, in his manner, much like us.

We still talk about the grouper all right, but when we do we automatically disconnect that prize fish from Willie— whether that's right or wrong is not for me to say—and we talk about it hanging in the air off the scale reeking a powerful smell of creation, Day One, so to speak, and it sounds like it appeared among us like ... well, like an immaculate moment in sport. We've been outside things for a long time here on the very edge of the continent, so what I'm saying, maybe, is that we, like Issabell, we're only just discovering what it's like to be part of the world.

HiDALGOS

You're in for it, *gringo,* if you've been seated alongside a Latin businessman on a flight south out of Miami, assigned to the simmering paramilitary looks that emanate from behind his sunglasses. And the rhetoric will be compounded, you can be sure, if there's whiskey, the ostentatious use of money, and it will escalate to the unchallengeable if the businessman is also an exile or expatriate, making his residence in Dade County, with warehouses down on the river. And if he is wearing narrow shoes shined with absolute principles, and dressed in the blue suit of his moral insight, you should know, *gringo,* that you are in for it.

"What's wrong with Americans? *Bueno,* I will tell you."

He was a Dominican—not only a grower but an exporter of coffee—going on to Puerto Plata. Thus he began to brief Mitchell Wilson, a businessman of sorts himself, not too long after they had lifted off. Wilson listened with one ear, showed interest with one eye, smiled insincerely with half his mouth, all the while concentrating on his newsmagazine. "One minute," the Dominican interrupted himself as a flight attendant walked up the aisle. "Sssstt, *be-be*, two Johnny Walker Negro." He looked at Wilson. "Wha' you want, man?" he asked, making a curling smile when Wilson declined. "Hey, come on, *dígame*." And Wilson permitted the Dominican to stand him a rum.

"So now I tell you. Americans don' like to hunt when it's warm. This I don' like."

The attendant returned with four miniatures, two cups of ice; the businessman insisted he could only pay with a hundred-dollar bill. There was a discussion and he somehow won.

Wilson flipped a page, not admitting outright that he was indeed curious about the peccadilloes of nationality. The page he had turned to was dominated by a color photograph: Iranian speedboats, machine guns mounted in their bows, the boatmen in T-shirts and camouflage pants and *mujahadeen* scarves. Although most of the guns were bare, and some tarped in olive canvas, one had been draped with a Persian blanket, its patterns aqua, powder blue, swirls of white, and the weapon and the struts of its mount were transformed into a beautiful shape, like a blue heron flared to land on a tidal marsh. Something lovely to take to war.

"What's right with Americans? I will tell you."

No participation was necessary; the Dominican would talk without it. He wiped the long, full line of his lips with a paper napkin. "*Bueno*, it is *fantasía*. It is *el sueño*, the dream, dreamland, *tierra de hadas*, make-believe from sea to sea. Every little insect a *hidalgo*, son of something. No one else has this particular advantage. Do you agree?"

A Korean student pitched a Molotov cocktail into the air. The photo was unrealistically cropped, forcing the protester to act in isolation, deprived of support, robbed of an enemy. Triumphant only in the random infinity of reproduction.

The landing gear shuddered into position; the jet banked for its approach to the Salt Islands, where Wilson would disembark. The Dominican neither stopped smoking nor fastened his seat belt. Wilson turned to a photo essay of Presidential candidates, eating the first watermelon of the political season. The photographs had no impact on his imagination; he thought of them as foreign, culturally obscure, void of cause or consequence or even symbol.

"You getting off at this crazy worthless place?" the Dominican said, his eyebrows lowered in disbelief as Wilson lifted his briefcase. "Jesus! No, you must come to the Republic with me." Wilson squeezed around him into the aisle. "Where you from anyway, *hermano?* Washington? Yii, no shit. *Vaya con Dios.* I love you green-ass *maricones.* Truly, I do." And, incredibly, he choked with manly emotion and two tears appeared, as unexpected as guerrillas, from under the black lenses of his sunglasses. He reached for Wilson's hand to cement their short encounter with a vigorous shake. "I love you fuckers. *Hidalgo,* true? An excellent word. We are all together, no? *Los Hidalgos Unidos de las Americas.* Good-bye, bye-bye, good-bye."

⁓

Hidalgo, you'll find no uglier islands in all the tropic latitudes than the Salts. Think, if you will, of the drive between San Antonio and Laredo, that dry and ominous countryside, armored with spikes and thorns and stingers. The Salts are pieces of the same geographical mood, chipped off the continent to float in a sparkling paradisiacal sea, its reefs the same tinted color of the glass that contained the Korean

179

student's defiance. On the resort island of Flamingo, where Wilson had deplaned, there were a few hundred yards of expertly paved road leading from the airport along a stagnant lagoon, defunct salt pans hosting junked cars; then seven miles of badly paved road; then an unpaved road to leeward; and finally two ruts across a chalky surface laked with milky water. No dirt to speak of, and no trees: Flamingo was brittle thorn acacia, wild cotton and dwarf palms, pigeon pea bushes and palmetto, impenetrable thickets of cacti and bayonet plants, and throughout the vistas of unfriendly stunted growth, dead, blackened, limestone coral knolls lay scattered like slag deposited from creation's furnace. Yes, ugly, flat, yet where the ironrock of the shore relented, Flamingo had beaches as exquisite as the lace collar at the throat of a deformed princess, and the bone-white strands attracted *turtles*—the native metaphor for tourists—by the tens of thousands since the new runway was built a few years back.

Wilson's government driver veered away from the nearby sea, off the main unpaved road to a lesser one probing lower land, moist air laden not with oceanic brine but with the earthy aroma of mineral wealth, and now they braked in front of the lone few acres of honest fecundity on the entire length of the atoll, an outpost of organic prosperity.

"You don't have to wait around." Wilson removed his garment bag and briefcase from the bed of the pick-up. "Someone here will give me a ride back to town."

The knee-high hedge of oleander was now head-high; behind it they had actually gotten a lawn to grow, Faye and Alberts had, a yard to be mown, probably the first in Flamingo, not like the sand-spurred mangy patches of runners scrupulously tended by the hotels, fed a daily drool of desalinated liquid. The citrus trees were twice their height since Wilson had been here last; pole-trunked papayas and other foliage embowered the tin roof of the cottage Faye and Alberts had built themselves for a pittance. Neems and ficus fanned the lot in back, bougainvillaea with harlot colors, a youthful revolution of casurina pines . . . all of this the labor not of redemption—the Salts were in a state that preexisted grace—but of conversion, a gradual and painstaking baptism of pagan land.

The black lab mix charged from beneath the potting shed, barked once for the sake of reputation, and then flopped on his back, exposing his flea-bitten genitals for inspection. The blacks on the island were terrified of black dogs—somewhere in their collective past was a notorious one—and this mutt's name was Blackie, a former runt raised to gnarly island standard by Faye. Tacked to the door of the screened porch was a computer-printed notice, which Wilson read.

```
SALT ISLANDS NURSERY AND LANDSCAPING LTD.

Hours: 8 A.M.-5 P.M. Mon-Fri . . . except
when
• There is no one here between 8 A.M.-5 P.M.
• The trucks are both broken down on the road.
• We're fishing, diving, or partying.
```
(Wilson grunted—Alberts hadn't fished or dived in years.)
```
• Alberts is drinking his lunch in one of the
local bars, which means we're only open from 8
A.M.-noon.
• Anyone comes by on the way to the beach, we
might have gone with them.
```
(Faye, yes; Alberts, no. He was sick of the beach.)
```
. . . The nursery will then be open any time
that day when we are not at the beach. 8
A.M.-5 P.M.
• Something unusual happens, then we'll
probably be gone, but you can come in and look
around provided the attack dogs will let you.
If they won't, perhaps you should come back
when we're here between 8 A.M.-5 P.M.
  If there's a problem, leave a message with
Bozo and we will get back with you.
```

181

Bozo, a well-known personality on Flamingo, was a macaw, inherited from a restaurant gone out of business. He was a volatile bird at times, not to be trusted with fingers, given to brooding existential moods and swift infatuations. He had been enamored with Faye, followed her everywhere like a psychedelic duck, repeating, as she had taught him, one rudeness after another.

"Alberts," Wilson hallooed, unsticking the warped frame of the screen door. He set his luggage down on the concrete and stood on the threshold of the living area—office, bedroom, salon for the high and the low—lulled by the homestead serenity that was the atmosphere of every tent, shanty, sailboat, or house inhabited by the two vagabonds, Faye and Alberts, the secured do-it-yourself clutter, the professionally makeshift life, as comfortable as a rag rug.

"Alberts?"

So recognizable, this island peace back in the bush. There, on the worktable, was Faye's typewriter, a white hand towel spread over it to keep out dust. He lifted the covering—well, it didn't have to be, but the carrier was empty. No letters-in-progress, reports to Burton's clinic in Freeport, to Archie Carr or some other authority about sea turtles, the porpoises or blue-shelled lobster, the iguanas unique to the Salts. That was over and now, finally—why had it taken so long?—Wilson was feeling it with guilty relief, the subtle arrangement of her leavetaking expressed in objects on the table: a cheap wristwatch, a brand of unopened cigarettes, a used syringe.

Alberts's voice. "Back here," he called, a voice that never got loud without being murderous.

Wilson took the five steps necessary to cross the depth of the cottage, then went out a second sliding door to a deck to the open-air kitchen. Alberts was on duty at the gas stove, heating refried beans in an iron skillet. They would be tasty, knowing Alberts. And, knowing Alberts, the glass he saluted with contained rum and water, half and half, medicine for the vanities of freedom. Wilson relaxed—at least the man was eating as well as drinking, not yet so much a part of the everyday shifts of alignment that he had gone, as he deserved, as white men were supposed to anyway in the tropics, to pieces. Crawl on their hands and knees, let pathos ride their backs like a monkey. Faye had died— Alberts had taken her to Miami two months ago to do it. First, though, he had spent a year with her on the road, a hopeless vacation at the clinic in the Bahamas, then to Mexico and Arizona for experimental treatments, a faith healer in West Palm, another clinic in Greece, what must have been a sorrow-stricken one-day return to Flamingo, back on the plane the following morning to Miami, a damn hotel room off the interstate near the hospital, from where she had called Wilson but hung up before she finished a sentence. Alberts had taken her ashes out to the reef about a week ago. What was left was to continue the process, a sort of scorched-earth policy, leave nothing behind, carry what you could afford to with you in your heart, clear out—and he had asked Wilson to help if he could.

"Until this minute . . ." Wilson began, his throat hardening around the loss. "Oh boy. I really miss her."

"Listen." Alberts delivered a soothing reproach. "Knock it off. She's here, she's all around us, you're a fool if you don't know that, so stop worrying about it." He took the skillet off the heat and smiled. Even at outrageous moments, even in merciless conflict, Alberts's smiles were disarming; quick, dangerously true, offerings of affection. "I'll tell you what her last words were—'Tell Wilson to go fuck himself.'" He laughed at his own sense of humor. "You want a drink or not?"

Alberts wore mechanics jeans sagging below negligible hips, belted under the puff of his stomach. The sleeves of his workshirt were rolled up past his elbows, the front left unbuttoned, the tails tied loosely at his waist. He had on a bill cap too, a relic of the Tesoro Corporation, a salvage outfit he nearly got off the ground, and though his neck and forearms were athletically tanned, everywhere else his skin was pallid, much too protected, slack beginning to threaten in the flesh. His beard, carefully groomed to the line of his jaw, and much of his hair had whitened prematurely. He was worn out, had stepped in his mind through the bottoms of his shoes, and he intended to repatriate himself to the States, where he had not lived for twenty-three years. Wilson figured he should stay put, but he wasn't going to say it without an invitation, and knowing Alberts, there wasn't going to be an invitation.

Up until the past year, when she had no choice but to resemble a dying middle-aged woman, Faye had unconsciously, perhaps naively, managed to seem a prototypical hipster, a character in a photograph, taken, say, in 1958, at a café poetry reading. Alberts had met her in the Village, an errant daughter of a First Family of Virginia, doing her dissertation in psychology at NYU. She had known all the writers, all the spooks, the geek intellectuals. He tended bar on MacDougal Street, kept company with the folk musicians, all the queer actors and actresses, but he had been to war in Korea and to jail in Cuba, married and divorced to a model who had been given pearls by Sinatra, as if he, Alberts, a kid from Kansas City, had let his life be defined by Hollywood and the Pentagon. But only for a while; by the time he met Faye he had focused elsewhere, settled right in with the Beats. She and Alberts talked too much, two late-night visionaries; the type of fast and faraway delusions everybody indulged en route to bed. But when they drove together to New Orleans, telling themselves they would buy a boat, neither of them turned out to be bluffing. Alberts, justifiably, had the daylights scared out of him. Faye, goddamn her, was fearless. Some life they were cutting themselves loose into.

Wilson first ran into them in '74 when he was working for International Development in Costa Rica. They were out on the coast, Puerto Limon, preposterous *yanquis,* shark fishing, trot lines baited with offal strung across the rivermouth. Next, there was a copra plantation up north, then a bogus gold mine in Colombia, tedious and cold, unforgiving; a charter business, a restaurant one place, a next place, then still another one, a three-table enterprise; a schooner taken by storm. When her breasts were removed she was given six agonizing months to live. But Faye was a headstrong and difficult woman. Anybody who had ever been in a room with her for five minutes could have guessed her reaction. All she had to say was, *Wrong.* She reserved the right to disregard fatal pronouncements until she was ready to make her own; her revenge against the arrogance of science lasted eight willful years. They arrived in the Salts with nothing—little money and Faye's cancer, two suitcases and a box of tools coated with axle grease. But the archipelago was wide open at the time. The evolution of opportunities was discreet and bizarre. They fried chickens, packing box lunches for smugglers; babysat shopping bags of cash for a thousand dollars an hour; inherited hundreds of five-gallon pots of South Florida dirt, each one centered with a withered sprig, an unlikely bounty from one of the high priests of the substance trade, his scheme to ornament his hideaway estate with flowering extravagance preempted by a hitch in one shipment that led to jail.

Given the history of the first and only nursery on Flamingo, a desolate island on the verge of a boom of speculation, Faye and Alberts were hardly pathfinders forging ahead, come to create the world anew. That was it, *hidalgos*—what had taken place was the alleviation of blind courage, or rather the transition of courage, the maturation of its impulse. Alberts, armed with a shovel, declared himself at home.

———

Wilson accepted the highball glass of rum, adding juice and ice from the refrigerator. Alberts asked what his schedule was. He lumped beans into two mugs and handed one to Wilson.

"Get pissed to the gills with you . . ."

"Ah, yes."

". . . but first, as soon as we can, sit down with the people at the Ministry, get over to Cockburn Cay, meet their man. Does he know how to manage an operation like this? Can he tell a customer from a pH content? Talk to your lawyer, talk to the government lawyers, whoever writes a contract that can be approved. Does anybody have plans to hand out licenses? You have to be protected from that."

From behind a rough lattice screen separating the kitchen from the grounds, its diamonds woven solidly with passion fruit vine, materialized one of the Haitian laborers. His face was a shadow beneath the brim of a straw hat that would have looked right on Huck Finn. He held a fat green pumpkin, an ever-present machete.

"Keep it for yourself, Raicees." Alberts, paternal intimacy in his voice, went over and laid his hand on the small black man's shoulder. "Cook it for yourself and Luciano. Or sell it to one of the ladies in the Bight." The worker held out the pumpkin, as though he expected his employer to take it. He raised his chin, light falling across his round boy's face, deferential and puzzled. "Anything else out there—cucumbers or squash—you and Luciano take it home with you." Faye had scattered vegetable seeds throughout the compound, let them grow wild.

"He doesn't understand you. Does he?"

Alberts shook his head, abstracted, thinking of something else. "Well . . . yeah, mostly. Faye would only speak to them in Spanish, which is better." He took his hand away from Raicees and the Haitian was gone, transported, a refugee spirit absorbed into a manufactured jungle.

"They don't believe me."

The beans were too dry, like spackling; Alberts was losing his touch. Wilson reached for the bottle of red salsa on a shelf. "You're always leaving," he reminded Alberts. "You're always coming back."

"Not this time."

Raicees returned, explaining in his child's English that there was a problem with the water pump. Alberts told him he would look at it tomorrow.

They went inside the cottage and sat down, one at each end of the convertible couch. Alberts and Faye had slept right there for four years, molested by no-see-ums, no privacy, as if they were still on one of the boats, often waking with hangovers to customers on the porch rapping on the glass door—until, after the Club Med landscaping contract, Alberts had added on the bedroom.

Alberts slouched, balancing his drink on his belly. "Look," he began, "the propagation unit over on Cockburn Cay isn't worth seeing. They've rooted some cuttings; Faye gave them a sack of neem seeds, but they couldn't get them sprouted. They have papaya seedlings in Dixie cups. Their shade shed was knocked down in the last hurricane and it's still down." Alberts smiled ruefully. "I'm sorry I asked you to get mixed up in it."

Wilson, now that he understood Alberts was retreating from the emergency deal, was apologetic himself. "I wanted to come down earlier, before Faye died, or at least for the wake," he said. "This was the best I could do."

There was another buyer, Alberts admitted. "A white kid, French, here with his wife and baby. Nice guy, same figure, he's ready to do it, you don't get tangled up as broker, so why not? The government would let this place go to hell, right?"

Righter than right. The point all along had been expediency; swift, irreversible release. It was no skin off Wilson's nose; better, really—an individual with a family would prove a more reliable debtor than any government in power in the Salts. Profits before politics, payments deposited on schedule. According to Alberts, the closing was already set for Thursday morning, so nothing important had changed.

"You can stay here if you like. We fixed up one of the tool sheds into a bungalow. It isn't fancy. It isn't even clean. Cholly still bunks here, or you could have the couch."

Wilson wanted to stay, he said he wouldn't leave until he saw the papers signed—just in case. Bozo came to the door, rocking from foot to foot, eavesdropping, and Alberts flattered the bird, saying how pretty he was, poured him a cup of orange juice, two more rums to celebrate the smooth resolution of Wilson's arrival, the alteration of plans. They might as well go ahead and get soused, Alberts proposed, and not worry about a damn thing. The bird gargled with his juice; the voices of the Haitians could be heard out on the lot, their creole like the singsong of effeminate boys. Boat people, working without papers—

Wilson was introduced to something new in his picture of the world the first time he heard the way they responded to their employers; the endearments, the childlike intimacy, a code of filial love claimed by the dispossessed. *Yes, Mommy. Merci, Mommy. Drink of water, Mommy.* I can't believe them either, Faye had said, giggling. Cubans raise hell, Haitians kiss the foot that holds them down in their own filth. She gave them anything they wanted except mechanical things, because she'd once given Raicees a padlock for a shed and he had broken it. Tell me, she had asked Wilson, how do you bung up a lock and key in five minutes? *Poppi?*—Luciano, five years ago, pointing at Alberts's wristwatch—*How much?* Not how much time left to work, because what did that matter, but how many holes would a man have to dig for an American to purchase such an object of distinction? It was only a ten-dollar Timex; Alberts gave both men new ones for Easter, the next available holiday. They made enough to buy their own, no problem, but always sent their money back to Cap Haitien, kept nothing for themselves, like drone bees.

Back on the couch with a fresh drink, Alberts's eyes wandered the room. There was a plaid recliner chair of unguessable origin, its foam stuffing in pieces on the floor, ejected by nesting mice. Nails in the plywood hung with foul-weather oilskins, diving gear, Faye's sextant and binoculars, rusty fishing lures, a bwana sun helmet Faye sometimes wore for fun. A gun rack for a shotgun, a BB rifle for feral cats. A short-wave radio, a citizens band that would have been crackling if the nursery was open for business, a cassette player with speakers wired into the shade shed. The Arum Family—caladium, dieffenbachia, ceriman, Hunter's Robe—was being introduced to Nina Simone and Eric Von Schmidt the last time Wilson was in the Salts. Shells and seed pods, shards of Amerindian pottery, nautical charts, photos of boats and one of Alberts's son by his first wife, now at college in Madison. All the remaining space, the shelves and the floor, were warehoused with books, gorged with encyclopedia, manuals, coffee-ringed alternative-health bulletins, horticulture newsletters, entomology journals, seed and equipment catalogs.

"I have to pack," Alberts said, but they both stayed as they were.

⤳

In the early evening, Wilson mentioned he was starved, repeated it twice before Alberts agreed they should take the truck—Cholly had the other one—to the harbor for something to eat. The curse of a captain's license—there never was a time when Alberts hadn't taken the most pleasure in travel as a passenger, so Wilson drove, assuming Faye's place. On his previous visit, the final night or possibly the first, the three of them had closed down a waterfront bar. Leaving, Faye stumbled and her eyeglasses fell off; Wilson found them, she put them back on, myopic as a fish, not even realizing the lenses had popped out. A quarter-mile down the road she stopped. I can't see a blasted thing, she said, unable to recall ever drinking herself into a state of blindness. She was more intrigued than disturbed by her condition. You better drive, she told Wilson, and they changed places. A mile farther down the road, a bug flew into Faye's eye; she doubled over, head on her knees, strangled by laughter, whooping and choking that infected the two men until they were doing it too, and Wilson parked in the middle of the dark island lane, unable to hold the wheel.

They had few choices—it was no longer turtle time, the

tourist season. The yacht club, a club more by name than by practice, seemed to be the best place open. They sat at the bar and studied a chalkboard menu. "Get whatever you want," Alberts insisted. "Get a lobster. I'm a day away from twenty-five grand."

"Crown Prince of Flamingo." Wilson cleared his head. "Ten percent down? I thought you were asking more."

"I was, I did." Alberts nodded. "I got it . . . the other share goes into Cholly's pocket."

"What!" In a fool's pocket is where it was going. Wilson had strolled through the grounds after putting sheets on the mattress in the bungalow. Cholly had let the nursery run down. He had lounged out there in his underwear for twelve months, a model castaway, reading mysteries and warrior adventures and drinking gin and quinine while Alberts followed Faye from treatment to treatment.

"Don't talk to me about it," Alberts said. "What do I care? Order anything you want if you're my friend."

Whoever walked in, Alberts bought a drink, as long as they refrained from speaking as if he were a victim of Faye's death. Raconteurs held precedent, anyone with a joke; he had no patience for rituals of mourning. Wilson devoured his fish and chips when they came from the kitchen. The sterile atmosphere of the club receded in alcoholic laughter, and by the time he finished eating, the bar was packed two-deep, the tables occupied in the restaurant section. "Would you sleep with an old soft-brained mullet like me?" he heard Alberts, making the rounds now, tease a young woman out of habit and style, a vestige of appreciation; that afternoon Alberts had hinted at impotency and his general indifference to a cure. Cholly arrived, Flamingo's premier ne'er-do-well, to a fanfare of vulgarity from his competition. A portly London Jew with a tuft of wild hairs on the tip of his nose, no member of

Parliament, no Labor Party wag, was as cavalier as Cholly. Wilson had never known him to wear anything but a uniform of aggressive unemployment: an epauletted bush shirt, baggy khaki shorts, plastic sandals, and a beard that grew high on his cheeks. There was nothing a white man couldn't do in the Salts that Cholly hadn't done—except get rich or move on.

"Caveat emptor," he grumbled to the bartender, demanding his regular tonic from the Salt Island woman. "Let the buyer bloody well beware with a girl like you." The exchange of haughty looks was no more than a game, Cholly's detachment timed to her most poignant sneer, at which he turned to scrutinize Wilson with an arrogant smile. "What brings you poking around?" he challenged, in command of a thousand affectations, measuring Wilson through half-lidded eyes. Suddenly his manner changed and he pumped Wilson's hand, blustering with good-natured fellowship. "Good to see you, sir. We missed having you aboard when we dunked Faye." It was as if Cholly were Noel Coward's younger brother, banished to the tropics, there to corrupt the art of theatrics and dramatize the craft of personal corruption.

"How's Alberts been holding up?"

Cholly blinked, pursed his fleshy lips, acting out the act of evaluation. Finally he spoke. "How the bloody hell does he seem to you?"

"He seems all right. Thrown off a cliff, but the same."

"Ah," said Cholly, "very well then. That's all there is to it then, isn't it. Let the man be, I say. He's drinking himself into the crematory fires. It's a proper tradition here. However"—Cholly held up a blunt finger—"I'm afraid it will not travel well. What shall the poor bastard do in the Great White North? Bag groceries? Carpool with your Mr. Hasenfus?"

Alberts emerged from the muddle and wrapped an arm around Wilson, patting his shoulder. He looked disoriented and swollen, and leaned with most of his weight. "Look who's here." Next to Alberts stood a lank man, square-jawed, a head of bleachy hair, a beard thin and colorless, with pock-marked skin and bright predatorial eyes. He was Scandinavian, a Norwegian, Wilson remembered, but he couldn't think of his name. A builder or another architect—Flamingo was thick with both. "Nils." A fresh round of drinks spontaneously appeared. Nils had housed Faye and Alberts for a couple months when they first showed up on the island.

"What did they do with all the black people around here?" someone—an off-season turtle or escapee from Club Med—questioned the bartender.

"Dey is teefin you room dis very minute," she answered, and punished him with a scowl.

Alberts turned gloomy and wanted to leave. "Let's all go on out to the nursery," he lobbied. "I want Wilson to hear the song we played when we took Faye out to the reef."

"Camilla," Cholly's stentorian voice boomed above the noise, "my dear, fetch us our bill." When it came, a four-page tab, the recurring but temporal issue of honor was raised by Alberts, and so they argued with unnecessary sincerity for the privilege to pay. Cholly hovered over the green chits, calmly unfolded his reading glasses. "Goddamn it," he growled, examining the first column of figures. Nils crushed against Wilson, leaving a wetness behind on his ear as he confided that he would take care of Alberts, and asked for the keys.

"Camilla," Cholly demanded, "bring me the calculator."

Wilson blanched. "You mad Jew," he said, but insults never worked on Cholly. "Pay it and let's go."

In due time Camilla obeyed, slamming the machine down in front of them. Cholly punched haphazardly at the buttons while she stood by, erect, ready for battle, shoulders rolling, never in her life dismissed as a stupid island girl, black and stupid. Cholly eventually removed his reading glasses and tucked them away, meeting Camilla's eyes.

"It's not enough," he pronounced wickedly, rearing back as Camilla feigned a slap to his face.

⁓

All the lights were on, in the compound and in the cottage, but the bulbs were inferior and weak. No radiant aurora announced the nursery in the sky; you wouldn't have known you were anywhere at all until you made it past the front hedges and entered a grotto of foliage strung with shy electricity. Riffs of Thelonious Monk crackled down the rows of botanic platoons, marshaled in fluid shadows that made the glossy leaves of the sea grapes shimmer marvelously, made the roots of the scheffleras burst through their plastic tubs. Down the white path flanked with crotons, Cholly and Wilson bumped and wobbled, a light-headed midnight dance. Inside, Nils and two girls—well, young women—sprawled on the couch, smoking cigarettes, cans of beer in their hands. Cholly, as formal as a circuit magistrate, fit himself into the recliner, ready to pontificate. Wilson looked at Faye's desk and decided he should not sit there. When he went out to the porch for a chair, the screen door nudged and rattled and he opened it for Bozo to come in for the soiree.

"Oh God, look," one of the girls exclaimed. The stylized edges of her hair looked blown back from her scarlet face by an explosion. Where had they come from? thought Wilson. Did they live on Flamingo? Guests of their fathers, brutal wizards of real estate? Off a boat? Sorority field trip? "It's a parrot! Isn't he gorgeous." Bozo scaled the couch, zeroed in on the females, the gender of his preference, using his enormous black beak for leverage to haul himself up. The other girl sprang to her feet and stood by the rear door, no friend to feathered things, watching the bird waddle along the spine of the couch and stop, inspecting her companion.

"That, ladies, is not a parrot," Cholly said, hunched down, his eyes nasty slits.

"What is it then?"

"It's a macaw, macaw, ma-*caw*." He squinted across the room. "Have you ever seen Bozo at Club Med, Wilson? He is a fan of tennis, he flies over to the courts and sits all day atop the fence—ping, pong, ping, pong—keeping his eye on the ball. Early in the morning he attacks joggers. Swoops down on them from behind. They bloody well have it coming too."

"Polly want a cracker," said the girl on the couch, reaching out her hand slowly. The bird cocked its head, appraised the rings on her fingers; the feathers bristled at the back of his neck, a request to be scratched.

"Polly want a cracker," she persisted. Bozo straightened up, realizing she wasn't really going to touch him.

"Polly want a cracker."

Bozo eyed her keenly. "Fuck off!" he shrieked, and Cholly rumbled with demonic chuckling. Faye had taught the bird to be indignant when people annoyed him with the cracker routine.

"He despises crackers," Cholly explained. "Why don't you ask him if he wants oral sex."

From the bedroom at the back of the cottage came

195

Alberts, loaded down with clothes still on their hangers. "I want you all to have these," he announced; you could see his mind turning, trying to match the top pair of slacks to a body. Nils and Cholly ignored him, but Wilson and the two girls raised their eyebrows at each other, avoided looking at Alberts. He was entirely nonplussed by the lack of response, then his eyes flashed with enthusiasm and he dumped the clothes in the middle of the room. Wilson stared uncomfortably at the pile. "I've got something for you ladies too," Alberts said, winking, and turned on his heels. One of the girls lit a joint.

Wilson thought he would strike up a conversation with Nils. "What is this music?" he asked. "Is this . . . Monk?"

He was astonished when the Norwegian snarled. "You don't know anything about jazz. First, you're an American. Second, you're not old enough."

"You're kidding me." Wilson couldn't get rid of his moronic grin. Cholly passed him the joint as Alberts clumped back into the room, waving something long and pink.

"Gaw!" The girl on the couch looked at her friend, their jaws dropped, and they both tittered. "Are those dildos? Look how big they are!"

"Take them if you want them," Alberts recommended happily. There were four of them, which he sailed across the room one at a time, flipping like throwing knives. "Someone traded them for a plant. They've never been used. Faye didn't go in for that stuff." Alberts shrugged; after a moment he wandered over to the cassette player. The music stopped and began again, something different, poorly recorded and scratchy, an almost familiar maudlin voice singing about a dolphin. Out of the corner of his eye, Wilson watched the girl with the peeled-back hair handling a dildo, place it to her lips and crack up, raise it back and part her mouth. Good Lord, he thought, don't do that. Nils tapped him hard on the knee.

"Listen to this, Wilson," Alberts encouraged from the corner.

Cholly leered at the girl. "Naughty, naughty."

Nils spat his accusation a second time. "You're too young to know shit about jazz." He was, inexplicably, angry, and Wilson was getting there.

"Listen to this, would you? Do you know who wrote this?"

He had no idea why the Scandinavian thought Americans were disenfranchised from their own music, but at least he could argue that Nils was no more than a few years older than him. He felt his attention splinter. "What the hell are you talking about?"

The tape was suddenly ejected, leaving behind a static buzz that paralyzed the room. Wilson ducked just in time to avoid being hit by the cassette Alberts whipped at his head. An opposing wave of fury surged through him; he wasn't a kid anymore, he didn't have to sit there and bite his tongue and take an offense from Alberts he didn't deserve. Still, he gaped at Alberts, utterly stupefied, and couldn't move.

"You rotten son of a bitch," Alberts slurred, his head wagging, flushed and bitter. "I wanted you to hear that song. I put it on for you. Faye loved that song."

Wilson stammered, he fought the trembling in his hands and knees. "Why did you throw it?" he protested. "Why would you do a thing like that?"

Cholly, firm and steady with genuine authority, rose from the recliner. "Okay, old salt," he said with surprising tenderness. He carefully slipped his arm around Alberts and led him, docile, defeated by the impulse of his generosity, back through the cottage. "Let's put you to bed."

197

"I'm freaked," the girl who had been apprehensive about the bird complained. "I miss Faye."

Wilson told her to shut up about Faye.

~~~~~

Sometime soon after dawn, with the nursery flooding with damp, heavy light, Wilson awoke on his pallet in the primitive bungalow and rolled on his side to gaze out the ceiling-to-floor screening. Mosquitoes whined throughout the room, and there were remarkable conversations, like convergent streams of consciousness, taking place out in the compound. He listened intently but couldn't determine the sense of what people were saying. Jesus—Wilson sat up—no wonder Alberts's going crazy. He slipped on a pair of running shorts and went outside. A woman talked on a telephone, which was not possible—no service.

"Hello . . . Sal?"

" . . . "

"The things people do these days."

" . . . "

"I'll be sure to tell him. Ha ha ha ha ha."

Wilson peeked around a corner barrier, a wall of incestuous vegetation, saw no customers, only a potting table, the aviary of two parrots housed in separate cages, a Green and an African Grey. The Green became a little girl, chanted a nursery rhyme, switched to a soundtrack for exorcism. When Wilson approached, the bird fell silent; the African Grey, apparently psychotic, cowered at the bottom of its cage, its breast visibly pounding, riven with fear. The Green started again, playing the role of an old hooker, and Wilson watched amazed as it calmly mimicked a woman's orgasm, *Don't stop, don't stop baby, don't stop.*

Alberts was up and dressed, making coffee in the kitchen. He moved around with a wooden gait, as if his hips were damaged, and his face looked doughy, his eyes bloodshot. Nothing was wrong with his mood though—he gave a frail smile but a hearty greeting, reconciliation a form of auto-response for both men, all the mornings down through the years, forgiving each other the trespasses and crossed signals of the previous evening. Wilson went straight to the refrigerator for juice and cut himself a slice of papaya.

"Whose disgraceful birds are those out back?"

"Cholly's," Alberts replied. "Cholly," he called into the cottage, "you've got to get the birds and everything else that's yours out of here today." The Frenchman Bruno, the new owner, wanted to scrub down the house inside and out and have its bare walls whitewashed. The Frenchman couldn't stand Cholly anyway, and had asked Alberts to make sure to put him out. Cholly, his nose in a book, waved acknowledgment from the couch.

"The Grey is mentally disturbed."

"Victim of a broken home," Cholly sniffed, hobbling outside to make himself a cup of tea.

Descending into lethargy, Wilson went back to the bungalow, spent a half hour under the cold shower until he woke up to a more tenacious spirit. He reappeared at the cottage in a bathing suit, a towel slung around his neck. Alberts, in the recliner, pawed through a carton of loose photographs, his brief abstinence broken by a rum and water next to him on the floor. Wilson could see he wasn't feeling well either.

"Something to eat?"

"Naw," Wilson said. "I'm going to walk down to the beach."

Who would have believed it, but Alberts told Wilson to

wait, he would go with him. He handed Wilson a set of snapshots while he went to change. They were pictures of Faye's burial, all the local expat crowd and a few somber island faces, going to sea on one of the dive boats bedecked with flowers. Alberts, grim immobility, on the stern, while a heavyset man with a walrus mustache and a military beret shook out Faye's remains from a shiny can, a plume of white fragments entering the frothy wake of the engines. The other passengers each held a hibiscus blossom to throw, or a bottle of beer, or both. Wilson shuffled through the pictures. Alberts on the boat alone, white hair wisping from under a black Navy bill cap, wearing an ironed white shirt and camouflage pants, a posy of vermillion impatiens clutched in both hands, his eyes black crescents behind the glare off his glasses. Next picture, Faye in better times. Bozo atop her sun helmet, Blackie at her feet on a leash, his punishment for chasing cars. Her smile of tenability, as always, said, Your information is reliable—of course, we survive. The young nursery proliferated in the background. Wilson shuffled again and Faye rose dying, propped with pillows in a motel bed, her blond hair stuck with poisonous sweat to her gaunt face, hands together but you can bet not in prayer, and her expression, the warm confidence of belief, was the same, infuriatingly the same. Alberts lay beside her, clearly repressing his rage at whoever pointed the camera.

He returned to the front room in a faded bathing suit and long-sleeved shirt, his legs as pale as an Edwardian banker's. "Can I have this photograph, Alberts?"

Disgusted, Alberts stifled an expression identical to what his face revealed in the picture. "Why do you want a picture of her when she was sick? What's wrong with you?"

His remonstration embarrassed Wilson deeply, and he

couldn't think of what to say. "I don't know," he mumbled. He tried to palliate his request, to make it seem less morbid. "She was the bravest person I ever knew." Alberts relented. "Keep it if you want, then," he said, "but take one of the other pictures too. I don't want you to have just that one."

At the beach, they lay in the shallow water, groaning with relief. They sipped from cans of warm beer and Alberts, trying to keep his cigarette from getting wet, seemed to constantly pantomime a man asking for quiet. "I love this," he said. "This is the life, and I've led it." Wilson pointed out to him that Faye, who had strived for six years to bring him back to the glorious water, or get him on one of the cays for a picnic, would kick his backside if she were there. "I was tired of it all," explained Alberts. "Hey, I'd had enough." And wasn't it Faye who said the opposite of a good life is not by nature a bad life? The opposite of a profound truth may very well be another profound truth? "This is the greatest thing on the planet, this water," Alberts crowed with pleasure, and under he went, glasses, cigarette, beer, and all. Yet by the time they toweled themselves dry and left, Alberts's face resembled a pomegranate, his shoulders and back forewarned blistering, his legs looked like they had been scraped with a wire brush, and he avowed that the sun was killing him.

The Frenchman waited at the cottage, overwhelming them with his energy, his boiling competence. "Alberts," he lectured, both amused and impatient, "what are you doing? You never go to the beach and now you go to the beach? You're supposed to be moving out, eh?" He gestured at a five-gallon drum of paint he had lugged in. "Look, I stole that from the airport—they're too disorganized to know what's going on," he confessed with laughter. "I think it should be enough, yes?" He paced around the room, surveying for other reasons to be there. "Alberts, where are the Haitians? I want them to start throwing out all the junk in the main shed. Today—okay with you? Are they around? How did you get so much junk out there? It all has to go." He walked out back, shouting for Raicees.

"Jesus Christ," said Wilson. "A capitalist."

"He's all right. It'll be good for the place. He'll unwind."

"He's going to burn up trying to make this into a white man's business."

Bruno hurried back into the room. "Alberts," he rattled on, "I meant to ask you, where's the other truck? I tell Cholly he can't drive the truck anymore, eh? Come with me to find him and drive it back."

"Not me." Alberts was letting Bruno aggravate him; he was also in pain, smearing a film of aloe across his skin. "I feel lousy. I'm going to have a drink and go back to bed. The truck isn't yours until tomorrow anyway."

Undaunted, Bruno turned to Wilson, and he agreed to go to town with the Frenchman, not so much to hunt down Cholly, but so Alberts could have some peace.

He found Cholly in the bar of the yacht club, lulled by sentimental boasting, the brisk trade of youthful exploits of his brethren of the Indies Nouveau. Again and again, Cholly and his cronies toasted the next new world, a place where they wouldn't have to give back what they had once conquered. Long after the sun lowered and the harbor blackened, Wilson finally decided that everything—the insanely loud copulatory music, the aggressive glamor of the clientele, the hauteur of the women, the unpredictable rapport between the males, the perfumed crush of bon vivants, the chic Eurotrash, the long-haired renegades with tattooed forearms—*everything* and everyone was insufferable, yet he stayed on, hoping for one thing good and rich to happen, a clear sensation of potentiality without a face or a name to it, and when that too seemed futile, he had one last drink and left.

Driving down the inky island lane to leeward, he tipped his head out the window of the truck, relishing the velvet breeze of the latitude, sighted the road ahead with quick instinctive looks, and mostly concerned himself with the diamond spray of the constellations. Faye, a little screwy, had been a dilettante of the paranormal; she believed in ghosts and the afterlife, and most of all in mystery. Wilson wanted, expected, then even stopped the truck and got out under the celestial loneliness and its shock of stars and ordered her to offer a sign, *right now,* let it be a meteor streaking through the desolation or a fluttering shape, a half-glimpsed animal in the headlights, anything, some message to obliterate the yearning, some gesture that all was satisfactory in the beyond. He waited for a while, hurt by the silence and then cursing her for being too inebriated with death to pay attention, and went on. The crickets were in full orchestration at the nursery; the lights were cut, and the air was pungent with smells of compost. Yet when he neared the cottage he thought he noticed a flickering behind the bedroom curtain, so he walked in instead of veering off to the bungalow, through the bathroom to the other side of the residence, Alberts's sanctuary, to check on him. He was prone on the bed, awake and clothed but barefoot, his skin aflame, his eyes meditating on a lizard eating insects attracted to the candlelight.

"*Compadre,*" Alberts said. He was his most gentle self. "*Tome una Cuba Libre conmigo, si?*"

"*Bueno,*" Wilson agreed, and in a minute was back on the edge of the bed with the drinks. "You making it through the night?" He knew Alberts wasn't sleeping these days without pills.

"She betrayed me, my friend," Alberts said, his voice

no louder than the fluid sound of water outside, pressure-driven from the hand-dug wells, soaking the nursery. "You knew how it was with us. Then she kept getting sicker and sicker . . . and she wanted to live."

Not betrayed. Faye refused to let Alberts inject her with an overdose of morphine, as they had planned, nor would she absolve him from the obligation of his life. He was trapped into surviving her. Not betrayed. Condemned to live by the charity of the dead.

⁓

By morning a front had settled upon the Salt Islands, weather the locals called *bleaky*. Listening to the BBC on the radio, Wilson and Alberts shared a pot of coffee. Bozo gnawed on the screen door, wanting social access; Alberts picked him up and put him on his shoulder, but the sunburn was too sensitive, so he let the bird hop around, stealing toast, sticking his black tongue in the pot of jam. Blackie was asleep on the deck, twitching, curled around his empty food dish.

"I don't know what I'm going to do about these animals," Alberts fretted, staring red-eyed at the dog. "I should shoot them, I suppose."

"What shit," protested Wilson. Macho melodrama. "They'll be fine."

Alberts conceded, too exhausted to be offended. "You're right," he groused. The Frenchman Bruno parked outside in a swirl of dust and honked several times before he bounded merrily into the cottage, his personality unaffected by the drop in barometrics, there to make certain they were out of bed, preparing for town.

"What did you do with Cholly?" Bruno questioned Wilson. "Where is he? Did you abandon him last night?"

"Not at all. I gave him willingly to the mob."

"Don't worry," Alberts reasoned. "Cholly will show up. He'll be there," and Bruno, more zealous than skeptical, sped off into a horizon of lowering gray clouds.

When Alberts had brushed his teeth a second time and combed the stiffness in his paper-white hair, they left too. The road was jammed with traffic racing toward them, buses and vans carrying the day shift of workers to Club Med or farther down to leeward, where a marina was under construction. Four times Alberts instructed Wilson to pull over to pick up a walker, pedestrians too poor for transport, old black women toting bundles on their skulls. "Mistah Alberts," the last one said, much like the others, "tank you, sah. Is nobody else does stop dese days. Me hear de news about Miss Faye, rest she soul. We ahll shall meet again in heaven, sah. Drop me here, please."

Wilson let off Alberts at the two-story yellow stucco offices across from the new supermarket, watched him walk up the steps that led to the upper arcade like an old man, which is how he wanted to think of himself now. A person compelled to treat the corners and sharp surfaces of the world with caution. Wilson drove on. Last night he had decided to leave on the afternoon flight, a day early, but at the airport the computer was down, climatic interference, and he wasn't going to get off Flamingo without a fight in the chaos of check-in.

A rain squall had just finished drenching town when he returned to the office lot, leaving behind a lingering drizzle, creamy mud, steam. Wilson climbed the steps, went down along a balcony, opened a door upon a woman typing who told him the number of the conference room. He knocked once and sauntered in. At the head of an oblong table, the commonwealth lawyer, a Canadian, a robustly optimistic man, thumbed through a portfolio of documents. Never had Wilson heard a bad word said against this man. The two of them had been bone-fishing once, in fact, and the solicitor, unmindful of the interruption, rose to offer his hand.

"How's it been going?" Wilson asked. "Anybody cut anybody's throat yet?"

"Speeding along." The lawyer grinned and sat back down. "Keeping these magnates happy." He opened a hardbound ledger of Royal Bank checks.

"You're alive, I see." Wilson nodded at Cholly.

"Quite." Not only was he alive, he seemed shrewdly pleased about it. He reeked eau de cologne, sat composed and erect in his chair, smug with the dubious talent of his resiliency, which could rescue him from every folly but the fractured perseverance of himself. And Bruno, casting thin smiles around the room, consumed by entrepreneurial foreplay approaching climax, double-checked inventory sheets and scanned the contract, his knees clapping methodically, his fingers drumming the arm of his chair.

Alberts—whatever remained of Alberts appeared to have turned radically inward, taken mental leave of the transaction. He hunched forward, his elbows on the table and eyes downcast, sun poisoned, despondent as an inveterate jailbird whose good behavior has mistakenly resulted in parole.

The lawyer tore the check he had written from its book. "Seventeen thousand five hundred and so on." Cholly pressed it to his obscene mouth, folded it into the bottom pocket of his bush shirt. "Cholly, we know each other well," the lawyer stated diplomatically. "When you leave here, go right to the bank, would you please, and deposit it." Impossible to insult Cholly. He was presented the appropriate document for his signature, then the Canadian left the room to make a copy of it on his machine.

Wilson found it unbearable to look across the table at Alberts's wordless inertia, his wounded sobriety, unbearable because his sympathy was limited—Alberts should be stronger, take a lesson from Faye; after all, he was getting what he wanted. Wilson got up for a cup of coffee from the electric pot and stood at the plate-glass window. Behind the offices, he saw, the foundation of another building was under construction. It was going to be big, ambitious, maybe the biggest structure in the Salts, by the looks of it. The first circle of workmen—Haitian laborers; no one else would do what they would—went about their business, exposed to the solemn drizzle, the paste of the disturbed ground. They were stripped to the waist, lean torsos glistening, their heads wrapped in bright bandannas—colors vibrating without sunlight, color full of sap, color that would burst with juice if the surface was penetrated. The men had dug footings that from above composed a checkerboard pattern, each black up to his hips in his respective hole bailing rainwater with buckets and calabash gourds, their dark muscles smeared with gluey sand, ragged pants caked with muck. As Wilson observed their movements, the rain started again and one by one, tic-tac-toe, the field cleared as the men sought shelter. Though he never carried one, he wished he had a camera to record the strangely vital image of the men as the squall passed and they resumed their positions on the checkerboard, and the game started again. He would expect such a picture to explain what he couldn't, to be its own news, about the tides of balance among men.

"Let's wrap this up," the lawyer said as he came back to the table, handing out identical sets of documents for each of the three to sign. "Austin," he called quietly, and waited for Alberts's attention to form before the accounting continued. Over five years of representation, the nursery had not paid a cent to the Canadian. Three thousand—a fair and decent sum—was subtracted from the top figure.

"Now accounts due. Let's clear them out."

Seven thousand four hundred thirty-two etcetera. The sale had been ill-timed.

"I don't like this any more than you do," the lawyer sympathized. "Taxes."

Twenty-five hundred.

"Closing fees."

One thousand.

"Utilities."

Nine hundred something.

The mortgage remaining on the property. Three thousand more.

In the name of Austin Alberts, the lawyer filled out a check for seven thousand two hundred forty dollars and eleven cents, U.S. There would be more, of course, monthly payments on the lien for twenty years to come. Alberts tucked the check into his pocket without looking at it.

Together the five of them strolled to the yacht club for Bloody Marys, but the intended celebration was flat and half-hearted, so they disbanded before their glasses were emptied. Wilson drove Alberts home, put him into his bed, and kissed him on the cheek. After he had collected his gear, he took himself in one of the nursery trucks to the airport, leaving the key in the ignition, and entered the competition for a seat on the plane that would take him to Puerto Plata, then to Miami, finally back to D.C. *Hidalgos* today? *Hidalgos?* . . . Such were his thoughts as he sat alone among the many in the terminal. Nobodys and the sons and daughters of nobodys. *Hijos de nadie.* The saints of the New World lived on in history, but their descendants, bastards of the bastards of the bastards, left in the night for America. Perhaps when they were somebodys, or the children of somebodys, they came home.

Faye and Alberts—their vagabond marriage, the stubborn precious questing of their failures—how had they measured their lives, against what standard? Mitchell Wilson once thought he knew, but now he knew he didn't. What remained was for Alberts to enter, like the millions before him in these times, the draft of cooling current, and without further hesitation or loyalty remit himself to the north.

Whistler's
Lane

ALSO BY ANTHEA FRASER

Laura Possessed

WHISTLER'S LANE

Anthea Fraser

A NOVEL OF SUSPENSE

DODD, MEAD & COMPANY · NEW YORK

Library of Congress Cataloging in Publication Data

Fraser, Anthea.
    Whistler's Lane.

    I. Title.
PZ4.F8413Wh3 [PR6056.R286]   823'.9'14   75–12780
ISBN 0–396–07143–0

Whistler's
Lane

prologue

THE doorknob, old and heavy, was unmoving in the weak grip of her rubbery fingers. Half sobbing now with fright and frustration, she fought it desperately, head perpetually turning back toward the mist-shrouded gate. Nothing moved there but her exertions were at last rewarded: all at once the knob turned, the heavy door swung open, and she almost fell inside. She closed it quickly behind her and leaned weakly against it while the deep, choking breaths tore at her lungs.

Gradually the warmth of the house stole comfortingly over her. On her right the old grandfather clock, face mellow with age, ticked like a metronome measuring her heartbeats. Slowly she raised trembling hands to her mist-wet hair, brushing it back from her face. From the half-open door of the sitting room his voice came, and she steeled herself to force down the irritation it awoke in her.

"That you, love?"

"Yes," she answered tightly, barely loud enough

1

for him to hear. She pushed herself away from the door and walked, still unsteadily, to the brightly lit room.

"Thought I heard the door." He turned with the slow smile that had been her undoing, but at the sight of her it checked and was replaced by a look of concern. "Good Lord, love, what's up? You look—"

"As if I'd seen a ghost?" She gave a short laugh. "As a matter of fact, I think I have." Patience snapped without warning. "Well, don't just stand there staring. Get me a drink, for God's sake!"

He moved obediently to the cabinet and she went toward the fire, stretching out numbed hands to the blaze. The mirror above the hearth gave back her disheveled appearance, hair lank and sprayed with moisture, face paper-white. His reflection loomed behind her and she turned and took the glass he held out, drinking quickly the cold liquid which turned to fire in her throat. Defiantly she raised her eyes to his troubled gaze.

"Well, aren't you going to tell me I imagined it, that it was a trick of the light, all the usual glib explanations?"

He said slowly, "I must admit I never expected it from you, but as you know, plenty of folk hereabouts are ready to swear they've seen the Whistler."

She drew a deep breath and turned back to the fire, setting the empty glass down on the mantelshelf with a sharp little click. "No doubt," she replied in a clipped, staccato voice. "The only thing is, it wasn't the Whistler that I saw."

He stared at her with dawning excitement. "You

2

don't mean it was the girl? They reckon she's never—"

"It was *a* girl, certainly, but not poor Lizzie Earnshaw, if that's what you mean. This was a very modern ghost!"

She sensed his bafflement, his inability to understand, but all he said, quietly, was "Tell me." She let him take her arm and ease her down into one of the deep armchairs and waited until he had seated himself opposite her, leaning forward expectantly with his elbows on his knees.

"I went into Clitheroe, as you know, to meet Ellen for lunch," she began a little reluctantly. "When she went back to work, I did some shopping and caught the three-forty bus home, and it wasn't until I was on the bus that I realized I still had Mother's birthday card in my bag. If it hadn't gone today, it wouldn't have arrived in time."

"You could always have pushed it through the door," he said dryly, and she flung him an impatient glance.

"It's not the same thing at all. Anyway, I got off the bus at Tanner's Lane and dropped it in the box outside the post office. The last collection hadn't gone." She paused.

"And," he prompted, "it was quicker to come on along Whistler's Lane than retrace your steps. I presume it was there that you—saw it?"

"Oh yes, it was there all right." She let her hand fall palm up into her lap in a gesture of helpless resignation. "It's so ridiculous; all my life I've heard that gibberish about a horseman and I've never believed a word of it—you know that. Actually, there have

3

been times when I'd positively have welcomed a handsome, seventeenth-century ghost—it might have livened things up a bit. But this—" She shivered uncontrollably. "This was something else entirely."

If he had been aware of the bitterness in her voice, he gave no sign of it. "What happened?"

"I crossed the little bridge beyond Cobwebs—Ellen was still at the office, of course—and started back down the Lane. It wasn't quite dark but the mist was drifting along above the stream, about waist-high. I was looking down because the path's uneven with all those loose stones, but I could hardly see my feet. Then suddenly, I don't know why, I looked up and—there she was, standing right in front of me."

She put a hand up to her face and after a moment he said gently, "It couldn't just have been someone you didn't know, hadn't seen before?"

She shook her head positively. "I could see *through* her, the Lane and the bushes lining the path. It was —horrible."

"You say she seemed modern. How was she dressed?"

"In a long white robe—the traditional ghostly garb, I grant you." She gave a small, shaky laugh. "It wasn't that. I don't know how I knew, I just did. Something to do with her hair, perhaps—it looked modern, loose round her shoulders."

"No doubt most girls have hair loose round their shoulders at some stage, particularly if they're wearing long robes. Could it have been a nightdress?"

"I don't know. It was very plain. Just long and

4

white and rather ugly. She didn't look much more than a child, and she seemed as frightened as I was."

"According to legend, Lizzie Earnshaw was only seventeen."

"For pity's sake forget Lizzie Earnshaw. It certainly wasn't her. Anyway, it was all over in a flash. I just saw her, we stared at each other, and then she was gone."

"Gone how—past you?"

"No, she just—disappeared. I told you I could see what was behind her. Suddenly, it was simply—unclouded."

A log shifted in the grate. She said flatly, "You don't believe me, do you?"

He leaned forward and took her small cold hands in his large warm ones. "I believe *you* believe it. I think you've had a bad fright but, as you said yourself, it was probably some trick of the mist and the half-light. You were hurrying along and whether you consciously believe it or not, you've known all your life that Whistler's Lane is supposed to be haunted. So— conditions were right and your mind obligingly conjured up a ghost for you."

She moved restlessly, withdrawing her hands from his. "Perhaps. Heaven knows I'd like to think you're right."

"Was there any reason why it should have happened today particularly, anything you can think of that might have triggered it off?"

"Not exactly." But she didn't sound as sure now.

"Anything you and Ellen were talking about over lunch?" he persisted. "Something that perhaps you

5

were still turning over in your mind on the bus home?"

"I suppose it could have been that, now that you mention it. Ellen had taken a book out of the library on the history of Clitheroe. You know the kind of thing, the marching soldiers of King and Commonwealth, and witch fires burning on Pendle Hill."

"There you are!" he said triumphantly. "Obviously that was what caused it—a direct link."

"But it wasn't the Whistler I saw," she began again.

"All right, so your subconscious rejects Whitaker and substitutes something it feels might be more acceptable—a girl you can identify with."

She eyed him resentfully. "You're always so bloody plausible, aren't you?"

He sat back. "I'm sorry," he said a little stiffly. "I thought you wanted a logical explanation."

"I don't know what I want! How would you feel, if it had happened to you?" Infuriatingly she was close to tears. "Oh, I don't know. I *thought* I saw something, but it was so brief and I suppose I had been thinking of Ellen's book." She gave a short laugh. "I'll tell you one thing. I don't envy her reading it alone at Cobwebs, with Whistler's Lane just beyond the garden!"

"Is she going to stay on there?" he asked, sensing she wanted to change the subject now to more mundane matters.

"I don't know. It's too early to say, really. She'll have to wait for probate to be granted on her mother's will, anyway."

"Poor Ellen, it's been a difficult year for her."

6

"Yes." She stood up, relieved to find that her legs had stopped trembling. "I'd better go and tidy up. Is the meal nearly ready?"

"I imagine so. Mrs. Hancock put it in the oven before she left." He stood with her and she knew his eyes followed her as she went to the door. Out in the hall the grandfather clock ticked steadily. He was probably right; her mind had been, if not on ghosties and ghoulies, at least on the witch hunts of the early seventeenth century, and there was no denying that they were inextricably woven into the history of Whistler's Lane. In any case—as fear dropped away excitement moved in her, lending wings to her feet as she sped up the shallow worn stairs to the floor above—that had not been all that she and Ellen had talked about over lunch. She stood in the center of the bedroom hugging herself for warmth, and the dressing-table mirror gave back a very different image from that in the sitting room a few minutes earlier. Hair dry now and falling softly about her face, cheeks flushed from the fire, she was once more herself, and her lips curved into a smile. For Ellen had agreed that they might meet secretly at Cobwebs, safe and warm away from the shifting shadows of the Lane or the cramped confines of the parked car. Even better, she had finally, although reluctantly, accepted her own refusal to reveal the identity of the man who would meet her there. "I'll tell you just as soon as I can," she had urged, "but for the moment it must be a secret, even from you." Praise heaven for friends like Ellen!

"My darling," she said softly in the cold, silent

7

room. Then, with an unwelcome recurrence of superstition, she moved swiftly across the room and drew the heavy curtains over the window, shutting out the nebulous uncertainties of the fog-shrouded night.

chapter

❦ 1 ❧

SOMETIMES I wondered whether it was the
gypsy who had set the whole, macabre sequence in motion, whether by her obscure warnings
she had in some way preconditioned events to take
their grim course. But that, of course, was impossible.
The woman had merely seen the future—or was it
the past?—irrevocably mapped out in the palm of my
hand, a future which had been predestined in a time
far removed from that blustery Saturday morning.

At that time I had been with Jake about three
months. Or rather, he had been with me. I was still
in the flat I had shared with Carol before her marriage; Jake divided his time between it and his rooms
at the University. It had never occurred to me to
demur at the arrangement he had so casually suggested. One did not demur with Jake Petersen; one
gratefully accepted any favors he felt disposed to
bestow. I knew, of course, that my parents would
have been scandalized, but fortunately they were
safely out in the Far East, blissfully cushioned from

awareness of the change in moral clime which affected the England of the seventies. Even Beryl, for all her eccentricities, did not approve. On the rare occasions that she and Jake had met, they had eyed each other with mutual and barely concealed dislike.

"You're living with him, of course?" she had said, that first time, with characteristic abruptness.

"Off and on, as you might say." I had been defiantly flippant.

"Huh. He's not in love with you. I suppose you know that."

"Yes, dear aunt, I know that."

"Well, it's your life, but I'm hanged if I'd let him make use of me the way he does you."

I had smiled brightly, but her disapproval distressed me as much as did her only too accurate assessment of the situation. I was fond of Beryl; she had been a substitute mother to me all through my schooldays, providing a base in which to spend the holidays when time or money did not allow me to fly out to join my parents. I had always been aware, though, that my mother particularly was not altogether happy with the arrangement. Beryl was her elder sister, tragically widowed during the War after only six months of marriage, and in the family's opinion the shock had left her slightly "peculiar." However, since she was my only relative in the country, there had been no alternative.

Jake, for his part, had, on the way home in the car, been equally uncompromising. In reply to my tentative "What did you think of her?" he had replied without hesitation, "She's dotty. Mad as a hatter!"

"Oh, not as bad as that," I'd protested loyally. "Actually, she—"

"My dear, any woman who goes around in midwinter—or any time, come to that, in ankle socks and gym shoes *must* be mad."

I smiled in spite of myself. "Perhaps I should have warned you about the gym shoes. I never even notice them now."

"Well, I've met your relative as you desired. I just hope I'm not expected to do any more."

"I have to keep in touch," I said placatingly.

"You, perhaps. I, definitely not."

And such was my weakness that I was reluctant to drag myself away from him to pay the visits which my conscience kept insisting that I should. Then, just a month before, the situation had changed. Without warning, Beryl sold the house in Biggin Hill from which we had all been convinced she would never move—Peter had been killed on a bombing mission from Biggin Hill—and moved, without word of explanation, to a village I'd never even heard of in the depths of Lancashire.

"Thank God!" said Jake devoutly when I relayed the news. "At least she can't expect you to keep dropping in at that distance!"

Which was how the situation rested at the time of the gypsy's call. I shouldn't, of course, have let her in. All my life I'd been surrounded by strong-minded people of definite opinions, and this constant hammering of my own will into submission had over the years diminished it to the point where I had the greatest difficulty in coming to even the most basic decision. And when, on that Saturday morning, the

11

woman stood whining on the step, the inevitable basket of heather and clothespegs over her arm, I was unable to summon up the strength of mind to say firmly, "Not today, thank you," and close the door. Instead, weakly, I hesitated. And was lost.

"Some heather for luck, missy," she repeated, sensing an easy victory, and as I fumbled in my apron pocket for the purse I had just needed to pay the milkman, she added, "Cross the gypsy's palm with silver and she'll tell your fortune!"

"Oh no," I said hastily and too late, "I don't think—"

"There's a tall dark stranger coming into your life," she began in tones designed to wear down token opposition, "and a letter from a stranger, too. Cross the gypsy's palm and she'll give you a full reading."

From behind me Jake's voice said irritably, "For God's sake, Sophie, either cross her palm or close that door; the whole flat's getting cold."

"What shall I do?" I asked laughingly over my shoulder.

"If you want to hear all that twaddle, give her something, but for Pete's sake, at least bring her into the hall and close the door."

The woman and I looked at each other for a moment, each of us equally reluctant to obey his command, myself to issue the invitation, she to accept it. For myself, I saw in that glance a small, bent old woman with a face like a wizened walnut, her jet-black hair scraped back into an uncompromising bun and her little eyes burning like black coals. She saw —what? Surely at that moment nothing untoward, or

12

fear would have overcome greed and she would never have stepped over the threshold. Perhaps her hesitation was simply the dislike of her kind for a roof over their head, the formalized life style of the despised "gorgio."

At any rate, the die was cast, she stepped cautiously into the hallway and I pressed the door shut against the wind's sudden thrust. I dropped a tenpenny piece into her small hard palm and held out my own. It's difficult to describe now exactly what happened, because memories of the incident are necessarily confused with what actually followed, but she took my hand and immediately, on that initial contact, a long, shuddering tremor shook her frail body and her head jerked up, her eyes raking over my face as though seeing me for the first time. She looked down again at my hand still resting lightly in hers, and then she dropped it, fear spreading over her face, and backed against the door.

"No," she said breathlessly, "there is nothing there. My powers can detect nothing."

She turned while I stared at her blankly and fumbled at the handle, but at this point Jake took command. He stepped forward and firmly caught her arm as she shrank away from him.

"Oh no you don't! You insisted on telling the lady's fortune, you took the silver she gave you, now we want to hear it."

She thrust a dirty old tapestry purse toward him. "Take back the money, pretty gentleman. I see nothing!" Jake caught hold of my hand and dragged me forward, thrusting it under the woman's eyes. "Let-

13

ter from a stranger," she gabbled frantically. "I see a tall dark stranger—" Her voice cracked into silence, broken only by her rapid, shallow breathing. I was acutely aware of the strange, musty smell that came from her, a mixture of dust and old clothes and woodsmoke and a faint waft of lavender from the little sachets in the discarded basket. Ever since that day the smell of lavender has awoken in me a deep, primeval feeling of fear.

"Sorry, that's not good enough," Jake had begun, when suddenly the gypsy broke in: "Beware of yesterday!"

We stared at her and Jake, still not grasping what was happening, remarked facetiously, "Isn't it a bit late for that advice?" Aware of the change in the woman, I gestured him quickly to silence. She had taken my hand again at last, and a shuttered, in-looking expression glazed her eyes and unaccountably raised the hairs on my scalp in a prickly sensation of unease.

"Danger," she went on, and her voice had changed from the classic wheedling tones to a curious sing-song. "Mortal danger I see—" There were a few words at this point which were incomprehensible, probably Romany, and then: "Caught in the time wheel—death—violent death—"

By this time I had had more than enough, and was trying to withdraw my hand, but her gnarled old fingers had closed immovably round it. "The time wheel spins—your past is tomorrow, your future yesterday."

I cried desperately, "Jake, stop her!" and

wrenched my hand free. A tremor passed over her again and she gave a low moan and covered her face with her hands. Jake, with a glance at my white face, picked up the basket of pegs and flowers and thrust it against her while he opened the door with his other hand and half lifted the tiny figure over the threshold. I caught one glimpse of her terrified face as she raised it to him and murmured something, could not distinguish his terse reply, and then he was back with me, the door safely shut, leading me into the kitchen and sitting me down at the table.

"Well," he said, "that's what you get for being gullible!"

My tongue was dry and heavy in my mouth and I found it difficult to speak. "What did she ask you just now?"

"It was rather weird, actually. She wanted to know what she had told you."

"Didn't she *know?*" I heard my voice rise.

"Apparently not. Presumably she was in a kind of trance. That's what comes, my girl, of meddling with the occult. You should know that, after the research you've been doing on demonology! Come to think of it, that's probably what threw her. She was confused into thinking you'd actually been dabbling in the Black Arts yourself."

" 'Violent death,' " I said in a low voice, and shuddered involuntarily.

"Oh, come on now, sweetie, snap out of it! What does an old fraud like that know about anything?"

I said imperatively, "Jake, I'm frightened!"

He moved swiftly round the table, pulled me to my

15

feet and wrapped me in a bearlike embrace. "Now look, sweetheart, you're too intelligent to be taken in by all that mumbo-jumbo, surely? As I said, she might have detected in some way that you had some knowledge of rituals and so on. She wasn't to know you were simply researching for old Carruthers' blasted book!" And, as I continued to lean trembling against him, he raised my face and stared down into it. "Hey, Sophie! This is nineteen seventy-four, not the sixteen hundreds!" He kissed my nose. "She was just an ignorant old woman who got rather carried away." Another kiss, on my chin this time. "Okay?"

"But what did it *mean*, Jake, all that talk of the time wheel and my past and future being upside down? It's—it's mind-bending!"

He sighed. "Well, at least it was more interesting than the usual rigmarole about going to cross water." He kissed my mouth lightly. "Talking of time wheels, by my reckoning it's just spun round to coffee time." Another kiss. "So how about it?" But as I still clung to him, he bent his head and started to kiss me in earnest and the familiar reassurance of his mouth and hands and his rangy, loose-limbed body against my own at last began to dilute the terror which had gripped me. When eventually we moved apart and smiled at each other, he said with a slightly unsteady laugh, "Come to think of it, perhaps you are a witch after all. You seem to have bewitched me without too much trouble, don't you?" He lifted a strand of my hair and pushed it gently behind my ear. "All right now?" And, as I nodded, "In fact it's been quite an entertaining morning. It's not every day that I'm

16

called a 'pretty gentleman'! Now, how about that coffee?"

Obediently I filled the kettle and reached for the grinder. The smell of the fresh beans, pungent and strong, drove the last clinging remembrance of lavender from my nostrils.

"Anyway," I said, "she didn't say the violent death would be mine. Perhaps I'm going to stab you with a carving knife!"

"That's a reassuring thought!"

I paused and looked across at him, at the strong, square chin, deep-set eyes and sensuous mouth, uncertain what had arrested my attention. I had, of course, meant the remark as a joke and he had taken it as one. Why, then, was it suddenly necessary to analyze his response? Possibly it was unacknowledged resentment that the shallowness of his own emotions enabled him to pass off so lightly any suggestion of violence in others. He was, after all, a clever—some said brilliant—lecturer in aerodynamics, an ultra-civilized man essentially of his own time and place, attractive, self-assured, inclined to be ruthless and self-seeking. But for all that his emotions, easily roused and easily satisfied, were all on the surface and he was content that it should be so. Not for him the rack of unrequited love, the despair which could lead to desperation, perhaps even, in uncontrollable frenzy, to murder.

I pulled myself together with a little jerk and turned back to the boiling kettle. It must have been the strange undercurrents of the gypsy's warning which had promoted this in-depth analysis of the

man I loved and up to now had accepted unquestioningly. For I did love him, a love that was quite separate from the surprised and delighted gratification of having been singled out by the much-sought-after John Jacob Petersen. His reputation with women had preceded him, and this too I had perforce accepted. Now, in a hard, clear light of perception, I knew that our affair would not last much longer, that already, though he was still attracted to me, he was beginning to tire of the association, was perhaps already looking round for another adoring, grateful girl with whom to pass some pleasant weeks. It was important to my self-esteem that he should not know how deeply that would hurt me.

"A penny for them!" he said curiously, as at last I set the mug of fragrant coffee on the table in front of him. "You've been miles away! Not still chasing the veiled illusions of our Romany friend?"

Now, had I been strong, was the time to have made the move, to have had the dubious satisfaction of being the first to hint that our relationship was coming to an end. Of course I couldn't do it. Looking down into the quizzical, attractive face, I knew despairingly that, though I would have to let him go, it must be at a time of his own choosing and in the meantime I would humbly hold on for as long as was left to me.

He reached up and snapped his fingers under my nose. "Sophie! What is this? What about all the light, bright chatter I depend on at weekends to ease the strain of my long hours of toil?"

"Sorry." I sat down opposite him with my own

18

mug. "I don't feel particularly light or bright today. How about you entertaining me, for a change?" I looked at him with the first hint of challenge I had ever shown him and noticed his surprise.

"I' faith, the gypsy woman hath much to answer for! All right, I will entertain you!" He smiled as though the unexpectedness of the request had somehow amused him. He had thought he knew all there was to know about me; the possibility that he did not was faintly intriguing. "First," he went on, "I shall take you to lunch at one of those little riverside pubs and then we'll go to Kew Gardens and look at the early spring flowers. Later we can come back to town, perhaps by way of the river, and go to a show. There are sure to be odd seats spare if we're prepared to take a chance, ballet perhaps or a concert somewhere. We can decide over lunch. And then, candlelit supper at some discreet little Soho restaurant. Would that help to disperse the vapors or whatever?"

"It sounds quite wonderful," I said.

And it was. The fact that I had been unable to shake completely free of the strange mood which possessed me sustained Jake's heightened interest and lent an added magic to the day. That night, after the enthrallment of a concert at the Festival Hall, a dimly lit *diner à deux* and a walk home hand-in-hand through the streets of London, there was an added zest and intensity to our love-making which foolishly made me wonder if after all I could ever make him love me. Perhaps it was as well that neither of us knew it was our last time together.

The Sunday, as always, was spent lazily with Jake doing what he called his "Noel Coward act" and drifting round the flat in his red silk dressing gown. We had brunch, we spent the afternoon lounging on the sofa reading the papers, we had supper on a tray making intellectually critical comments on the banality of the television serial. It was how we had spent most of our Sundays during the last three months, but I could find no reassurance in the fact. Instead the day seemed to be a lull, a marking-time between the thunderclap of the gypsy's visit and the destruction of the storm which would surely follow it. I pleaded a nonexistent headache and went to bed early. I was asleep before he came.

Monday morning, then, and the next distant rumble of the approaching storm—metaphorically, that is. The March sun streamed into the flat, glinting on the cut glass jar of marmalade and on Jake's thick fair hair as he tossed an envelope onto my plate.

"One for you this morning, and not the usual missive from abroad, either."

I stared down at the unknown writing, spidery and difficult to decipher, and frowned. "I've no idea who it's from."

"Perhaps the 'letter from a stranger' you were promised," Jake said flippantly, digging his spoon into the marmalade, and he didn't seem to notice my tremor of apprehension. Then, as I picked up the envelope, my eyes fell on the postmark. "Pendlemere, Lancs."

"Pendlemere? Isn't that the place where Beryl went? But it isn't her writing." Fear clutched at me

as I tore open the envelope and my eyes raced down the single sheet of paper it contained. My anxiety must have reached Jake, because he said impatiently, "Well?"

"It seems to be from some doctor or other but it's not all that serious. Apparently Beryl slipped the other day and wrenched her ankle rather badly."

"I suppose the laces of her gym shoes came untied."

"The point is she's not really ill and in any case she's apparently refused pointblank to go into the cottage hospital because it would mean leaving the dog."

"God, don't tell me she's got a dog now!"

"She mentioned it in her last letter, a King Charles spaniel."

"Oh, I remember. Called, predictably, Charlotte, but 'usually answering to Lottie.' Unquote."

"And he goes on: 'As your aunt has only been in the village a short time, she does not know many people and is unwilling to "impose on anyone"—her own words. She was also extremely reluctant that I should write to you but I managed to convince her that as her nearest relative you would at least like to be told of the position and may perhaps be able to suggest a satisfactory solution.' "

"Bloody cheek! In other words, get up there at the double and play nursemaid! These officious medicos need putting in their place. Let me reply!"

"Don't be silly, Jake," I said quietly. "Of course I must go."

He stared at me. "But it could take weeks! You

can't just drop everything and dash up there at a moment's notice!"

I moistened my lips. "But you see, I can. I can work up there as easily as here. That's no doubt why Beryl finally gave in and let him write to me."

"And where do I fit in to all this?" His voice was ominously quiet and my resolve faltered.

"Jake, try to understand. She needs me."

"And I don't?"

I met his eyes. "Do you?" And then, cowardly as ever, hurried on before he could answer. "At least I must go up and see the position. I might be able to arrange something, get one of the village girls to move in with her till she's better." I put my hand pleadingly over his. "Jake, please. You know I have to."

"As long as you make it as brief as possible." Which grudging comment I took as a form of consent.

"I'll go into College this morning and explain to Dr. Carruthers and stock up with library books. The work's well in hand. I'm sure he won't have any objections."

"Bully for Carruthers," said Jake sulkily. He sounded so like a small boy who has been unexpectedly thwarted that I almost smiled.

"Then I can get an afternoon train up there," I continued artlessly.

"Where to, for heaven's sake?"

"I'll have to find out. Manchester, perhaps, or Preston, in the first place, and then on to—" I turned the envelope over. "Pendlemere." Interest quickened suddenly. "Pendlemere—the name hadn't registered before. That must be near Pendle Hill."

"So?"

"The heart of witch country, Jake!" My rising excitement must have been apparent in my voice because his mouth tightened, but I hurried on: "I only came across the more well-known place names, of course, like Rough Lea, Malkin Tower, and so on, but I imagine every little hamlet round there had its own Dame Demdike or Chattox. It'll be fascinating to see it all first-hand, having just written it up. I might even be able to go and visit—"

"You still haven't told me how you propose to get from the mainline station to this back of beyond. By broomstick, I take it?"

I smiled. "If that's all I'm offered!"

"Meaning," he said heavily, "that I have no lectures today and a perfectly adequate car in the garage."

"Would you, darling? Knowing how you drive, we'd be up the motorway in no time. Even if you stayed overnight you'd still be back in time for your first lecture tomorrow afternoon."

"Don't you mean that *we* would?"

"Oh—I might not be able to fix anything quite as quickly as that."

"Well, at least remember that you're going up expressly to arrange help for your aunt and not on a gallivanting witch hunt all over the county."

"Yes, Jake," I said meekly.

His eyes held mine for a moment. "Right. Well, I'd better go and get dressed if I've got to run you to and from College first." He went through to the bathroom and I heard the water running.

Thoughtfully I turned back to the table and picked

up the letter. I couldn't decipher the signature, but the name Graham T. Lethbridge was printed at the top of the sheet, with a string of qualifications after it. My letter from a stranger, after all. Again I felt a breath of disquiet, as though—what was the rather macabre phrase?—as though someone had walked over my grave. And the words "violent death" surged into my mind on a renewed wave of fear.

Hastily, with hands that shook a little, I started to clear the table.

chapter

❧2❧

THE sun stayed with us all the way up the motorways until, conscientiously following the map spread out on my knee, we left the M6 at junction 31 and turned east in the direction of Clitheroe. Low in the sky by that time, it gradually became more obscured until, as we bypassed the ancient town of Whalley, it finally slid behind a bank of cloud. Very appropriate, I thought with a superstitious quiver, since it was an abbot of Whalley whose curse was reputedly responsible for the long line of the Lancashire witches.

"It feels a good ten degrees cooler up here," Jake remarked, mistakenly interpreting my shiver. "And judging by the buds on the trees, they seem to be at least a month behind us."

I nodded, pulling my coat about me. After the warmth of the sun, its withdrawal was certainly noticeable and he bent forward to switch on the heater. "It's only another three miles to Pendlemere from here. When we get there, we'll have to stop and ask directions. What's the name of the cottage?"

I dug Beryl's last letter out of my handbag. "Cobwebs, in Tanner's Lane. Sounds very countrified."

"There's probably no indoor sanitation," Jake prophesied grimly.

I dimpled. "A pump on the village green and a dubious shed at the bottom of the garden? How picturesque!"

"That's one word for it. Sophie, what's got into you? You're up and down like a yo-yo today. Personally I dislike this place already, and the sooner our noses are pointing south again, the better I'll be pleased."

I leaned forward suddenly. "Here we are now, this turning."

Jake swung the wheel and we went more slowly down the twisting lane. After a mile or so we came to a noticeboard leaning rather drunkenly to one side and bearing the name "Pendlemere." The road had risen to form a bridge and beneath us as I looked out of the window I could see a sheet of water, unmoving, gold-flecked from the setting sun. I said abruptly, "Jake, I know this road!"

"How can you possibly? You've never been here, have you?"

"No, but I do. There's a rough road immediately to the right after the bridge—Starling's Way, it's called, and over on the left are the walls surrounding the grounds of Ashley Hall. Look!"

We had come over the bridge and the scene I had described a second earlier lay before us. I said slowly, "It's ludicrous and quite impossible, but we won't have to ask directions. I know the way."

26

"What are you trying to do, scare the daylights out of me? Look, I like this whole thing less and less. Let's turn back and say we had a puncture. At least if we wait till morning we can get a good look at the place. This spooky half-light doesn't help at all."

I said shakily, "The High Street is a continuation of the road we're on. Tanner's Lane is almost halfway up on the right, just opposite the end of this high wall. The doctor's surgery is on the corner—here." I didn't look at him, though I knew he'd turned to stare at me as, swinging into Tanner's Lane, we saw the brass plate on the gate.

"Go on past the shops and cottages," I said expressionlessly. "There's a space for some yards with open fields on either side, and then you come to Cobwebs on the right. That's as far as you can go by car, anyway. The road ends in a little humpbacked footbridge over the stream leading into—" I broke off, horror slowly washing over me.

"You might as well finish," Jake said, his voice as toneless as mine. "Leading where?"

"To Whistler's Lane," I said in a whisper.

Beyond the lighted shop windows the road was dark and Jake switched on his headlamps. On either side cottages huddled behind their garden walls. In most of them a light shone in one of the downstairs windows. Then, past the cottages, darkness again and finally, right at the end of the Lane, Cobwebs, as I had described. Jake stopped the car and after the noise of the engine which had been with us for so long, the silence was somehow eerie. He said harshly, "Look, Sophie, this has gone far enough. I presume

27

it's all some kind of joke? Your aunt described it to you this morning, didn't she, when you phoned to say we were coming?"

My face must have been answer enough. "I see," he said after a moment. "I'm beginning to think I owe our gypsy friend an apology. Did you borrow her crystal ball?"

I licked my lips. "Let's go inside."

He said something under his breath and abruptly got out of the car. Without the headlights it was now almost dark and the few street lights that Tanner's Lane boasted stopped short of Cobwebs. Without waiting for me, Jake strode ahead up the path and knocked with, I felt, undue violence on the front door. As I ran breathlessly to join him, the door opened and light spilled onto us. A girl's voice said hesitantly, "Who is it? Who's there?"

It wasn't the girl I had expected. I said quickly, "I'm Sophie Woodburn and this is Dr. Petersen. I phoned this morning. We've come to see my aunt."

Her face cleared and I heard Beryl's voice, blessedly normal after the last few unnerving minutes: "Sophie? Is that you? Bring them through, Polly, quickly, it must be cold out there."

And so once again I entered Cobwebs, Jake at my heels, and turned automatically toward the archway on the left—because, I assured myself in that split second of wonder, it was where Beryl's voice had come from. With a thankfulness that almost overwhelmed me, I realized that the long, low-ceilinged room was totally unfamiliar to me. Quickly I ran to where Beryl was propped up on a sofa before the fire and dropped to my knees to hug her.

"Sophie, poppet, how sweet of you to come!" She returned my almost hysterical embrace with enthusiasm. "Welcome to Cobwebs. I'm sorry it's not under more propitious circumstances! Good evening, Jake."

Jake, who had remained just inside the archway, gave her a curt nod. "We were sorry to hear of your accident."

"So stupid, such a silly thing to do!"

Something warm and wet inched into my hand and I started violently. Beryl said with a half laugh, "Don't be so jumpy, child. It's only Lottie come to say hello."

I looked down at the small body wriggling ingratiatingly against my side and gave her a perfunctory pat as I rose from the rug.

"Pull that chair up to the fire and let me look at you!" Beryl instructed. "I've asked Polly to bring in a pot of tea. Won't you sit down, Jake?"

He said abruptly, "You appear to have someone with you after all."

"Polly? Yes, her mother keeps the post office down the Lane. She comes in three times a day to get my meals. There was a little confusion at first, until I learned that lunch up here is what we've always called elevenses. Our lunch becomes dinner and anything eaten thereafter is automatically 'tea,' even if it's roast beef and two veg!"

Jake was not to be distracted by a dissertation on the peculiarities of the north. "We understood from your doctor that there was no one available to help."

She met his eyes levelly. "And you wouldn't have bothered coming if you'd known the position? I'm

sorry you were misinformed. I did tell Sophie on the phone that I was perfectly capable of managing, but she insisted on coming."

Jake's eyes, bleak and accusing, were on my face. I said quickly, "We had to come and see how you are, and anyway, someone only coming in three times a day doesn't sound very satisfactory. How do you manage the stairs at bedtime?"

"I can hobble up all right if I take my time. As for Polly, she's willing enough, even if her attentions do leave something to be desired!"

"Mrs. Latimer—" Jake, having obediently seated himself, leaned forward urgently. "Did you this morning, or at any time, give Sophie directions how to get here?" My immobility matched his.

"I'm afraid not—how stupid. I was so thrilled to hear she was coming, I just didn't think. I'm so sorry. Did you have trouble finding it?"

"On the contrary," Jake said slowly, "from the moment we turned off the bottom road, Sophie 'recognized' it. She described the layout of the village accurately before we'd even crossed the bridge."

"*Did* you, darling? But how fascinating! It must have been telepathy!"

"Or déjà vu," put in Jake expressionlessly.

Beryl clasped her hands. "You believe in that? I've misjudged you, Jake. I always thought you scientists never looked beyond your noses and wouldn't admit of anything that hadn't a chemical formula or a mathematical equation!"

"I *don't* believe in it," he said flatly. "At least, I never have."

30

A rattling of teacups heralded the arrival of Polly with a tray. I pulled out a little polished table and she set it down. "I'd best be getting back now, Mrs. Latimer. It's almost dark. I've put the hotpot in the oven for your tea."

"Thank you, Polly, and thank you so much for all your help."

"Mum said to tell you if you need me at any time, you've only to ask." But it was obviously assumed in the village that I had come to take up my duties and that Polly would not be required again. Without looking at Jake, I started to pour the tea. A draught of cold air followed by the slamming of the front door signified Polly's departure. Into the silence that followed it I said the first thing that occurred to me.

"Surely she doesn't always leave so early? I suppose when you're alone she stays at least long enough to give you your meal and clear away?"

Beryl's eyes, keen and alert as ever, turned speculatively toward me. "I'm lucky she comes at all in the evening. Very few people will come this way after dark."

I stared at her, the teapot heavy in my hand. "What do you mean?"

"Whistler's Lane, my love, has the reputation of being haunted, and it's just beyond the garden wall."

"Whistler's Lane?" Jake repeated, and his voice cracked.

"You've heard of it?"

"Only from Sophie," he said heavily.

Beryl's eyes were thoughtfully on my face, but she made no direct comment, merely continued: "It's

31

also the local lovers' lane. Fear of the supernatural adds a touch of excitement, I suppose. At least it provides a good excuse for keeping close together!"

Jake took the cup and saucer I handed him. "I dare say people still believe in that kind of thing in out-of-the-way places like this," he remarked carefully.

Seeing Beryl open her mouth, I said quickly, "He's also afraid such 'out-of-the-way places' may not have the benefit of twentieth-century plumbing!"

Beryl's eyes went from my face to his. "There's no need to worry on that score," she said quietly. "We have all the mod. cons here, even unto a minute downstairs cloakroom which, I don't mind telling you, has been a cause of thankfulness to me since my accident. Well now, tell me how the job's going. I don't like to think of you spending your days poring over stuffy books in dim, dusty libraries! You should be striding out over our lovely moors breathing in the fresh country air."

"Powerfully laced with cow dung!" I said with a laugh. "Not to mention, I suppose, wrenching my ankle in one of the numerous rabbit holes! How did it happen, by the way?"

"Oh—it was nothing. I tripped over Lottie, actually. She suddenly shot under my feet."

A dull thud from the rug intimated that Lottie had heard her name and duly acknowledged it without bothering to open her eyes.

"They're very highly bred," Beryl said a little inconsequentially. "Anyway, I was asking about your work. How's it going?"

"Oh, fine. I haven't a great deal more to do, but I

brought a few books with—" I broke off under the force of Jake's warning gaze.

"I forget what the research was this time?"

"Jacobean England. Beryl, that is Pendle Hill we saw looming in the distance as we came up the High Street? I had to wade through James I's treatise on demonology and of course it was all centered round here."

"Oh yes, Pendlemere had its fair share of witches, from all accounts. The local haunting is tied up with one of them. It really doesn't do, you know," she added, her eyes on Jake, "to proclaim your skepticisms too loudly in this vicinity. The whole area has been steeped in the supernatural since time immemorial."

He set his cup down on the tray with an exasperated little bang. "Mrs. Latimer, I haven't any immediate intentions of proclaiming anything, but if I had I assure you that rather extraordinary warning would carry no weight with me whatsoever."

Beryl shrugged. "On your own head be it. It's perhaps just as well that you've made it very clear you don't intend to stay around long enough to cause any friction. Tell me, though, Jake. I've a fairly good idea of the many things you *don't* believe in, but I imagine there must be something rather more positive. What exactly *do* you believe?"

I said hastily, "Oh, now, really, that's not quite fair."

"It's perfectly fair. He's just assured me he has no inhibitions about airing his beliefs." And, as Jake, suddenly presented with something of a poser, still hesi-

tated, she added, "How about God, for instance? Does He fit into your concept of the universe?"

Jake shifted uncomfortably and cleared his throat. "Well, that's rather a difficult one. I believe in a force for good, of course—"

"And therefore, obviously, in a force for evil as well. But you're evading the issue."

"Well then, perhaps I don't believe in God per se. I believe that men have a fundamental need for a father figure, someone greater and much more powerful than themselves, whom they can turn to in moments of crisis. But I can't honestly see that it makes much difference whether it happens to be Jupiter, God, or even a totem pole, as long as it serves its purpose."

"I see. And the reverse side of the coin?"

He smiled a little. "Well, that's really just a case of passing the buck, isn't it? So much more face-saving if we can blame all our misdeeds on the devil!"

Beryl said dryly, "Very rational and just what I expected. You're quiet, Sophie. Do you go along with all that?"

"No," I answered in a low voice, "I'm afraid I want the best of both worlds. I've always believed in God, but I must admit I'd never given much thought to Satan until I started researching into ritual sacrifices, black masses, and so on. Now I'm not so sure."

"And which of you, do you suppose, has the more open mind?"

"Sometimes," said Jake crisply, "an open mind is more indicative of credulity than intellect."

"I'm well aware, of course," Beryl remarked calmly, "that you have a poor opinion of my intel-

lect." She lifted a hand to silence him as he moved protestingly. "Let me put my case before you and see what you make of it. I'm not sure how much of it you already know, but to start with I was married at eighteen and my husband, a bomber pilot, was killed six months later. A common enough story in wartime, I know, but to me it was the end of the world. I was a very highly strung girl and for a while I believe I almost was insane with grief." She looked down at her tightly laced hands. "Even when I was supposed to have recovered, I was regarded as 'medically unfit' for any of the women's services and eventually I was drafted to a factory making component parts for aeroplanes. Fortunately the war was nearly over anyway, but the point of all this is that it was at the factory that I met a girl who gave me the most concrete offer of help I had yet received. She introduced me to spiritualism."

"I didn't know that," I exclaimed involuntarily.

She smiled a little. "No, my dear, it was hushed up, rather as though I had some unsavory disease. Believe me, when your mother had no alternative but to entrust you to my care, I was given a list of instructions as long as my arm, the main one being that under no circumstances was I ever to mention such things in front of you. I think she envisaged me as a kind of devil's disciple on the lookout for recruits! Well, I kept my side of the bargain, but you're not a child any longer."

"And do you still—I mean, are you—?"

"Do I still attend séances? Of course. That was why I sold the Biggin Hill house and came up here."

"I—don't think I understand."

35

"Peter wanted me to," she said simply.

I stared at her and a pulse began to beat insistently in my temple. *"Peter?"*

"He was a northerner, you know, and I believe our own family originally came from round here, too. I chose this particular place partly, I admit, because of all the legends and superstitions clinging to it, which have always fascinated me, and partly because it was within easy reach of a medium who'd been recommended to me."

Across the hearth Jake's eyes met mine with an expression which clearly said, "What did I tell you?" A log shifted in the grate and my heart shifted with it. I became aware that beyond the fire and the tiny circle of light from the lamp by the sofa, the rest of the long room lay in shadow. And no one had drawn the curtains. Our little group would be clearly visible to anyone—or anything—who cared to look in.

Jake cleared his throat. "Yes, well, that's very interesting. You're entitled to your own beliefs, just as I am. Thank God we no longer persecute people in this country at least."

"I gather you haven't changed your opinion of me, though."

"I never stated any opinion, Mrs. Latimer; you did. However, I must say that I share the concern Sophie's parents felt. She may not be a child, but these last few days she seems to have become unduly— susceptible and, not to put too fine a point on it, I feel very strongly that any more talk in this vein could be positively harmful to her."

"My dear man, what rot! Talk never harmed anyone."

36

"On the contrary, it's always been one of civilization's most insidious weapons. Look, I don't want to argue with you, Mrs. Latimer, I'm just trying to get it across that Sophie's a sensitive girl and—oh, hell, do I have to spell it out for you?"

"But of course she's sensitive," Beryl returned calmly, "and from what you said earlier it sounds as though she may have some paranormal gift which needs careful handling. The whole point of going into my own beliefs in such detail was to reassure you of my very genuine interest. And I might remind you that it was you who first brought up possibility of déjà vu."

"I wish to God I hadn't. Believe me, I'm not trying to be rude, but I honestly feel it would be better for Sophie if we could find someone else to come and live in until you're fit, and I'll take her straight back with me tomorrow."

"That, of course, is for Sophie to decide."

I said, just above a whisper, "I don't think it will help to run away, Jake."

He stood up abruptly. "Aren't there any bloody lights in this place?" He went to the archway and flicked down a switch. Pools of light blossomed down the length of the room from the sconces on the wall. Beyond the arch the hall leapt back into contrasting darkness.

I said automatically, "Wasn't there a door there at one time?"

"I believe so, yes. Originally this long room was two small ones."

Which was why I hadn't recognized it. I said aridly, "When were the alterations done?"

"About eight years ago, I think. The house was bought by an architect and his wife. They knocked down a few walls to make larger rooms, but although the effect is pleasing downstairs, it resulted in only two bedrooms and an unnecessarily large bathroom. As most people interested in this type of property want a minimum of three bedrooms, it was a distinct drawback when they came to sell it."

"If they bought it with the express purpose of modernizing it and then selling at a profit, that was surely rather shortsighted of them," Jake put in.

"Oh, but they didn't; they fully intended to stay here. In fact they were in the house about seven years, until someone left them some property down in Suffolk or somewhere. It had been empty about six months when I bought it, and fortunately was going pretty cheap."

"It's most attractive," I said, "but I must admit I'm not too keen on open-plan. I like to have a door I can close!"

"It depends what you want to shut out," Beryl said with a smile. "Doors wouldn't be any use against ghosts!"

"I wasn't thinking of ghosts," I replied shortly.

"Oh? I rather thought you were." Her eyes met mine innocently.

I stood up. "Anyway, the lack of doors is allowing a rather gorgeous smell to drift through from the kitchen, and it's reminding me that we only had a snack lunch. Will the meal be ready yet?"

"Almost. I got Polly to cook it this morning so it would only need heating through."

"Then perhaps we can take the cases up and have a wash first?"

"Of course. As I said there are only two bedrooms, so for tonight I've had a camp bed put up for you in my room. If you decide to stay on for a few days, you can move through to the other room when Jake returns to London."

"Thank you." I didn't look at Jake as I moved past him into the hallway.

"Just a minute," he said quickly. "I'll strike a match so that we can find—" but my hand had gone unerringly to the light switch round the corner. The walls had been distempered white. There was a gold-framed picture opposite the arch where we stood and beneath it a carved settle with a model ship on top of it. Before, there used to be an old-fashioned coat stand—

Without a word Jake picked up the two cases and followed me upstairs. I turned right unhesitatingly and snapped on the light in Beryl's bedroom. Darkness stared back at me from beyond the mullion-paned windows and beneath them, obviously made up by Polly's untidy hand, was the camp bed, decently sheathed in a patchwork quilt.

"A bit pointed, isn't it?" Jake said.

"Only to be expected. You're through here." He followed me again across the creaking boards of the small landing to the left-hand door. A washbasin was in one corner, with a clean towel draped more or less evenly over the rail beside it, and a narrow bed stood chastely in the center of the room. A corner of his mouth lifted. "Barely room for two, admittedly. So-

39

phie, you're not going to stay, are you? Not after that weird business downstairs?"

"As I said, it's no use running away."

"But she's mad! Oh, I know she sometimes talks like a pseudo-intellectual, but don't let that fool you. It doesn't alter the fact that she's not all there. She *can't* be, for Pete's sake. All that nonsense about her dead husband wanting her to come here —it gave me the willies."

"I know, but she really is extremely bright, all the same. I remember Mother saying how brilliantly she did at school. She was all set for University when she met Peter and dropped everything to get married."

"Well, you know the cliché about genius and madness. It was her husband's death that unhinged her, she more or less admitted it herself." He caught hold of my arms and turned me to face him. "Sophie, listen, love. I admit that before I tried to get you to agree not to stay for selfish reasons. After all, I do need someone who knows how long to boil my egg! But now it's you I'm thinking of. I honestly believe it would be harmful for you to stay here."

I sighed. "You still don't understand, do you? Stop and think for a moment about the lead-up to all this. The gypsy's visit, for instance. You've laughed about it since, but at the time it shook you, didn't it? So did finding that I seemed to know my way round Pendlemere. It's all very well being down to earth now, but who was it who wanted to turn back so we could see everything in broad daylight? It can't just be explained away, Jake, and it's no use pretending that it can."

"Then what is your considered opinion, Professor Woodburn?"

"Simply that I was meant to come here. I've no idea why. I certainly didn't receive any messages from Peter, I assure you. It's just a feeling I can't put into words, a kind of—accepting."

He turned away from me, running a hand through his hair. "Well, at least I tried. Obviously I don't believe in all these signs and portents myself, but that doesn't alter the fact that if *you* do it could be dangerous. Believe me, Sophie, it doesn't do to meddle in these things—it could send you round the bend."

"But I'm not meddling, Jake, merely acquiescing." I reached up and kissed his cheek. "Don't worry about it. Have a wash if you want one. I'll go down and see to the supper."

Sloppy bed-maker or not, Polly had done a good job with the hotpot. The brightly lit sitting room on my return revealed a dining table at the far end which had been lost in the shadows but now emerged as laid for three, complete with a bottle of wine. We ate our meal hungrily and for the most part in silence, each of us busy with our own thoughts. Beyond the table a further set of windows, originally belonging to the back room, presumably gave onto the garden.

"Plug in the percolator, will you, Sophie," Beryl requested as we finished our cheese. "These small luxuries have been a boon to me since I was incapacitated. Polly usually leaves a tray and I can make myself coffee any time I feel like it without

41

having to leave the room. If I can just take your arm, Jake, we'll go back to the fire."

"I'll clear the table," I said.

"Oh, leave it for now."

"I'd rather get these things out of the way. I'll take my coffee through with me."

Jake as requested held his arm out to Beryl and I smiled at her momentary hesitation. If she had expected him to offer to help me load the tray or dry the dishes, it was more than I had. Jake did not concern himself with such mundane tasks.

The kitchen had been modernized tastefully to fit in with the rest of the house. Cupboards and shelves were of pine and the large chimney breast had been used to accommodate the central-heating boiler. I washed the supper things as hurriedly as hygiene would allow, aware of the hall stretching quietly behind me and the darkness of Tanner's Lane beyond the front door. My mind fluttered helplessly from topic to topic like a frightened bird, not daring to settle anywhere. There were suddenly so many things I dare not dwell on.

With an audible sigh of relief I hung the tea towel on the hook and forced myself to walk at a reasonable pace back to the sitting room. Beryl was talking earnestly over her coffee cup and Jake's mouth had a stubborn line to it.

She looked up as I joined them. "Sit down, dear. I'm still trying to convince this obstinate young man that I'm not as addle-witted as he seems to suppose. I've just been quoting his beloved scientists at him, since presumably he respects their opinions. Did you know, for example, that Isaac Newton was a student

42

of the occult? And when asked rather scornfully if he really believed in it, he replied stiffly, 'I, sir, have studied it. You have not.' "

"I've already acknowledged that people did believe in it in those days," Jake said with heavy patience, "even the early scientists."

"Newton's other theories still haven't been discredited, for all your modern advances. Well, Carl Jung then, he's nearer our time, though perhaps you haven't a very high opinion of psychologists anyway." She glanced over her shoulder at the table behind her. "Pass me that book, will you, Sophie? I was looking at it only this morning. I marked what I felt to be rather a significant passage. Here it is: 'There is this peculiar faculty of the psyche that isn't entirely confined to space and time; you can have dreams or visions of the future, you can see round corners'—take note, Sophie!—'and such things. Only the ignorant deny these facts. It's quite evident that they do exist.' There!" She looked across at Jake triumphantly, snapping the book shut. "That's pretty unequivocal, isn't it?"

"I know, of course, that Jung later turned to mysticism—"

"Which, ipso facto, nullifies his theory? Come, come, Jake, you're deliberately holding the telescope to your blind eye! Anyway, that last was really for Sophie's benefit, to reassure her about her little incident this afternoon. It's nothing to be frightened about, poppet, really."

"Thanks," I said briefly, replacing the book she handed me on the gateleg table behind the sofa.

"Have you ever experienced anything like it before?"

I shook my head positively. "Never, thank goodness."

"Nothing at all? No precognition, dreams that came true in detail soon afterwards?"

A childhood memory flickered in my brain and, as always throughout the last ten years, was instantly suppressed. "Nothing," I repeated firmly.

"You see, the gift often runs in families. I just wondered—"

"Gift?" I broke in harshly. "It seems more like a curse to me!" I was remembering the transparent terror her so-called gift had brought to the gypsy woman on Saturday morning—but that was something else it was safer not to think about.

Beryl folded her hands in the lap of her ancient tweed skirt. "I see. I gather, then, that you'll be returning to London tomorrow?"

I looked helplessly across at her. With her bright eyes and the short hair curling softly close to her head, she looked almost birdlike as she waited, head slightly cocked, for my reply. Her injured leg was stretched out on the sofa, and on the rug the solitary gym shoe seemed somehow pathetic. But the decision I had to take was not as straightforward as she supposed. Though she didn't realize it, she was asking me to choose between her claim and Jake's. If I stayed here more than a very few days, I knew with certainty that I should lose him. Even so, I really had no choice.

"Of course not," I said quietly. "I can't go rushing

44

straight back leaving you in this state. In any case"—
the hint of defiance that had crept into my voice was,
of course, for Jake—"I haven't seen you for some
time. We've a lot to talk about, and as I said I've
brought some work with me so I can get on with that,
too." Greatly daring, I added less than truthfully,
"Jake understands."

He neither confirmed nor denied it, but Beryl exclaimed gladly, "Jolly good show! I was so hoping
you'd stay, but of course I didn't want to put any
pressure on you."

So it was settled. I smiled dutifully, but my mind
was on the flat in London and how empty it would
seem when Jake had gone.

chapter

❧3❧

I AWOKE the next morning to bird song and the gentle, rhythmic puffing of Beryl's sleeping breath. My mind swung uneasily back over the unaccountable remembrances of yesterday, including my initial surprise at seeing the girl Polly in the doorway. Whom had I expected? Not Beryl—it was not her tall, ungainly figure I had looked for. In what unmeasured time had I been to Pendlemere before? What deeply buried memory had been strong enough to reach out and draw me back to Whistler's Lane?

Slowly and determinedly I fought down the grey tide of panic and as fear gradually began to recede, a more healthy curiosity rose to the surface. I slipped out of bed, picked up my dressing gown and soundlessly let myself out of the room. The house stood sideways on to Whistler's Lane, but the bathroom window might give me my first conscious view of it. Fumblingly I slid the bolt and pulled back the gaily striped toweling curtains.

Below me, the back garden of Cobwebs stretched

for some eighty feet, ending in a grey stone wall. Away to the right I could see the gardens of the cottages further down Tanner's Lane; to my left, despite my frantic straining, the side wall of the garden cut off any sight of the Lane beyond it. All I could see were some distant farm buildings, humpbacked and indistinct in the early morning mist. It was not enough. Hurriedly I washed and, returning to the still-sleeping Beryl, dressed rapidly and stole down the staircase to the silent hall. A moment later a soft scurrying spun me round, fear leaping again to my throat, to see with relief a shiveringly expectant Lottie, tail hopefully signaling her desire to join me in my explorations.

"Quiet, then," I told her, and together we went down the pathway to the gate. I hadn't stopped to put on my watch, but somewhere to my left a church bell began to chime insistently. It was probably almost eight o'clock. Lottie, running ahead with tongue lolling, had already set off down Tanner's Lane. I hesitated, unwilling to raise my voice in the sleepy stillness, and after a moment she turned to look for me.

"This way," I said softly, and turned toward the little footbridge. She gave a soft whine and hung back. "Come on, girl." I was suddenly glad of the unlooked-for company of this fellow creature, but the dog was no longer at ease. Her tail drooped and she slunk at my heels instead of racing on ahead. Slowly we went together over the bridge and on to Whistler's Lane. I stopped, heart pounding, and stood still, ridiculously poised for flight back over the

47

bridge. Still the church bell chimed, but here all was quiet. To left and right the Lane stretched away into the mist. Along the pathway low bushes lay festooned with spiders' webs, fairylike and ethereal under a cascade of dewdrops. My straining ears could detect the faint sucking sound of the stream we had just crossed as it went on its way, presumably down under Starling's Way to the mere over which Jake and I had entered the village. Abruptly the church bell stopped and I shivered, as though a benediction had been suddenly withdrawn. My eyes went to the trembling dog at my side.

"What is it, Lottie?" I asked softly. She looked up at me, still panting, and her tail gave a perfunctory swish, overridden by a repetition of the low whine deep in her throat.

Well? I asked the Lane silently, why have you brought me back? Alongside the stream behind me and slightly to my right ran the comforting garden wall of Cobwebs. Perhaps Jake was already awake and stirring. In another few hours he would be leaving Pendlemere and I wished with a dull, futile ache that I could go with him. Down at my feet the dog still waited, unhappy, frightened, but trained to obedience.

"All right, girl, home!" She needed no second bidding. With a swift turn she was back on the bridge and scuttering over its boards to the relative security of Cobwebs' gate. I slipped the key I had brought with me into the lock and let myself into the hall. The dog's prints, muddy and wet, left a telltale trail to the kitchen. Later, when they had dried, they would re-

spond to brush and dustpan. I wiped my own shoes conscientiously and followed her down the hall, ready, after the chill outside, for hot toast and coffee. Swiftly, keeping my mind blank, I set about preparing them, laying the kitchen table for two and a tray for Beryl. A transistor radio stood on a shelf and I switched it on, needing the balm of everydayness to soothe away the disquiet that still held me.

Mentally I checked the contents of the tray, slid the toast into the rack, and carried it upstairs. Beryl was sitting up in bed, a fluffy bed jacket of a rather violent orange draped round her shoulders.

"I didn't hear you get up. That looks good, dear, thank you." She took the tray from me and set it on her knees. "Good gracious, your hand is frozen! What have you been doing?"

I avoided her eyes. "I just took Lottie for a short walk to get my bearings. I'd better give Jake a knock now; he'll be wanting to make an early start." I hurried from the room before she could question me further, but I had the feeling she did not need to ask which direction I had taken.

A quick tap on Jake's door brought an immediate response. He opened it, fully dressed. "Breakfast ready? Good girl. Some blasted church bell woke me. Lord knows why, it's not even Sunday."

"Some saint's day, perhaps. A cup of coffee will soon warm you."

"Warm me? I'm not cold. The central heating at least seems reasonably efficient."

I went ahead of him down the stairs without replying. We had shared so many breakfasts. I knew in my

49

heart this would be the last. As though echoing the thought, he said, "I suppose there's no hope of your changing your mind?"

"Not at the moment, Jake. She needs me. I have to stay."

"I might as well move back to the University for the time being, then. No sense in hanging round the flat and having to fend for myself."

"Of course not," I agreed with a dry mouth.

"Sophie, whatever you do, don't let all this nonsense prey on your nerves. Don't let her ladyship try to foist her spirit friends onto you!"

"No," I said with a faint smile.

"She'll be glad to see the back of me, anyway." He drank quickly and my eyes went over his face in a mute farewell. Already he was impatient to be gone, his mind racing ahead to the lecture he had prepared and to all the other matters that might arise during the day.

"What's today, Tuesday? I'll phone on Friday evening and if you're ready to come back, I'll drive up for you on Saturday."

"Thank you," I said quietly. I was being offered one last chance.

He pushed his chair back. "I'll just go and say good-bye to the old girl. I presume she's decent?"

"Perfectly."

He smiled briefly and strode from the room. Slowly I followed him, and had just reached the foot of the stairs when he came hurrying down again, his case in his hand. He put it on the floor and pulled me toward him. "Good-bye, then. Take care, and if you're worried about anything, if you want me to come before

50

the weekend, just give me a ring. You know the number."

"Yes," I said without hope. I returned his kiss, smiled brightly and handed him the case. "Good-bye, Jake; thanks for coming with me."

He nodded, patted my shoulder absently and went down the path. I stood in the doorway watching as he got in the car, made a U-turn and, with a wave of his hand, started back down Tanner's Lane. Then I closed the door and, fighting down desolate tears, went into the sitting room. The cushions were still dented on the chair he had sat in and his cigarette ends lay in the ash tray. Methodically I erased all physical traces of him, plumping cushions, rearranging chairs, moving round the room in a dull misery that I had no means of dispelling.

Seen for the first time in daylight, the long low room was even more attractive, the respective turquoise and amber of the two fireside chairs echoed by tall vases on the mantelshelf above. The hearth needed sweeping and the fire relaying. I moved automatically to do it, remembering also to remove Lottie's muddy prints from the hall carpet. There were still the breakfast dishes to wash and later I must move my things through to the other bedroom. Somehow, no doubt, the hours would pass.

"Sophie!"

I went quickly out into the hall. "Yes?"

"I forgot to tell you, Dr. Lethbridge said he'd look in today. He usually comes straight after morning surgery, about ten-thirty. Is the place reasonably tidy?"

"Yes, I've just dusted and relaid the fire."

"Bless you! I'll be down in two minutes."

"I'll come and help you." Between us we got her safely installed in her usual position on the sofa. "Shall I light the fire or is the warmth from the radiators enough?"

"Let's wait awhile and see if the sun breaks through. When it does, it heats this room beautifully. Perhaps you'll go shopping for me after the doctor's been? Most of the shops are in Tanner's Lane, but there are a few further up the High Street."

"Near the library?"

She looked up quickly. "That's right. You *do* know it, don't you?"

"I can't think how," I said unsteadily.

"The important thing is not to let it worry you. A lot more people have this faculty than is generally realized, you know. Just relax and give it its head, so to speak, and we'll soon find out what it's all about." She hesitated. "You are, of course, perfectly free to refuse, but I should dearly love Madame Zelda to see you."

"Who?" I stared at her blankly.

"The medium I visit up here."

I said violently, "I want nothing to do with mediums, thank you."

She sighed. "Just as you wish. Pass me the morning paper, will you, dear? Are you going to sit down yourself?"

"Not at the moment. I'll peel some potatoes and tidy up a bit in the kitchen." She nodded and I went back to the uncleared breakfast table.

It was about an hour later that I was coming up the

hall when the front door suddenly opened and a tall thin man came quickly inside and stopped short on seeing me.

"I do beg your pardon! I'd quite forgotten you were here. Miss Woodburn, isn't it? I'm Graham Lethbridge. I usually walk straight in so that Mrs. Latimer doesn't have to get up. I hope I didn't startle you."

"It's all right, doctor. How do you do? My aunt's in the sitting room." Beryl introduced us again formally and I took my place across the hearth and watched while he examined her swollen ankle. His hands, long and narrow, were swift-moving and dextrous but as gentle as a woman's. After a moment he re-wound the bandage and sat back on Jake's chair.

"It's coming along very nicely, Mrs. Latimer, but you must continue to rest it as much as possible and keep your weight off it. It's only a matter of time till the swelling goes." He smiled across at me, and I was surprised how that smile, peculiarly sweet, illumined his gaunt face. "I see you have a resident nurse now. I'm sure that we'll soon have you leaping about again like a spring lamb."

"I certainly hope so. I'm not the kind of person who enjoys sitting still for long."

He smiled and got to his feet. "I'm aware of that. Be patient and it won't be more than a week or so. At least you have congenial company now."

I went with him to the door. "I'll call again at the end of the week, Miss Woodburn, but it'll really only be a courtesy call. The ankle will heal of its own accord now. Try to make sure she doesn't do any-

53

thing foolish, like running up and down stairs the minute she can bear to put it to the ground."

"I'll do my best. Thank you for letting me know about the accident."

"I thought you'd come up if you could. Good morning, Miss Woodburn."

"What did you think of him?" Beryl asked as I went back to her.

"Charming, and apparently very capable too."

"He's an incredible man; the whole village adores him. There's nothing he won't do for you and he goes to endless trouble over the most trivial complaints. You feel he really cares."

"Well, I'd better go and see if I can find something for lunch. Any preferences?"

"Not really. Blackburn's usually have some nice fish in on a Tuesday. You could see what they have. You'll find them—" She broke off and smiled. "You tell me!"

I shook my head. "Sorry," I said, not feeling sorry at all. "I've no idea."

"Pity! They're a couple of doors past the post office. And I could do with a few stamps too. I owe your mother a letter as well as some friends in Biggin Hill."

"Right. Is there anything I can get you before I go out?"

"No, thanks. I haven't finished the paper yet and when I have, I'll do the crossword. Don't hurry back, dear. Get your bearings and try to discover just how much of the village seems familiar to you."

The sun was breaking through as Lottie and I set

out once again, and when I turned along Tanner's Lane, she bounded excitedly ahead of me with obvious relief. My heart lifted as well and I looked about me with interest at the small grey cottages and the first of the shops. Mrs. Briggs, a small woman with tightly waved hair, greeted me with interest from behind the grille in the post office.

"You'll be Mrs. Latimer's niece from London? Our Polly said as how you'd arrived." Her sharp eyes behind the extravagantly winged glasses went immediately to my left hand, informing me that Polly had also advised her I had not come alone.

I smiled brightly. "Please tell Polly how delicious the hotpot was last night. I gather she's been a great help to my aunt."

Mrs. Briggs looked pleased. "Aye, she's a good girl right enough. Bit daft when it comes to the lads, but she'll grow out of that. Six three-and-a-halves, you said?"

"Yes, please, and an air letter."

"Dr. Lethbridge wanted her to go to the Cottage but she wouldn't, on account of yon dog, that as caused the accident in the first place. Have you met the doctor?"

"Yes, he called just before I left."

"A lovely man," Mrs. Briggs said complacently. "We're lucky to have him in a village this size, specially on the National Health. None of that 'Keep taking the tablets' and pressing the buzzer for the next patient."

"So I believe." I slid my money under the grille and retrieved the stamps.

"You'll be staying till your auntie's fit, then?"

"Yes, I imagine so."

I turned from the counter as a woman came hurrying into the shop, tall and fair and in a beautifully cut tweed suit. She paused for a moment, surprised no doubt by my unfamiliarity, and then went over to the counter. Behind me, Mrs. Briggs's voice had altered subtly, become almost subservient.

"Good morning, Mrs. Ashley, ma'am. And what can I do for you this morning?"

Mrs. Ashley. The name rang a strident, jangling note in my head. Mrs. Ashley of Ashley Hall, whose high walls I had pointed out to Jake last night. Despite the sunshine some of the coldness had returned. I walked blindly past the next couple of shops and it was only a pungent smell of fish which recalled me to my surroundings in time to turn into Blackburn's doorway. I bought some fillets of plaice and two pairs of gleaming kippers and, as I came out onto the street, I again had to swerve to avoid the hurrying figure of Mrs. Ashley. This time she stopped and smiled.

"Forgive my bad manners in the post office—it's so seldom we see a face we don't recognize here!" She held out her hand. "I believe you're Mrs. Latimer's niece, but Mrs. Briggs's information didn't extend to your name! Mine is Rowan Ashley."

"Sophie Woodburn," I murmured.

"As a matter of fact, I'm afraid I don't know your aunt, either. She hasn't been here long, has she?"

"No, only a few weeks."

"I was so sorry to hear of her accident. Please give her my best wishes for a speedy recovery."

56

"Thank you, I will."

She went on down the road to a parked car and was unlocking the door as I came alongside. "Can I give you a lift anywhere?"

"No, thank you, I'm on a voyage of exploration this morning!"

"I see. Well, do go as far as the village green, at the top of the High Street to your right. There are the remains of some fifteenth-century stocks there and we're very proud of them."

I smiled and thanked her, but a cold shudder had zigzagged down my back, leaving me trembling inexplicably. Gripping my basket, I went doggedly down to the bottom of Tanner's Lane and paused on the corner by Dr. Lethbridge's house. Opposite me the walls of Ashley Hall left the road to curve back round the grounds, and their grey stone, I saw, doubled as one of the boundaries of the school playground which lay alongside. I imagined that their height ensured that no errant ball ever disturbed the peace of the Hall.

A little farther on, the school itself, small and grey as were most of the buildings in Pendlemere, lay behind its high railings and as an ever-present backcloth the slopes of Pendle Hill rose against the sky, its top still shrouded in mist.

With Lottie at my heels I started to walk up the High Street. On my own side of the road houses lined the footpath without benefit of a garden to separate them from passers-by, and one or two had converted their front room into a little shop, knitting wools, baby linen and newspapers arranged temptingly in the respective windows. The road bore round to the

57

right and now I could see at the top on the far side the squat outline of the old church whose bell had woken Jake that morning. In questionable proximity to it on my own side was the village inn, its name, The Fleece, reinforced by the sign that hung creaking overhead. Beyond the inn I suddenly found myself on open ground. Grass stretched back from the road and the ancient remains of the stocks were clearly visible hunched in the background. The village green.

Across the road the church clock chimed the four slow quarters of midday and from further down the hill, almost simultaneously, it seemed, the school must have opened its doors, because I could hear the children's voices as they poured out en route for home and "dinner." The sun shone steadily in a clear sky but all of it, clock, children and sunshine, were suddenly removed from me, held apart by a searing blast of fear which, without warning, scalded over me, leaving me weak and gasping and leaning for support against the wall of the inn. Before my staring eyes church, sky and grass started to spin in a dizzy arc and I would have fallen had not my arm been grasped firmly as an anxious voice reached me out of the mists of my recoiling withdrawal. "I say, are you all right? You don't look at all well."

I was beyond replying. The voice went on, "Come and sit on this bench and get your breath back for a minute." Its owner was trying to propel me gently onto the green, but with an almost manic frenzy I pulled violently back. "No!" With my last ounce of will power I forced the words out: "Please—not on the green."

58

It must have sounded insane, but he merely answered, "All right, there's a seat in the church porch
if you'd rather." Numbly I let him lead me across the
road and through the lych gate, up the path to the
doorway of the church. Sure enough there was a
stone seat on either side of the porch, warmed with
the sunshine, and my deliverer lowered me gently
down onto one of them. And as I felt the solid stone
beneath my spread-eagled hands, sanity shudder-
ingly returned, and I looked up into the anxious face
of a young man only a few years older than myself.

I moved my tongue over my lips. "Thank you," I
said weakly. "I feel much better now."

"What happened, do you know?"

"No, I—I just felt faint all of a sudden." I looked
about me, remembering Lottie for the first time. "I
had a dog with me—"

"It's all right; it's here." And the faithful Lottie,
ignored in my preoccupation, was indeed crouched
beside me on the floor of the porch. I reached down
a hand and she licked it wetly, unreproachful, glad to
be acknowledged at last.

"You're not local, are you? I haven't seen you
before."

"No, I've come to look after my aunt. I only arrived
last night."

"Your aunt being—?"

"Beryl Latimer. She lives at Cobwebs."

"Oh yes, I heard it had been sold. By the way, my
name's John Phillips. I teach at the school down the
hill."

"Sophie Woodburn."

"Are you sure you feel all right now? I can walk

59

home with you if you like. I'm lodging with the Graysons and they live in the same direction."

I thought wearily of the walk all the way back down the High Street and up the length of Tanner's Lane. But John Phillips had not turned down the High Street when he came out of school, but up toward the church. He was obviously going to take the short cut home—down Whistler's Lane.

I nodded my head across the road toward the stretch of grass which had so bewilderingly terrified me. "Does Whistler's Lane lead off there?"

"I was forgetting you wouldn't know. Yes, it's much quicker than going the long way round. The Graysons are nearer this end than Cobwebs, but there's not much in it."

I tried to smile, but it was rather a rocky one. "Isn't Whistler's Lane supposed to be haunted?"

He laughed. "Oh, you don't want to pay any attention to all that nonsense. I've lived just off it for four years now and it hasn't lost me any sleep, I assure you! Anyway, you needn't worry. I'm sure no self-respecting ghost would appear in broad daylight!" He helped me to my feet. "Sure you can manage now?"

"Yes, quite."

We went slowly down the path and across the road and a tremor reached out for me again. "Do you mind if we walk along the path instead of cutting across the green?"

He looked at me curiously. "I was going to show you the village stocks. They're reckoned to date from the fifteenth century."

"Not—just now," I said as firmly as I could manage.

"Okay." We walked along the path and I knew, though I couldn't stop myself, that I was holding onto his arm with a grip which must have been almost painful. Slowly and carefully we skirted the green and came to a cinder track running from the road alongside it. I was still trembling as we started down it and then after a few yards we left the green behind, the cinder track degenerated into loose stones and mud, and we had reached Whistler's Lane. At my side John Phillips said awkwardly, "You're not really frightened, are you?"

I forced myself to relax my grip on him. "I'm frightened of falling, that's all," I lied. "I still feel a little shaky."

"Of course; how stupid of me. It's a pity I haven't got the car with me—I could have run you home in comfort."

"Probably the fresh air will do me good."

"Yes, you're beginning to get your color back now. You were as white as a sheet up there. Why didn't you want to go on the green?"

"I—don't know. I think I was still a bit groggy and I was—afraid the stocks might have been a bit gruesome." It was totally untrue but he accepted it without question.

"You needn't have worried; they aren't at all, really. Anyway, you can look at them another time."

On our left a large farmhouse stood solidly in front of its yard and in the field beyond cows were grazing. I said with an effort, "I suppose there are a lot of farms round here."

"Quite a few, yes. That's Claythorpe's, one of the biggest. It's at the top of Whistler's Lane and—Starling's is at the bottom." He glanced sideways at me, seemed about to speak, to change his mind, and went on, "There are one or two leading off in between, of course, Grayson's among them, and several more on the outskirts of the village beyond the Hall. This is my turning down here."

I stopped. "Then I'll say good-bye, and thank you so much for coming to the rescue in my hour of need."

He said quickly, "No, no. I'll come down to Cobwebs with you. I can't leave you here."

"Really," I insisted, "I'd rather. For one thing, I'm the one who's supposed to be looking after my aunt, not the other way round, and if she sees me being escorted home, I'll have a lot of explaining to do. Also, you've already wasted quite enough of your lunch hour on me. Honestly, I'm all right now."

He hesitated. "Well, if you're sure. No doubt I'll be seeing you around. Try to take it easy for the rest of the day."

"I will, and thanks again." I gave him a reassuring little nod and went on down the Lane, Lottie close to my heels, preparing to give Beryl a carefully noncommittal account of my morning in Pendlemere.

chapter
4

IT was two mornings later, as I was sweeping the hall after settling Beryl on the sofa with the paper, that the vicar called.

"I must apologize for not coming sooner," he remarked as he sat down. "I'd heard, of course, that Cobwebs had been sold but it was only this week I learned via the grapevine that you had met with an accident. Most unfortunate. How did it happen?"

I excused myself to make some coffee and when I returned, he was saying, "I think what troubled me most was the news that your niece had to be sent for because there was no one here to look after you. I felt I'd slipped up on my duty considerably, and my parishioners with me."

"Oh, not at all," said Beryl a little awkwardly. "It's probably my own fault anyway. I'm rather a solitary bird and don't go out of my way to make friends. Anyway, Mrs. Briggs kindly lent me Polly to cook my meals and tidy up generally."

"All the same, one of the advantages of village life

over town life is supposed to be that it is friendlier, even if that does sometimes entail knowing rather too much of one's neighbor's business!" He smilingly took the cup of coffee I handed him. "I'm sure Miss Woodburn will return to London with a much easier mind if we can convince her during her stay that we're really a very friendly little community always ready to welcome a new member." He stirred his coffee. "I presume you are C of E?"

"Yes," I said quickly, and caught Beryl's amused glance.

"As is usual, of course, the church is at the center of most social activities. We have the usual affiliated societies and quite a full program of meetings, talks, and so on. As a matter of fact, two have combined to hold a wine and cheese party this coming Saturday, in aid of the church restoration fund. We should be very happy to see you there if you'd care to come. It would be a good opportunity of meeting everyone."

Beryl said hesitantly, "I rather fear I'm not up to—"

"We would, of course, arrange for a car to call for you, and you'd be able to sit quite comfortably, so your ankle would be none the worse. I don't suppose Miss Woodburn has had the chance to meet anyone and we have quite a few young people in the parish. In fact, I have a son and daughter myself not much older than she is, and they're both making an effort to get home this weekend."

"It sounds very pleasant," I murmured, and tried to close my mind to the fact that Saturday was the deadline which Jake had ambiguously given me. "I

did meet one of the masters from the school the other day," I added. "I think he said his name was John Phillips."

"Ah, yes, John does a very good job with our scout troop." He leaned forward to put down his cup. "May I take it we'll have the pleasure of seeing you, then? I'll make inquiries and let you know later who will be collecting you. It starts at eight o'clock. In the meantime, I hope you'll forgive me for not calling sooner, and I trust your ankle will soon be as good as new."

When I returned from showing him out, Beryl was looking down at the card he had handed her. "The Reverend Stanley Postlethwaite," she remarked caustically. "How about that? And look what you've landed me in, my girl!"

"I? I didn't do anything!"

"You know very well that the orthodox church frowns on spiritualism, though I can never understand why. After all, we offer them positive proof of their own creed, life after death. Perhaps they prefer to live in doubt! Well, I shall put him in the picture at the first opportunity. I have no intention of sailing under false colors. For the sake of your social life, though, I'll keep quiet till you've gone!"

I said a little stiffly, "I'm not particularly interested in the social life up here."

"Well, I dare say it won't measure up to the West End, but it'll do you no harm to meet some people of your own age." She paused. "Is Jake coming up this weekend?"

"Only if I'm ready to go back with him."

"And are you?"

"It doesn't look like it, does it?" My eyes rested on her bandaged ankle.

"Will he come for you later, then, when you are ready?"

"I doubt it," I said bleakly.

"You mean it was an ultimatum, now or never?"

"He didn't say so, but I felt it was implied."

She looked across at me, then away again. "Sweetie, I know it's none of my business, but don't you think you're being rather a clot? I mean, he's not really a very decent type, is he?"

Her occasional lapses into dated, nineteen-forties slang I found embarrassing in company and touching when we were alone. I found myself wondering rather irreverently if Peter still used such expressions during her alleged conversations with him.

"I mean, he does expect you to dance attendance on him, doesn't he?" she persisted as I didn't reply. "All right, well, I've had my two cents' worth and I'll shut up. If you don't see it my way, then I can't expect you to make sacrifices for my sake. You have your own life to live, after all. You'd better tell him when he phones—tomorrow, did you say?—that you're ready to go home."

I shook my head. "No," I said unwillingly, "you're right. I knew it wouldn't last much longer anyway. This is probably as good a way as any of ending it."

"You're sure? It has to be your own decision."

I nodded and she sat back with a sigh of relief. "Well, I can't say I'm sorry. Cheer up, my pet; there are many more fish in the sea."

I gave a little protesting laugh that was more than half a sob. "The only trouble is that I love him."

"I know." Her voice was gentle. "He was the first, wasn't he? I imagine you never forget the first man you love, even if you don't happen to marry him, as I did. What about this John Phillips? Would he make an adequate temporary escort for maypole dancing or muck-spreading or whatever they do up here?"

I laughed as I was meant to. "He might."

"You might even make a hit with Postlethwaite junior—a catch indeed!"

"Don't be wicked, Beryl! No, I certainly shan't trot meekly back to London just because Jake Petersen lifts his finger. If he loved me, he'd be prepared to wait, and if he doesn't—and I know he doesn't—it's pointless to let the thing drag on. But don't expect me to fall immediately into the arms of some local yokel, because I've had quite enough for the moment."

She said musingly, "It's rather frightening to think that by the time I was your age, I'd been widowed for five years."

I stood up and smoothed down my skirt. "I'd better go and do the shopping. Lottie's hinting that her walk is due. I haven't much to get so I shan't be long."

"Take your time; the fresh air will be good for you, especially since you say you must spend the afternoon working."

By this time most of the shopkeepers in Tanner's Lane knew me and I kept having to repeat my assurances that Beryl's ankle was on the mend. My last stop was at the butcher's, on the corner opposite the surgery, and it was only eleven-thirty when I emerged, too early to go back and start preparing

lunch. Lottie waited hopefully for my decision, one paw lifted interrogatively.

I had no wish today to turn in the direction of the waiting green, and as the thought materialized, I quickly turned left instead and started down the High Street toward the mere. Across the road were the walls of Ashley Hall and I remembered Mrs. Ashley and wondered how many of the vicar's committees she was engaged on.

At the bottom of the High Street I paused. To my right, the high walls turned along the side road and a few hundred yards farther on I could see tall iron gates. John Phillips had said there were farms beyond and presumably the road eventually petered out onto the moors and the lower slopes of Pendle. I would need a complete afternoon ahead of me to set off in that direction.

Opposite me was the bridge over which I had driven with Jake, and the still reaches of the water lay beneath it. To my left Starling's Way meandered into the distance, and I knew that Whistler's Lane led down into it. "Come on, Lottie; we'll go home this way."

The roadway was rough and unpaved. Deep grooves obviously worn from the repeated passing of tractors had filled with the overnight rain. There was no footpath and on the far side beyond a narrow grass bank stretched the waters of Pendlemere. Lottie and I crossed over and started to make our way along the rather muddy grass. There was a continuous movement of frogs along the shallow edge of the water. Once one hopped from the reeds almost under Lot-

tie's nose and she leaped back with a startled yelp, shaking herself vigorously as the frog's leap landed it in the water with a shower of spray. In another month or so the dark green pads of water lilies would blotch the surface and the bank would be lined with the purple and yellow spikes of flag irises. Spring would be lovely in this northern village, even if it were not so luxuriantly verdant and prolific as the southern springs I had known.

Lottie cocked her ears suddenly and raised her nose from the delightfully mysterious scents of the grass to stare up the road. A moment later I too caught the noise of an engine, and almost at once a tractor came into sight. I bent down and held onto her collar and we waited while the great, lumbering vehicle moved toward us. My eyes went to the driver, prepared to return the almost inevitable greeting which I had come to expect of acquaintances and strangers alike in Pendlemere, but the chance did not arise. The man who was driving was, at a guess, in his mid-thirties, with broad shoulders and thick black hair. His thigh-length boots were spattered with mud, as were his strong, muscular arms, bare to the elbow. But it was his face that held my attention. His eyes, dark and unwavering, were fixed straight ahead and there was a hard, bitter twist to his mouth. Completely ignoring Lottie and myself, he passed within a contemptuous foot of us and went by without so much as a turn of his head, the progress of the tractor liberally spraying my legs with a shower of muddy water. I stared after him in impotent fury.

"Charming!" I said at last, in an attempt to relieve my feelings. I released Lottie and she ran on ahead, nose to the ground, while I followed more thoughtfully, wondering who the man could have been. Presumably someone from the farm at the end of the lane, since this road led nowhere else. Perhaps, I thought suddenly, it was a private road and my presence had annoyed him? But there was no notice to that effect, and after all, Whistler's Lane led off it so it must be open to the public. And here, in fact, was Whistler's Lane, just short of the farm gates on the other side of the road.

"Up here, Lottie." The dog trotted obediently across with me and then, almost as though she could read the board tacked onto a tree, she hesitated, looked up at me beseechingly, and uncertainly thumped her tail.

"Don't be silly," I told her, and added, paraphrasing John Phillips, "No self-respecting ghost would show itself in broad daylight!" But as I set off up the Lane suddenly, ominously, the sun went in and in spite of myself I quickened my footsteps. At first I associated the sensation with the withdrawal of the sun, a coolness easily accounted for. But gradually it intensified and spread all over me, bringing in its wake a positive flood of conflicting emotion: excitement, anger, apprehension, and above all a wild, singing happiness which caught hold of me and set me running up the Lane in a frenzy of impatience.

Heart thumping against my ribs, I forced myself to slow down, almost having to press backward in order to do so, as though some force were pushing me

onward from behind. Beside me the dog cringed, panting, her ears flat against her head and eyes rolling.

"All right," I said jerkily, "you were right and I was wrong, but we still have to get home." A stitch in my side knifed into me, but I was in no mood for hesitation. "Race me, Lottie!" I urged, and together, as though the furies were at our heels, we sped over the loose stones and chippings of Whistler's Lane until at last the garden wall of Cobwebs came into sight. Together we clattered over the bridge and the garden gate rocked back on its hinges under my frantic push.

Unfortunately we erupted into the hall to find that Beryl, en route from the kitchen, had witnessed our precipitate approach. Lottie, no actress, flopped to the ground, saliva creaming at the corners of her mouth, the pumping of her heart making her sides rise and fall rapidly. Vainly I struggled to compose myself, but Beryl cut across my preliminary dissemblances.

"I presume you've come from Whistler's Lane?"

I stared at her wordlessly. There was no point in denying it. A smile lifted the corner of her mouth. "You're lucky you didn't twist your ankle, as I did."

"You mean that was how—?"

"It was. Lottie suddenly yelped and shot under my feet—not that I blame her, mind, but the result was that I lost my balance, slid on the mud and came down heavily, my ankle underneath me." Her eyes traveled down me. "And talking of mud, you seem to have encountered quite a lot yourself. Come into the

sitting room, pour us both a stiff drink and tell me all about it."

I took her arm and helped her to the couch. My breath was still coming in great, tearing gulps and my hands shook so much that the liquid spilled.

"Never mind mopping it up." Beryl was all impatience. "What happened?"

I lowered myself into a chair, took a sip of the drink, and said as steadily as I could, "I imagine I've just experienced your local ghost!"

"Ah! What form did it take? I'm compiling a report to send to the Society for Psychical Research. Did you hear the whistling?"

"Whistling? No. It was just—just a bombardment of emotions, really. It was—very odd."

"Fear?"

I shook my head slowly. "No, not fear this time."

Beryl pounced. "This time? What's happened before?"

I sighed. "Well, I don't know that it was anything to do with the ghost. It was up on the village green, of all places."

"The *green?* When were you up there?"

"On my way back from the shops on Tuesday. Actually, that was how I met John Phillips. He helped me to a seat."

"You were as frightened as that?"

I shuddered. "It was horrible—absolutely terrifying."

"But what were you afraid of? The stocks? They weren't really too horrific, you know. It was an undignified punishment rather than a painful one. Personally I'd much rather have them than the remains of

72

a gibbet as some of the villages round about have. Now that *is* gruesome, and I don't doubt gives off the most appalling vibrations."

"It wasn't the stocks," I said definitely. "I was only faintly aware of them in the background. It was the location itself. As though at some time someone had stood in the same place and experienced that—that paralyzing terror, and somehow branded it on the atmosphere. Actually," I went on hesitantly, feeling my way, "that was how it was today, too, a kind of *remembered* feeling of excitement and confusion."

"I'm surprised you braved the green again, after all that."

"But I didn't. I came up from the bottom, off Starling's Way. That, incidentally, was where I received this deluge of mud. A most unpleasant man passed us driving a tractor, sloshed this all over us in the process, and for good measure cut us completely dead. Big, dark, in his thirties. Who would he be?"

"I don't know. I've never been down that way. One of the farm workers, I expect."

"I wouldn't have a man like that working for me," I said with feeling, but Beryl wasn't interested in the tractor driver.

"He would have known the green, of course," she said musingly. "After all, he obviously used to go to Claythorpe's, but I've never heard of him being seen there. It's always in the Lane."

" 'He'?" I broke in sharply.

"Richard Whitaker, your ghost."

"Oh, no." I shook my head positively. "It certainly wasn't a man."

"But of course he's a man, child. A rather gorgeous

73

chap in full seventeenth-century rig. I've seen him myself."

"Beryl," I said slowly, "whoever or whatever it was, on the green and again in the Lane, it was definitely female. There's no possible doubt about it."

She stared at me. "You're quite sure?"

"Quite."

"Now that's interesting. Perhaps it's the girl, then, Lizzie something. I've only ever heard about Whitaker appearing. It was he, of course, who was the Whistler."

"Why?" I asked curiously.

"Well, apparently he was a yeoman farmer in the early seventeenth century, young, good-looking, but with not much money. Being a sensible young man" —her mouth quirked—"he wooed and won himself a wealthy bride, one Alice Claythorpe, a plain, homely woman about five years older than himself. Then, with her money comfortably behind him, he continued his dalliance among the more comely village girls." She took a sip of her drink. "All was well until he was hoist with his own petard and fell very heavily in love with one of them. He lost his head completely, threw caution to the winds and the inevitable result was that not only his wife but her very influential family came to hear of it. And to add insult to injury, this was the one girl who would have nothing to do with him."

"So what happened?"

"The luckless Richard was hauled up before a family conclave and sternly told to account for himself. The story goes that he'd just returned from a

74

very fraught meeting with this Lizzie, who had laughed in his face, and he really hardly knew what he was saying. At least, that's my belief. At any rate, he started trying to wriggle out of it, muttering about it not being his fault, that the girl had put a spell on him. Not unnaturally in the climate that then prevailed, the Claythorpes seized on this. It was much less degrading to claim that he had been bewitched rather than had voluntarily looked elsewhere, and of course it didn't stop there. There was some distant relation who was a clerk to the judges on the northern circuit and almost before anyone knew what was happening, Lizzie Earnshaw had been convicted of witchcraft and burned on Pendle Hill."

"And she hadn't done a thing?"

"Only rejected a philanderer she hadn't cared to become embroiled with."

"But that's awful!"

"Of course it's awful. What's more, the Claythorpes were careful to press the lesson home and insisted on Richard accompanying them to watch the proceedings. Whether it was bravado or sheer callousness I don't know—I prefer to think the former—but legend has it that he stood on the fringe of the crowd whistling as the faggots were set alight."

"Small wonder he can't rest in peace," I said shakily. "What happened to him?"

"Only a few months later he was thrown from his horse—in the Lane, of course, and killed instantly. The story goes that Lizzie's shade had suddenly appeared, causing his horse to rear, but how they knew that since he certainly couldn't have told them, I've

75

no idea! Straight from the horse's mouth, perhaps! Anyway, that's the only report there's ever been of Lizzie's ghost, though down the years many people have seen and heard the Whistler. So if it *was* she you were aware of, you see what exciting possibilities it opens up."

"Not really," I said reluctantly. "In fact, I think it's rather a horrible story. That poor girl!"

"Yes, she was only sixteen or seventeen, they say."

"And is it still the same family at Claythorpe's farm now?"

"Yes, Alice's brother's descendants. I saw the son and daughter-in-law one day at the library with their little boy. Perhaps they'll be at this riotous cheese and wine party." She looked across at me. "What is it, Sophie? Has my little saga depressed you?"

"It has rather, but it's not only that. It's all very interesting but I don't think it throws any light on what happened to me. Mine seems to be a much more personal link, since I know so much about the village. After all, the library surely wasn't there in Jacobean times, so Lizzie couldn't have made me aware of it."

Beryl clasped her hands tightly. "You mean there might be another, more recent ghost?"

"I'm not sure what I mean. I don't understand any of it, but—" I broke off. Incredibly, I had almost forgotten the ravings of the gypsy in London last week. I went on hesitantly, "I had my fortune told on Saturday, if it can be called that."

"Go on."

"Come to think of it, that was the start of it all. Life

76

was perfectly normal until then. Less than a week ago! I can hardly believe it."

"What did she tell you?"

"Very little that made sense, but she did say, 'Beware of yesterday.' "

"How very strange." Beryl's voice was soft and thoughtful.

"And—something like 'Your past is tomorrow, your future yesterday'—I remember that bit because it had a scansion almost like poetry. And something about being caught in—the time wheel."

"The time wheel!"

I licked my lips. "Do you think it could have any bearing on what's happened since?"

I longed passionately for her to deny it, to laugh me out of my fears. How, in that moment, I needed down-to-earth, scientific Jake! Yet even he had looked at me oddly since we came to Pendlemere, and Beryl, of course, made no attempt to console me.

"I'm almost sure of it. The time wheel—that's a conception new to me. I've always thought of time as a network of strands, wires which occasionally get twisted and fuse together or short-circuit to cause an electric shock—a ghost, that's overstepped its own barrier. But a wheel; that suggests that the same time keeps recurring in a cycle, history quite literally re-peating itself, though of course slightly different each time round, as if the axis has shifted a little. What is it the French say—'Plus ça change, plus c'est la même chose.' Beware of yesterday; I wonder if rein-carnation is implied?"

"Oh, Beryl, no!"

77

"The thought distresses you?"

"Absolutely!"

"Yes, I know what you mean. I used to feel like that. It's the apparent loss of identity, I think, the negation of self as we know it. But I've worked out a very comforting analogy for myself and I think I can just about accept it now if I have to." She leaned forward intently and winced as the movement pained her ankle. "Imagine for the sake of argument that you're looking at your own family snapshot album. There's a photo of you at six months, say, another at six years, one at sixteen, and so on. In time there may be others of you, at twenty-six, forty-six, even eighty-six: in other words, a whole collection of different selves. Now—which is the real you?"

She leaned back triumphantly. "I think the instinctive reaction is 'As I am now,' but you were no less real twenty years ago nor will be twenty years hence. So who's to say that there isn't another, unchanging entity, a four-dimensional you, of which all the others are just passing likenesses? And that being so, all these different you's are one and the same and therefore, logically, must co-exist."

"Didn't H. G. Wells mention something on those lines in *The Time Machine?*"

"Good girl, he did indeed. There have been various similar theories put forward over the years, but to the best of my knowledge no one has yet gone one step further and reached what seems to me the almost obvious conclusion, that this is the root of the reincarnation idea too. And this theory makes it so

78

much more palatable, because if you yourself actually exist eternally in a different dimension, *unchanging*, mark you, then it is *you* in each incarnation just as surely as it is you in each of those different photographs. I wonder if we'll ever have proof of that, be able to see all the different selves through the ages. I doubt if man's mind could withstand it—we're not programmed to take in the full meaning of infinity. Yet I don't know. Time travel may seem like science fiction now, but so did walking on the moon thirty years ago."

I said with a little shiver, "I hope it wasn't one of the 'me's' who was burned at the stake. I don't really think it could have been, though. I don't feel the empathy with Lizzie that I did with—the other one." I gave a shaky laugh. "Oh, Beryl, why couldn't you have stayed in dear old Biggin Hill?"

She smiled. "I'm sorry if you've become entangled in something you'd rather have left severely alone, but I must confess I find it all tremendously exciting and challenging. But, darling, you must be completely open with me, no more hiding these experiences. You never even mentioned your first visit to Whistler's Lane, the morning after you arrived. I only knew of it because of Lottie. I can always tell when she's been there. She's off key somehow for the rest of the day." She put the empty glass down. "You know, it's strange. You say you wish I'd stayed in Biggin Hill. I was quite content there, but Peter insisted I should come here. I still don't know why. And a little later fate brings you

here too, with all these nebulous, half-formed impressions and awarenesses. It must all be part of the same thing. I have a feeling that you're the important one. The only way to get you here was through me, so I had to come first."

"I don't know that I believe in all this—predestiny," I said, making what I felt to be a last defensive stand before accepting her view of the affair, which I still found very disturbing. "I chose quite freely to come here and not to go back with Jake. I can still change my mind and tell him I'll go this weekend."

"But you won't," Beryl said with quiet certainty.

"No," I agreed after a moment, my defiance collapsing, "I won't. And the strange thing is, I wouldn't even if your ankle had completely healed."

"Exactly. This thing, whatever it is, has to be played out to the end. Sophie my love, I really think I must insist that you see Madame Zelda. For one thing you might be in urgent need of help. She'd know what to do."

I moved awkwardly, remembering Jake's warning. "Look, I don't want to upset you, but I'm afraid I really can't believe in all that—that table thumping, and so on. How can you prove it isn't faked?"

"Because," she answered quietly, "I hear Peter's voice. His actual voice, Sophie. Not always, but it's happened several times, and as long as there's a chance of it happening again, I shall keep on going. How can it be faked? No one but myself knows how he spoke. He uses our own private code that we never told anyone."

Telepathy from her own mind? I wondered, but I hadn't the heart to suggest it.

"His actual voice," she repeated softly. "Can you understand what that means?"

I rose unsteadily to my feet. "I think I'd better see to the lunch," I said.

chapter
❦5❧

WHEN Jake rang on the Friday evening, I told him quite calmly that it was impossible for me to return yet. I did not, of course, say why, and he assumed it was because of Beryl's ankle. Perhaps it was. It no longer seemed to matter.

"Has there been any more of that funny business?" he asked abruptly. The choice of words brought a vivid picture of him into my mind, his light, quizzical eyes, the way the thick hair grew into his neck, the line of his jaw and mouth. A twist of longing for him drove the breath from my body.

"Nothing to worry about," I faltered. "Jake, do you miss me?"

"Of course I miss you," he answered irritably. "When *are* you coming back, for Pete's sake? There's a button off my blue shirt and my brown slacks need pressing."

"All you need is a valet," I said sharply.

He laughed and the old teasing note was back in his voice. "Not all, my love, I do assure you!"

"Can you—is it possible for you to come up just for the weekend?"

"With petrol the price it is? I haven't paid for last weekend's yet."

"By train, then." I knew I was pleading and was powerless to stop myself.

"Sorry, sweetie, no way. You come back here. That place gives me the creeps anyway. And don't be long. This monastic existence disagrees with me."

The stupid tears were back in my eyes when I turned from the phone. I brushed them angrily away under Beryl's keen but sympathetic gaze. "Sorry," I said brusquely. "Withdrawal symptoms. I'll be all right in a moment."

I sat down in my usual chair, leaned my head back and gazed moodily up at the ceiling, returning monosyllabic replies to Beryl's attempts to solicit my help with an extra-stubborn crossword. And then, alarmingly, the outlines of the room began to blur, to slip out of focus, and I was aware of another image superimposed on them, a picture which grew in clarity as the rest of the room faded behind it. I was no longer looking at the familiar sitting room of Cobwebs but at a gate set in a high wall, a narrow wooden gate with grass and flowers at its base, leading, I knew, to a garden. And all the time I was dimly conscious of Beryl's voice irrelevantly in the background: "Twelve letters beginning with M." But even as the picture came fully into focus, so it began to fade, slowly blurring at the edges like an old snapshot and reverting once again to the arm of the sofa and Beryl's after-dinner coffee cup. Yet I knew with

certainty that it hadn't been just a picture that I was looking at. I had actually, for an undefined space in time, been outside that gate. Had my own personal time wheel simply jarred fractionally, jolting me back—or forward?—and then almost immediately righted itself?

"Four and six," Beryl was saying, "probably an anagram." I gazed at her incredulously. How long had that taken? Wasn't she even aware of my temporary absence? Who or what had been here in my place while I had been standing looking at that gate? Whatever had happened, Lottie had noticed. She'd left my feet, where she'd been lying like a heavy, fur-covered hot-water bottle, and was crouching, whining, in the archway. The sound finally penetrated Beryl's hearing and she looked from the abject animal to my stunned, uncomprehending face. Immediately she laid down her paper.

"Tell me."

Stumblingly I did so.

"You were outside a gate? Really there?"

"Yes. I could actually feel the grass under my feet, but the ridiculous thing was I could still hear you reading out clues."

"Infuriating that I didn't look up, notice your face while it was happening. Were you aware of anything that might have led up to it?"

"No. I was still thinking of Jake."

"Love? Desire? Anguish?"

"Perhaps," I said with difficulty.

"It must have been a strong emotion to evoke that reaction. Someone, sometime, felt such a combina-

tion while staring at that gate. Does it sound feasible?"

I said shortly, "I don't doubt millions of people the world over feel that combination every day of the week, whether they happen to be staring at a gate at the time or not."

"Sophie"—her voice was gentle—"don't fight it, darling; just relax. Ride with it, or it could destroy you."

I drew a deep, shuddering breath. "I'm sorry. I know you're trying to help. It was—unnerving, that's all."

"I'll phone Madame Zelda in the morning and make an appointment for one day next week. In the meantime, since it upsets you, try to put it out of your mind and help me with this confounded crossword." But it was some time before Lottie ventured to return to the hearth rug.

The next morning the telephone rang soon after breakfast and a pleasant voice inquired, "Miss Woodburn? This is Phyllis Harcourt. I believe you and your aunt would like a lift to the church hall this evening? I'd be pleased to call for you. I live just along the road in one of the cottages in Tanner's Lane."

I duly reported back to Beryl.

"Yes, I know her by sight. I believe she teaches at the school. There's a son sometimes in the offing, a boy of about eighteen, but I've never seen a husband."

"Well, she's calling just before eight," I finished, and went upstairs to wash my hair.

Mrs. Harcourt was as good as her word and took

great care to settle Beryl comfortably on the back seat of the car. "You needn't worry about being conspicuous sitting down," she remarked cheerfully. "Several ladies always make a point of doing so, Mrs. Lethbridge among them."

"Will the doctor and his wife be there, then?" I asked, closing the car door.

"Not his wife, his mother. Graham isn't married. Have you met him? A charming man, and so dedicated. Apparently he was once offered an extremely good position at a teaching hospital in Manchester, but he preferred to stay on here. He's devoted to his mother, too. It does you good to see them together."

"Is your son not coming with us this evening, Mrs. Harcourt?" Beryl inquired from the back.

"No, I'm afraid he's going through a phase of being extremely antisocial. There's obviously no point in trying to force him, but I do wish he'd go out more. Of course, he works hard during the week—he's at agricultural college—but at the weekends all he wants to do is stay at home and read. It might help if my husband were here more frequently, but he's in the Merchant Navy and on the Pacific run at the moment, so we don't see all that much of him."

We were already pulling off the High Street into the small car park alongside the church hall. From across the road a burst of laughter reached us as the doors of the Fleece swung inward, and I thought of the deserted green lying in the darkness alongside it. A little tremor of revulsion shook me and I was glad to make my way quickly into the lighted hall behind Beryl and Mrs. Harcourt.

It was a pleasant and sociable evening. Once Beryl

was settled in a chair, with a stool on which to rest her foot and several people to talk to, Mrs. Postlethwaite firmly removed me from her side. "Now, my dear, you don't want to spend your time sitting quietly in a corner, do you? You must meet some of the young people. Harry!" she called to a young man over by the buffet table. "Come here, will you, and introduce —is it Sophie? Such a pretty name!—introduce Sophie to some of your friends. My son," she added to me, somewhat unnecessarily.

Harry, tall, shock-headed and red-cheeked, moved over, a girl clinging to his arm. "Hello." He held out his hand, his eyes frankly appraising. "I, as you'll gather, am Harry Postlethwaite and this is Carol. She teaches at Sunday school, poor child." The girl smiled a little shyly. "My sister Sue is busy being officious with the Camembert, but I'll introduce you to her later. Have you met Jim and Amy Claythorpe?"

I looked at them with interest, wondering if there were any remnant of plain, unfortunate Alice in her progeny. It appeared not, physically at least. Jim Claythorpe, though slightly below average height, was a good-looking man in his early thirties with a mane of reddish brown hair and quick, intelligent brown eyes. It was his wife who was the plain one—small, thin and nondescript, with a discontented droop to her mouth. I had the uncomfortable impression that they'd been on the verge of a private disagreement when Harry had distracted them, and was rather relieved when, after the barest civilities, they moved away and he led me over to another couple.

"And these are our resident librarians, Dick and

Frances Cope." They looked more like brother and sister than husband and wife, both thin, dark and bespectacled. "I might add," Harry went on, "that we're the envy of a lot of the villages round here who have to rely on the mobile library. We owe it to the generosity of the Ashley family, Adam's grandfather, actually."

"Adam?"

"The present incumbent." He nodded his head across the room and I saw that Mrs. Ashley and her husband had just come in. In another corner, Mrs. Briggs, hair waved more ferociously than ever and glasses flashing with enthusiasm, was conversing with a crowd of people whom I recognized as fellow shopkeepers. So much for the classless society, I thought dryly. In a village as old as Pendlemere, social levels were carefully and proudly maintained from both ends of the scale. I also caught sight of Polly, giggling and blushing in a corner with a gangling spotty-faced youth, one of the "lads she was a bit daft about," no doubt.

Behind me a quiet voice said, "I see you're being initiated. Will you be able to remember all these names?"

I looked round to find Graham Lethbridge at my side, and smiled. "I rather doubt it."

"Never mind, everyone will remember yours. We don't see many strange faces in Pendlemere, except when new teachers come to the school and they're soon swallowed up and digested into the common maw, if you'll excuse the somewhat medical metaphor. You must come across to meet my mother

later. I left her talking happily to your aunt." He turned to accept a glass of wine from a tray which Sue Postlethwaite was now offering and stooped even more than usual to catch what she was saying.

"Sophie!" I looked round to see John Phillips making his way through the now quite crowded room. "Hello, I hoped you'd be here! Have you been meeting the local populace?"

"Yes, Harry's introduced me to quite a few people."

"Good. How are you? No more dizzy spells? I wasn't at all happy leaving you to make your way home alone. In fact, I'd have rung to make sure you were all right but you'd said you didn't want to alarm your aunt."

"It was only a few hundred yards, and I'm fine now, thank you."

He took my arm and led me over to the buffet table, giving me swift and sometimes scandalous thumbnail sketches of several of the worthies we passed. "I automatically divide people into two groups," he confided, handing me an empty plate and gesturing for me to go ahead of him to serve myself. "Parents and The Rest. Give me The Rest any day. I have to watch my step with parents in case they feel I'm not a responsible enough person to instruct young Johnnie! Try some of this cheesecake; it's Mrs. Ashley's speciality and a great weakness of mine." He ladled some onto my by now rather full plate. "There are a couple of chairs over there—let's grab them."

We did so, balancing our plates on our knees.

"That's Ringate, my revered Head, across the room now, bowing somewhat obsequiously to the Ashleys." The Headmaster was short and heavily built, with receding hair and a small mustache. "His offspring are at the school, of course," John added, "which naturally doesn't make for an easy life. His daughter particularly is a real horror. One of her charming little ways is to go up to the other kids in the playground and pinch them. When they retaliate, she comes out with the inevitable shriek, 'I'll tell my daddy of you!' The majority, greatly to my regret, back off at once. All very trying but it's not exactly politic to inform one's superior that his child is a potential delinquent! That's Jim Claythorpe he's speaking to now. Have you met him? He's all right— a bit of a lad for the girls, from all accounts, but who can blame him with a wife like that? She really is a dead loss. I can't imagine what Jim ever saw in her, always niggling and complaining. No wonder he seeks consolation elsewhere."

"Perhaps that's the original cause of the complaining?" I suggested from a dutiful sense of feminine loyalty.

"Could be, I suppose, it's the old question of the chicken and the egg. Anyway, they fight like cat and dog and aren't too worried who hears them."

"Have they any children?"

"A little boy of five. He's due to start school after Easter. No doubt that's what Jim's talking to Ringate about. Anyone else I can give you the lowdown on? I suppose you've met our worthy doctor? Vowed to chastity, it would seem, though half the girls in the

village would be only too ready to fill his syringe and disinfect his instruments!"

I laughed. "Jealous? Who does the privilege fall to in the meantime?"

"One Barbara Simpson. She works as his receptionist and is obviously eating her heart out for him."

"Is she here?"

"Too right, she's never far away. Over there, talking to the Copes."

I saw a pale, fair girl, whose long hair was swept attractively into a French pleat. "She looks very pleasant."

"Oh, she is."

"But he's not interested?"

"I doubt if he even knows she's there."

"And what does Harry Postlethwaite do?" I asked, my eyes going back to the vicar's son.

John grinned incorrigibly. "Not a lot! He's always been a wild one and still doesn't seem to show any signs of settling down. I have a theory that basically it's reaction from an overstrict upbringing. The old question of discipline," he grimaced, "never far from a schoolteacher's mind!"

"But he must have a job of some kind, surely?"

"Not so that you'd notice. As long as he has enough cash for a pint or two in the Fleece on a Friday night, he's not bothered. Believe me, he's caused his parents no end of a headache over the last ten years or so."

"Well, well!" I laid my knife and fork down and sat back. "If I ever aspire to writing an English *Peyton*

Place, I shall certainly know where to come for my material!"

He laughed a little shamefacedly. "Sorry, I have been going on rather, haven't I? It's not often I get a chance to let my hair down with someone virtually unconnected with village life. Anyway, what about you? What have you been doing with yourself since I saw you?"

"Not a great deal, really. I'm finding my way round the village by degrees. I walked along by the mere the other day, and home up Whistler's Lane from the other end."

He glanced at me quickly. "I shouldn't make a habit of going that way alone; it's pretty deserted."

I turned to him in surprise. "You're surely not warning me about the ghost? I thought you assured me he never appeared in full daylight!"

"It's not ghosts you have to worry about down there," John said a little grimly.

"What then?"

"Oh—nothing. Just don't make a habit of going there, that's all."

"John, for goodness' sake don't be so mysterious! What—"

"Look, it's nothing. I spoke without thinking. Would you like another piece of French bread? Mary!"

The woman across from us turned, a stick of celery in her hand.

"Pass me the bread plate, there's a love. By the way, this is Sophie Woodburn, who's staying at Cobwebs. Sophie, meet my landlady, Mary Grayson!"

Mrs. Grayson came across and joined us and I had no chance to return to the subject which intrigued me. I had wanted, too, to find out if John could enlighten me on the identity of the man who drove the tractor. His cavalier treatment still rankled.

The meal over, the various groups shifted and reformed. I found myself talking to the little headmaster, Tom Ringate, and his wife Muriel, to the local police constable, tall, red-faced and jovial, and to Mr. and Mrs. Claythorpe senior. To the latter I said cunningly, "I've met your son and daughter-in-law, and the Graysons and the Sickleburys, but so far no one from Starling's, at the bottom of the Lane. Are they represented here too?"

A swift, warning glance passed between them. "No," Mr. Claythorpe answered after a moment, "the Starlings keep very much to themselves, and that suits the rest of us."

"Oh?" I waited but no further explanation was apparently forthcoming. "I walked that way the other day," I persisted hopefully, "and a man on a tractor passed me. Who would he be?"

Again the wary glance between husband and wife. "What did he look like?" Mrs. Claythorpe asked a little nervously.

"He was big and very dark, and not exactly friendly."

"Aye, that's him. Ben Starling himself." Mr. Claythorpe might possibly have been going to elaborate on the statement, but his wife touched his arm quickly and he glanced over his shoulder and lowered his voice. "I shouldn't mention him in the Ash-

93

leys' hearing if I were you. There's—bad feeling between them."

"Oh. Thank you." More mystified than ever, I answered Mrs. Ashley's approaching smile and the Claythorpes, seemingly glad to escape from my ingenuous questions, moved quickly away.

"Miss Woodburn, may I introduce my husband? Adam, this is—"

"Sophie," I put in quickly. Adam Ashley smiled and took my hand.

"Delighted to meet you, Sophie. I've just been having a fascinating conversation with your aunt on, of all things, Byzantine art!"

"She's very knowledgeable," I said with a smile.

His wife laughed. "She'd need to be, to keep up with Adam. It's one of his hobbyhorses. Well, Sophie, what do you think of our village? Did you get a look at the stocks the other day?"

"I—no, I didn't actually. I will though, when I get the chance."

"I bumped into her outside Jackson's," she explained to her husband, "and suggested she might like to walk up by the green."

"I presume you mean outside Blackburn's?" Their voices needled against my eardrums like darting mosquitoes. Jackson's—of course, the fish shop. No wonder Blackburn's had sounded so blessedly unfamiliar.

Mrs. Ashley was saying, "What? Oh, Blackburn's, then. I never remember."

"Of course not. After all, it only changed hands five years ago!" Adam Ashley smiled at me. "My wife is

a die-hard conservative. She refuses pointblank to move with the times!"

"That," she replied with dignity, "is because at heart I'm a historian. Have you heard any of our local history, Sophie? We've an abundance of it. If you're interested, you should drop into the library and ask the Copes for the relevant books."

"As a matter of fact I am very interested. I'm just finishing some research I've been doing on Jacobean England and of course that touched on the Lancashire witches and all the associations round Pendle. I'm determined to fit in a visit to all the famous places before I go back to London."

"I'll come with you," Rowan Ashley said promptly. "I've not been for several years myself."

"You know, of course, that we have our own local ghost?" Adam put in in his dry voice.

"Yes indeed, I was hearing all about him. Most lurid! It was fascinating just now to meet the Claythorpes, a direct link with the legend."

"Most of the local families have lived here for generations. I often think that if our ancestors could come back and have a look at the Parish Register they'd recognize nearly all the names. I must admit it gives one a comforting feeling of continuity."

"Now who's being reactionary?" Rowan demanded. "Anyway, Sophie, we were just telling your aunt you must both come round one evening. She and Adam can discourse on Byzantium while we stick with rather more recent history."

"I'm sure we'd love to, thank you. And that reminds me, I really must go over and see how Beryl's

getting on. I haven't seen her since we first arrived."

Fortunately, Beryl had been quite enjoying herself, and introduced me to old Mrs. Lethbridge, a fragile, grey-haired woman in her seventies. "Adam Ashley has some fascinating books on art, he was telling me. He said we must go round sometime and have a look at them."

Mrs. Harcourt leaned over us. "The evening's finishing now, so I can take you home any time you're ready."

"Actually," Beryl said with alacrity, "I'm ready now. I'm getting quite stiff with sitting so long in one place, and I'm not sufficiently well padded to be really comfortable on this wooden chair!" Rather guiltily I helped her up and we made our good-byes and followed Mrs. Harcourt out to the car. As I settled myself against the cushions, my mind was revolving round the people I had met and the scraps of gossip John had so willingly given me on everyone I asked about—except one.

I said casually, "I gather the Starling farm crowd don't join much in village life?"

"No." Phyllis Harcourt concentrated on getting the car back onto the road. It was closing time at the Fleece and there were quite a lot of people milling about. I was afraid the distraction had put an end to the conversation, but once we were moving down the High Street she went on, "They seem to be a closed community down there. In fact I've only ever seen Ben Starling once and can't say I have any wish to repeat the experience. Those dark, brooding eyes sent a shiver up my spine—a veritable Heathcliff of a man!"

Yes, I thought silently, it was an apt description, though I doubted if there was any gypsy blood in Ben Starling. And the word "gypsy" set different speculations moving round my head, but by then we were already drawing up outside Cobwebs. Mrs. Harcourt, despite my protest, insisted on helping Beryl up the path and brushed away our thanks.

"Any time you need a lift, don't hesitate to ask. It's no trouble. So pleased to have met you!" And with a wave of her hand she was gone.

Beryl said briskly, "Well, I don't know about you, but all that wine has made me thirsty. Be a lamb and bring me up a mug of hot milk, and then you can tell me how you enjoyed your evening. That young schoolmaster seemed quite attentive."

"He was quite informative, too!" She shook her head to my offer of help and, leaning on the banister, managed the stairs reasonably well. As Graham Lethbridge had predicted, her ankle was now improving rapidly. As long as she was careful, there would be nothing to keep me in Pendlemere after another week or so.

In the kitchen Lottie mutely demanded her evening walk and was most indignant when I merely pushed her out of the back door into the garden. I boiled Beryl's milk, added some cocoa to my own and let Lottie back inside. Reproachfully she slunk straight to her basket. I checked the locks on both doors, turned off the lights and followed Beryl upstairs. She was already in bed, her face shining from its recent scrubbing, the orange bed jacket round her shoulders.

"Now," she said, patting the bed invitingly, "spill

97

the beans! My conversation was all most correct in deference to Mrs. Lethbridge's ancient ears. I have a feeling yours was more interesting."

I smiled and sipped at the milk. "What do you want to know? I rather suspect that John's comments were exaggerated, not to say slanderous, but for what it's worth, the young Claythorpes lead a bickering existence generally attributed to his attentions elsewhere—happy marriages don't seem to run in that family—the vicar's son hasn't finished sowing his wild oats yet, and half the village is in love with the doctor!"

Beryl gave a bark of laughter. "Not bad for starters! I'm not surprised about Graham Lethbridge, anyway. That gaunt, hollow-cheeked look has a way of bringing out the maternal instinct."

"John reckons his receptionist has first claim, but he doesn't hold out much hope for her!"

"Well, I must say I've learned more about my fellow villagers in the last five minutes than I had in the preceding five weeks! I thought Pendlemere was such a quiet, respectable place!" Her keen eyes came back to my face. "There's something else, though, isn't there?"

I said flatly, "I discovered why I didn't recognize the name Blackburn's. It's only been there for the last five years."

"The fish shop? What was it before?"

"Jackson's."

"And that did seem familiar?" I nodded. "Well, that helps a little in dating your time switch. I wonder how long Jackson's was there."

I stood up and put my empty mug on the table. "Actually," I said tightly, "it doesn't help much. I'd already realized my memory must be at least eight years old, if that was when Cobwebs was converted. When I knew it, the sitting room was much smaller and there was a door under the archway."

"When you knew it?" Beryl repeated, and gave a little shiver. I met her eyes for a moment as my brain cringingly tried to analyze the words which had come so naturally, and then shuddered away from the explanation.

"Good night," I said abruptly, and left her. As I undressed in the room across the landing, I wondered half fearfully whether it was that same sense of familiarity which made me feel so much at home in Pendlemere, and once again my rational mind forcibly rejected the idea. At home, when the village green held some nameless terror for me, when Whistler's Lane was alive with impressions and emotions that buffeted me mercilessly, when I was inexplicably warned not to go alone down Starling's Way? And I thought of Ben Starling, grim and unsmiling, passing close by me without a turn of his head. At least I now knew that I was not the only one he treated in that way. "A veritable Heathcliff of a man."

I was aware suddenly that my bare feet were cold and a draught played across my shoulders. Quickly I climbed into bed and pulled the blankets up to my chin. London was where I belonged, with or without Jake Petersen, and it would be as well not to lose sight of the fact.

chapter
❧6❧

WE awoke the next morning to leaden skies and a thin, persistent drizzle of rain. With nothing to tempt me outside, I set out my reference books and worked solidly for three hours in my bedroom, until, in fact, a delicious smell of roast beef wafted upstairs and reminded me both of the time and my own neglect of duties.

Beryl, hobbling cheerfully round the kitchen with an improvised crutch under her arm, discounted my guilty apologies. "Nonsense. Of course you have work to do and I've thoroughly enjoyed pottering round. First time I've been able to contemplate it for over ten days. I reckon the ankle's almost as good as new again, but I'm not taking any chances. There's a sherry poured for you on the sitting-room mantelpiece. Go and sit down with the papers for half an hour. I can see to lunch quite comfortably."

Since she was determined to establish her independence, I did as she directed. It seemed barely credible that it was only a week since Jake and I had

lounged about the London flat with no inkling of the change in our lives the next morning's post would bring about. A letter from a stranger . . .

By the time we had finished our meal and I, to salve my conscience, had insisted on washing the dishes, the rain had eased off and a watery pale gold sunshine began to filter through the clouds. I stood at the window and stretched inelegantly.

"After that big meal and a morning poring over books, I feel in need of some fresh air. I think I'll take Lottie out for an hour or so and we can both work off some steam."

"Good-o. I'll put my feet up and have a snooze. I'm quite tired after all our socializing last night; out of practice, obviously. But I should go prepared for the rain to come back; it doesn't look too settled to me."

I borrowed a pair of her boots, since life in London only called for the fashion variety and anyway I hadn't brought any with me. They were rather too big but at least they would protect my feet and legs from the muddy crevices and puddles.

I had reached the gate before I realized my rather limited scope for a walk. Every morning I had set off along Tanner's Lane and I felt like a change, but the only alternative in the immediate vicinity was Whistler's Lane. What was more, I was extremely reluctant to walk up to the top of it since that would bring me within reach of the green, and if John were to be heeded, it was apparently, and equally mysteriously, unwise to venture alone to the bottom. It seemed that Lottie's walk must be within prescribed boundaries, and she was not fond of the Lane anyway. I saw

101

her tail plummet and ears droop dejectedly as I turned in that direction.

"It's this or nothing," I told her briskly. "You'll have to make the most of it. I've brought your ball, so we can have a game with it."

The magic word "ball" revived her spirits a little and she trotted complacently enough over the bridge beside me. "We'll go up as far as Claythorpe's boundary," I continued, crystalizing my own intention, "and on the way we can explore the tracks leading off to some of the other farms." It was in my mind that we might possibly meet John Phillips, and his company would have been welcome on this still rather overcast afternoon. Luck, however, was not with me on that score. Lottie and I made our leisurely progress up the Lane, I throwing the ball along the path as often as possible since the long grasses on either side were still drenched and rain-laden, and she skittering along after it, ears flying in the breeze of her movement. We set off along one of the promising-looking tracks to the right, but once we'd rounded a bend, the farm gates were disappointingly close and we had to turn back. All too soon, since my intention had largely been to fill in time, we had reached the lower wall of Claythorpe's farmyard and I dared go no further in that direction.

"So now," I told Lottie, feeling rather like Alice Through the Looking-Glass, "we go as far as we can in the other direction." She wagged her tail amiably and I thought with relief that the normality of the ball game appeared to have dispelled her usual disquiet in Whistler's Lane. Cobwebs loomed on our

right and she turned inquiringly to see if we were going back over the bridge, but when I shook my head trotted on quite happily, apparently content to prolong the outing. Below Cobwebs there were no more farms with access to the Lane before Starling's down at the bottom. Yet again I found myself thinking of Ben, with his stony, unyielding face, and wondered why he was apparently at loggerheads with the rest of the village. From the Claythorpes' comments, it seemed I should not inquire of the Ashleys, and they themselves, like John, had clearly been unwilling to discuss the matter.

Lottie returned from her quest in the grass and jumped up at me, begging for another game of ball. I started to throw it, lost my balance slightly, and instead of a smooth flight along the footpath, the ball arched over the long grass and with a distant but unmistakable plop landed in the stream below.

"Damn!" I said under my breath. Lottie had gone flying after it, and I could imagine that the long, feathery fur of her under parts would need a good rub, if not a wash, when we reached home. I called her but she was not to be distracted. There was no help for it but to make my way through the sodden undergrowth and fish the ball out of the water. Fortunate indeed that I was wearing Beryl's boots. Gingerly I swished through the almost knee-high grass to where the dog, yapping excitedly, was jumping up and down on the bank while the ball bobbed tantalizingly just out of reach. The trouble was that, swollen with the overnight rain, the stream was a little wider than usual and as my fingers touched the cold wet

rubber, the ball spun infuriatingly further over to the other side.

"Oh, hush, Lottie!" I said irritably, in an attempt to quieten the now almost hysterical barking. "I'll have to wade in and get it. At least it will test the boots' seaworthiness."

I lowered one foot into the water. It seemed to sink in an alarmingly long way and the soft mud at the bottom felt far from firm. With even more reluctance I tested the other foot and began to move cautiously after the ball which, in the ripples caused by my descent, had now gaily started to float downstream. I bent over to retrieve it before the whole thing got out of hand, seeing the circle of my face clearly reflected in the moving water. And, suddenly, another face as well.

I looked up so sharply that I teetered for a moment, my feet treading the mud and clouding the dual reflection. On the bank of the stream stood a girl in trousers and a short white mackintosh. For a moment we stared at each other. She looked vaguely familiar with her large grey eyes and rich chestnut hair which, damp now, hung about her shoulders. Perhaps she had been among the people at the hall the previous night to whom I had not been introduced. I was about to mention the possibility when the dawning recognition on her own face froze, to be replaced, incredibly, by fear. One hand went up to her throat, but her eyes never left mine.

"You again!" she said in a low, unsteady voice. "What is it that you want?"

"I was getting the dog's ball," I faltered stupidly,

but she did not seem to hear. Her eyes were moving slowly over me and a frown had appeared on her face.

"You're dressed differently," she said almost accusingly.

"Well, of course! I'd hardly—"

"And you're older. I can't see through you this time."

I stared at her, a slow, creeping suspicion stealing up the small of my back like the prickle of icicles. I said rockily, and it was suddenly, appallingly, true: "But I can see through you!"

The effect on her was immediate. She said sharply, "Nonsense, it's *you* who—" And then, looking down at herself, an expression of total, indescribable horror spread across her face. "Oh my God!" she said, on a high, shrill note of terror. "I remember now! Does that mean—?" Her whole being shuddered violently, as though a stone had been thrown into a reflected image in the water, and then, sickeningly, there was only the long wet grass.

With numb icy fingers still clutching the slippery ball, I floundered out of the stream, skidding and sliding on the bank, and, with the heart-stopping idea that some trace of her might remain, that I might unknowingly be walking *through* her, I swerved violently. Sobbing now with reaction and terror, I came at last back onto the path of the Lane. Lottie's hysterical barking had given way to a series of short, agonized yelps and I looked frantically round for her.

"Lottie!" I tried to call but the word came out a croak. Then I saw her, her quivering body pressed

105

down into the grass on the other side of the Lane as though seeking the only concealment offered. I put my hand down to her but she recoiled abruptly, flecks of foam spinning from her mouth.

"It's me, Lottie," I shuddered. "Let's go home." And, able to rein myself in no longer, I started, with legs as helpless as flower stems, to run shamblingly in the flapping, too-big boots toward the bridge. I didn't even turn to see if she was following, but her adrenalin appeared to work better than mine, for a moment later she shot past me, short legs bunched for speed, giving me as wide a berth as possible. She was waiting, trembling, for me to open the gate, though her eyes rolled wildly and she cringed down as though to avoid any contact with me.

Gasping and choking from our headlong flight, we went up the path and into the house. Once inside, all strength left me and I stood idiotically knowing I should remove the muddy boots before taking another step but totally unable to summon the right muscles to respond to the brain impulse. Lottie, with no such inhibitions, shot like a streak of lightning down the hall and straight into her basket.

Beryl's voice called, "Well-timed; the kettle's on! I've only just woken up. Did you have a good walk?"

Still, through unmeasurable seconds, I stood there. There was a sudden, apprehensive shuffling and she appeared in the archway.

"Sophie!" The word seemed wrung out of her. "Come in here, for pity's sake." She hobbled toward me, clutched my arm and started to propel me toward the sitting room.

106

"Boots," I mumbled inanely, pulling back.

"To hell with the boots!" A moment later she had pushed me onto the sofa in her own place, boots and all. Limp as a bundle of rags, I just lay there and after a minute she bent and pulled off one heavy boot and then the other and eased the cold, slimy ball from the convulsive grip of my clenched hand. My mouth was slack and incapable of forming speech.

"Hot, sweet tea—good for shock." She almost hopped from the room in her haste and the next thing I knew she was bending over me holding a cup to my lips. "Come on, poppet, drink up, there's a good girl."

Obediently, mindlessly, I took too large a gulp and the nearly boiling liquid ripped over my tongue and seared its way down my throat. The pain was welcome, since it restored feeling at last. I bent stiff cold hands round the cup, drawing the heat into my frozen palms, and then the trembling started and Beryl hastily took the cup away before the scalding liquid spilled over me. She limped into the hall, moved the model ship and opened the oak settle, then came quickly back with a thick tartan traveling rug over her arm. This she proceeded to wrap as tightly as possible over me, while I concentrated on trying to still the violent, agonizing chattering of my teeth. Almost frenziedly she threw a couple more logs on the already blazing fire and pushed ineffectually against the sofa to move it nearer. Beneath the rug the damp mackintosh clung clammily to my skin and my hands, imprisoned in the confines of the rug, fluttered helplessly.

"Can you speak yet, or shall I phone the doctor?"

Experimentally I tried to shake my head and discovered that I could. Like a released dam the torrent of words gushed past my lips, incoherent and confused, leaving her frowning in perplexity. I forced myself to stop, draw a deep, painful breath and start again more lucidly.

"What was so unbelievably awful," I repeated, once the story was more or less told, "was the look on her face when she realized that—when she discovered it was she who—"

"Yes," Beryl said quietly, "I understand."

Suddenly I was unbearably hot. I fought my way almost desperately out of the rug and it dropped to the floor while I tugged at the buttons of the mack and pulled it off too. Sweat began to pour enervatingly down my body and my hair clung wetly to my scalp. I said violently, "That, without doubt, was the most horrible experience of my life, even worse than the fear I felt on the green. The look on her face—"

"That's enough, now. Sit up and drink your tea."

"It'll make me even hotter."

"Never mind, it will steady you."

Meekly I drank it. She refilled the cup and I drank that too. "Why me?" I demanded suddenly. "Why should all this happen to me? Who was she, for heaven's sake?"

"I've no idea, but I sure as hell intend to find out."

"She looked so *real*, so solid at first. She was dressed more or less as I was, in mack and trews, and the incredible thing is that she seemed so familiar.

108

She recognized me, too. She said, 'You again!' But I don't know anyone like that and it's no use saying it was in some previous incarnation because obviously it couldn't have been—she was very much of our own time. And why should I see her, when everyone else only speaks of the Whistler? What possible connection could she have with me?"

I stopped as something occurred to me. "Beryl, didn't you say our family came from somewhere round here?"

She nodded. I noticed for the first time that she looked pale and shaken and made an additional effort to speak rationally. "How do you know?"

"It was in the old family Bible. I haven't opened it for years, but I do remember reading some of the marriage entries once. 'In the county of Lancaster' stuck in my mind."

"Where is it now?"

"The Bible? Goodness knows. I haven't seen it since the move. Wait a moment, though. There was something under the rug in the settle just now."

"I'll get it." I swung my feet to the floor and stood up, waiting till the wave of dizziness that the rapid movement brought had cleared. Away from the direct heat of the fire I was shivering again. I lifted the heavy lid of the settle and knelt down, feeling inside it. My fingers touched something large and heavy and slid round to a brass clasp. A smell of dusty old leather seeped into my nostrils and I sneezed.

"Here it is!" I carried it back and laid it triumphantly on the sofa, dropping down on the rug in front of it partly to see the book more clearly and

partly to allow the blazing fire to warm my chilled back. Inside, the writing was squiggly and badly faded. A stain had spread across one page, possibly caused by damp. Together, Beryl perched on the arm of the sofa above me, we tried to decipher it.

"The earliest legible entry seems to be around eighteen hundred," I said after a moment. "William George Howarth, born at Morecambe in the County of Lancaster 30th September 1799. You were right about Lancaster, anyway. And on this side, Isabella Robertson, born at Kendal in the county of Westmorland, 28th November 1802. Married at St. Margaret's Church, Kendal, 18th December 1820. She was eighteen, like you were. I can't see any other link, though."

"Turn over the page," Beryl instructed. "Ah, these entries are a bit more abbreviated. They just trace the family line, without any details about whom they married. I suppose the first couple started the Bible, which is why they had a page to themselves. All their children have to share this one."

"Isabella Jane Howarth," I read aloud, "born at etc., etc., 1821, married Robert Henry Anderson 1841, died October 1842. Oh, how dreadful! It was probably in childbirth." I flicked over a page. "Yes, here it is: George Henry Anderson born October 1842, married Abigail Ashley March 1865, died—"

I looked up suddenly. "Ashley! Look!" Excitement came into my voice. "George Henry Anderson married Abigail Ashley 4th March 1865 at St. Botolph's Church, Clitheroe, in the County of Lancaster. Beryl, imagine that! We might be distantly related to

the Ashleys! I wonder if there are any other branches of the family round here?"

"Even if there are, I imagine they'll all be connected. It's an interesting possibility, but I don't think it helps us much. I can't imagine why any ancestor we might conceivably share with the Ashleys should want to bring you back here."

"No." I closed the old book carefully and smoothed my hand over the intricately cut binding. Somehow I had thought some clue to the whole affair might be contained in it, but apparently I had been mistaken. I stood up, folded the traveling rug and took it and the Bible back to the oak settle and replaced the model ship on top. As I turned from doing so, the telephone just across the hall shrilled sharply. My shredded nerves reacted out of all proportion, but I was relieved that my voice sounded quite normal as I replied.

"Sophie? It's John Phillips. I've just surfaced from correcting a sheaf of exam papers and I'm in need of a little sparkling company! I see from the local rag there's quite a decent film on in Clitheroe. Would you like to come? We could have a bite of supper afterwards."

"Oh, John, I would!" The thought of his normal, gossip-spiced conversation was balm after the experience of the afternoon.

"Fine, I'll pick you up in about an hour. We can see an early performance and then go somewhere to eat."

"You don't mind?" I asked Beryl rather belatedly as I replaced the receiver.

111

"Of course not—do you good to have some young company."

"You—won't worry about what happened?"

"I'll try not to think about it. Did I mention that I phoned Madame Zelda when you were out yesterday morning? She's made an appointment for us for Tuesday afternoon. It's a great relief. I can unload all these worries onto her. She's better equipped to cope with them."

"I suppose so." I was still not enamored of the idea of visiting a medium, but perhaps Beryl was right and she might be able to help. "I think I'll have a leisurely bath and then get ready to go out." The abnormal coldness had left me now as had the alternating waves of intense warmth, but a soak in soothing hot water might restore my mind as well as my body, and Beryl's strained face was certainly not conducive to regaining a more balanced outlook on what had occurred.

I leaned over the bath to sprinkle in a sachet of bath salts and the movement of the water brought an unwelcome return of the pale disc of the girl's face in the stream, my first glimpse of her. I tried to blot out the memory of the whole episode but her face was clearly etched on my brain, a lovely face in that first instant before fear had marred it—large grey eyes with lustrous lashes, a small, tip-tilted nose, full passionate mouth, all framed by the rich nut-brown hair. I knew it almost as well as my own, I thought despairingly.

"You're older," she had said. Older than what, than whom? And again the faint flutter of that ten-year-

112

old memory, instantly succumbing to the censorship of my brain. Old enough anyway in my knowledge of Pendlemere to remember the fish shop which five years ago had sold out to Blackburn's, and Cobwebs in the days when a door had closed under the archway and an old hatstand stood in the hall.

I stepped quickly into the still too hot water and sat down, watching the pinkness spread over my skin. Obviously the girl, whoever she might be, was a vital part of that unaccountable memory. Perhaps that was how the house and village had been when she knew them? Yet there was still no conceivable link with myself. With a little exclamation of dismissal I reached for the soap.

John was casual in cravat and sweater and as I settled beside him in the car, my fears fell away to a large extent and I prepared to enjoy the evening ahead. I had not been to Clitheroe before and he chatted interestingly about its long and eventful history, pointing out the shell of the old castle skeletoned against the cloudy sky and the park below splattered now like an artist's palette with the riotous colors of spring flowers.

"There's not much left of the castle, as you can see, but there's still a breath-taking view from up there on a clear day. The de Laceys who built it certainly made sure they would never be taken by surprise. You should look round the church sometime, too, it's a real treasure-trove. There's a brass engraved with the horoscope of John Webster, for instance, who was headmaster of the grammar school and an astrologer during the witch-hunting days."

113

"You can't get away from witches round here, can you?" I remarked with a superstitious little shiver.

"Not with Pendle glowering only three or four miles away! I doubt whether it bothers the present inhabitants much, though. To most of them Clitheroe is just a pleasant little market town with a fair bit of cotton manufacturing going on as well." He drew in to a carpark across the road from the cinema. "Right, this will do us very nicely. Let's hope the rain keeps off. I haven't brought a mack."

The film we had come to see was a comedy, which suited me very well, and every time that my mind wandered to less pleasant topics, I painstakingly brought it back to the screen. After a while John reached for my hand and I let it lie passively in his. If the gypsy hadn't come, if, somehow, the mere fact of her not coming had been able to cancel out all that had already happened, such as Beryl's accident, would I now, as last week, have been sitting back in the London flat with Jake's arm flung carelessly along the back of the sofa behind me?

In the vicious onslaught of pain which without warning leaped out at me I instinctively tightened my grip on John's hand, almost immediately releasing it as the quick turn of his head made me aware of my action. But the misery of severance from Jake, total now, as I well knew, was not banished as easily as less tangible problems. Quite suddenly I ached for him in a hopeless void of loneliness, longing for the feel of his thick, springy hair, for the dimple in his chin, even for the quick, easily roused irritability which could chase suddenly across his face. I craved

114

the smell of him, compounded of tobacco smoke and wet tweed and the faint spiciness of after-shave, for the sound of him, with his quick probes and occasional gentle teasing, and all my senses flailed me simultaneously with a combined torture of bereavement which left me weak and gasping. John mistook the small, choked sound I made for mirth, and whispered enthusiastically, "They make a marvelous team, don't they? I'm so glad I discovered this was on."

By the time we left the cinema, I had only a very dim idea of what the film was about, but a precarious control had been regained. It was dark by now, with rain blowing in the wind. I remembered the proximity of Pendle Hill and shivered. We drove out of the town for a short distance and stopped at a roadside restaurant which, John told me, was a well-known local landmark for good though unpretentious food. Unfortunately the large lunch I had eaten at midday, followed by the shattering experience in Whistler's Lane, had left me with little appetite.

John brushed aside my apologies and I could only hope that not too large a proportion of his hard-earned salary would metaphorically find its way into the bin with the food remaining on my plate. Several times as we idly discussed the people we had been with the previous evening, I tried to steer my way round to inquiring about Ben Starling, but whether John was aware of my intention and adroitly steered me away from it, or whether my traumatic day had simply robbed me of subtlety, I was not sure. In any event, the name was not permitted to intrude in our

115

conversation and yet another riddle therefore remained unsolved.

"If you're sure you don't want any more coffee, I suppose we might as well be making a move," he said at last. "Wrap your coat round you, it's pretty chilly now." He took my arm and guided me through the darkness to the outline of the car. "Okay?"

"Yes, fine." I settled back in the seat, trying to anchor my irresponsible thoughts to safer matters. Beside me John was equally silent as he drove expertly through the twisting roads until we came to the top of Pendlemere High Street, with the church on one side and the impenetrable darkness of the green on the other. At the end of Tanner's Lane outside Cobwebs he made a U-turn and drew up at the gate.

I fumbled in the darkness for handbag and gloves. "Thank you for a lovely evening," I said dutifully. "I did enjoy it."

"Good; so did I." He turned toward me and put his arm rather tentatively along the back of the seat. "I'd better say good night, then."

"Good night, John." I knew I should move quickly, but was suddenly incapable of it. Slowly, still not quite sure what my reaction would be, he bent his head and his lips brushed against mine. I don't know quite what happened then, whether it was an upsurge of the longing for Jake I had been trying to obliterate or simply a desperate need, here in this shadowed place, for the comforting proximity of a warm human body. Whatever the reason, almost without thinking, I reached up quickly and dragged his mouth forcibly back to mine, turning what had

116

been a light, questioning kiss into an unexpectedly passionate embrace. His response was immediate. I felt his arms close round me and in exultant selfishness I continued to cling to him, draining my need and reassurance from him as an alcoholic might from a bottle of raw spirit.

At last shortage of breath forced us apart and as I dazedly moved my head aside I felt his lips, warm and searching, on my neck and throat. I drew back a little and he gave an unsteady laugh. "God, Sophie, you seemed such a quiet little thing! I never imagined—" His shaking fingers were fumbling at the buttons of my coat. Gently I pushed them away and sat upright.

"I'm sorry, John, I don't know—"

"Lord, don't apologize! It was wonderful! I just—"

"I must go in now."

He moved protestingly, reaching out for me again. "Oh, now look, you can't just—"

"I'm sorry," I said rapidly, "I have to."

"But hell's teeth, after—"

"I know, I'm very sorry. I—" Desperately searching in my mind for a reasonable excuse, I said the one thing which was totally unforgivable. "I was—thinking of someone else."

There was a tense, brittle silence. Then he said stiffly, "I see."

Too late, I realized what I had done. Close to tears now, I repeated frantically, "John, I'm sorry. I didn't really—"

"Don't mention it." Still the cold, bitter humiliation. "Glad to have been of service!"

"That's vile!" I flung at him, and at last the car

117

handle gave way to my frantic clawing. I half fell out and set off at a run up the path of Cobwebs. I need not have hurried; he made no move to follow me. At the door, with sanctuary within reach, I turned and gave a small wave in the direction of the car. There was no acknowledgment and after a moment I pulled the door shut and stood inside, listening. It was some moments before I heard the engine start up and the car move away.

chapter
❧7❧

ALTHOUGH it was only a week since I had arrived in Pendlemere, it was by now so deeply etched into me that apart from the still acute loss of Jake, it was hard to cast my mind back to that other life in London. However, one pressing reminder of it existed in the batch of work I was engaged on for Dr. Carruthers, which still needed a few hours spending on it. Since Beryl was once again moving fairly freely about the house, I was relieved to accept her assurance that she could manage without my ministrations and settle down to work. The recurring memory of my parting from John suffused me with a hot wave of shame and I was not sorry that my preoccupation with work would that day allow me to go no further afield than the post office in Tanner's Lane.

With an effort I put such distractions behind me and became engrossed in my papers. In fact, it all took longer than I had expected and it was almost four by the time I took the completed package along to the post. A milky sunshine was spilling onto Tan-

ner's Lane, sheening the pools of water which still lay
after yesterday's rain into stretches of pale, rippled
silk and intensifying the colors of the flowers in the
cottage gardens. The air was fresh-washed and new,
with an underlying smell of wet earth and at my side
Lottie, her suspicions of yesterday mercifully forgotten, trotted briskly.

"Enjoy the social, did you?" Mrs. Briggs inquired
amiably, franking the parcel I handed her. "I saw you
hobnobbing with that young schoolmaster. Nice lad,
by all accounts." The sun reflected in her glasses
made them into miniature mirrors and I couldn't
read the expression behind them. "Your auntie's
looking more perky, too. I said to Polly as there'll be
nowt much to keep you after the next few days."

"Possibly not," I prevaricated, "but I don't want
her to try to do too much at once." Only when I was
outside again did I define my reaction. A week ago
it would have been impossible to imagine this feeling
of reluctance at the prospect of leaving Pendlemere.

That evening, to counteract it, I tried without success to phone Jake. It was no surprise when the
phone at the flat rang unanswered, since he had told
me he was moving back to the University while I was
away, but he was not in his rooms there either. Perhaps he had already taken up more congenial accom-
modation.

"We'll have an early lunch tomorrow," Beryl said
over dinner. "It's not much more than an hour or so
on the bus to Downhurst." She flashed me a darting
glance. "You're not apprehensive about the séance,
are you, poppet? There's no need to be. Madame

Zelda has a most comforting aura about her. I know you'll feel quite at home with her."

"I hope so," I said resignedly, and added with a touch of skepticism I tried to cloak with innocence, "Perhaps Peter will be more forthcoming about why he wanted you to come up here."

To my relief she took my remark at face value. "I certainly hope so. I'm afraid Madame hadn't much for me last time. Not her fault, of course; it's something that you just have to accept. Often people make long journeys to see mediums only to be disappointed. There's no guarantee attached to making an appointment and you can hardly ask for your money back if you're not satisfied. In fact, the occasions when Mrs. Prendergast down in Kent didn't manage to establish a contact seemed to tire her more than when she did." Another quick look in my direction. "Perhaps I should warn you that Madame Zelda has a 'guide,' a red Indian called Silver Cloud."

"A guide?" I repeated blankly.

"Someone through whom she works," Beryl explained. "You can't just tune in at random and hope for the best."

"I didn't know I'd be expected to play cowboys and Indians," I said lightly.

"And you can leave that attitude at home, my girl. There's nothing so negative as facetiousness. Whatever you may feel inside, do try to leave your mind open. If you don't, the whole business will be pointless, and don't forget this visit is really for your sake, not mine."

I shopped as usual the next morning and wondered

121

what the reaction of the solid, down-to-earth people would be if they knew how I should be passing the afternoon. To be honest, my own reaction was not far removed from their hypothetical one. I wished Jake were available to share the joke, because that was how it was beginning to appear to me. That three grown women should solemnly sit round a table trying to conjure up the spirit of a man who had died thirty years ago seemed too ludicrous even to be macabre. At least it would be a new experience, one which, safely back in London, my brain underlined carefully, I could laugh over with my friends.

This attitude cushioned me against apprehension throughout the bus journey along densely wooded valleys and high moorland roads, and may have continued to be my salvation had Madame Zelda been the flamboyant medium I had subconsciously expected. In fact, her house turned out to be one half of an unprepossessing semi-detached just along the road from the bus stop, with a child's tricycle in the garden. It would have been hard to find a more ordinary place. She opened the door to us herself, a small, thin woman with a rather shy smile, and the presumed owner of the tricycle, a rosy-faced four-year-old, clung to her hand.

"Off you go then, love," she told him, adding for our benefit, "this is Tommy, my grandson. Straight back to your Mum now, like a good boy." She acknowledged Beryl's introduction of me a little absently, her eyes on the child until he was safely across the road and apparently cycling in the right direction. Then she gestured us into the hall and shut the door.

"Been having an accident, have you, Mrs. Latimer? That'll never do!"

"It's almost better now," Beryl murmured. "My niece came up from London to look after me and since her arrival she's been having some experiences which I think will interest you."

We had been directed into the back room of the house, a plain, homely room obviously doubling as the family dining room. An overlarge sideboard took up more than its share of floor space along one wall and there were framed photographs on the mantelpiece. Impossible to believe that this ordinary little grandmother believed herself to be in contact with dead red Indians! I was almost inclined to think that Beryl had been making that bit up, but the quiet, businesslike way that Madame Zelda was now preparing the room for its more doubtful usage overrode this comforting idea. She drew a small round table into the space between dining table and fireplace and covered it with a green cloth, chatting easily about her family as she did so. It occurred to me suddenly that she was deliberately putting me at my ease, and contrarily I felt the first tremor of apprehension.

"Now, Miss Woodburn, love, I'm going to draw the curtains. Not to make the place spooky or anything soft like that, but just because it's easier to concentrate when I'm not being continually reminded that the grass needs cutting!"

The heavy rust serge swung over the windows and my heart fluttered foolishly at the base of my throat.

"Now, if you'll sit there, opposite me, with your auntie to your right, we'll see what we can find out.

123

Just relax and sit with your hands loosely clasped together on the table. That's it."

"It really started the day she arrived," Beryl began, but Madame Zelda held up a restraining hand.

"I'd like it in her own words if you don't mind, love."

So, haltingly, I began to speak; firstly of the gypsy's visit in London, then of my unexplained recognition of Pendlemere when Jake and I first approached it; of the extreme terror I had experienced on the green, the time slip which had transported me to the gate in the wall, and lastly of the—materialization could be the only word—of the girl in Whistler's Lane. And Madame Zelda sat silently listening, her head nodding from time to time but forbearing to prompt me even when I hesitated, as I did increasingly. I was becoming aware of a heaviness coming over me, weighting down my eyelids, and it was an effort to keep talking. The bus drive must have tired me, I thought confusedly.

Madame Zelda began to ask questions at last, her quiet voice more like an internal jogging of memory than outside stimulation, and I tried to concentrate on what she was saying, but there was a strange, rumbling sound in my ears like the distant thunder of an approaching storm. I shook my head to clear it and the rumbling resolved itself into the murmuring of a vast crowd and some element latent in it triggered my heart to a frenziedly rapid beating. I tried to lift my hands from the table but was powerless to move them. To blot out the crescendo of sound, I

124

abandoned the disjointed remarks I had been making and instead began to recite the words which were jostling in my head, demanding to be spoken.

". . . did feloniously practise and use her devilish and wicked arts, called witchcrafts, enchantments, charms and sorceries, in and upon Richard Whitaker . . . contra pacem Domini Regis, Coronam et Dignitatem suas."

I don't remember any more. Wave after wave passed over me. I think I continued to speak for some time. At last, like coming out of a deep sleep, my eyes focused once more on the quiet room and the tense faces across the table from me.

"Sophie?" Beryl's voice was shaking. Madame Zelda laid a restraining hand quickly on hers. I noticed with rising alarm that she too was trembling.

"What—what happened?" I demanded.

"I think we got our wires crossed somewhere!" Beryl said with an attempt at lightness, but her face was shining whitely in the dimness.

I moistened my lips. "Please tell me what happened." My eyes went to Madame Zelda, small and intent, her eyes fastened on my face. Without speaking, she left the table and went into a corner of the room. I saw her stoop and lift something off the floor.

"A tape recorder," she said briefly. "I always use it. It helps me to know what takes place when I go into trances myself."

Beryl said sharply, "Madame, I really think it's better that she shouldn't—"

"Look, Beryl," I interrupted with mounting impa-

125

tience, "I only came to please you. I have a right to know what happened."

"What happened, my dear," Madame Zelda said slowly, "is that you established direct contact. Unfortunately it wasn't one I would have chosen for you." I stared at her uncomprehendingly and she went on, "What I mean is that you're a sensitive yourself. You didn't need me at all. Once your powers were properly channeled, you were away."

"Will you—play it, please?"

Into the room came the first stumbling words I had spoken about the time wheel—"Beware of yesterday!" In tense silence we sat listening to the medium's gentle prompting and then, suddenly, to my recitation of the words I have already recorded. As my voice trailed away, Beryl's broke in agitatedly. "What was all that about? Ought we to stop her?" Then, presumably before Madame Zelda could do more than shake her head warningly, my voice again. But it was not my voice. It was a horrible, cracked treble and I listened to the words with growing horror.

> "Hunchbacked demon, foulest fiend,
> On myrrh and hemlock juices weaned,
> With hag and warlock now convened,
>   I bid thee come.
> White-robed abbot, vows defiled,
> With lust for power nigh driven wild,
> Who friend betrayed and saint beguiled,
>   I bid thee rise."

There was more in the same vein, but I'd heard enough. I made a blind, uncertain movement with my hand and Madame Zelda switched off the machine at once.

"That couldn't have been me!" My voice shook violently. "Whatever did it mean? I don't understand!"

"Well, love, it wasn't very pleasant, I admit. I imagine it was one of the incantations that the witches used when they wanted to raise evil spirits. I'll be able to verify it later, but I'm sure that's what it was. I've never heard anything like it before, and that's the truth."

"You mean—" My voice shook with incredulous horror. "Was I actually being used to—to bring back—" The idea was unspeakably appalling.

"Nay, love," she cut in quickly, "don't you go thinking anything like that."

"But you can't deny that some evil thing was communicating through me! You never told me there was a possibility of that. How can you be sure that simply by repeating those—those obscene words I—"

"Look, love, try to think of it this way. The air round about us is as full of these voices and sounds as it is of radio waves. Now, you don't actually *hear* the radio until you switch it on, tune in, as we say. It's the same with this business. For a time there you were acting as a radio set, transmitting, like. But what came through can no more harm or change you yourself than any words or music can alter the actual

127

fabric of a radio set. They were other people's words, not yours."

"Thank you," I said after a moment. "I think I can accept that. What about the other part? About the king's crown and dignity?"

"That was a more or less standard charge of witchcraft, probably used at Lancaster Assizes."

"Lizzie Earnshaw?" I said in a whisper, my eyes going to Beryl's strained face.

"Who's Lizzie Earnshaw?"

I left Beryl to explain the story of the Whistler and as she finished, the medium sat back.

"Well, it's clear enough how all that came about then. You picked up vibrations from the Lane and later, when switched on, as it were, you simply repeated them, just like the tape recorder here."

"But I've never paid that much attention to the Whistler; it all seemed so remote. I'm far more interested in the girl I saw and the fact that we seemed to know each other."

"I know, dearie, but we never had a chance to get round to that and I think you're too exhausted to try anything else today. If you like I could attempt a trance myself, but it might start you off again."

"I certainly don't want to risk that," I said vehemently.

"But what interpretation would you put on the things Sophie was telling you about?" Beryl demanded.

"It sounds very much as though this girl, whoever she was, was somehow responsible for bringing Miss Woodburn to Pendlemere, though whether it was

intentional or not I can't say. It could have been her memory that guided your niece to your house that evening, but we'd need to find some link between them. There must be one, especially since they seemed to recognize each other. And of course the other thing we need to know is *why* she brought her." She looked at me. "We really didn't have a chance to discuss this before you started to go under. The gypsy's reaction, for instance, was very interesting. How did it go? Something about yesterday and tomorrow changing places?"

" 'Your past is tomorrow, your future yesterday.' "

"Aye. Fascinating. I've never come across that before. She must have had very strong powers."

I said slowly, "Almost the same thing happened to her as happened to me just now. She went into some kind of a trance and afterwards she didn't know what she'd said." I looked across at the thin little woman. "I suppose you're used to this, but the feeling of—of someone or something taking over from you—it's terrifying."

"I know. That's why it's never wise to dabble in things you don't understand. Any form of power is a responsibility; you can use it well or you can use it badly. I like to feel I've been able to help a lot of folk over the years, but sometimes a message comes through that the recipient would rather not have received. I can't help feeling upset when that happens, but it's not a question of paying half-price and only hearing the good news!" She held out her hand. "Give me something belonging to you, a powder compact or pen, something you've had for some

129

time. We won't risk another trance at this stage, but vibrations from some personal object might be a bit of help. Psychometry, we call it."

I reached under the table for my handbag and passed over the compact as she had suggested. She held it for some moments, turning it slowly round in her thin, large-jointed fingers. From the rapt expression on her face she seemed to be listening rather than feeling and my mouth was dry as I waited for her analysis. After a few minutes she stirred slightly.

"I'm not getting anything very unusual, love. There's a lot of water separating you and your parents—water that they'll be crossing before long. I can see a pleasant room and a tall, fair man standing in it, but this picture is in the past and doesn't appear again. In many ways you are weak, and people find it easy to use you, like the forces that spoke through you a few minutes ago. That could also be how the girl you're interested in was able to draw you back. There's something else, though—" Her voice quickened with excitement. "Something a lot more promising—about ten years in the past. I can hardly—"

She stopped and turned to me abruptly. "You've blocked it off, haven't you? You won't let it come through. What is it, love? This could be the answer to everything."

I said tightly, "There's nothing. Nothing at all."

"But I almost had it! It was just on the fringe of—"

"Nothing!" I said again, a little more loudly.

She sighed and handed me back the compact. "I can only work with your co-operation. If you won't trust me—"

Beryl, with a glance at my set face, said quickly,

130

"Let's recap on what we know about this girl. She seemed about your age, Sophie?" I nodded. "And dressed more or less in current fashion?"

"Yes."

"If it is her memory that keeps coming to you, we know she either lived in Pendlemere or knew it well and it must have been at least eight years ago, judging by the conversion of Cobwebs. If it's also she who is responsible for the sensations you've been aware of, she must presumably have had some very strong emotions associated apparently with the entire length of Whistler's Lane. Is there anything else we can pinpoint?"

"I don't think so."

"Then we come to a full stop. It's not enough to identify her."

"I think," put in Madame Zelda, "that we'll just have to be patient. If she brought you back for some purpose, it will be revealed in due course."

I said suddenly, "But surely she can't have brought me back knowingly, or she wouldn't have been so frightened to see me."

"That's true. Well, as I said, it could have happened involuntarily. Such things have been known—simply a question of mind over matter, but whatever caused it, there must be some basic connection between the two of you and until we know what that is, we've nothing to go on."

"But Sophie can't stay up here indefinitely," Beryl interjected. "After all, my ankle's almost better now and you've more work waiting to be collected, haven't you?"

"I suppose I could always arrange for them to put

it on the train and meet it this end. There's no real urgency about going back." The flat without Jake was something I still couldn't face. "This picture is in the past . . ."

"Right." Madame Zelda pushed her chair back. "If that's all the work we can do for the moment, I'll go and put the kettle on and we'll have a nice cup of tea." She went over and pulled back the curtains and the pale spring sunshine flooded into the room with all the joyful abandon of a readmitted exile. We blinked in its brightness.

"I'll put the table away," I said, and started to fold the green chenille cloth. "Beryl, did you say you've seen the Whistler several times?"

She looked up at me a little uneasily. "Darling, I really think we should change the subject. You've had quite enough for now and I don't mind telling you it's shaken me up quite a bit, too."

"I just wondered what he looked like, that's all."

"Oh, rather hard to describe. He's always on horseback, of course, and never comes particularly close anyway. He has a sweeping plume in his hat and a cloak wrapped round him, and long elegant boots—thanks, no doubt, to his wife's tidy dowry! But I've never seen his face and it's always all over in a flash. I don't hold any kind of conversation with him like you did with your—what?—apparition?"

The door opened to admit Madame Zelda with the tray. The teapot was hidden under a hand-knitted cozy of apple green and there was a plate of assorted biscuits. In full daylight the room had taken off its rather sinister mask and was blandly an ordinary din-

132

ing room again. There was a bowl of fruit on the sideboard, a couple of oranges and a few wizened apples. Could this be the same room which had echoed to those terrible words that had come through me? It remained innocently untainted by their utterance as, Madame Zelda had assured me, was I.

The tea was sweet and rather strong and my cup had a hairline crack in it. I was seeing everything in hard, clear focus as if a heightened awareness had resulted from my temporary loss of it. To this day I could accurately draw the pattern on the worn carpet, the uneven folds where the curtains had been drawn quickly back without being rearranged. The clock on the mantelpiece was framed in a dull metal and had stopped at six o'clock of an afternoon long gone.

Madame Zelda was saying, "I'm sorry I didn't get a chance to do anything for you today, Mrs. Latimer, love. I feel I can hardly charge for this visit anyway. It was Miss Woodburn that put on the performance; not me. Come again whenever you're ready and we'll waive the fee—two for the price of one. How's that?"

Beryl made a token protest but was overruled. When we had finished tea, it was time to make our way to the bus stop. Madame Zelda took my hand in both of hers. It was rather like being sandwiched between two sheets of emery paper, warm, rough and rasping.

"You come back too, love. Don't let your rather frightening experience put you off. It may never hap-

pen again. If you just relax and let the spirits do what they will they'll never harm you in any way and you might have the chance of passing on some much-needed help."

Beryl and I were silent most of the way back. Around us were children traveling home from school, women returning from market with baskets of eggs and vegetables, a baby crying fractiously for its bottle. I was apart from them, an outsider. How would they react to the words that had poured out of me without my volition? I smiled grimly, thinking that if the facts were known Beryl and I would have the whole bus to ourselves. I didn't blame them. Ten days ago I had thought as they did, before the shades of Whistler's Lane had cunningly used natural means to draw me back into the maelstrom of myth and mystery that awaited me there.

Beryl turned from staring out of the window and said in a low voice, "Sophie, before we drop the subject altogether, what was your first intimation that something extraordinary was happening? Can you remember what brought those words into your head?"

I frowned, trying to clarify the memory. "I began to feel sleepy, as though I couldn't be bothered to speak, and then there was this strange rumbling."

"Rumbling?"

"It sounded like thunder at first and then I realized it was the collective murmuring of a huge crowd of people. I couldn't distinguish any words, but there was a most horrible atmosphere about it, a strong feeling of ill-will, as though they were all eagerly waiting for something terrible to happen to me. It

was to drown the noise that I said the first words that came into my head." I glanced at her white face. "Have you any idea what it could have been?"

She looked away. After a moment she said expressionlessly, "I believe large crowds always gathered to watch the witch burnings."

A shudder ran through me, my chattering teeth nipping my lip so that I could taste the warm blood. "Lizzie," I said softly, "her trial and her death. But not her incantations, because she was innocent. Something else must have taken advantage of the prevailing atmosphere, something really evil. Do you remember once saying you couldn't understand why the orthodox church wouldn't accept spiritualism? That must be part of it, the fact that evil spirits are as likely to be conjured up as good ones. It says something about that in the Bible, doesn't it? 'Try the spirits, whether they be of God.'"

Beryl put her hand over mine. "Look, sweetie, I know you didn't want to go this afternoon and I more or less talked you into it. I'm—sorry it turned out the way it did."

"It doesn't matter," I said listlessly. "Perhaps subconsciously I knew that might happen and was trying to fight against it."

"I'll never try to persuade you again, though of course if you want to go, I'll be glad to take you." She shivered. "I couldn't believe it was you, my little Sophie, with all those foul rhymes spilling out of you."

Her words still hung between us as the bus lumbered past the church and the village green and down the High Street to Tanner's Lane.

135

interlude

HE said patiently, "Look, love, I'm sorry but I can't take you tonight. I promised weeks ago to attend this meeting, and after all it concerns us more than most, since they're proposing to lay the pipes under Starling's Way."

"I'm not interested in your stupid meeting," she said with controlled impatience. "Really, Ben, it would be very gratifying if your mind occasionally rose above such things as drainage and cesspools!"

He flushed darkly. "That's not fair, and you know it. Only last week we went to that damn-fool party at the Schofields', and a more thorough waste of time—"

"And you didn't trouble to conceal your boredom, did you? But I hadn't realized that little outing would have to last me till—till next muck-spreading! Ye gods, the joys of being a farmer's wife!"

He rubbed his hand over his face. "Do we have to go on like this? I know it amuses you to make out I'm a tame village idiot with straw in my hair, but frankly I find the joke's wearing a bit thin."

She leaned forward tensely. "But don't you understand, I'm bored? Bored, bored, bored! Can't you see it would be to your own advantage to give me a bit of social life—and that doesn't mean discussing drainage at the church hall!"

"My advantage? How?"

She sat back again, breathing quickly. It was enjoyable needling him to a certain extent, but she had never dared go too far, being unsure how he would react. Tonight, disappointment had proved a dangerous addition to the seething emotions which already had hold of her and she was more inclined to be reckless.

"I might amuse myself elsewhere," she retorted challengingly. His eyes, dark and unreadable, held hers for a moment, and something she saw in them disturbed her. But he merely said flatly,

"I'm sorry if you're bored, but you knew well enough the kind of life we'd lead and it didn't stop you wanting to marry me."

"Ah!" Furious triumph blazed across her face. "That's what I was waiting for! I wondered how long it would take you to get round to it!"

"Actually, that wasn't what I meant—"

"Actually," she mimicked savagely, "I think it was exactly what you meant! I don't doubt your ego's been nicely flattered all this time by the thought that it was I who made all the running? God, if you only knew how it started!"

"Dinah, this has gone far enough. I wasn't trying to insinuate any such thing, but when you get down to it, we both know that—"

"That if I hadn't made a play for you, the thought

of marrying me wouldn't have entered your head?"

His anger rising now to meet hers, he returned her baleful glare. "All right, since you're determined to put words into my mouth, I dare say it wouldn't!"

"You insufferable boor!" she said with difficulty, and the last shreds of caution disintegrated and were gone. "It's obviously high time I told you the full story. I did it for a dare! Do you hear me, a dare! My God, and all this time you've been imagining that I fell hopelessly for your bucolic charms!"

He said in a strangled voice, "I really don't see the point in bringing this up now."

"But it was you who brought it up, wasn't it? Oh, all right, so your family turned out to be respectable and reasonably well-to-do, but I didn't know that at the time. To me you were just Joe Starling's boy, who brought vegetables to the back door twice a week. I didn't pay any more attention to you than—than to the pony that pulled the cart!" She paused, trying in vain to steady her chaotic breathing. "But one afternoon Ellen and I were playing tennis when you arrived—remember? We'd just been reading *Lady Chatterley's Lover* and our minds were on the—how shall I put it so as not to offend your bourgeois prudery?—on the *romantic proclivities* of the lower classes!"

"Dinah—for God's sake—"

"And Ellen said, 'I wonder what it would take to rouse that one? He looks about as responsive as a clod of earth!' And I bet her I could do it. God, I didn't mean to *marry* you!"

"Then why did you?" She could hardly make out the words.

"I can't imagine." She sat back, breast still heaving convulsively, and added a little more calmly, "I suppose it was a combination of things. You were so different from all the other men I'd known. I wasn't used to all that old-world courtesy and being treated as though I might break and I enjoyed it, just as I enjoyed always having to make the first move. It was a new experience for me and it—relieved the boredom, I suppose. And before I realized what was happening, the joke rebounded on me. Heaven help me, I really thought I was in love with you. The rest is history. As you so charmingly reminded me, I finally managed to persuade you to marry me and after a lot of prodding and shoving, you went cap in hand to see Father."

She flicked the wheel of her lighter, but her hands were trembling so much it took several tries before she could achieve a flame. "Will you ever forget the storm that conjured up? All the ranting and raving, with me screaming that I'd marry whom I liked and the family could go to hell." She gave a hard choke of laughter. "Of course, the trouble was that Mother had decided when I was in my cradle that I should marry into the nobility, and after all the expensive education and what-not geared to that end, the fact that I should come home and settle for Ben Starling from the village was just too much to swallow."

She leaned her head back and blew out a cloud of smoke. "Anyway, they came round eventually, except for Adam. I knew they would. But they were right after all, weren't they? It didn't work, and you can't accuse me of not trying. My God, how I tried,

if only to stop the family being able to turn round and say 'I told you so.' "

She glanced across at his stunned face and the expression in his eyes made her look quickly away again. What had she done? Lord, what in heaven's name had she said to him? "Ben—" She broke off and licked her lips, belatedly aghast at the extent of the devastation she had caused. "Ben, I'm sorry. I shouldn't have said all those terrible things. I can imagine how you—how I—" She took a deep breath. She had gone too far this time and there was no going back. "It's no use saying I didn't mean to hurt you because of course I did, but I truly am sorry now. If it's any comfort, you won't have to put up with me much longer." There, she'd said it! She waited like a statue for his response.

He wiped an unsteady hand across his face. "And what's that supposed to mean?"

"Just that I'm going away soon. With somebody else." She tried to speak matter-of-factly but the crescendo of her heartbeats reverberated in her voice. "Try to understand, Ben, and be glad for me. It really is love this time."

"Dinah—"

"Let me finish. I'm sorry things didn't work out for us. It wasn't anybody's fault. I should never have meddled in your life and mixed you up in all this, but at least it's over now. There's time for both of us to find happiness with someone else."

He was staring at her unbelievingly. "Do you really imagine you can just— Who is it, this man you're talking about?"

140

"I—can't tell you at the moment. Ben, I didn't mean this to happen, please believe that, and nor did he. It just—came up on us without warning and completely swamped us." She shuddered. "I never knew love could—"

"I said who is it?" His hand crashed down on the table, setting the glasses tinkling.

"Ben, don't look at me like that! I told you, I promised not to say yet. In fact, I didn't mean to say anything about it until we'd had a chance to work things out properly but—well, once I'd started, it all seemed to follow on somehow. Anyway, I'll go and see him tonight. Now that you know, there doesn't seem much point in waiting any longer. It will mean going away, of course, starting a new life somewhere, but at least we'll be together."

He went on staring at her, seemingly unable to speak, his face dark and cords standing out like ropes in the column of his neck.

"Ben?" she faltered, "I should have thought after all this you'd be glad to get rid of me! If the marriage was a failure from my side, it must have been a downright disaster from yours." She paused, eyeing him nervously. "I've told you I'm sorry for the things I said. I never meant to, it was just—just your calm assumption that you'd only had to sit back while I— Well, say *something*, for pity's sake!"

"All right," he said thickly, "I'll say something, if that's what you're waiting for, but you won't like it. There's one point you seem to have overlooked in all your careful planning. You're my wife, God

141

help me, for better or worse, as the preacher said, and so you'll stay. You can call it lower-class morality or what the hell you like, but the Starlings have been at Pendlemere as long as the Ashleys and we have our pride too. I'm not going to be cast off like a worn glove because you imagine you've found someone more to your taste. Like it or not, it was you who did the choosing and now you're stuck with me. In the meantime," he added, and his voice had gone flat, "until I've had a chance to sort things out a bit, you're not to leave this house."

She stared at him, her eyes widening incredulously. "And how, might I ask, do you propose to stop me?"

"I'm telling you, that should be enough." She gave a quick choke of derisive laughter and he went on heavily, "If it isn't, I'm quite prepared to lock you in your room."

"Lock me in? Do you really imagine—"

"Dinah!" His voice echoed frighteningly round the room and for the first time she felt a touch of apprehension. She had goaded him beyond bearing, she really shouldn't have let it go so far. "By fair means or foul I intend to keep you indoors until I've sorted out this—this disgusting mess. Is that clear? Your fancy man can think what the hell he likes. If he's any sense, he'll gather what's happened and just accept it."

Slowly she rose to her feet. "And you really imagine that after all this we could go on living together, even if it weren't for him? Ben, be reasonable! Is this

some sort of revenge for my hurting you? I said I'm sorry—"

"And that makes it all right, I suppose, just washes everything away. No, Dinah, as you quaintly put it, it isn't revenge. Incredibly enough I happen to believe in the marriage vows and I've no intention of having them broken."

Her temper flared again. "Of all the sanctimonious — Let me tell you something, Mr. Morality! They've already been broken, several times, and I'll go on—" She broke off with a cry as, finally stung beyond control, his hand streaked across her face. Caught off balance, she stumbled and fell, knocking her head against the leg of the table. Immediately he was down beside her, helping her unsteadily to her feet, his horrified eyes on the red imprint of his hand against her white cheek.

"Dinah, I'm sorry, I should never—" but she was fighting frantically now to get free of him and instinctively his grip on her arm tightened.

"Let me go!" she sobbed distractedly. "You're mad! Let me go to him now and I won't bother you again."

His breathing was out of control again. Beneath his, her white face with the terrified grey eyes had never looked lovelier. "I did it for a dare!" she had said.

"You're not—going anywhere," he said with difficulty, fighting down a surge of desire as unwelcome as it was inopportune. "You're going to stay here with me if I have to strangle you with my bare hands!"

She gave an inarticulate little cry, twisted suddenly and broke away. The next moment she was scrabbling at the door, but it took him only two strides to reach her. He had never realized before how slender her neck was, or how big his hands.

chapter
〜8〜

THAT evening after our return from Downhurst exhaustion overtook me, mentally and physically, and it was Beryl who answered the phone when Rowan Ashley rang to invite us to dinner.

"Thursday evening," she informed me, coming back into the sitting room. "I shall look forward to it. It's not often one gets a chance to see round a stately home without forking out fifteen pence or whatever for the privilege!" She eyed me keenly. "I think you ought to go to bed, honey."

"I can't be bothered! I'm all right, as long as you don't mind my taking over your place on the sofa."

"You're very welcome. I don't really need it any more anyway. I've done a fair bit of walking today and my ankle isn't aching at all. Most gratifying! That dog shouldn't be up there with you, though. She knows quite well she's not allowed on the furniture." Lottie, whose ear had twitched guiltily at the word "dog," put her nose prudently down on her paws and lay still.

"She's all right," I said lazily.

"Are you ready for supper yet?"

"I doubt if I'll want any."

"A bowl of soup, perhaps? Try, darling. We had early lunch and you haven't touched a thing except that cup of tea at Madame Zelda's."

"Soup then, thank you." It was easier to agree than to argue.

"I'll go and see to it. You stay where you are—both of you!" she added with a resigned laugh.

In fact it was Lottie who moved first. She lifted her head suddenly, ears pricked, and looked quickly in the direction of the archway.

"What is it, girl?" I fondled her silky ears but she shook my hand away, growling softly.

"It's only someone passing in the Lane," I told her, but her body had started to quiver and I was aware of uneasiness. She stiffened abruptly, eyes moving across the room as though following someone only she could see. I reached out to pat her again and was suddenly assailed by a wave of dizziness. Instead, I gripped the sofa cushion on either side of my body, pressing my head back. Before my frightened eyes the room began to shift and spin in a slowly turning arc. I tried to call out to Beryl, but I could make no sound. The spinning room started to revolve more quickly and I shut my eyes tightly. Perhaps I was going to faint; I never had, but presumably the sensation was something like this. Gradually my reeling head steadied and I drew a breath of relief and opened my eyes: to a fresh horror.

In the space of those few seconds Cobwebs had

changed, retreated into that recent past which kept intruding so disturbingly on my own present. Lottie, of course, had vanished and although I was still sitting in the same position, the room about me was utterly different. A wall a few feet to my left separated this room from one at the back of the house and the furniture was not the glowing amber and turquoise of Beryl's sitting room but a rather nondescript beige moquette.

I became aware of two more things; firstly, that I was dressed in a strange, loose-fitting white garment and secondly that I was not alone in the room. Beside the fire where, in another time, Jake had sat—would sit—how could I know which tense to use?—was a girl, head bent over a book. And, of course, I had seen her before, though I didn't know when. She had short hair hanging in a sleek cap to the level of her chin and in the lamplight shining down on her it glowed like strands of copper. This, I knew sickly, was the girl I had instinctively expected to open the door to us instead of Polly that first evening.

Then, just as I was looking down with some curiosity at the white robe I was wearing, which also seemed to strike some dim chord in my mind, the reeling began again and I only had time to clutch at the cushions and close my eyes before I was spun back—forward?—to the present, and opened them again to find Lottie, hackles up, still growling.

I said tremulously, "All right, Lottie, all over now." Gradually the fur on her back smoothed down. She turned her head and looked up at me and I gave her a reassuring little nod. Against my thigh the banner

147

of her tail moved once in acknowledgment and after a moment she laid her head back on her paws.

"Right, soup coming up!" Beryl hobbled cheerfully into the room, pulled the low coffee table in front of me and, seeing my face, halted abruptly. "What's happened now?"

"Oh, not much, just another time trip," I said bitterly. "The room was suddenly several years younger, that's all, and a girl was sitting reading over there. Lottie knew."

"The girl you saw in the Lane?"

"No, another one, but I seemed to know her, too."

"No one spoke?"

"No. I'm beginning to see what was meant by my future being yesterday, though. After all, today was in the future that Saturday, but part of my today happened years ago. I just hope that's not the only kind of future I have to look forward to."

"Don't be silly." Beryl spoke briskly. "If you're alive here now, in nineteen seventy-four, nothing can have happened to you in nineteen whatever it was, because it must already have happened, if you see what I mean."

"Incredibly, I do! What about my past being tomorrow, though?"

"Isn't that just another way of saying the same thing? A kind of poetic rhetoric, like in the Psalms? In any case, the same argument applies. Poor lamb, you're having quite a day, aren't you? I'll bring in your soup now and then the sooner you get to bed, the better. A quiet day is indicated for tomorrow, I feel, and then you'll have regained your equilibrium

in time to enjoy smoked salmon and grouse at the Hall on Thursday!'

As it happened, however, even my "quiet day" was not without incident, although this time of a more down-to-earth nature. I had insisted on doing the household shopping as usual, and volunteered to return two of Beryl's library books at the same time. I lingered for some time at the library talking to the young Copes who, in their own environment, triumphed over their innate shyness to become both learned and helpful. I made use of Beryl's returned tokens to select a few books on local history for myself, as Rowan Ashley had suggested. It was after twelve when I finally left and started back down the High Street toward Tanner's Lane, and as I rounded a bend I came almost face to face with John Phillips on his way to lunch.

Neither of us had time to maneuver. After only a second's hesitation he came on toward me, said quietly, "Good morning," and would have passed if I hadn't instinctively put my hand on his arm.

"John, at the risk of repeating myself, I really am terribly sorry if I hurt your feelings the other evening. I honestly didn't mean to."

He glanced at me briefly, then away up the road. "It's all right, Sophie," he said quite pleasantly. "Obviously there was some misunderstanding somewhere. I'm sorry for my part in it."

"It was all my fault; I know that. The fact was that I'd had rather a bad fright that day and I was—in need of comfort, I suppose. I'm just sorry it rebounded on you, after such a pleasant evening, too."

149

He waited politely to see if I had any other excuses to offer, and as I apparently had not, he said again, "Well, it's all right; no harm done." His eyes came back to my face, he gave me a brief smile and a nod and went on up the road. He had, of course, behaved impeccably; it was not his fault that I felt as though a door had been shut in my face.

"I wonder if anyone else will be at the Ashleys' tomorrow?" Beryl remarked over dinner that evening. "They might have invited your buddy John Phillips as company for you among us old fogeys!"

"I hope not," I said shortly; "it could be embarrassing."

"Oh?" Beryl's sharp nose quivered in much the same way as Lottie's after a new scent.

"We had a slight difference of opinion on Sunday," I enlarged awkwardly.

"Pity. I hoped he might help to take your mind off that arrogant so-and-so in London!" To which I smiled bleakly and did not reply.

Rowan had promised Beryl on the phone to "send the car" for us, but I doubt if either of us was prepared for the formality of a uniformed chauffeur knocking at our door. Feeling like landed gentry ourselves, we allowed him to settle us tenderly on the back seat of the gleaming limousine and assured him we had no need of the rug he offered for our knees. Later, when I mentioned our awe to Rowan, she laughed.

"Old Charlie? Bless his heart, he's really just the general dog's-body around here, gardener, odd-job man or chauffeur, whichever happens to be re-

quired. But he always rises magnificently to the occasion, and addresses me as "Mrs. Hashley, ma'am.' In these days he's worth his weight in gold."

As it happened, we were the Ashleys' only guests and they proved themselves charming and considerate hosts, quickly dissipating our rather stilted formality with a request for Christian names. I hadn't known quite what to expect of the Hall, which had so far been invisible behind its high walls. In fact it was rather smaller than I had imagined and even in the half-light of our arrival, the different styles of architecture could easily be distinguished where succeeding generations had added a wing or turret.

There was an imposing entrance hall resplendent with a vast open fireplace and graciously winding staircase, lined with the portraits of unsmiling ancestors. Rowan remarked that it was very useful when they held parties. "It's rather gorgeous sweeping down that staircase with your skirts trailing behind you; it appeals to my historical bent!" The sitting room into which we were led was altogether more informal and welcoming. "This is where we usually entertain, though when we're alone we retreat still further into the little Blue Room to save fuel!"

"And you've a library as well, haven't you?"

"Yes, we'll save that till after dinner and then perhaps we can discuss the hobbies that we have in common. Beryl and Adam will no doubt retreat to the art corner and Sophie and I to the history one!"

"I took two books out of the library yesterday on local history," I commented. "I've not had time to look at them properly, but they seem very interest-

ing. From what I could see, the Ashleys of Pend-lemere seem to go back to the dawn of time!"

"Beyond!" Adam claimed with a laugh. "In the early days, all the big families round about intermarried and we have liberal portions of Hoghton, Read and Assherton blood mixed with ours."

"As a matter of fact," Beryl broke in with a laugh, "we may well have some of it, too! We found an Ashley among our forebears in the family Bible!"

"Really?" Adam leaned forward interestedly. "I'd no idea your family originated up here."

"Nor had I, till Beryl told me," I confessed. "Of course, it might not have been your particular branch."

"Can you remember the name? That could give us a lead."

"Abigail," I said, and was surprised when Adam and Rowan exclaimed and laughed in unison.

"That's us all right, the one name there is no mistaking," Rowan assured us. "There's been an Abigail Ashley in our family for several hundred years. In fact, to this day every female Ashley is saddled with the name, usually buried among several others. Even Dinah—" She broke off, shot her husband an anxious look, and reached for her glass.

Missing her apparent confusion, Beryl inquired innocently, "Dinah? Is that your daughter?"

"No—no, we have two boys. Dinah was Adam's sister. She—died tragically some years ago. But to get back to the Abigails, apparently one of them in the early seventeenth century had 'secret powers,' if you please!"

152

"You don't mean she was a witch, surely?"

"Well, strictly of the white variety! Even so, it didn't make for comfort in those days, as you'll appreciate. She used to brew simples from herbs and so on and was well-known and loved in the village for her healing powers."

"I'm afraid our Abigail was a good two hundred years later," I said a little regretfully.

"Never mind, the power's supposed to be handed down, you know. It bypasses the males and comes out in their daughters, and strangely enough there has been at least one daughter in every generation of Ashleys until now. And of course all these girls grew up and married into other families and may well have passed their gift on to their own daughters ad infinitum. Was your connection on your mother's or father's side?"

I stared at her for a moment as the implications of her question sifted into my understanding, bringing with it an instinctive recoil.

"My mother's," I said dryly.

"Then you may well have it yourself!" Rowan said with a laugh.

"You're quite sure it was always white magic?"

"Oh, quite! If it hadn't been, we'd have kept quiet about it! Anyway, the one who started it all was quite an old lady at the time of the witch hunts. It's even been suggested that poor Lizzie Earnshaw was her son's illegitimate daughter, but I feel that's stretching it a bit. In any case, the general opinion today is that Lizzie wasn't a witch at all. It's too bad for her that her contemporaries didn't see it that way."

"But have there been any other instances of witchcraft in following generations?" Beryl persisted avidly.

"Oh, the odd hint here and there, but of course, as I said, most of those descendants are pretty widely scattered about the country, especially since people tended to move about more. But this—sixth sense, call it what you will, has shown itself in various forms from time to time—odd instances of pre- and retrocognition, spiritualism, the ability to see into the future—that kind of thing." Which covered Beryl as well as myself, I thought shakily.

"It seems such a shame to let it all die out. Every now and then I frighten the life out of Adam by suggesting we have another baby and try for a girl this time!"

"Which," interposed Adam humorously, "I feel is carrying traditionalism too far!"

A knock on the door brought the announcement that dinner was ready, and rather to my relief the subject dropped. The menu was not as grand as Beryl had facetiously suggested, but it was an extremely good meal of traditional English fare, ending with a delicious syllabub and an assortment of cheeses. After we had finished our coffee, Rowan led the way to the library. This was a magnificent room lined from floor to ceiling with books, most of them beautifully bound in soft leather and suede. In one corner was an impressive desk with a lamp and card index on its wide surface, and on either side of the fire stood a deep leather armchair, surely specifically designed for settling into with a good book.

As Rowan had predicted, Adam and Beryl moved

154

over to a far corner where the books on art were grouped while she and I became absorbed in those dealing with medieval Lancashire.

"I'll be sorry when you go back to London," she said once. "There's no one round here who shares my interests except dear little Frances Cope and she's so painfully shy it takes all the pleasure out of it!"

"In some ways I wish I could stay. It must be my ancestral threads pulling, but I certainly feel very much at home in Pendlemere."

"I wish I did!" Rowan said ruefully. "Oh, I'm not really serious, of course, but I do find it hard to make friends up here. Adam and I have been here about five years now, but all the worthy matrons of the parish insist on keeping me at arm's length. I'm 'from the Hall' and therefore not one of them, quite apart from the additional crime of having been born a Southerner! My family comes from Sussex," she added by way of explanation. "Adam and I met at Cambridge."

"You didn't come to live here when you were first married, then?"

"Lord no. Adam's parents were in residence then."

"And you only moved here when they died?"

"When his father died, yes. His mother's still alive, but she lives abroad now." There was a note in her voice which subtly indicated that further questions along those lines would not be welcome.

The evening drew to a close, our two little groups merged, and Beryl said with genuine regret that we must go. Old Charlie was duly summoned and escorted us with great rectitude back to Cobwebs.

"What a pleasant couple they are," I said as I let Lottie in again at the back door.

"Yes. Mind you, I think there's more to our Adam than meets the eye. I imagine he could be a hard man if things didn't go his way."

"Is that just an impression or an informed guess based on your supernatural ancestry?"

She smiled. "That was rather strange, wasn't it? Your mother would have been furious, bless her! For thirty years she's been trying, as she puts it, to beat some sense into me, and all the time the explanation was there, in code, in the family Bible! I must be a throwback, and you too, my pet!"

"I certainly hope it wasn't Abigail who was croaking that hair-raising incantation at Madame Zelda's."

"I'm sure not. Probably one of her contemporaries, though. I suppose you didn't give any hint of what you've been experiencing when you were talking with Rowan later?"

"No, I did not! It's one thing to shudder deliciously over abstract witches, quite another to find you may be entertaining one to dinner!"

"Well, I shouldn't worry about it. It's only legend, after all, and I imagine the power must be pretty diluted after all this time."

"It's still quite strong enough for me, I can tell you!" I said grimly as I went after her up the stairs.

The next morning there was a long, rather disjointed letter from my mother, who was inclined to write as she spoke and therefore made an interesting if sometimes incoherent correspondent. She had been upset to hear of Beryl's accident and was relieved that I'd been free to go and look after her. No

156

doubt by now I would be back in London. She still couldn't understand why Beryl had sold "that nice little house" and gone traipsing up to Lancashire. It would make visiting so difficult next time they were on home leave.

This reminded me that there would probably be a similar letter awaiting me at the London flat and that it was more than time that I wrote to my parents myself. I made a note to buy some airletters when I went shopping, but as it happened Mrs. Briggs informed me they were sold out and my slightly guilty conscience was temporarily assuaged.

However, as Beryl and I were sitting at the kitchen table with our after-lunch coffee, there was a knock at the back door and I was somewhat surprised to find Mrs. Briggs outside with a few airletters in her hand.

"They came in just after you'd left," she explained, her eyes going past me to the coffeepot on the kitchen table. "And since I thought it might be urgent, like, I decided to bring them round myself."

"It's very kind of you," I said a little awkwardly. "I'm not sure where I put my purse—"

"Perhaps you'd like some coffee, Mrs. Briggs?" Beryl asked resignedly.

"Well, now that you mention it, I could do with a cup. Thanks."

She stepped past me with alacrity and sat down at the table while I perforce found another cup and saucer. I was not overfond of Mrs. Briggs and was at a loss to guess the real reason for her visit. As it happened, I was not left long in doubt.

"I hear you were up at the Hall last night," she

157

began, her long nose pink-tipped above the steaming coffee cup. "Have a nice time, did you?"

Beryl raised her eyebrows. "Very, thank you."

"Real lady, Mrs. Ashley, I've always said. Lucky for her she wasn't here during all the trouble."

There was a brief, expectant pause. Beryl and I exchanged a look, acknowledging that we should let the remark pass unchallenged and aware that it was almost impossible to do so.

"What trouble would that be, Mrs. Briggs?" asked Beryl, taking up her obvious cue.

"Why, the murder, of course! Surely you've heard of the murder? Such a to-do there was, and policemen up from London and all. Sometime back now, of course, but there's things you never forget, as I told Briggs at the time. He was alive then," she added somewhat unnecessarily.

"And—er—who was it who was murdered? Someone from the village?"

Mrs. Briggs savored to the full her moment of glory. "Well, yes and no, as you might say." She paused and triumphantly brought out her trump card. "It was Miss Dinah herself. Not that she rightly was Miss Dinah by then."

"Adam Ashley's sister?" Beryl demanded in dawning horror.

"Aye, the very same. And Ben Starling's wife."

"Dinah Ashley was married to Ben Starling?" Beryl's voice rose incredulously. I said nothing, but a dull, insistent beating in my head told me that every word was of vital importance to me.

"She was that!" Mrs. Briggs announced, setting her

158

cup back on its saucer. "And got murdered for her trouble!"

In my mind's eye I could see the hard, cold face of the man who drove the tractor, the man the whole village appeared to ostracize.

"I think," Beryl said firmly, "that you'd better tell us the whole story."

Mrs. Briggs needed no second invitation and launched into it immediately, delighted to have a fresh audience. "Well, she were a lovely young lady, were Miss Dinah, pretty as a picture with her charming ways, but very spoilt, they said. If she set her heart on summat, she had to have it—and she set her heart on Ben Starling. Fine-looking man he were and all," she conceded grudgingly, "tall and dark, with them black eyes of his."

"When—when was all this?" I interrupted faintly.

"Oh, twelve, thirteen year since, I dare say. Anyway, it said in the papers as Miss Dinah were twenty when she was wed and twenty-three when she died, and that's a good ten years back now."

Twenty-three. The same age as myself.

"So she set her heart on Ben Starling," Beryl prompted. "What happened next?"

"Well, the family near went wild, as you'd imagine. Young Mr. Ashley, Mr. Adam, that is—he adored her and they say he took it harder than the old man. Never forgave her, so likely never forgave himself when she died without them making it up, like. But as usual Miss Dinah got her own way in the end and wed she was in the village church and moved to Starling's farm and after a while the fuss died down.

159

After all, there was nowt really wrong wi' the Starlings, a good respectable family even if they weren't gentry, like the Ashleys. After a bit we gave no more thought to their affairs and the first we knew of any trouble was when Constable Rushton came hammering at our door at six o'clock one morning with the news that her body had been found in Whistler's Lane! Fair turned my blood cold, I can tell you. If there's any more coffee in that pot, Miss Woodburn," she continued in the same breath, "I wouldn't say no."

Silently, with shaking hands, I refilled her cup.

"Ta. Well, there was a right carry-on and no mistake. It came out that Mr. Starling had been expected at a meeting the night before at the church hall but he'd never turned up. We weren't surprised at that, because Briggs had already told me as how he'd showed up at the Fleece, looking like death, he said, and sat drinking in a corner and talking to no one till he was so tight he could hardly stand. But when Len Jackson went and tried to help him, he got right violent so they kept their distance after that. In the end he passed out cold and several of them managed to get him out and took him home. Well, that caused enough of a stir because he wasn't what you'd call a drinking man at all—leastways, not in public. For all we knew he could have been drunk regular down at the farm, knocking his wife about, poor lady."

"And what happened? Did they find out who killed her?"

"They did and they didn't," Mrs. Briggs answered characteristically. "After questioning the whole vil-

160

lage and taking fingerprints and Lord knows what, they settled on him."

"*Ben Starling* was accused of his wife's murder?"

"He was. But as soon as they got onto him, he started shouting that she'd had a lover and he must have done it. Never mentioned it before, mind, and they weren't too ready to believe him, specially since he couldn't say who the man was. And her family, as you'd expect, swore she hadn't been with anybody. But then, rather late in the day to my way of thinking, Miss Wainwright, who used to live in this cottage and was right friendly with Miss Dinah, she came forward and said yes, right enough, she had allowed them to meet here but—now can you credit this?— *she* didn't know who he was, neither! I reckon no one believed her, but they couldn't shake her story. And it didn't do Mr. Starling no good, neither, since it was a ready-made motive for him to kill her."

"Did he have an alibi for the time of the murder?"

"Not him. They worked out she must have died between seven and eight o'clock, and he didn't appear at the pub till gone nine."

"And what did he say had happened?"

"Oh, that they'd had a row because he wanted to go to the meeting and then she told him about this other man and how she were going away with him. He said he told her not to leave the house, but she got out anyway and he didn't bother going after her. *But* —" Mrs. Briggs paused significantly. "Would she have run out like that without even stopping for a coat? It was a bitter night—November. And if she'd really been meaning to go away for good, it stands to

161

reason she'd have taken something with her, but they couldn't find a thing missing, not even her toothbrush."

"And who did her lover turn out to be?"

"They've never found out to this day. And after the trial going on for weeks they had to let Mr. Starling go for lack of evidence, if you please! In my mind there was enough to hang him, and that's what he deserved."

"So that's why no one has anything to do with him?"

"Aye, that's why, and quite right too. And even that weren't the end of it. Old Mr. Ashley was so shook up about it all that on the day Mr. Starling was acquitted, he had a stroke and though he lingered another four or five years, poor gentleman, he never left the house again till he was carried out in his box. That's why I say young Mrs. Ashley was well out of it all, down in London. Well!" She pushed her cup away from her and stood up. "I'd better get back and see young Polly's keeping the books straight. Thanks for the coffee," and she was gone, well pleased with the result of her bombshell though only aware of a fraction of the impact it had in fact made on us.

chapter
~9~

NEEDLESS to say, after Mrs. Briggs had left, Beryl and I spent hours discussing the story she had told us and its possible relevance to myself. I think I knew straightaway that the girl I had seen in the Lane was Dinah Starling, that the sensations I'd felt down near the farm would have been hers as she hurried to meet her lover here at Cobwebs. At last it seemed we might be able to answer the questions of who and when, but why I had been brought here was still wrapped in mystery.

"The most obvious solution would be that she wants you to reveal the murderer," Beryl said with a worried frown, "and I don't like the thought of that at all."

"I assure you I don't either, though how I could possibly find out after ten years when Scotland Yard detectives failed to at the time, I can't imagine."

Beryl seemed about to say something and to change her mind. "Except that with your time hops you have rather more scope than they had," she sug-

gested at last. "Also, don't forget that you and Dinah were distantly related. Perhaps it's your common link with old Abigail that's responsible for a certain amount of ESP between you."

"A certain amount of what?"

"Extrasensory perception, honey. I was forgetting you're not au fait with the parlance."

A ring at the doorbell put an end to the discussion at last. This time it was Phyllis Harcourt who stood on the path.

"Hello, Sophie. No, dear, I won't come in. I'm on my way home from school and have masses of exercise books to correct. I just wanted to let you know there's a whist drive at the church hall tomorrow evening, and you'd both be very welcome if you'd like to go."

"Well, it's kind of you, but—"

"Sophie would love to, Mrs. Harcourt," Beryl said firmly from behind me, "but I hope you'll excuse me. I'm not much of a hand at whist, and I'm committed to watching the serial on BBC 2!"

"I'm really not sure—" I began, but again Beryl briskly cut across my excuses.

"Nonsense, child, you'd enjoy it. You need a bit of social life."

"Unfortunately I can't go this time," Mrs. Harcourt said. "Bernard has some function on at the college which he wants me to attend, so I'm afraid I won't be able to offer you a lift, but if you like I could ask—"

"I won't need a lift, really," I said quickly, afraid she might have been about to suggest John Phillips, "and since Beryl seems to want me out of the way to

watch her serial in peace, I'll be pleased to go!" After all, I told myself, I couldn't spend the rest of my stay in Pendlemere studiously avoiding any place where I might come into contact with John.

"Good, then please accept my ticket and I hope you enjoy it." She brushed away my offer of payment and left us to return to her exercise books.

"Did you have to let me in for that?" I asked Beryl a little resentfully.

"You might patch up your quarrel with young Phillips, or alternatively strike up with someone else."

"Still trying to exorcise Jake for me?"

"Merely to provide you with a little entertainment, dear child!" returned my aunt with infuriating complacency.

As I had expected, it was much the same crowd as on the previous Saturday. In a village of this size people made their own entertainments and for the most part they were loyally supported. On this occasion there were eight or ten card tables set up round the room and Mr. Sicklebury, whom I'd met briefly the week before, was acting as master of ceremonies. I saw John almost at once at the far side of the hall and he gave me a noncommittal wave. I sat down rather hastily at the nearest table, finding myself partnering Harry Postlethwaite, the vicar's son. He grinned at me cheerfully.

"Good to see you, Sophie—very good, in fact! I was roped in tonight by my fond mama and must admit this is not my chosen way of spending a Saturday evening. Have you met Frank Denton, here? Teaches maths at the school down the hill. Sophie

Woodburn, Frank. I don't think you were here last Saturday."

"No, I was at a concert. How do you do, Miss Woodburn?"

One of John's colleagues, I reflected, but not one of his contemporaries. Frank Denton looked to be in his late thirties and there were furrows between his eyes and joining mouth and nose. On my other side, playing opposite him, was the attractive Barbara Simpson, Graham Lethbridge's receptionist.

Play started and at the end of each game, two players left the table and two more took their place. As the evening progressed I discovered with a faint sense of guilt that I had been subconsciously assessing all the men present and trying to imagine how they would have been ten years ago. Could Dinah Starling's lover—and perhaps murderer—be among them? Frank Denton appeared to suit the role admirably. There had been no mention of a wife, I noticed —"I" was at a concert, he had said. And Harry Postlethwaite was acknowledged to be wild. Although he would only have been in his late teens at the time, he might well have appealed strongly to a spoiled, willful girl only a few years older.

Of course, I reminded myself, absent-mindedly returning my partner's lead, the fact that Dinah and her lover had occasionally met at Cobwebs didn't necessarily mean that he came from this village, though the strictly kept secrecy seemed to indicate that he did. Jim Claythorpe, for instance, was known to have a roving eye and not much love for his nagging wife. Or there was Jack Grayson, at whose farm

166

John lodged, or even the small and rotund headmaster, Tom Ringate. One by one I lined them up in an imaginary identification parade, but Dinah alone could have told me whether or not the right one was among them.

Halfway through the evening, Mrs. Postlethwaite and some other ladies brought trays of coffee and sandwiches to the tables and it was unfortunate that this prolonged partnership should have been the one I shared with John Phillips. The Copes had been our opponents in the last game and I was thankfully able to chat with them about local history, which I knew also interested John. But I was remembering his words when I had mentioned walking along Starling's Way: "It's not ghosts you have to worry about down there." Where had he been ten years ago? I was considerably relieved when the trays were removed and play resumed, leaving me free to move to the next table.

At ten-thirty the score cards were added up and prizes awarded for the highest score. In the ensuing mêlée I slipped quietly away. I had no wish to give the impression that I was hoping for a lift home from John, or, for that matter, from anyone else. I was, however, a little perturbed to find that a mist had come down, restricting visibility to a few yards. Obviously there was no question of braving Whistler's Lane under such conditions. Cautiously, ears strained for approaching traffic, I crossed the road and started to walk as quickly as I could down the High Street. Disembodied sounds reached me from time to time: voices, a dog barking, a burst of laugh-

ter, but the mist played unreliable tricks with distances and it was impossible to gauge their nearness. At least it was a comfort to know I was never far from occupied houses all the way home.

Tanner's Lane manifested itself by the mere gap of houses and I turned thankfully into it. The familiar, everyday shopfronts were shrouded with drifting barriers of mist and the streetlamps hung like blurred haloes overhead. Once I inadvertently walked through a spider's web and its clinging strands moved eerily over my face, making me choke back a gasping scream. Cobwebs, I thought confusedly.

Then at last here was Cobwebs, waiting in the mist at the end of the path. My fingers fumbled with the catch of the gate, and to my surprise it creaked and swung back crookedly as though a hinge were broken. I resolved to have a look at it the next morning. I hurried up the path, and only as I felt for my handbag to get out the key did I realize with a jarring sense of shock that I was not carrying it; not, in fact, carrying anything, and the warm tweed coat in which I had hurried from the church hall had unaccountably changed into the cold, stiff cotton of a long white gown.

I rocked back on my heels in a wave of sheer, unadulterated terror. What had happened? There had been no blurring of images this time, unless they were already blurred by the floating strands of mist. Numb with horror, I stumbled the remaining distance up the path and started hammering frantically on the front door. But though I beat and beat at its

panels, no sound came from my banging. Then, behind me, the gate squeaked again and footsteps came hurrying toward me. Pressing my fingers against my mouth, I shrank back against the lintel, eyes straining fearfully for the figure that must appear at any moment.

And here she was, scarf slipping back off her rich brown hair, cheeks flushed and eyes alight—a girl hurrying to meet her lover. For a second I held myself rigid, braced for her scream, but her eyes passed over me apparently unseeingly as she reached for the bell. The door opened at last and Ellen stood there. I was beyond wondering how I came to know her name.

"Come in, Dinah. Heavens, what a night!"
"Dinah"—the final proof, if any were needed. Soundlessly, unseen by either of them, I slipped inside with her. On my right, where in another time the oak settle stood, was an old-fashioned hallstand with mirror and hooks. Dinah hurriedly pulled off her coat and draped it carelessly over a hook, leaning forward to peer at her lovely reflection and smooth down her hair. Beside her I too stared into the mirror, but no reflection looked back at me.

"Ellen, you're an angel! What would we do without you in this weather? It's not even safe to drive on a night like this."
"Do you think he'll come?"
"If he possibly can."
They went together into the front room and I, ghostlike and unnoticed, went with them, but for a while their voices, Ellen's quiet and slightly disap-

169

proving, Dinah's vibrant with excitement, did not penetrate my understanding. For quite suddenly I had recognized the gown I was wearing, and with that recognition came all the detailed memories which over ten years I had fought so successfully to batten down. Weak and paralyzed with fear, I leaned against the prickly moquette of a fireside chair. Suppose on this occasion, which had already lasted considerably longer than the previous two flashes, it proved impossible to return to my own time? Suppose I was locked back in 1964 and would have to live the intervening years all over again? And if so, what would happen when I once more reached this point in 1974? Would the time wheel keep endlessly spinning, sending me over and over the same ten-year period forevermore? "Your future yesterday" . . .

Ellen was saying, "I really think you might tell me who he is. Surely you can trust me? Under the circumstances I do feel I have a right to know."

"Ellen darling, you've been just wonderful, but please hold on a little longer." She shivered suddenly and looked round, staring straight across to where I stood cowering.

"What's the matter?"

"I don't know. I suddenly got a weird kind of feeling. Probably just someone walking over my grave."

"You're sure Ben doesn't suspect anything?"

Her mouth curled contemptuously. "Of course not. The only things he notices are crops and silage!"

"Oh, come on, Dinah, you know quite well he's not the bumpkin you try to make out! I've seen him get the better of you before today!"

Before Dinah could reply, the doorbell rang and both girls jumped.

"Ellen, please!"

"Oh, all right. I'll go into the dining room and promise not to peek. But I warn you I'm getting fed up with all this secrecy."

"It won't be for much longer, I promise." Dinah almost pushed her out of the room and as the dining-room door closed behind her, ran to open the front door. With palpitating heart I went after her, every nerve straining to see who stood there. But as the door opened, it was as though the mist rushed inside, wrapped itself round me and swept me out again, fighting helplessly against its blanketing hold as it carried me back through time and space, finally leaving me abandoned, a cold, crumpled heap on the footpath of Tanner's Lane.

"Miss Woodburn? Miss Woodburn, is that you?" Someone was pulling gently at my shoulder. "Are you hurt? What happened?"

It was some time before I could force my eyes open, to see a figure bending over me in the misty darkness. I said indistinctly, "What year is it?"

Perhaps fortunately, he didn't understand. "You don't seem hurt in any way. I think you'd better come inside for a moment." But to my spinning mind, "inside" still meant the Cobwebs of 1964 and I pressed myself in silent desperation against the pavement, resisting the pressure of his hands.

"Miss Woodburn, there's nothing to be afraid of. It's me, Graham Lethbridge. I think you must have

171

fainted. Let me get you into the house and I can examine you properly."

Cold now and dazed, I allowed him to help me up and half-carry me into his surgery. How I had got from one end of Tanner's Lane to the other, I had no way of knowing. The bright light hurt my eyeballs and I covered my face with my hands. I heard a quavering voice say, "What is it, Graham? Has there been an accident in the fog?"

"No, Mother, it's only Miss Woodburn. I don't know what's happened yet. Just give me a moment while I examine her."

I said with an effort, "Was I outside your house?"

"Yes, on the corner of the Lane." His long, expert fingers moved over me, testing, probing gently. "Have you had these spells before?"

"Just—lately I have, yes." I was afraid to let my mind come down from the safe, accepting level where it now hovered. I knew vaguely that during my "spell" I had remembered something that I would prefer to forget again immediately.

"Where had you been this evening?"

I had to think for a moment before I could reply. "To the whist drive at the church hall."

"With your aunt?"

"No, alone."

"And no one offered to see you home?" He was frowning.

"I didn't really give them the chance. I hadn't realized it was misty until I got outside, but I could still see where I was going—just. But—I passed your house, doctor, I remember. And Jackson's, and the post office."

"Jackson's?" He was looking down at me, puzzled.
"Blackburn's," I mumbled. But I remembered
now that it had indeed been Jackson's I had passed.
At what stage had 1974 slipped backward—when I
walked through the spider's web? I hadn't noticed
my clothing until I reached the other Cobwebs.

"Were you feeling nervous in any way, overex-
cited?"

"I don't think so."

"Perhaps you were hurrying and out of breath?"

"A little, perhaps."

"The sharp cold air after the heat in the hall may
well have made you feel faint. It's lucky I was so late
getting home, or you might have lain there till the
morning. You have young Mrs. Warburton's latest
baby to thank for that; it took its time! Are you feeling
a little better now?"

"Yes, thank you. Just—cold."

"We'll go through into the house and Mother can
get you a hot drink. The surgery always depresses me
at night; I don't know why."

He took my arm and led me through the connect-
ing door into the hallway of the house. Old Mrs. Lethbridge came to a doorway. She was wearing a dark
blue dressing gown and a thick plait of grey hair
hung over one shoulder.

"Could you possibly rustle up a pot of tea,
Mother?"

"Of course." She moved away in the direction of
the kitchen and my hand suddenly tightened on her
son's arm as my returning senses detected a faint
scent of lavender. A picture flickered in my mind of
the gypsy woman with her basket, and having iden-

173

tified the source of fear, I was thankfully able to dismiss it. I sank gratefully into a comfortable old chair whose cushions closed protectingly round my cold, shaking body. Graham Lethbridge knelt down and shoveled some more coal onto the fire.

"How is your aunt, by the way? I called on Tuesday but you were both out, which seemed a good sign."

"Yes, she's very much better, thank you."

"I suppose you'll soon be going home, then?"

"Soon, I expect." I didn't want to think about it. The flickering firelight played over his face, creating cavernous hollows round his eyes. I leaned back with a faint sigh, safe and relaxed at last. "You must be tired yourself, after such a long day."

"Yes, but it's been a very satisfying one. For all the croaks of doom about the population explosion, I never fail to feel a tremendous sense of wonder and achievement when I've delivered a new baby."

"Is that the best part of your job?"

He laughed. "I suppose so, but it's also wonderful when someone who has been desperately ill at last turns the corner and begins to improve."

I said curiously, "Someone told me you'd been offered a fabulous job in Manchester and turned it down to stay on as G.P. here."

He turned toward me, his eyes smiling. "And you find that hard to understand? I don't see why. We Lethbridges have been in Pendlemere a very long time, Miss Woodburn. My father was the doctor here for thirty years before me, and his father before him. These people are my friends. I know

174

and understand them and they trust me. I feel this is as worthwhile a job as any Manchester might have to offer."

"But not as lucrative, surely."

"I have more than enough for my needs. Also, it would upset Mother to have to leave the village and all her friends, and I obviously couldn't have considered going without her."

"Not that I didn't keep telling him to seize his chances and not be so sentimental!" Mrs. Lethbridge remarked with mock severity, coming into the room with the tea tray. He stood up and took it from her, putting it on a low table before the fire and the old lady sat down carefully on the sofa and held out her gnarled hands to the now blazing fire.

"Mother knows all there is to know about Pendlemere and its families," the doctor commented, sending her an affectionate glance. "I tell her she should write it all down, but she won't be bothered."

I was very tempted to bring up the subject of Dinah Starling's murder, but the idea seemed almost sacrilegious in the quiet warmth of the listening room. I took the cup and saucer handed to me and sipped slowly at the hot, sweet tea. "Mrs. Ashley was saying the other evening that most of the families living here now have been here for hundreds of years."

"Quite right. It gives one a wonderful sense of belonging."

"My aunt and I were most intrigued to find we're distantly related to the Ashleys ourselves."

"Really? So you're one of us, too! The Ashleys were

175

squires of the manor in the old days, of course, with all the respects and privileges that went with the position."

"*Droit de seigneur?*" I asked idly, thinking of the rumor about Lizzie Earnshaw.

"Quite possibly, but we don't inquire too closely! I'm afraid we Lethbridges came of somewhat humbler stock."

"My grandfather was the first headmaster of the village school," Mrs. Lethbridge put in with quiet pride. "Back in the eighteen-sixties, that was."

"Has Mr. Ringate been here long?"

"About twelve years. He came as a newly married man and I delivered both his children. Little horrors they've turned out to be too, from all I hear!"

On the mantelpiece the clock struck half-past eleven. "I must go," I said reluctantly. "Beryl will be getting worried and I'm keeping you up."

"Don't worry on my account. I need to unwind before I have any chance of settling for the night and in any case I don't need much sleep."

"He spends most of the night reading and studying," his mother said sternly. "I tell him he's burning the candle at both ends, but he never listens to me."

I leaned forward and put down my cup.

"Sure you're all right now?"

"Yes, thank you; just very, very tired."

"I'll run you home, then."

"Thank you for the tea, Mrs. Lethbridge. I'm sorry I disturbed you."

"Not at all, my dear. Graham's always bringing people in, usually far less presentable than yourself!

His lame ducks I call them, like June in *The Forsyte Saga*. It was very pleasant to have an attractive young lady for a change!"

It took all my will power to school my sagging muscles to propel me as far as the car. Though I hadn't consciously admitted it, there was an unnerving fear in my mind that Cobwebs would still be ten years in the past. It was with indescribable relief that I saw the gate, new and painted, swing easily back on well-oiled hinges, and before it had clicked to behind us, Beryl had the front door open.

"Sophie, is that you? I was beginning to wonder where you were. Dr. Lethbridge! Did you bring her home from the whist drive? That's very—"

"No, no, Mrs. Latimer. Your niece is all right now, but she felt rather faint and I found her at my front gate. I should have thought to let you know. I'm afraid it never occurred to me. I'm sorry if you've been worried."

"I wasn't really. I thought she might have gone back somewhere for coffee. Found her at the gate, did you say? I don't quite understand."

I swayed in total exhaustion and Graham Lethbridge said quickly, "She should get to bed straightaway. If you don't mind, we'll postpone discussing it until the morning. I'm sure it's nothing to worry about, but I'll call round to make sure there are no aftereffects. Perhaps you could see that she stays in bed until I come. Good night, Mrs. Latimer, Miss Woodburn."

Anxiously Beryl shepherded me inside and my eyes moved in infinite gratitude to the open stone

archway, the lightly painted walls and the gleaming wood of the oak settle. Dear Cobwebs, safely back with me in 1974.

With Beryl's arm supporting me, I stumbled up the stairs and within the space of ten minutes was in bed and sound asleep.

chapter
⤜10⤛

THE deep and blessedly dreamless sleep lasted until Beryl woke me with a tray of toast and coffee at half-past nine the next morning. "I thought if I left you any longer, you wouldn't have time for a wash before the doctor arrives. Also," her bird-bright eyes fastened on my face, "I'm nearly bursting with curiosity to know what happened."

Slowly, while I ate my breakfast, I told her of the time slip, of my seeming invisibility, the acute anxiety I had felt to see the face of Dinah's lover, and my swirling, spinning removal down the length of Tanner's Lane to be deposited, most opportunely, outside the doctor's surgery.

"You're quite sure you didn't—dream it? I mean, could you simply have fainted and lain there for half an hour or so before he found you?"

"You mean never have come back to the house at all?"

"Isn't it a possible explanation? You say everything was vague and disembodied because of the mist. You

179

didn't even register it was Jackson's rather than Blackburn's that you'd passed until speaking of it later."

"It was just as real as the other time lapses but more frightening because it lasted so much longer and was much more detailed. Dinah and Ellen were as real to me as you are now."

"And how much of this are you going to tell the worthy doctor?"

I grimaced. "What's the point? If I mention any of it, he'll think I'm psychotic or something. He might even be right."

"I'm sorry, Sophie." Beryl laid her warm, hard hand over mine. "I'd no right to doubt you, even for a moment. Of course it happened exactly as you said. After all, it fits the pattern. You're gradually being shown more and more of the events leading up to the murder."

"It's all layered, isn't it?" I said slowly. "Time, I mean. Like an archaeological dig, where you slice through a slab of rock and can actually see all the different strata of previous civilizations, one on top of the other. The only difference is that with time they're not static but continuing to run on their own level."

Beryl was watching me with a slight frown. I knew what I meant but found it hard to elaborate. "On one of the lower levels there's Richard Whitaker still galloping to his death along Whistler's Lane—occasionally people still see him. Much higher up, but still below us, Dinah Starling goes along the same Lane to her own death. And I still see her. I wonder if

180

already there are people born who one day will see me walking there with Lottie? Perhaps without knowing it, we all leave imprints on our own time band, little grooves like a gramophone record which only need some sensitive person in the future to act as a needle to start it all playing again."

So, when Graham Lethbridge called later that morning, I was able to assure him that I felt perfectly well again and to thank him and his mother for their care of me the previous evening. And I meekly accepted at face value his explanation of the whole thing. Beryl, however, was not so easily satisfied, and after he had gone she came and sat on the bed again.

"I've been trying to think, Sophie, what we were doing ourselves ten years ago. I mean, how was it you were available, if that's the right word, to flit effortlessly around without anyone apparently noticing anything?"

My heart began its hard, painful thudding. This thing I had feared for so long could, I knew, no longer be hidden away and deliberately consigned to forgetfulness. Blindingly terrifying as it was, at last the time had come to examine it.

"We know now that Dinah was killed in November '64," Beryl was saying. "Presumably you were at school. Was there anything special about that term? Anything that—Just a minute!" Her voice quickened and I knew sickeningly that she had remembered. "Wasn't that when you had that bad time with your appendix? Surely that was the Christmas you weren't well enough to fly out to Hongkong and spent quietly with me at Biggin Hill?"

181

"Yes," I said tonelessly.

"You were very seriously ill," she went on softly. "In fact there were times when they actually thought you had stopped breathing. Sophie darling, I think you do remember. Tell me."

I reached mindlessly for her hand and it gripped mine strongly, reassuringly. "I thought I was going insane," I said from a dry mouth. "Later, I convinced myself it was delirium, hallucinations from the strong drugs they were giving me. And after that I didn't allow myself to think of it at all. It only really came back to me last night. I realized then that it was the hospital gown I was wearing, and that was when I remembered, before I could stop myself."

"What was it that you remembered?"

I closed my eyes on a spasm of rejection but there was no escape now. "Floating somewhere just below the ceiling and seeing myself lying in the bed below, and all the doctors and nurses bending over me. I—thought I was dead."

"Oh, God!" Beryl said in a whisper. "Astral travel —of course! It's the only explanation."

I turned glazed eyes toward her. "You mean—it is possible?"

"Of course. Oh, poor darling, what hell it must have been for you! No wonder your subconscious blotted it right out. But it's a known phenomenon, sweetie. There's no need to be so terrified. What else did you see?"

"I'm not sure. It happened more than once. On one occasion it was night and I floated out of the window and the town lay below, the main roads

picked out by the yellow lines of their streetlamps. And then there was just darkness and mountains and—" I broke off as the mere process of allowing myself to remember brought in its wake a whole host of new memories I had not had a chance to examine and the enormity of which clutched at me with a new wave of fear.

"And what?"

"Pendlemere High Street."

"Ah!" Beryl sat back with a deep sigh. "Do you see now what must have happened? Temporarily free of the restrictions of your body, you instinctively came here."

"But—why?"

"I'm not sure, but you familiarized yourself with the High Street and you obviously had some close affinity with Dinah. She was going through a turbulent emotional upheaval at the same time. She might even have seen *you* as a ghost, though you say she wasn't aware of you last night."

"I suppose we have Abigail to thank," I said shakily with a rather pathetic attempt at lightness.

"Yes. Sophie—" Beryl's hand had tightened on mine. "I've just thought of something rather horrible. Perhaps—it's possible you were actually there—when she was murdered."

I stared at her whitely, incapable of speech, and after a moment she moistened her lips and went on. "That would fit, you see. You've been—called back as an eyewitness. To bring the murderer to justice."

"No!" I said violently, jerking my hand out of her clasp. "Oh no, Beryl, please!"

"I can't think of any other motive strong enough to account for it."

"But even if I did, who would believe me? Can you honestly imagine dear, solid Constable Rushton solemnly accepting that ten years ago I was here as a—a disembodied spirit and actually—" I broke off in a confusion halfway between tears and hysterical laughter.

"Obviously that would do no good, but I don't doubt a way will be shown to you in due course. The whole thing seems to be beautifully—stage-managed."

I said unevenly, "I'm beginning to wish very strongly that I'd gone straight back to London with Jake."

"But don't you see, darling, it reached out for you there in the first place. The gypsy was aware of it, wasn't she?"

"Yes, she said I was caught in the time wheel. How right she was!"

Beryl said tentatively, "You haven't any vague stirrings, have you, which might identify—"

"No, I have not!" I threw back the blankets and swung my legs to the floor. "I haven't the remotest idea who her lover could have been, and if I'm supposed to come up with cast-iron proof of Ben Starling's guilt, I haven't the faintest notion how to go about that, either. And what's more, I rather resent being forced into the role of an avenging angel."

"Yes, I can understand that. How would you feel about seeing Madame Zelda again? Now that we have so much more to go on—"

"No, thank you, I'm not going to risk a repetition of what happened last time. If Dinah or Abigail or whoever it is wants to contact me, she'll have to manage without Madame Zelda."

After Sunday lunch, which once again Beryl insisted on preparing without my help, I decided, as last week, to take Lottie for a walk, but in my present volatile state nothing would have induced me to cross the footbridge into Whistler's Lane. Instead I walked the length of Tanner's Lane and turned left down the High Street. I had decided to explore the road at the bottom of the hill which formed the crossroads with Starling's Way and led past the wrought-iron gates of Ashley Hall.

It was a very different day from last Sunday's hovering rain, tender with the unmistakable approach of spring, the twigs on bushes and trees blurred with a soft wash of green. Beside me the tall grey walls hid the Ashley grounds. Even when I passed the large gates through which Beryl and I had driven in splendor on Thursday evening, the Hall itself was not visible from the road and all I could see was the gracefully winding drive, tree-lined and immaculately graveled.

I had not gone much further when I heard my name called and, turning, saw Rowan Ashley emerge from the gates with two dogs at her heels.

"Are you going anywhere in particular?" she called.

"No, just walking the dog."

"May I join you, then?"

"Please do." I waited for her to catch up.

"I don't usually use the big gates on such occasions, but I saw you vanishing from sight as I rounded a bend in the drive and it was the quickest way to catch you. Isn't it a glorious day?"

"Lovely, yes. I haven't been along this way before. Does it lead out to Pendle?"

"Eventually, but it's a pretty stiff walk. I must confess my usual constitutional is just round the walls of the estate. That's five miles or more and quite enough for me. The wall leaves the road further on and winds its way through fields and a little copse. It's rather a pretty walk. Can I lure you away from Pendle today if I promise to take you in the car some other time?"

I laughed. "Oh yes, five miles is my limit for today, too, but I would be very grateful to go with you sometime to Rough Lea and Whalley Abbey."

"Still witch-hunting?" Rowan asked with a smile.

"I feel I have a personal interest now!"

"Yes, I envy you your Abigail. She's no use to me, since I'm only an Ashley by marriage."

"She could prove a mixed blessing," I remarked enigmatically. "By the way, I've been meaning to drop you a note to thank you for a lovely evening, but I'm afraid I haven't got round to it yet."

"Take it as read. We enjoyed it too. As I told you, I don't often get the chance of a good talk on topics close to my heart."

I glanced sideways at her. If I could find the courage to bring up the subject of Dinah, there would never be a better opportunity. Hurriedly, before my habitual cowardice could intervene, I began, "I was

186

very sorry to hear about Adam's sister's death. It must have been a terrible time for you all."

"You heard what happened?"

"Yes. I didn't know about it on Thursday, though."

"I'm sorry I was rather evasive. The fact is it still upsets Adam considerably. He was extremely fond of her and—well, I don't know how much you've been told."

Stunned now by my own temerity, I said awkwardly, "I didn't mean to pry. If you'd rather not—"

"It's all right. Actually, it's quite a relief to talk about it. Poor Dinah, she was headstrong and selfish, but she didn't deserve that."

"You weren't here at the time, were you?"

"No, I didn't really know her well at all. When I first met Adam and spent weekends during the vac at the Hall, she was away in Switzerland. She came home for the wedding, of course, but then we moved to London and didn't see much of her. When the row blew up about her wanting to marry Ben Starling, Mr. Ashley sent for Adam post-haste to try to talk some sense into her. He was seven years older than she was and had always had quite a lot of influence over her. Not this time, though. It's tragic to think how different things might have been if she'd only listened to him."

"What had they actually got against him, though?" I asked curiously.

"You know, I've often wondered that. I can't believe in this day and age all the fuss was just because she preferred a farmer's son to a belted earl! After all, the Starlings were very well thought of locally. It

certainly wasn't as if Dinah would be expected to milk the cows or anything like that. They'd plenty of money. I have a feeling there was some personal element in it, but I've no idea what. At the time Adam was so upset I didn't like to question him and gradually, being away from them and caught up in our own interests, I more or less forgot about it."

We had come to the place where the wall left the road and we went with it, onto the soft, springy grass. "Dinah wrote to Adam several times," Rowan continued, "but he never replied. I'm afraid he can be very hard. Then of course when she was killed, he was beside himself. I honestly thought for a while that he would have some kind of breakdown. It would have been bad enough if she'd been killed in an accident or something, but at least it would have been over quickly. As it was, it put an unbearable strain on everyone, all the suspicions, then the arrest and trial and the endless going over of everything. And the last straw, of course, was when Ben got away with it."

"You think he did it?"

"Oh, beyond a shadow of doubt. Everyone was convinced of it. I mean, his story was so thin. As if she'd have gone out of the house with not even a coat, let alone a suitcase, if she'd been intending never to come back! It's my belief she never left the house and he dumped her body in the Lane later, perhaps on the way to the pub. Mind you, there were extenuating circumstances. It was obviously done in the heat of the moment when, on top of the row they were having, she suddenly came out with the exis-

tence of this mysterious lover. A *crime passionnel,* as the French call it. Although the death penalty was still in force then, I doubt if he'd ever have hanged. All the same, when he got off scot-free, it was too much for the old man and he collapsed. He was never the same again, so that's another thing Adam blames on Ben Starling."

Ahead of us the grey expanse of wall was temporarily broken by the insertion of a narrow wooden gate. Grass grew in thick tufts at its base as though it had not been unlocked for some time. It was the gate I had seen in my first time switch, and I recognized it almost without surprise. No doubt it was here that Ben used to come and wait for Dinah to slip out and meet him. "She was so young," I said sadly.

"Yes, and so, of course, was he. He was only twenty-four when he stood trial for murder."

"I wonder how he could bear to go back to the farm and live there all this time with everyone regarding him as a reprieved murderer."

"Pride," said Rowan briefly. "That's what's kept him going. He's as proud as Old Nick and damned if anyone should drive him away from his own home. You can't help respecting him in a way. I'm quite sure Dinah drove him to it. She could be maddening. I found that out myself."

"And the identity of her lover was never discovered."

"No. It's my belief that he was married anyway, hence the need for secrecy. If it hadn't been for Ellen's testimony, no one would have believed that he ever existed."

189

"What about Ben's family? Were his parents alive at the time of the trial?"

"His mother was. When he married Dinah, she went to live with her daughter in Barrowford. Lally had married a man a lot older than herself and he died soon after Mrs. Starling joined them, so when Ben was cleared they both came back here. Mrs. Starling died last year, but Lally still keeps house for him. She never had any children and it seems to work quite well. At least, I presume it does. She's as uncommunicative as Ben is. No one has anything against her—in fact, most people are sorry for her—but she won't have anything to do with anyone. Out of loyalty to Ben, I suppose. She does all her shopping in the next village. You never see her in Pendlemere."

We walked in silence for a few minutes, our eyes on the dogs gamboling ahead. Away to our left the land began its gradual rise to the lower slopes of Pendle and in the afternoon sunshine the ancient hill took on a false benignity, like the wolf lurking beneath the grandmother's lace cap. I wondered fancifully if some residual evil in the atmosphere roundabout was responsible for the recurring violence which ran through Pendlemere's history and whether it could ever be fully expurgated.

Rowan said suddenly, "It's only three weeks till the boys break up."

"Your sons? How old are they?"

"Twelve and fourteen—great, gangling lads, both of them. It'll be good to have them home. What about your family? I know your parents are abroad. Have you any brothers or sisters?"

"No, I've always wished I had. I was rather a solitary child. I went to boarding school and spent the holidays with Beryl."

"She's quite a character, isn't she? Adam was most impressed by the depth of her knowledge on early art forms."

I smiled. "Yes, no one really knows what to make of Beryl. She has many facets and she shows different ones to different people."

"I imagine we're all guilty of that."

"Yes." Jake crossed my mind. "Some people never get past the gym shoes!"

Rowan gave a spurt of laughter. "I'm all for a bit of eccentricity. How dull it would be if we were all the same!"

We had come round another bend of the wall and now in the distance I could see the low shape of the school building over to the left. We had almost completed our tour.

"You fare better than I do," Rowan joked. "When we reach the High Street, you've only the length of Tanner's Lane to walk, whereas I have to go down the hill and along the bottom road. Unfortunately there are no gates let into the wall along this side, though it's probably just as well or we'd have the school children breaking in. They're a wild bunch, some of them."

"Come back with me for a cup of tea," I suggested, but she shook her head.

"I'd love to but Adam will be back from golf soon and we're invited to a cocktail party at six."

So we approached the road, walking in single file now along the narrow pathway between the wall and

191

the school playground. The dogs had been called to heel and, tired by all their mad dashing about in the fields, were happy enough to obey. Rowan and I parted at the end of Tanner's Lane and I walked with Lottie back to Cobwebs. My mind was full of the additional details I had learned that afternoon and I wondered whether any one of them would prove to hold the clue as to why I should be caught up in all these affairs which were finished and done with ten years ago. And then I reflected that perhaps from Dinah's point of view they were not yet done with, which was why she had been unable to rest in peace.

"I think," I said to Beryl the next morning, "that I'll take the bus into Clitheroe today."

"Why on earth?"

"I imagine that's where the nearest newspaper office is. I want to look up the files that covered Dinah's death and Ben's trial and see if there's anything there which could be of help."

"Good idea. I'll come with you. I've some things I want which I can't get in the village so we might as well have lunch there and make a day of it."

We left the house soon after ten and stopped at the post office with the back door key and a request that Polly should slip along to Cobwebs to give Lottie her meal and a brief run in the garden.

Yesterday's sunshine had brought a definite advance in the emergence of green along the hedgerows. Blossoms and leaves were beginning to break out on all sides and I was aware of the pulsating miracle of new life bursting forth in the relentless, uncheckable advent of spring. No wonder our ances-

tors had thought it expedient to worship this all-powerful life force which flowed so strongly through seemingly dead twigs and branches, quickening them to renewed procreation. The ancient rituals of spring must have been celebrated since time immemorial along this very route where now the lumbering bus carried us in solid, unimaginative comfort.

We found the newspaper offices without difficulty and were given the necessary permission to look through the files. It was strangely disturbing to read the account in uncompromising headlines. "Ashley Bride Found Murdered in Haunted Lane" ran the most lurid. With Beryl beside me I carefully read through them all, but nothing really new came to light. There were pages and pages of verbatim reporting from the court. Ellen Wainwright had admitted under cross-examination that Mrs. Starling had met someone secretly at her home but she had consistently claimed that she was unaware of his identity. And as a final rebuttal of Ben's version of the affair, she insisted that Dinah had told her on the morning of her death that she wouldn't be seeing her lover again "until the weekend."

So why, demanded the prosecuting counsel triumphantly, had she suddenly told her husband that she was not only meeting him, but actually going away with him that very night? "I put it to you, Mr. Starling, that your wife never left the house, that you strangled her in a fit of jealous rage and later dumped her body in the Lane." Which was the point of view that Rowan had also adopted. The medical evidence

193

was more or less straightforward. Death was due to strangulation but there was also extensive bruising of the right cheekbone and eyebrow, as though the deceased had been struck shortly before her death. When confronted with this evidence, Ben had apparently muttered something inaudible and the judge had to request him to speak up. "She fell and banged her face," he had repeated more loudly, and when the prosecutor had "put it to him" that he had caused her to fall he had at first not replied and then, when instructed to do so, claimed that the fall had been accidental.

"It all seems rather pointless," I said to Beryl in a low voice. "Whatever I uncover, he can't be tried twice for the same crime."

She stretched and pushed the dusty pile of newspapers aside. "I don't know about you, but I've had enough of this. Outside the sun is shining and here we are poring over all these mountains of print just as though you were back in your stuffy library in London!"

"I don't think there's much to be gained from them anyway," I said regretfully.

Our spirits had been dampened by the dreary reading through of old news but they lightened a little as we looked round the shops. Beryl bought a new salad bowl in preparation for the summer she appeared to consider imminent and I bought myself a blouse in sunshine yellow. We had a pleasant lunch in an unpretentious little café and caught the three o'clock bus home.

"You know something?" I said thoughtfully as we

left the post office after reclaiming the key. "It's just struck me that the only person I haven't had any contact with is the principal character in the whole affair—Ben Starling himself."

She stared at me in consternation. "And if I were you, I'd keep it that way. I don't fancy your getting mixed up with the likes of him. Surly devil, from all accounts."

"All the same, that seems to be the only course left open to me. Rowan told me all she knew, so, heaven knows, did Mrs. Briggs. Ellen Wainwright seems to have disappeared in a puff of smoke, and anyway I doubt if she knew more than she said at the trial. Since we've no lead on the unknown lover, the only person left is Ben."

"And since no one speaks to him and he speaks to no one, might I ask how you propose to go about it?"

"I don't know yet," I replied, pushing back the gate of Cobwebs and holding it open for her. "But I'll think of something."

chapter

❧11❧

I AWOKE the next morning with the sinking feeling which, before full consciousness returns, reminds one that something unpleasant lies ahead. As the last layers of sleep melted away, the unpleasant prospect resolved itself into my determination to seek out Ben Starling.

Fighting down my extreme reluctance to go ahead with it, I reasoned that since the only time I had encountered him had been in Starling's Way, the obvious course would be to go down there again. It wouldn't be necessary, I assured myself encouragingly, to do more than establish an acquaintance in the first instance. Perhaps even the exchange of a few words would be enough to trigger off a vibration which might develop into something useful.

So, still with an apprehensive knot in the region of my stomach, I did the household shopping as usual and then made my way down the hill. But this time no tractor came toward me up Starling's Way. Out in the fields I could see distant figures moving, but the farmyard as I approached it was deserted and I had

no excuse to go any nearer. Disconsolately I turned into Whistler's Lane, and there was not even a flicker of the powerful emotions which had assailed me there the last time. All in all, it was a thoroughly negative morning.

The next day I followed the same procedure and again without any success. Obviously if I wanted to see Ben Starling I should actively have to seek him out. Yet even though it might be possible to make some excuse to knock at the farmhouse door, it was extremely unlikely that Ben himself would answer it. Nor, in my city ignorance, had I any idea of the hours he would work or the time he was most likely to be at home. If I were to be of any use to Dinah, it seemed she would have to give me some positive help.

"You're not going hanging round Starling's Way again, surely?" Beryl asked as we finished lunch and I mentioned my intention of a walk. I looked at her defiantly.

"Have you any better suggestion?"

"You know I have. Come back to Madame Zelda with me. She invited you."

I shook my head decidedly. "I'm sorry, Beryl, no. Spiritualism isn't my thing, I'm afraid. I went once to please you and also to see if it would help. It didn't. After all, I'm not interested in calling up anyone. Someone is already contacting me and seems to be managing very well without the help of mediums or any other outside agent. When you think I've only been here just over two weeks, it's incredible the amount I've learned already."

"Just as you like," she returned a little sulkily, "but

it seems much safer to me to go to a medium than to try to smoke out a murderer single-handed. What he's done once he can do again, especially since he got away with it last time!"

"Thank you," I said feelingly; "you've made me feel much better!"

"But you haven't changed your mind?"

"No." I tucked my shirt into my trousers and picked up the jacket from the back of a chair where I'd dispiritedly thrown it on my return that morning. "Come on, Lottie, walk! If nothing else, our figures should benefit from all this exercise."

"In another few days I'll be able to come with you," Beryl said. "Can't you at least wait till then?"

"He'd be even less likely to talk if there were two of us. Don't worry, Beryl, I can take care of myself and Lottie will protect me."

It was Wednesday afternoon and the shops were closed, their blinds pulled down over the windows. It gave Tanner's Lane a depressed, deserted air. The children were out in the playground as I turned down the High Street, their shrieks and screams strident on the air. I was grateful that the sounds of their merriment didn't reach as far as Cobwebs.

Once more Starling's Way stretched emptily ahead of me. If Ben were so unattainable, might there perhaps be something to be gained from his sister? She must lead a lonely life, widowed and voluntarily sharing her brother's exclusion from village life. The figures I'd noticed the day before had moved away to a more distant field and were now just dots on the horizon. At the bottom of the slope,

the mere spread its rippled surface, disturbed every now and then by the soft plopping of fishes rising to the water insects.

Slowly, inevitably, my now dragging footsteps brought me nearer to the gates of Starling's farm. The tractor stood in one corner of the yard, great cobs of patterned mud clinging to its heavy tires. An aged sheep dog slept outside the barn. The sun shone warmly on the back of my neck. I hesitated and looked down at Lottie, my decision wilting as the moment for action approached. Quickly, before I could change my mind, I went into the yard, carefully closing the big gates behind me. On my left the rear of the old farmhouse formed one side of the square, and I wondered uncomfortably whether perhaps suspicious eyes were peering out at me from the windows which the rays of the sun had transformed into two-way mirrors.

The old dog awoke and barked surprisingly shrilly, making Lottie flatten her ears and press against my legs, hampering my already reluctant progress. Our presence having been announced, there was no course but to advance. I lifted my hand and knocked on the back door and almost immediately it was opened and a woman stood staring resentfully at me. I recognized her easily as the sister of the man I had seen before. Her skin was sallow and her black hair dragged harshly back into a heavy bun low on her neck. She wore no makeup and her skin had a polished sheen to it, but it was her eyes which held my gaze—large, somber and very black. She was probably about forty, but there was an agelessness about

her which was strangely disconcerting. She could as easily have been twenty or sixty.

"I'm sorry to disturb you," I faltered as she made no attempt to speak. "I wonder if you could help me? We've run out of eggs and the shops are shut. Could you possibly let me have a dozen?"

Her eyes moved slowly over my face. "Why come here?" she asked at last. Her voice was deep, slow and strangely musical. "There are plenty of other farms round about."

"It's—just that I was passing and the idea suddenly came to me. Of course, if you can't—"

"You're new here, aren't you?" she broke in, her eyes still continuing their minute inspection of me.

"Actually I don't live here at all. I'm staying with my aunt at Cobwebs."

Her colorless lips tightened fractionally. "Oh, yes, Cobwebs." Keeping her eyes on my face, she reached behind her for a shallow basket. "You can have a dozen if there are that many in the nesting boxes. The ones that were collected this morning have already been packed and delivered. We don't cater for passing trade." There was heavy irony in her voice.

"Thank you," I said awkwardly. I wondered for a moment if I were expected to go and forage for eggs myself, but then she stepped outside and led the way to the hen-run at the back of the yard. Her shoulders were narrow and bony under the thin blouse and a few strands of soft black hair had escaped from the severity of the bun and straggled against the pale skin of her neck with a strangely touching vulnerabil-

ity. This, I felt instinctively, was a woman who had almost completed the defensive armor she was building around herself, but there were still a few chinks in it through which she might be reached and even hurt again.

She unlatched the wooden doors and her long, work-worn fingers reached expertly into the warm straw, disturbing a clucking hen which squawked and batted its wings, sending Lottie into another frantic dive for my legs.

"Nine," the woman said over her shoulder. "The best I can do, I'm afraid. That will be thirty-five pence." She handed me the punnet which she had layered with straw to prevent the eggs cracking.

"Thank you. I wonder if I could ask one more favor, a glass of water? I'm thirsty after my walk."

She straightened and looked at me intently. Then without a word she went back to the open door and I followed her uncertainly, feeling in my pocket for my purse. The farm kitchen looked large and cheerful. A tray of freshly baked scones lay on the table and beyond was an open door leading into the hall. I could hear the loud, asthmatic ticking of a grandfather clock.

"There's milk if you'd rather," said Ben Starling's sister. Her voice was flat and unemotional—strictly take it or leave it.

"Thank you, I would."

She moved to the fridge, large and up-to-date, I noticed, and the milk frothed creamily into the glass. Silently she picked up the tray of scones on her way back to the door and held it out to me as well.

"That's very kind of you." They were still warm from the oven, crisply brown outside, soft and crumbly within, with large moist raisins. I added spontaneously, "I don't know when I last tasted home baking."

A faint flicker of interest moved in the unlit depths of her eyes. "You don't bake yourself?" It was the first voluntary comment she had made and I seized on it gratefully.

"I'm afraid not. In London it's easier to nip down to the corner shop!"

"Oh, London," she said, as though that explained everything.

I sipped at the cold milk as slowly as I dared. She could hardly close the door while I still held the glass, much as she obviously longed to.

"Nice little dog," she offered dispassionately after a moment and Lottie, ever conscious of a compliment, thumped her tail. "Perhaps she's thirsty too." She filled a saucer with water and set it on the path and Lottie lapped greedily, ears swinging.

Encouraged by this display of innate hospitality, I said tentatively, "I don't think I've seen you in the village, Mrs.—?"

She let the name hang uncompleted on the air, answering merely, "No, you wouldn't," and reaching out for the now empty glass. Aware of time rapidly running out, my eyes raked the kitchen and hall beyond but there was nothing to suggest Ben Starling's immediate presence. I handed her the money for the eggs, adding, "And the milk and scone?"

"We've not reached the stage where we have to charge for that," she replied tartly and, with a nod as

202

acknowledgment of my renewed thanks, she firmly closed the door.

Unsure how much progress I had made, if, indeed, any, I went back across the yard and let myself out of the gate. Lottie kept a wary eye on the sheep dog, but it had lost interest in us after announcing our arrival. So that was the woman who kept house for Ben Starling. At least, I thought with a flicker of amusement, remembering one of my grandmother's expressions, they were not a good couple spoiled.

I turned into Whistler's Lane, my mind still on the woman I had just left. A sweet, dusty smell rose from the hay in the punnet I was carrying. Perhaps I could make the excuse of returning it the next time I passed. Might the unresponsive Lally unbend a little further? I was convinced that basically she was a deeply sensitive woman, whose rejection by the world, even though voluntarily invited for her brother's sake, was still an intolerable pain. I tried to imagine that still, watching face lit with laughter, and failed utterly.

Beside me Lottie, never at her ease in the Lane, stopped suddenly, one paw lifted, and pricked her ears. A moment later I heard it too, or rather felt it in the ground I stood on, the approaching thunder of a horse's hooves. Immediately, idiotically, all the stories of Richard Whitaker flooded into my mind as I stared fearfully up the Lane, intensifying when I realized to my confused panic that although the sounds were growing louder every second, I could still see nothing.

I made a sudden violent movement preparatory to

203

headlong flight, and in the second that I did so, a horse and rider suddenly, terrifyingly, loomed over me, coming not from along the Lane but round a screen of trees which edged the field to my right. The horse, quite as startled as I was, reared, hooves lashing, and the man on its back, after a brief, ineffectual fight to control it, crashed heavily to the ground. For a moment the animal stood there, snorting and pawing, then with a toss of its head it turned and careered back across the field and I was left with pounding heart staring down at the inert form of Ben Starling. So this was Dinah's way of ensuring our meeting, I thought grimly, as fear of the supernatural receded to be replaced by anxiety for the still-unmoving man at my feet. Richard Whitaker had died after his fall—

"Mr. Starling," I said urgently, "are you—all right?" A lunatic question, since obviously he was not. Hesitantly I knelt down beside him. An outflung hand was hanging over the ditch and one foot was bent unnaturally beneath him. With my teeth fastened in my lip I carefully inched it out. He made no move. There was a dark gash at one temple from which a thin trickle of blood crawled down the side of his face. I pulled a clean handkerchief out of my pocket, hurried across the Lane to dip it in the running water of the stream on the other side, and came back to dab gingerly at the wound. So intent was I that I didn't realize his eyes had opened until a gruff voice demanded truculently, "Who the devil are you?"

I jumped and my eyes flew to his, as black and wary as his sister's had been.

"Whatever happened? Oh yes, you loomed up suddenly right under us. Of all the damn-fool things to do!" He tried to sit up and fell helplessly back. "Where's the horse?" And, as I still searched for the best way to answer him, he added tersely, "I presume you have a tongue in your head?"

"It ran away," I said at last, stung to reply by his tone of voice.

He made an impatient sound. "If you hadn't been so bloody useless, you could have caught hold of the reins."

"As a matter of fact," I answered tightly, "I was glad to see the last of it. The way it was thrashing its hooves about it might have done some real damage."

His eyes moved over my face. "I presume you don't know who I am or you'd be running for your life."

"On the contrary," I said tartly, amazed even as I spoke at my own courage, "no one but Ben Starling would be so appallingly rude."

He stared at me for a moment. "All right, you can go now. I'll see you're nominated for the bravery awards."

My temper snapped. "Will you for heaven's sake stop talking and try to be more constructive. I shouldn't be surprised if your left ankle's broken. Can you move it?" I stared defiantly back into his dark, unwavering gaze. Then, as he tried to move his foot, I saw the wince of pain and his lips whitened.

"As I thought," I said briskly. "I'd better go and get help."

"Save your breath. No one would lift a finger to help me."

205

"I'm beginning to see their point, but as it happens I meant from your own farm. I've just left there."

"The devil you have. Might I ask what you were doing?"

My eyes dropped to the basket of eggs on the path beside me. He moved his head slightly to follow their direction, then looked back at me. "Did Lally fall for that? She must be slipping. What did you really want? Are you another of those damned reporters? Every now and then we're still plagued with them."

"No," I answered steadily, "I'm not a reporter, damned or otherwise." If he was determined to conduct an interview from this recumbent position, who was I to stop him? After all, it was what I had wanted in the first place.

"I presume," he said heavily, "that you're well primed with the whole sordid history of myself and my family?"

"I am."

"Then what are you after?"

I bent forward with the handkerchief to stop the trickle of blood before it could reach his eye, but his hand shot out and closed bruisingly over my wrist. "Will you stop poking at me with that soggy rag and answer the question? Why can't you leave us alone? Most people are only too happy to!"

I stared down at his hand closed round mine. It was large, tanned by the weather, and very strong. I imagined it round Dinah's throat and remembered too late Beryl's words of warning. I had thought I was safe while he was incapacitated, but it would take more than a broken ankle to stop Ben Starling. Belat-

edly I reviewed my position and it brought little comfort. I was alone in a reputedly haunted lane with a man most people were convinced was a murderer. I licked my lips.

"Do you or do you not want me to get you back home?" My voice shook only a little.

"It would be interesting to see you try."

"Very well. Are you conscious of pain anywhere except your ankle?"

He released my hand at last and began to flex various parts of his body. "Apart from the crack on the head, I don't think so."

"Then there's no reason why you shouldn't get up, but first I'll have to take that shoe off."

"Like hell you will!"

"Look, the foot's swelling already. If I don't take it off now, it will be much more painful and the shoe will have to be cut away." I started to unfasten the thick, mud-caked laces. "If you'd been wearing boots, you might have been spared this."

"I usually do, but if it's any of your business I've been lunching with some customers." He stiffened, arching his back as with a final movement I removed the shoe as gently as possible. His eyes closed and he fell back, his breath rasping, and for a panic-stricken moment I thought he'd passed out again. Then his eyes flickered open and, masking my relief, I said rallyingly, "You'll be all right now as long as you don't put any weight on that foot."

His mouth twisted. "You're a hard case, aren't you? What's your name?"

"Sophie Woodburn."

"Well, Sophie Woodburn, if you're reasonably sure I'm not going to strangle you for the moment, come round to this side and give me a bit of support."

He was making a valiant effort to struggle into a sitting position and I could see the sweat starting out on his forehead. My usual feeling of inadequacy, strangely lacking in my treatment of him so far, rushed back over me and I started to vacillate. "Perhaps it would be better after all if you waited while I—"

"If you imagine I'm staying here any longer, you're mistaken. Stop dithering about, for God's sake, and let me use you as a lever."

I bent down and put my arm round him beneath his left shoulder. The tweed of his jacket smelled of horse and tobacco and general maleness. He fastened his teeth in his lower lip and started slowly to heave himself upward, I struggling to support his considerable weight. From the path Lottie watched us, head inquisitively on one side, wondering if this were some new game. His arm was heavy across my back and his hand gripped my shoulder almost painfully.

"Well, come on!" he said irritably. "You sag every time I put any weight on you! We'll never get anywhere at this rate."

Resisting a strong impulse to move away altogether and let him fall, I braced my aching shoulders and fought silently to raise him from the ground. After a few minutes of tense, desperate struggle, he was upright, leaning heavily on me, and we were both covered in sweat. Despairingly I looked back down the length of Whistler's Lane.

"Well, Sophie Woodburn, this was your idea. Have you bitten off more than you can chew?" He raised a hand to brush the sweat out of his eyes.

"The only thing I'm not sure about," I said levelly, "is whether I can keep my temper until I hand you over to your sister."

He gave a short bark of laughter. " 'Hand me over!' I like that. Come on, then, we won't make any progress standing here talking." So we began our long, painful trek back down the Lane. It was a shuffling, almost hopping progress, because by now the ankle was so badly swollen that any movement at all pained it.

"Don't you think we ought to rest for a while?" I asked breathlessly.

"Had enough?" His face was white and his lip shredded where he had chewed on it.

"If you can take it, I certainly can."

"Then what are we waiting for?"

There was no answer to that and our difficult progress began again. Step by agonizing step, we inched our way slowly down the Lane.

"No need—to go—as far as—the yard," he said at last in a series of jerks. "Try—the front—way." He nodded to our left, where a little path I hadn't noticed before branched off, obviously leading to the front of the farmhouse. Locked in our ungainly hold, we lurched into it. There was a pretty, cottage-type garden, but I paid it scant attention as for the second time within an hour I found myself knocking at Starling's farm. Ben, however, was not one to wait at his own door.

"Lally!" he bellowed. "Hurry, for God's sake!"

There was a grating noise from inside as a bolt slid back and a moment later the door rocked open to reveal his sister, eyes huge in her alarmed face. "Ben! What's happened?" Her bewildered gaze traveled from him to me. "What on earth—"

"This girl lunged out suddenly under Prince's hooves. He bolted. God knows where he is. Send Fred to look for him."

"Never mind Prince. What happened to you?"

"What do you think? I was thrown, of course." He added to me, "Since we've finally achieved a workable arrangement, you'd better help me inside."

I caught his sister's quick, reproving glance, but I doubt if he did. Together we hobbled over the threshold into the hall. Ahead of us a shallow staircase, bathed in mellow sunshine from a landing window, wound its way upward, and beyond it was the open door of the kitchen.

"Into the sitting room," Lally directed, opening a door immediately on our right by the grandfather clock. Swaying now with exhaustion, Ben and I staggered after her and I released him at last into her charge. She took his weight and gently lowered him onto a sofa. As I straightened, a shaft of pain lanced across my shoulders and I rubbed them gingerly. From the cushions below, Ben Starling, his face still white with pain, said grudgingly, "Well, I suppose you didn't do too badly for such a pocket-sized Florence Nightingale."

"You're too kind," I said acidly. For some reason, probably fatigue and reaction, I was close to tears.

From the past some memory of etiquette appar-

ently belatedly manifested itself. "Lally, this is Sophie Woodburn. My sister, Lally Masters." He waved a hand vaguely between us and let it fall. I kept my eyes on the woman. "I'd better go. My aunt will be wondering where I am."

"It's very kind of you, Miss Woodburn. I don't know what—"

"Oh, come on," Ben broke in briskly. "She caused the accident. It was the least she could do."

I said rockily, "Good-bye, Mrs. Masters," and without waiting for her to accompany me, I hurried across the hall and through the open front door to find Lottie dejectedly awaiting me by the gate.

As I came over the bridge into Tanner's Lane, I saw Beryl standing outside the cottage, and she visibly wilted with relief at the sight of me. "Sophie! I was beginning to get frantic! I hadn't really imagined you to be in any danger, but when you didn't come and didn't come— What have you got there?"

"Eggs," I said flatly, thrusting at her the punnet which I had retrieved on the way home.

"Good heavens, child, what have you been doing with yourself? You're filthy!" She hobbled excitedly up the path beside me. Whistler's Lane was a dangerous place for ankles, I reflected. As she closed the door, I said firmly,

"Beryl, I'll tell you everything in a few minutes, but first I'm going straight upstairs to soak in a hot bath. In any case I'll be as stiff as a board tomorrow."

"But—"

"Later," I repeated, and went on up the stairs. Half an hour later when I came down again I was slightly

211

more relaxed, though my jumbled thoughts had still not clarified themselves completely.

"Now," Beryl instructed, thrusting a glass of sherry into my hand, "what happened?"

I took a sip gratefully. "In a nutshell, I made Ben Starling fall off his horse and carried him home again." She stared at me, unsure whether to believe me. "Truly," I assured her. "We had a most interesting conversation." Another drink, and I looked across at her levelly. "Beryl, Ben Starling is without doubt the most rude, self-centered man I've ever met, but there's one thing I'm absolutely convinced of. He didn't murder his wife."

chapter
❧12❧

MY conviction, as far as it went, was not particularly valid. I had no more proof that Ben was not a murderer than the court had that he was. Unless I could uncover the identity of the real culprit, my carefully engineered meeting with the Starlings was virtually useless. And how to find a man who had lain low for ten years, who quite possibly had left the district and, having put his momentary madness behind him, might now be living an exemplary life as devoted husband and father? Yet there was still the certainty that if my goal was as hopeless as that, there would have been no point in my being brought here —and I was in no doubt that I had been. Somehow I should be given the vital clue to the identity of Dinah's lover—and murderer.

Two days after my meeting with the Starlings, I came out of the kitchen after lunch to find a square white envelope lying on the mat. There were only two words written on it: Sophie Woodburn. I tore it open and extracted the single sheet of paper. The

same writing, thick and black, began baldly: "On reflection I might have been less than polite to you the other day. If you feel disposed to accept a somewhat tentative olive branch, Lally says to tell you she'd be pleased to see you for tea tomorrow afternoon at four-thirty. Ben Starling."

Silently I handed it to Beryl.

" 'Will you come into my parlor,' " she quoted softly.

"Nonsense, it's all quite aboveboard. If it weren't, he wouldn't risk the incriminating evidence." I flicked at the paper with my fingernail. " 'Less than polite,' indeed! It will be interesting to see if his manners are any better this time."

"I don't know why you bother. The man's a boor."

"But a wronged one, Beryl, that's the important thing."

"You're going then?"

"Yes. I don't think a reply is called for. If I want to go, fair enough; if I don't, forget it. That seems to be the attitude. Anyway, it's only for a cup of tea."

"You forget," Beryl said dryly, "that up here tea is likely to be a three-course meal."

I looked at her quickly. "Do you think so?"

"I know so. Never mind. Go if you must, but just remember I'll be watching the clock till you get back."

Lally Masters had changed her blouse and skirt for a thin dress of red wool, whether for my benefit or not, there was no way of knowing. Ben Starling, his injured leg laid along the sofa as Beryl's had been, looked up as I came into the room. He was wearing

214

a blue sweater and a cravat was tucked into the open neck of his shirt. "You came, then."

"As you see."

"I'm instructed to ask you to forgive my appalling manners and to promise to try to behave better to-day."

"On that condition, I accept your apology." Lally, having seen her orders carried out, nodded and withdrew, presumably to the kitchen. "How's the ankle?"

"Pretty bloody." He nodded toward a chair. "You'd better sit down."

"Did your man find the horse?"

"Yes, it was still wandering round the field. It seemed none the worse of the experience. More than can be said of me."

"I suppose I should apologize in turn for startling it."

"Right; now all that's out of the way I want to know exactly why you came here the other day."

"So that's why you asked me back."

"Of course. You never gave me a satisfactory answer."

I looked at him reflectively. "All right, if you insist. I came because I don't think you killed Dinah and I want to find out who did. How's that for size?"

There was a pause and then he said, "Thanks for the vote of confidence, but if I'm not the murderer, you're not likely to find him at Starling's."

"I wasn't sure you weren't until I met you."

He raised an eyebrow. "When my diffident gentleness convinced you I was incapable of such an act?"

"Something like that."

215

He said slowly, "You're a funny girl, Sophie Wood-burn. You spoke of my wife as Dinah. Did you know her?"

I hesitated. "I believe we were very distantly related."

"You're connected with that insufferable mob at the Hall?"

I said stiffly, "Good manners include not being offensive about my friends."

"I *beg* your pardon. Right, this is the way I see it, then. Correct me if I'm wrong. According to Lally you came up here to stay with your aunt, but it all seemed pretty dull after London, so you seized on the only spot of excitement available, even though it was ten years out of date. Right?"

"Wrong."

"You'll have a job convincing me differently."

"I've no intention of trying."

There was another brief pause and then he smiled slowly, and his whole face changed. "I've done it again, haven't I?"

"You have." For the first time I could see the attraction he must have had for Dinah Ashley.

"The fact is I've forgotten how to behave in company. You might not believe it, but I am trying, really. So tell me: what possible interest can this dreary old business have for you? I want the truth."

"The truth," I said deliberately, "is that in some quite inexplicable way your wife and I seem to have become jumbled together. I don't expect you to believe this, but I saw her the other day in Whistler's Lane."

Long moments ticked away. Ben Starling sat with his eyes intent on my face. I don't know what I'd expected his reaction to be—laughter, scorn, sheer disbelief. Certainly I had never even remotely anticipated his actual words, for when he finally spoke, it was to say expressionlessly, "Don't tell me you were wearing a long white robe at the time?"

A wave of intense heat washed over me and receded again, leaving me shivering. "What do you mean?"

"When you met her in the Lane. She told me about it."

"Last week?" I stared wildly at him and he moved impatiently.

"No, of course not, idiot, before she died."

"She told you she saw *me?*" Beryl had hinted it was possible.

"A young girl with long hair in a white robe. She said you looked frightened. I tried to link it up with the legend of the Whistler but she wouldn't accept it."

There was an insistent throbbing of blood in my temples. "Ben, have you ever heard of astral travel?"

"No, and I don't want to. All right, so there may be more things in heaven and earth, etc., but I've no intention of meddling with any of them."

"Nor had I, but I wasn't given any option."

"Suppose you tell me everything from the beginning."

Simply and without embellishment I did so: the gypsy's visit, the promised letter from a stranger bringing me to Pendlemere and my instant recogni-

tion of it, followed by the three different time switches and my encounter with Dinah in the Lane. The only thing I omitted, why, I was not sure, was the terror which had gripped me on the village green. When I came to the part about her lover arriving at Cobwebs, his lips tightened and he sat forward slightly, leaning back again as he discovered I had never seen the man's face.

"My God," he said flatly, when at last I finished.

"I said you wouldn't believe me."

"But I do, so help me. Having spent my life in the shadow of Pendle Hill, I'm not disposed to discount anything, however weird. It's just—rather more than we'd bargained for when we invited you to tea."

"That I can well imagine." I hesitated. "Have you ever been aware of anything supernatural yourself?"

"No, thank heaven, but enough people have for it not to be brushed aside. I'm a farmer, Sophie, but not a dunderhead, which you city people seem to think is synonymous with living in the country."

"I didn't say—"

"No, I'm sorry, you didn't. Dinah did, though, and she should have known better. I dare say I've had a complex about it ever since. Anyway, suffice it to say that although my feet are firmly on the ground, I do occasionally lift my eyes to look at the stars." He stared at me for a moment and gave a short, embarrassed laugh. "I don't know what brought that on. I'm not usually given to such bursts of rhetoric."

The door opened and Lally Masters came back into the room. "Tea's ready if you'd like to come through, Miss Woodburn."

218

"Sophie," I amended quickly. She smiled in acknowledgment, and it was the same slow, arresting smile as her brother's. She reached down behind the sofa for an improvised crutch and with her help he got to his feet.

"Straight across the hall," she directed and I led the way as she lingered to help Ben. The dining-room table was laid with an assortment of cakes and scones, dishes of bread and pale farm butter and bowls of jams and honey. A silver teapot and hot water jug were laid at one end with a set of china cups. Obviously Lally too intended to indicate that they were not yokels. I wondered why it should matter to them. The Starling pride, I supposed.

Ben lowered himself into a chair at the far end of the table and his sister put a footstool under his injured foot. Then she moved to a side table and busied herself with a carving knife. A moment later a plate of succulent pink ham was laid before me, accompanied by parsley sauce, potatoes and green peas. I looked up from it to find Ben's amused eyes on me. "Were you expecting thin fingers of toast and seed cake?"

I smiled back. "No, I'd been warned. This looks delicious."

It was a new experience for me to eat my evening meal accompanied by thin slices of bread and butter and a cup of sweet strong tea, but I enjoyed it thoroughly and said so. Apple pie and fresh cream followed, the cream yellow-beaded from the warmth of the fruit, and thick wedges of crumbly Lancashire cheese were served with it. After that, Ben and his

sister moved on to the selection of jams, but I had had more than enough.

When the meal was over, she again supported him on his return to the sitting room and firmly refused my offer of help in clearing the table and washing the dishes. Ben had reached into his pocket for a pipe and started to fill it.

"Do you know something," he said, pushing down the tobacco. "You're the first person from the village to set foot in this house for ten years? Apart from the doctor, that is."

I said softly, "It must have been very hard for you, being shut out like that."

"It was hard all right. It mattered to me far more what my own people felt than what was officially said in court, but they're all as stiff-necked and stubborn as I am myself. They decided I was guilty and for my part I was damned if I would go out of my way to try to change their minds."

"Did no one make any attempt to contact you?"

"The vicar came a couple of times, but I wasn't in any mood for platitudes about turning the other cheek. In the end I lost my temper and told him not to bother coming back."

"And he was the only one?"

"Oh, Graham Lethbridge tried to be friendly, possibly with an eye to which side his bread was buttered. There's not a surplus of patients in a village this size. Perhaps I'm wronging him. Anyway, on the occasions when we've needed him over the years—when my mother died, for instance—he's been pleasant enough, but there hasn't been a cheep out of

220

anyone else. After a while I schooled myself not to mind."

I said awkwardly, "Apart from being accused of it, did—did your wife's death—" I broke off and he raised his head from the smoldering pipe and looked at me.

"Are you trying to ask if I was in love with her?"

I flushed. "I'm sorry, I—"

"You're right, it isn't any of your business, but as it happens I was. At first, anyway. Later—I don't know. Things hadn't been going smoothly for some time. She was bored and discontented and I suppose I resented that. The fact was of course that the marriage was doomed from the start and if we hadn't both been so young and pigheaded we'd have had the sense to see it."

"I believe there was quite a lot of opposition to it."

He smiled grimly. "You could put it that way. One hell of a rumpus. That brother of hers was the worst of the lot."

I looked down at my fingers, folding and unfolding the pleats in my skirt. "Rowan thought there was some personal reason why they were so set against it."

"How very astute of her. There was."

I looked up expectantly and he gave a short laugh. "Sophie Woodburn, I have a feeling I'd rather face the Spanish Inquisition than you, despite your gentle face and large, innocent eyes! All right, if you must know, there'd already been bad feeling between us." He hesitated. "It's strange, really, the way we Starlings keep brushing up against the Ashleys, and each

221

time the sparks fly. I didn't know about the first occasion and nor did Dinah until Adam told her, though why he should have imagined it would make a ha'-p'orth of difference, I can't imagine."

"And what was it?"

"Oh, apparently their mother, who was Charlotte Hoghton before her marriage, fell for my father many years ago and they had a brief affair. Since she was already engaged to James Ashley, you'll appreciate this wasn't very well received. She tried to break off the engagement but her parents were determined to marry her into the Ashley family and marry her they did. When Dinah fell for me, it must have seemed like history repeating itself."

I said thoughtfully, "It's surprising how often it does, isn't it? Perhaps time really is a wheel that keeps revolving and bringing back the same circumstances only slightly changed."

He looked at me curiously. "What other instances have there been?"

"Oh, countless little things I've noticed since I came here. Beryl hurt her ankle in Whistler's Lane, so did you. Richard Whitaker fell off his horse there and so did you, though fortunately with not such drastic results. Even your marriage could in a way be compared to his and in the end no good came of either of them. And Whistler's Lane links you both again; he died there, and so did Dinah."

"Most people are convinced she died in this house. You might have a point, though. And I dare say I was as much under Dinah's spell as Whitaker was under Lizzie Earnshaw's."

"What was the other occasion that you brushed up against the Ashleys?"

"That was rather more recent and I don't want to go into it."

"Presumably it concerned Adam, since he was so against your marriage?"

"Yes. And I'm damn sure he never mentioned *that* to Dinah." He hesitated. "Well, since you know so much—but I don't expect it to go any further. Years ago, when Dinah was still at boarding school, Adam started taking Lally around. It wasn't serious on his side, but he couldn't have helped seeing that it was on hers. Lally's a very gentle soul. Don't be fooled by that tough outer skin she's had to grow for protection. Anyway, it got to the stage where it had to be stopped, for her sake, and since my father was dead, it fell to me to do it. I was several years younger than Adam, which didn't help. It was all very unpleasant and he never forgave me." He glanced across at me under lowered brows. "As I said, that's strictly between you and me."

"Of course. Poor Lally. And I suppose she was married soon after?"

"Yes. I never agreed with that, but Mother felt she ought to be settled as soon as possible, to put all thoughts of Adam Ashley out of her head. And George, though he was so much older, had always been fond of her. Anyway, none of this has anything to do with your second sight or whatever it is."

"No. Did you know Dinah had an ancestress who was a witch?"

223

"Old Abigail? Yes, she was named after her, if you please!"

"She's my ancestor too, and according to Rowan a lot of her descendants do have second sight or something in that line."

"Meaning that's how you and Dinah stumbled up against each other?"

"It could be. Ben—"

"Back to the inquisition? All right, fire away."

"When did you first discover she—had a lover?" I wasn't looking at him. There was a silence and then he said flatly, "The night she died. Next question."

When I dared to look up, I saw that his knuckles were clenched on the stem of his pipe.

"That was the first indication you had?"

"It was. Sophie, I've been through this times without number. Is it really necessary—"

I leaned forward urgently with clasped hands. "But I'm trying to help you, Ben."

He said slowly, "I suppose that does make a difference. Apart from the formalities at court, no one's ever been interested in hearing my side of it before. Do you know the words I hate most in the English language? 'Circumstantial evidence.' Believe me, they nearly did for me." He was silent for a moment. "I still don't understand why you're bothering. What can it possibly matter to you?"

"It's Dinah who's bothering, Ben."

"You honestly believe she's responsible for bringing you here?"

"I don't know how else to account for everything."

"And what happened when you 'saw' her last week? Did she give you further orders?"

"No. Actually she—" I shuddered to a halt.

"She what?"

"At first she didn't seem to realize—which one of us was the ghost."

"Ye gods!" he said softly.

I went on quickly, "I'd rather not talk about it. It upset me considerably."

"That I can believe. What I can't quite swallow is that I'm to go over the whole miserable business for the umpteenth time and suddenly hey presto, you'll wave a wand and the murderer will stand revealed before us."

"Please let me try," I pleaded. "Surely any chance is worth taking?"

He leaned his head back, staring up at the ceiling. I heard Lally come into the room and quietly sit down, but my eyes didn't leave his face. At last he began tonelessly, "There was to be a meeting that night at the church hall, something to do with drainage and I'd promised to go. Anyway it concerned Starling's Way. After tea, Dinah suddenly announced that she wanted to go to the pictures. I said I couldn't take her, and almost before either of us realized it, the hell of a row had blown up. Well, she raked up all kinds of things which I've no intention of going into. Sufficient to say I was knocked sideways, completely poleaxed by all the bitterness she'd kept locked up inside her."

His voice cracked and I felt Lally make a movement, but after a moment he went on, "Then suddenly, almost as an afterthought, she announced that she had this lover and was going away with him. I

think she was a bit frightened when she realized what she'd said."

There was another long silence and I sat motionless, trying to equate the bewildered young man of ten years ago with the hard and bitter one in front of me. Ben Starling had learned a lot in those ten years and learned it the hard way. The raw edges had been knocked off and he would never again lay himself open to such intolerable hurt.

"She seemed surprised when I wouldn't agree to let her go," he went on at last. "I said something about preserving the marriage vows—fatuous I agree, in the circumstances—and she—she made it quite plain that it was too late to worry about that. It was then that I hit her. I'm not proud of it. I regretted it at once, but it knocked her off balance and she banged her face on the table. I tried to help her up but she twisted away from me. I went after her and caught her round the throat. Yes, I know," he added heavily at my involuntary exclamation, "I suppose you find it as hard to believe as everyone else that killing her simply never entered my head. Oh, I dare say I made a few empty threats but it was the extravagant way everyone does talk—'I'll murder you!' —that kind of thing. It had no meaning. I simply gave her a good shaking. I was beside myself by this time —and then I just let her go. I'd meant to lock her in her room, but of course there were no keys and all the bolts were on the inside. Anyway, she rushed straight out of the house and I made no attempt to stop her. That was the last time I saw her alive."

Feeling more like the Public Prosecutor than ever,

I whispered, "And what did you do between then and nine o'clock when you arrived at the Fleece?"

A bitter smile touched his mouth. "A familiar question. And I can only give you the same answer I gave to everyone else. I really don't remember. Not in the kind of detail they were trying to insist on. I know I walked round and round the house like a caged animal, still smarting from all the taunts she'd flung at me. My whole world had suddenly collapsed—can you understand that? I'd considered myself a reasonably happily married man and then suddenly—wham! Nothing! I discovered that my wife had despised me for years, had probably never loved me at all, and was calmly planning to run off with someone she really did love. I think most of my rage was directed against that unknown man who'd somehow managed to make her love him.

"When I couldn't stand the house any more, I strode off across the fields. I must have walked miles. I made a wide detour and finally came out on the main road some way beyond the village. I tramped back along it. When I got to the church, I saw the lights on in the hall and remembered the meeting for the first time, but I was in no state to go there and anyway it would have been almost over. So I went to the pub and, as no doubt you've heard, made an exhibition of myself and had to be carried home."

I seized on what seemed to me to be the most relevant piece of information. "So if you approached the village from the main road, you never went near Whistler's Lane?"

"No, ma'am. They tried to be very clever about

227

finding mud on my shoes, but I'd already told them I tramped the fields for hours on end. Anyway, the next thing I knew was the terrific hammering on my door which turned out to be the police with the news that her body had been discovered. I found I was lying on the bed fully dressed except for my shoes, which whoever brought me home had removed. So!" He turned to me with a suddenness that made me jump. "The facts are now before you, learned counsel. Who did the dirty deed?"

"You never had the slightest idea who her lover was?"

"Plenty of ideas, never any proof. Don't you imagine that during the last ten years I've gone over and over all the men it could possibly have been? So-and-so smiled at her at that party, so-and-so kissed her under the mistletoe. God, don't you think I've tried?" He crashed one hand into the palm of the other. A little anxiously I turned to look at Lally. The knitting she had been engaged on was lying in her lap. She seemed poised to go to him, but as unmoving as he now was.

I said dryly, "I'd no right to come here and make you go through it all again."

"Now you tell me!"

I stood up, aware that my legs were shaking. "I think I'd better go."

"You had, and what's more you'd better not come back."

"Ben!" It was Lally who had exclaimed.

"I meant for her own sake. It wouldn't do to let it be known that she's been here. Crippen is my middle name, don't forget."

228

I said hurriedly, "Thank you for the delicious tea."

"Just a minute," Lally said firmly; "you can't go rushing off like that. One of the men will take you home."

"No, really—"

"Of course. If Ben were able he'd take you, but since he can't, I arranged with Fred. He's ready when you are, but it's not nine yet—"

"I think I should go, all the same," I said a little more calmly. "Thank you for your hospitality."

"Well, if you're sure, I'll get your coat."

She went out and I turned back to Ben. He was lying staring up at the ceiling again. "Good-bye," I said. He did not reply. I doubt if he even heard me. I went out into the hall and met Lally with the coat. Minutes later I was in one of the farm cars bumping along Starling's Way beside a burly laborer.

"There's nowt wrong wi' Master," he volunteered abruptly as we swayed round the corner and started up the High Street.

"Er—no. Of course not."

"There's them as thinks wicked things, but we never believed 'em, not us as 'ave worked man and boy at Starling's all these years, wi' Mr. Ben and his father afore him. We're the ones as knows him."

"Yes." I found there were tears in my eyes.

"Cobwebs, Missus said?"

"Yes, please." Into Tanner's Lane.

"It's good to see him meeting folk again." It seemed heartless to disillusion him. I just smiled numbly into the darkness. Two minutes later I had taken my leave of the loyal Fred and fumbled my way into the house.

"Well," Beryl demanded eagerly, "what did you find out?"

"Among other things that he's not quite as alone as he imagines. Apparently all the farm workers are fiercely behind him as well as his sister."

"Hardly evidence to change the course of justice. Is that all?"

"No, there was something else." I hesitated, looking down at my clasped hands. "It was rather unnerving. He said Dinah told him she'd seen me in the Lane."

"Seen you? When?"

"Before she died. 'A young girl in a long white robe.'" I shivered and moved nearer to the fire.

"I thought it might tie up," Beryl said softly. "The time wheel again. Sit down, honey, and tell me what happened."

Shakily I lowered myself into a chair. "He told me the whole story from his angle. Frankly, I wouldn't have blamed him if he had killed her."

"From his angle," Beryl emphasized heavily, "that would obviously be the impression you were left with."

"But what can I do?" I cried despairingly. "I don't know how much he accepted of my links with Dinah, but if I raised his hopes and then nothing comes of it—"

She leaned forward and took hold of my hands. "But something *will* come of it, darling. You must keep believing that. If it doesn't, then the whole thing's senseless, without point. I just can't accept that. I'm sure Dinah's behind it; she was apparently

very strong-willed and you must admit, sweetie, that you're not. Whether she's aware of what she's doing, I don't know. Possibly not since she was frightened when she saw you. She may not even realize you're 'tuned in' to her memory bank, but *someone's* urging the thing along and I'm sure they won't give up till the whole thing's clarified."

"Yes," I said after a moment, "you're probably right. Part of the memory might be my own subconscious one from ten years ago and the fact that Dinah saw me in nineteen sixty-four would provide a ready-made connection, a kind of channel for the thought waves to pass along. Even if she's doing it unconsciously, she's still responsible for bringing me here, though, simply by being restless and unhappy and wanting to change things. Mind over matter, as Madame Zelda said."

"Which brings us back to square one. I can't say I'm happy about you going round killer-hunting, even if it is in the interests of justice."

"Who could it have been, Beryl?" I asked softly. "Who could it possibly have been?"

"I wasn't there, my sweet, any more than—"

"Any more than I was? But you said something about the possibility that I *was* there."

"I know." Her voice shook. "Sophie darling, that's what I'm really afraid of. I think you must have been and that was one of the reasons for the total mental clampdown you imposed on the whole thing."

"And I'll have to go through it again before I find out who killed her?"

She nodded, her eyes on my face.

231

" 'Beware of yesterday,' " I said, and some more of
the gypsy's words came into my head which I'd forgotten, or perhaps just not wanted to remember:
" 'Mortal danger. Death—violent death.' " Jake and
I had tried to joke about it. Now the words seemed
to underline an impending threat.

Beryl slipped to her knees on the rug and put her
arms round me, holding me close. "Just keep remembering that you're here with me, in this time. Nothing that has already happened can harm you."

"But even if I do discover who it is, what then? I
can hardly hope for Dinah to come forward and identify him!"

"Once you know who he is, you'll also know what
to do. I'm sure of that."

"I don't want to ruin the life of someone I might
not even know. If he's basically a decent man, he's
probably suffered enough already as it is."

"So has Ben Starling," Beryl said quietly.

I sighed. "Yes. The more I think about it, the more
sure I am that Dinah's more concerned about clearing Ben than revealing the real murderer, but of
course that's the only way it can be done. Anyway, I
haven't really any choice." I looked down into her
anxious face, trying to think of the right words to
reassure her, and brought out one of her own favorite
expressions with a certain quiet triumph. "So I'll just
have to press on regardless, won't I?" I finished, and
saw her smile and relax slightly in acknowledgment.

chapter
⇌I3⇌

I WASN'T sure why, but I had to get out of the house. It didn't seem to be as late as I had confusedly thought, only about seven o'clock, but the mist had come down a little and there was a hoarfrost on the garden. It was very cold, and she realized suddenly that she had no coat. What time did the meeting start? He had said he was going, she must catch him before he went in. He must be made to see that they couldn't wait any longer, not now that Ben knew. She could never go back to Starling's, not even for her coat.

Dazedly I stopped and put a hand to my head. I was Sophie. Sophie, not— Hurry, hurry, time's getting on. He might arrive early. It was silly not even to have stopped for a coat, but she was so frightened of Ben catching hold of her again. He'd hurt her when he held her throat and her face was burning, too, where it had been banged against the table.

No, I thought despairingly, stop! I'm Sophie, Sophie, not Dinah!

The stones on the path of Whistler's Lane were wet and slippery. Twice she almost lost her footing. Oh, darling, please be there! He wouldn't be expecting her, of course, they hadn't arranged to meet that night. If only she hadn't lost her temper and blurted everything out! It would have been so much better not to have rushed him, to work everything out properly as they had planned.

The outline of Claythorpe's boundary wall loomed toward her through the mist. Not far now. She cut across the village green, ran over the road and up to the hall. Lights were on inside and the committee, bustling and self-important, were already settling in their seats. One or two people were moving about in the body of the hall, but he wasn't among them. She moved back away from the light, shaking with cold. It would not do to let anyone see her standing here without a coat in this weather and she could hardly tell them whom she was waiting for! Not that it would really matter, of course. By the next day, when they had left together, everyone would know. Oh, come *on*, darling, please hurry! It's so cold—so cold.

I heard a soft little moan and realized I had made the sound myself. Please, Dinah, please! It isn't necessary to take hold of me like this. I'm here, as you wanted. Let me be beside you, not part of you. Don't let him kill us both! My teeth were chattering with a ferocity which made my jaw ache.

A car was pulling off the road into the carpark. Surely—yes, at last! She ran across and tapped on the window and he wound it down quickly.

"Dinah! What the hell are you doing here?" She

couldn't see his face in the shadows but his voice was a little off key. Only, of course, because she had surprised him.

"Darling, I've something to tell you—"

"Not now, for heaven's sake! The meeting—"

"Damn the meeting. Please, darling, it's urgent!"

He glanced at his watch. "Well, we've a few minutes in hand but we can't talk here, people will be arriving. Go and wait on the green, out of the light. I'll lock the car and follow you over."

Silently she sped back over the road. There was the sound of a piano coming from the Fleece. They were off to an early start tonight. She slipped round the corner of the building into the wonderful, welcoming darkness, trembling as much with excitement as with the cold. A moment later his tall shape turned the corner. She hurled herself into his arms, feeling them automatically go round her, but his body seemed stiff and unyielding.

Dinah, please—who is it? That's all I need to know, then I can go! Dinah, don't make me stay! Not again!

"Dinah." His voice this time. I recognized it but it fretted at the edges of memory without identifying itself. "Listen, dear, things have changed. I have to talk to you, too, but not now. Good God, girl, haven't you got a coat? You're frozen!"

"I didn't dare to stop for it. Oh, darling, Ben knows! He—"

"*What?*"

"It's all right, sweetheart; it had to happen sometime."

"You little fool, what have you done?" His hands

caught hold of her arms, hurting them in their frenzied grasp. "Look, Dinah, I tried to tell you last night —something's come up."

At last the almost alien note in his voice penetrated her understanding. "Something more important than me? Is that what you're trying to say?"

"Hush, someone will hear you! Dinah, please understand. It's desperately important; all that I've been working for."

"And I'm in the way." Her voice was rising again and his hand came none too gently over her mouth. She fought free of it. "Well, I'm sorry—sorry that's come too late for you. But if you think I'll ever let you go—you *can't* mean that, not after we've found each other! You can't really think that I'll be content just to fade into the background and go back to Ben! He hit me, do you hear? He tried to lock me in the house, that's why I hadn't time to stop for my coat. Darling, he knows about you! How can I possibly go back?"

"What exactly did you tell him?"

"Well, not your name, actually. That's what he was most interested in, of course, and I wouldn't give him the satisfaction of knowing. Anyway, he'll know tomorrow, when we've gone."

"Tomorrow? Are you mad, Dinah? Haven't you heard a word of what I've been saying? Look, I haven't time to go into it all now. I had prepared the best way of telling you but you caught me off guard. Listen, sweetheart, I really am terribly sorry but it did rather get out of hand, didn't it? I never meant it to happen and I'm sure you didn't, either. Let's just say we've both come to our senses. I'd never have

236

believed myself capable of so strong a—" His voice shook to a halt. "Infatuation," he finished firmly. "That's what it was, darling, you must see that. We both lost our heads for a while but obviously it can't go on. Please try to understand. I've been offered—"

"I don't care what you've been offered!" Her voice rose again. "You've got it all worked out, haven't you? All so tidy and civilized! It was just a pleasant little episode that is now closed, neatly tied up and ready to be put away. But not for me! Didn't it occur to you that I might feel differently? Doesn't it matter that I believed you when you said you loved me?"

"Be *quiet!*" His voice was low and frantic. "There are people just across the road. Do you want them to hear you?"

"I don't care who hears me! God, what a fool I was! You're just like the rest after all, all sweetness and light until you got what you wanted, and then—"

"No, Dinah!" There was anguish in his voice. "It wasn't like that, I swear it! I thought I loved you. I *did* love you at the time, but—"

"But now something more important's come up? Well, that's too bad because if you really do try to get rid of me, I'll shout it all from the rooftops, the whole furtive, horrible affair!"

He shook her roughly. "Be quiet! You don't know what you're saying! Dinah, you wouldn't—"

"But I would! What have I got to lose? I love you! Don't you understand?"

"*Will you be quiet!* Dinah, love, calm down. Let's talk it over sensibly."

"Sensibly!" The word broke from her in a harsh

bray of laughter and his hands came up to her throat as, barely an hour before, Ben's had done. In the wall above them a light flashed on in one of the windows, staining the patch of grass just beyond them a bilious yellow. "How can I be 'sensible,' as you call it, when—"

"Hush!" His hands were tightening round her throat and her own went up to loosen them. For a moment they swayed together in a ghastly mockery of a dance while, petrified and unseen, but heart-stoppingly thankful to have disengaged myself from her clinging presence, I, Sophie, pressed fearfully against the wall where, in another time, this same paralyzing terror would again grip me. Let me go now, but first I must see— And as though they had heard me, their silent, struggling gyration spun them slowly round until at last the light from the window shone directly onto his face. It was Graham Lethbridge.

I could hear a harsh, grating sobbing, dry and agonizing. Was she dead? Was she dead yet? Dare I look again? There was darkness swirling inside my head. Someone had hold of my shoulders. Not him! Surely I wasn't still with him? My eyes flew open and it was indeed Graham Lethbridge bending over me, in my own bedroom at Cobwebs. For a second which I will remember for as long as I live, we gazed deep into each other's eyes. Then all the light went out of his, his shoulders sagged and he straightened from the bed. He said over his shoulder, "She's come round now, Mrs. Latimer. Will you wait downstairs, please."

I licked my dry mouth. "Beryl—no!"

"It's all right, Miss Woodburn." His eyes, steady again, met mine with the old compassionate reassurance, but how could I trust them now? The door closed behind Beryl with a final little click. He pulled a chair forward and sat down, his eyes on my face. "You know, don't you? God knows how, but you do. No, Sophie—" as the terror came back to my face— "don't look like that. I won't hurt you. Don't you think it's enough to remember what I did to her?"

I said unsteadily, "If you feel like that, why did you never come forward?"

He gave a small, helpless shrug. "Partly, of course, because I'm a coward, but mainly because of Mother. It would have killed her, there's no doubt about that. Would I have been justified in sacrificing another life just to salve my conscience?"

"But Ben—"

"Yes." He sat back. "That was something I hadn't reckoned on. If he'd been convicted, of course, I wouldn't have had any choice, but when he was acquitted, as I was sure he would be, I didn't think that my silence could hurt him. I'd no idea they just wouldn't accept his innocence. God knows, I did everything I could to bring them round." His mouth twisted. "Correction—almost everything. But don't think I got off lightly, Sophie. Every second of every day since has been torture to me. The only way I could see of trying to atone for taking a life was to spare myself nothing in saving others. That was how I earned my reputation for being dedicated." His voice was sour with self-loathing.

239

"How do you think I felt, seeing the trust and respect people gave me? Believe me, it was a far greater punishment than whiling away the time in a prison cell. And then there was Barbara; I couldn't even let her know I loved her. Oh, there were dozens of times I almost gave myself up, but it always came back to Mother. I owed it to her to carry on, so I kept thinking up additional little penances, testing myself, I suppose, to see just how much I could take."

The fear had gone, leaving me drained of all emotion, all ability to move, even if those hands which had always seemed so gentle and soothing should again close round my throat. Again? I closed my eyes to dispel the clinging strands of nightmare.

"Perhaps if you knew how it happened," he began in that low, desperate voice.

"I do, Graham," I broke in quietly. "I know exactly how it happened."

"Yes." His eyes came back to my face. "Of course you do. It's strange that I can accept that, despite my scientific training. Then you'll know I never meant even to hurt her. When she went limp in my arms, I picked her up and started to run with her. I think I was making for the Claythorpes', theirs was the nearest house. But when I reached their gate, I stopped and looked at her, and of course it was obvious that she was dead. I just laid her gently down at the side of the Lane and went on without her." He put his head in his hands and then looked up again.

"The whole affair was my fault, you know. I started it. I'd known her all her life and then suddenly one day, I seemed to see her for the first time. It was—

240

overpowering and it just swept everything away, common sense, decency, everything. I think she was just flattered at first, and rather bored. I'm sure she agreed to those first secret meetings merely to add a bit of excitement to her life. The tragedy was that later, when I was beginning to regain my senses, she came to love me."

"And then you were offered that job at the Manchester hospital."

"Yes. It's ironic, isn't it, after all that happened, that I had to turn it down."

There was a long silence between us. He sat hunched forward beside the bed, hands clasped, staring down at the floor between his knees. I was aware of the constant, slow trickle of tears down my face, but I had no strength to raise my hand and wipe them away. At last he stirred and looked up and an expression of concern crossed his face. He took his own handkerchief and gently wiped my face.

"Don't cry for me, Sophie; I'm not worth it. In any case I feel better now that it's all come out. Isn't confession supposed to be good for the soul?"

I said with an effort, "Graham, surely—" but he shook his head and put a hand gently over mine. "Try not to worry. You won't have to do anything. I'll make all the necessary arrangements, for Mother as well as myself. My only regret now is the wrong I did to Ben. I wish there was some way I could make it up to him." His eyes moved thoughtfully over my face. "Perhaps you can." He stood up slowly, my hand still in his, and looked down at me for a moment. "It's strange to think it was my letter that brought you

241

here. Thank you for coming. I couldn't have gone on much longer."

"I'm sorry," I whispered helplessly.

"Don't be. Think of it as my sentence of hard labor coming to an end at last. All I feel myself is a wonderful sense of relief. Good-bye, Sophie."

I couldn't say the word. He laid my hand gently down on the bed, patted it, and went out of the room. Time ceased to have any meaning. Once or twice Beryl came to the room but I just turned my head away and she went out again. I can't describe the emotions that gripped me except to say I was filled with a vast and terrible pity. I had never realized it could be such a harsh, abrasive emotion, rubbing raw the edges of my soul: pity for poor, impetuous Dinah, for Ben, wronged and hurt beyond endurance, and for Graham, who had had an even more terrible burden to bear. I imagined him quietly making the preparations that he must, and I cried aloud in protest at the irreversibility of it.

Hour followed hour. I didn't know if it was night or day; it was all darkness to me. Formlessly I tried to pray, but no words would come except "Forgive —forgive." And eventually a kind of peace began to seep through me, a comforting assurance that my prayer had been answered. So at last, almost without a change in the level of consciousness, I slept, hour after hour as Beryl told me later, until she was alarmed and would have phoned for the doctor—if there had been one to phone. I was finally roused to full awareness by the sound of voices and a heavy, uneven tread on the stairs, and the door opened to

admit Beryl and Ben Starling. I lay passively looking at them, knowing what I was now called upon to bear.

Beryl said brokenly, "Sophie, oh, thank God! I was beginning to think you would never wake up." Beside her Ben stood leaning heavily on a pair of crutches, resting his injured foot. Slowly, awkwardly, he moved across the room and my eyes followed him unquestioningly. At last he said, "I felt it was my responsibility to tell you. Do you need to be told?"

I gave an almost imperceptible shake of the head.

"It was very peaceful," he went on, not quite steadily, "for both of them. Simply an overdose of sleeping tablets. The old lady, of course, wouldn't have known anything about it. He—left a full confession."

I closed my eyes, and after a moment I heard him turn and hobble back to the door, and Beryl's soft voice as they went together out of the room. When she came back a few minutes later, I had sat up and pulled forward the bedside clock. It was two o'clock, in the afternoon, obviously, but of what day in the week I had no idea. It had been Friday when I went to the Starlings' for tea.

"What day is it?" I asked as she came back into the room. She was very pale and there were dark rings under her eyes.

"Sunday, darling; Sunday afternoon."

"What happened?" My voice was calm, politely curious.

"Are you sure you're ready—?" I nodded impatiently. "Well, I woke early yesterday morning, I

243

don't know why, and for some reason I got up and came and looked in your room. You—weren't here."

"No." I had a confused memory of letting myself out of the house. That had been real, then, present time which had so intricately wound itself up in the past. Perhaps Dinah and I had hurried together along Whistler's Lane on that time-fused night. "What did you do?"

"I was nearly frantic with worry. There was no knowing how long you'd been gone. I flung a coat over my pajamas and rushed down to the doctor's. I don't know why; he just seemed the nearest person I could turn to. He got out the car at once and asked me if I'd any idea at all where you might have gone. And suddenly I thought of the green and how you'd been so frightened there. I'll never forget his face when we found you lying in a crumpled little heap. I think—I think I knew then."

"He didn't mean to do it," I said with a desperate kind of urgency. "Everyone does understand that?"

"Yes, darling. Try not to worry."

"He was only trying to stop her shouting. It had nothing to do with thinking she might give him away."

"I know, I know."

"How—what is everyone saying?"

"The whole village seems to be stunned."

"Did you ask Ben to come?"

"No, he arrived on the doorstep and demanded to see you. I wasn't even sure you were awake, but he's not exactly easy to argue with." She hesitated. "Was it very terrible, that last time switch?"

I nodded.

"I blame myself for not stopping you, but how could I? We never had any warning, did we? It was what I'd always been afraid of, that you'd have to go through it all again."

We sat quietly for a few minutes. So Graham had after all made the final, Biblical atonement which the State no longer demanded. A life for a life. And his mercy had extended to his mother, whom the news would have killed anyway. At least she had been spared that. My heart went out to Barbara Simpson, who hadn't even known that her love was returned. Perhaps one day I should be able to tell her.

Beryl stirred at last. "You haven't had anything to eat for two days. Could you manage something now?"

"I think so." The sadness was a clean wound now, with no lingering suspicions to cause festering. In time it would heal. And Dinah Starling would surely rest in peace.

epilogue

IT was autumn, and shining red berries festooned the briers in Whistler's Lane. The harvest was safely gathered in and the fields lay white and bristling with stubble. On the trees the leaves, red and gold and brown, clung tenaciously, reluctant to fall.

It had been a warm, mellow day and we walked slowly, enjoying all the rich country smells that hung in the air, lazily content with the pleasant hours behind us and the prospect ahead of an evening with Beryl at Cobwebs.

At first I was hardly aware of it, as though the sound grew gradually inside my head. I paused and glanced across at Ben. "What's that?"

"What's what?"

"That noise. You weren't whistling, were you?"

"No." He looked at me curiously and the same thought came to both of us, as so often happened. "Hey," he said slowly, "I thought we'd laid the ghosts!"

I said jerkily, "Not, apparently, all of them." The

whistling was now becoming louder, more insistent, as the everyday world faded slightly, not, to my relief, disappearing completely but simply merging into the background. And then, as clear as day, I saw him for the first time, Richard Whitaker galloping toward us on a beautiful black horse, his cloak flying out behind him. I stopped and stared, waiting for him to vanish, as Beryl told me had happened on the occasions when she'd seen him. Instead, incredibly, he suddenly caught sight of me. For one appalling second I wondered whether it had been my twentieth-century ghost rather than Lizzie Earnshaw's which, three hundred years ago, had caused him to fall to his death from the rearing horse. But that at least I was spared. He reined the animal in sharply and sat staring at me, only about six feet away. Then, to my amazement, he gave me a slow, grave smile, swept off his plumed hat and bowed to me.

I felt Ben pulling at my arm, heard his anxious voice, "Sophie! Sophie, for God's sake, what is it? Are you all right?"

He had gone, of course. Dazedly I turned to Ben.

"You saw him." It wasn't a question.

"Ben, it was fantastic—he saw me, too! He bowed to me!"

Ben stared at me, then he smiled slightly. "Well, they always said he had an eye for a pretty girl!"

"No, it was more than that. It was—like a gesture of thanks. Ben—" My voice was shaking. "No one else has ever been close enough to see his face."

"And you were?" He was watching me intently.

"Yes. It was incredible. He had a great look of Graham."

For long minutes we stood stock-still in the middle of the Lane, looking at each other. I moistened my lips. "Graham once told me his family had been here for hundreds of years. Could—could he possibly have been a descendant of Richard Whitaker?"

"I suppose it's possible."

But that wasn't all that I meant, though the conviction I was grouping toward was hard to put into words. That gesture of thanks—I had no doubt that was what it was. . . . Graham had thanked me, too, for bringing about his release. Was it possible that one man had atoned for two? Or were they the same? As Beryl would have put it, was Richard Whitaker merely an earlier snapshot of Graham Lethbridge in the album of one soul's eternity?

My eyes focused again on Ben's intent face. "I think maybe I have laid all the ghosts after all," I said unsteadily.

"You mean what you saw just now was by way of a farewell performance?"

"Yes, exactly that. I'm sure Richard Whitaker won't have to ride again."

Ben looked at my stunned face, took my arm and gave me a little shake. "Well, I know better than to argue with you. Now come on, sweetheart, snap out of it. Beryl will be wondering where we are."

With his hand held tightly in mine, we went on together down Whistler's Lane.

DATE DUE

DEC 8	1980
MAR 2 3	1981

APR

PRINTED IN U.S.A.